THE SAHARA LEGACY

A SEAN WYATT THRILLER

ERNEST DEMPSEY

ENCLAVE PUBLISHING

GET FREE BOOKS

PROLOGUE

T he young boy stared at the charts, images, maps, and books littering the wooden table that ran along the length of the room. The wall was covered with dozens more pictures and maps. Notes were attached from one item to another with red strings, kept in place by pushpins of varying colors.

It wasn't the kind of stuff a typical boy of nine years would be interested in, but he was no typical boy.

His parents loved history. More than that, they loved uncovering things that time forgot—artifacts lost long ago. They spent every waking hour entrenched in their study where the boy now stood. Now and then, his father would take a break to go outside and play catch or kick a ball around the yard. They may have loved their work, but they also knew what was important. The attention they gave their son helped plant the seed for his own interest in history. Even at a young age, he had a deep fascination with the past.

The study was more like a small library. The opposite wall ran all the way to the ceiling with shelves overflowing with books. Though he was too young to understand most of the contents, the boy knew they were books about history. Only a few works of fiction occupied space in the study, and if they did, it was likely because they contained some kind of historical importance.

Something creaked just outside the room, and the boy twitched, snapping his head around to make sure no one was coming. The doorway was empty. He sighed a breath of relief and returned his gaze to the incredible array before him.

His parents didn't want him going into the study without their supervision. They'd told him on numerous occasions to stay out unless one of them was in there. The boy couldn't help but feel like they were keeping something from him. He didn't know what it was, just a sense in his gut. At the moment, his mother and father were toiling away in the kitchen, making dinner as they almost always did together in the evenings. They were under the impression that their young son was up in his room, working on homework. As a third grader, he didn't have much to do in the way of homework, and so when he finished, he'd quietly made his way down the stairs and into the study for a little clandestine operation.

He moved closer to the table, one of three in the room and the longest of all. Worried his parents would notice if anything was even slightly out of place, he cautiously leafed through the overlapping papers and books.

He didn't have anything specific in mind with his search. Instead, he simply let curiosity be his guide.

One of the books on the table was open to a sketched drawing of some ruins. It featured tall columns and a triangular façade above them. Nearby were some notes under the heading *Socrates*. The boy didn't know what that meant, but he thought he'd heard that name before.

His feet shuffled unconsciously to the right, and he raised his eyes to the wall, following some of the red strings to a point in the middle of the wall amid a cluster of faces both in photographs and drawings. Some of the people in the pictures looked very old. One was bald with a long white beard. Another had a mustache and was in cowboy clothing from the 1800s. Placed intermittently between some of the faces were pictures of grand cathedrals, mosques, and temples.

In the center of it all was what caught the boy's attention. Seven strings came to a stop on an old piece of paper with a strange symbol drawn in the middle. It was nothing more than a circle with a four-sided cross in the center.

The boy's eyes narrowed as he followed one of the strings back to its origin—another symbol. It appeared to be nothing more than a sideways figure eight. He traced another string to a different sign, one with a square in the middle connected to four circles. One of the symbols linked to the center was something he'd seen before—a six-pointed star that was prominent on the flag of Israel. Another looked like a crucifix with a loop on top. One was similar to the four-sided cross but was done in graded lines. There was one that looked like an X with a circle around it. The last two he examined were more unusual, appearing to be something from Asian culture.

The boy eased a little closer to the table and leaned in toward the wall, staring at the symbol at the epicenter of everything.

"I thought I told you not to come in here without one of us," a familiar man's voice said from the doorway.

The boy spun around, nearly knocking some papers and books off the table in the process. His face flushed red, and his eyes were wide with panic.

"I'm...I'm sorry, Dad. I...I just wanted to see what you and Mom were working on." The boy stammered through his explanation. He didn't feel like it was good enough to keep him out of some form of punishment.

His father stepped into the room with a casual gait. At first, the man's arms were crossed, and he wore a stern look on his face. Once inside the room, though, his expression eased. He put his hand on his son's shoulder and smiled.

"It's okay, Son. I want you to be interested in what your mother and I do."

The boy's face curled in confusion. "Why did you tell me to stay out of here, then?"

The father took his hand from his son's shoulder and slid it into his pocket. "Because we have a very specific way of doing things. You see all this?" He motioned with his free hand.

The boy nodded.

"This is all a giant puzzle."

"A puzzle?" the boy asked as he scanned the room of mysteries.

"Yep. Unraveling most of the mysteries of the world is just like solving a puzzle. You have to figure out where the pieces fit and where they don't. It can take a long time with some puzzles, and often you have to start without some of the pieces."

"How do you solve a puzzle without all the pieces?"

The father laughed. "Well, you have to go out and find them."

"Find them?"

"That's right. You start with a clue. Sometimes it's a small one, something that everyone else has missed. That clue leads you to a puzzle piece. Or it may lead to another clue. Eventually, when you find the piece, you have to organize it with the other pieces to figure out where they all go."

The boy turned around slowly and gazed at the walls. His eyes shifted to the table full of what appeared to be random stuff.

"This doesn't look very organized, Dad."

The father snorted. "Well, everyone has their own way of doing things. This system works for your mother and me."

"System?"

"Yep. And all these maps, books, charts, and pictures are pieces to the puzzle. When we figure out how they all go together, we'll be able to see what we're looking for."

The boy frowned. "What *are* you looking for?"

"Well, that's part of the fun. We don't know exactly."

The father could see his son didn't fully understand what he was saying, so he went on. "Let me explain. You see that image over there, the one that's commonly called the Star of David? Although, that isn't what it's officially called." He lined up his finger with the six-pointed star.

The boy nodded, understanding. Even at age nine, he had a firm grasp on the difference between common cultural mistakes and historical facts.

"Well, we think there's a connection between that symbol and the one in the center here."

"And there's a connection between the other symbols and that one, too?"

"Yep. We think so."

"What does that mean?"

"Funny you should ask. Many of these symbols represent immortality."

"Immortality?"

The father's head bobbed up and down. "That's right. The ability to live forever. Since the dawn of time, mankind has been obsessed with immortality. No one wants to think that their life will come to an end, that their existence will blink out. So, throughout history, people have tried to find a way to keep on living."

"Did any succeed?" the boy asked.

His father chuckled again and rubbed the boy's head. "Not that I know of, Son. One of the more famous of the legends was the story of the fountain of youth. A famous explorer named Ponce de León tried to find it. He believed it was located somewhere here in America. He had a particular interest in Florida."

The boy fell silent for a moment as he gazed upon all the symbols, papers, and maps. "So, you have all this because you're trying to figure out a way to live forever?"

"Maybe. Our job is to find things that have been missing for some time. In the case of these symbols and their connection to one another, we're not sure what we'll find."

"The fountain of youth?"

"I suppose anything is possible, Son. But in this case, that isn't what we're looking for. We're looking for a lost city."

"A lost city?"

The father nodded. "That's right. You see, a long time ago, in the sands of the Sahara Desert, there was a thriving oasis city. You know what an oasis is, right?"

The boy gave his father a derisive glare. "Of course I know what an oasis is, Dad. It's a place where things flourish in the desert."

The father smirked. His son was growing up so quickly. *And what kind of nine-year-old uses words like flourish?*

"Right. Anyway, this city, called Zerzura, was supposedly the location of a vast, ancient treasure."

The boy's eyes brightened. "Treasure?"

"I thought you'd like that. Yes, a treasure."

"What kind of treasure?"

"We don't know. That's part of the legend. There might not be any treasure at all."

The boy frowned. "Then why spend so much time looking for it?"

"Because, Son," a woman's voice interrupted from the doorway, "the true value of things isn't always measured in terms of money."

The boy cocked his head to the side. He was clearly trying to understand what she meant.

"What your mother is saying, Son, is that there are things in this world that are more valuable than money. For example, there isn't enough money in the entire universe worth more than you are to me and your mom."

The boy blushed. "I think I understand what you mean."

"I thought you would."

"Dinner's ready, boys. Time to eat. And you, young man, need to get to bed right after."

His mother turned around and flitted back toward the kitchen. The young man continued to stare at the webwork of information.

The father came close and put his hand on the boy's shoulder. "We've been working on this for a long time, your mother and I. If we can ever figure out this puzzle, it will be our family's legacy."

"Legacy?"

The father grinned at the boy. "You'll understand when you get older." He shook his son to jar him from the information overload. "Come on, Tommy. Let's get something to eat. The Schultz family legacy can wait."

Chapter 1

RUB' AL KHALI (THE EMPTY QUARTER), UNITED ARAB EMIRATES

S ean felt the heat on his skin before any of his other senses kicked in. His eyes itched and burned, dry from a lack of moisture. Opening them was a painful chore. He blinked rapidly to wet them, but his tear ducts did little to ease the irritation. It took a minute before he was able to fully pry them open. When he did, he realized the source of the searing warmth.

He stared up into a perfectly clear blue sky. The white-hot sun blazed just over his left shoulder.

His body ached, like he'd lost a prize fight to someone twice his size. He tried to swallow, but his mouth was parched like the sands of a desert. Another epiphany struck him. He was lying on the slope of a sand dune. He looked over one shoulder and then the other, taking in the sea of rolling dunes around him. He *was* in a desert.

He tried to move, but his muscles screamed in pain. Aside from the soreness, his wrists and ankles were bound to metal stakes in the ground, the skin rubbed raw from the ropes—a result of wiggling around while unconscious.

"I must have really ticked someone off this time," he muttered to himself.

"I'm just so thankful you got me into your predicament, too," a familiar voice said from just above Sean's head.

"Tommy?" he asked through dry, cracked lips.

Sean strained to tilt his head back to see his friend, but the angle was awkward and his neck wouldn't bend far enough.

"Who else would follow your rear end into a scenario like this?"

Sean let out a sigh. "How did we end up here?"

"They must have hit your head pretty hard. We were in the market in Dubai, remember?"

Dubai? That doesn't sound right. Why was I in Dubai? Oh, right. Something about a river or a symbol or something.

"Kind of. Be a lamb, and fill me in on the details while my brain catches up."

"Really? You don't remember anything?"

"Do you really think this is the time to be critical? We're tied to metal stakes in what looks to be the middle of the desert. Wait, are you tied down, too?"

"Of course I'm tied down, you moron. Why wouldn't I be?"

"I don't know, maybe you were angry at me and thought you'd teach me a lesson. Where are we, anyway?"

Sean couldn't see his friend roll his eyes. "Still not coming back to you, huh?"

"I already told you it wasn't."

"We're in the Empty Quarter, Sean. It's pretty much the most desolate place on earth."

"I know what the Empty Quarter is."

"Sorry, you weren't exactly clear about what you remember and what you don't."

A hot wind rolled over the hill, kicking sand onto the two men.

Sean got a little in his mouth, which only made his thirst even worse. He spat out the sand but couldn't get rid of the gritty feeling between his teeth.

"Start with the immediate problem," Sean said after a few seconds of struggling with the sand. "How long have we been here?"

"You think I started a timer or something?"

"Tommy!"

"Fine. Best I can figure, a couple of hours."

That explained the dry lips and the burning feeling on his skin.

"You said we were in Dubai? What happened?"

"We were working on a case. We went there to follow a lead. While we were talking to our contact, someone ambushed us. We tried to fight them off, but they hit you over the head, put a bag over my head, and drove us out here, where they staked us to the ground. I assume they want us to suffer a long, slow death."

"You think?"

Tommy ignored the barb.

"Any idea who brought us out here?"

"You have as much info as I do about that. I didn't get a good look at them. Even if I did, they're probably working for someone else."

"Faceless goons."

"Always."

The two fell silent for a moment as another wall of sand blew over them from a gust of wind. They winced, squinting their eyes shut as tight as they could. Last thing either of them needed was sand in their eyes with no way to rub them or flush them out.

"Your parents' legacy project," Sean said after the wind subsided again.

"What?"

"That project your parents were working on when we were kids. That's what we were doing in Dubai. It's all coming back to me now."

"Glad you could catch up."

Sean's mind started to clear a bit. He'd made a call to a friend in Dubai, a guy named Hank Tillis. Sean and Hank went way back. They'd met in a cantina in Mexico. An assassin had been on Sean's tail. Hank helped Sean fight his way out. After that, Hank disappeared for a few years. Sean thought he'd been killed while looking for something in Mexico, a lost Mayan city. He'd warned Hank of the danger, especially in the area where Hank was planning on searching.

The jungles were full of guerrillas, drug cartels, and all kinds of dangerous wildlife. Sean remembered joking about how the frogs could even kill him.

It wasn't until a few years later that Sean found out Hank made it out of Mexico and ended up in the Middle East. Sean never asked what happened with the search for the lost city, but he had a feeling his friend struck out in a major way.

While Hank was a good guy, he had bad habits that had a tendency to get him into trouble. One of the biggest was his gambling addiction. After the night they met at the cantina, Sean learned that he wasn't the only one who had someone after him. Two hired guns from a Costa Rican syndicate were there to eliminate Hank.

Based on the huge knives hanging from their belts, Sean assumed they were going to cut off his friend's head and take it back to their boss. It was a popular way to take out a problem due to the vicious warning it sent to any others who might cause trouble.

Sean knew the hit men wouldn't try anything in the bar. While he'd seen his fair share of bar fights in the past, it was easy to tell these guys had no intentions of making it a messy incident—other than the possible decapitation.

He figured the men would follow them outside, herd them into an alley, and then kill them there—quietly if possible.

Sean and Hank finished their conversation, went out the front door, and ambushed the three men in the adjacent side street. After the smoke cleared, the three assassins were dead in a dumpster behind the cantina.

Even after Hank disappeared, Sean knew how to find the man—although it wasn't easy. Hank had become a master of staying off people's radar.

The whole reason behind Tommy and Sean seeking Hank's help was because the man always knew what was going on in the black market. Not only was Hank a highly trained historian and archaeologist, he knew how to spot a fake piece from nearly every culture that ever existed. It was a skill that made him a valuable commodity and was probably how he'd secured some sense of relative safety in Dubai.

"You and your family legacy," Sean muttered.

"What's that?" Tommy asked.

"I said I wish someone would turn on the AC."

"Funny."

The Schultz Family Legacy. It was the reason Sean and Tommy were strapped to metal spikes in the middle of the desert. Tommy's parents had been working on some big project in the 1980s but dropped everything abruptly when their leads ran out. They discovered something else, a clue to a great weapon from the ancient world, and completely abandoned years of research.

It was a decision that cost them years of their lives and kept them separated from their son while they were held captive in North Korea for almost two decades.

Tommy had approached Sean about renewing the search. He said he'd received a lead that filled in a huge missing piece to the puzzle. Now that his parents were safely back in the United States, it would be a glorious gift to them if he could find what they'd been searching for during his childhood.

Sean thought it was a fanciful notion, especially given what Tommy wanted to find. Not to mention it was the second time in the last few years they'd attempted to locate an artifact that could supposedly give the gift of eternal life.

He'd seen some strange things in his life working for Tommy's International Archaeological Agency, but he'd never witnessed anything that would make someone immortal.

Sean agreed to help out. After all, what was the worst that could happen? Apparently, the worst was ending up staked to the sand dunes in the world's most desolate desert quarter.

The question weighing heaviest on Sean's mind was, who knew they were going to be at Hank's?

"You think he stabbed us in the back?" Tommy asked, cutting into Sean's thoughts.

"Who?"

"Who do you think? Your friend Hank. He's the only one who knew we were going to be there."

"Hank wouldn't do that."

"You said he's a scumbag, owes money to bad people all over the Western Hemisphere."

"That might be true, but we can trust him."

Tommy sighed. "Fine. Who else?"

"I'm thinking."

"Well, while you're thinking would you mind thinking up a way to get us out of this mess?"

"Maybe try going into full rage mode and see if you can muster up some kind of mutant strength to rip the spikes out of the ground."

"You think this is funny? We're gonna die out here, Sean. And no one will know." His thoughts drifted to his new girlfriend, June. She was back home in the United States, working on a few projects of her own.

"Take it easy, man. We'll think of something." Sean did his best to project an air of confidence. Truth was, he had no idea how they were going to get out of this one.

"Well, I hope you're going to start thinking of something soon because we won't last long out here."

Sean glanced over at the watch on his wrist. It was a gift from his friend at DARPA and came equipped with a built in distress beacon. He never figured he'd need to use it, but now would be the opportune time. The only problem was that he had no way to hit the combination of buttons with his fingers. To make things worse, his wrists were tied so tightly to the stake, he couldn't bend his hand in such a way to set off the signal.

He squirmed and wiggled hard against the taut bindings, but it was no use. Their salvation was only inches away, and he couldn't move enough to activate the device.

An automobile engine groaned somewhere in the distance, startling both men.

"What's that?" Tommy asked.

"Your guess is as good as mine. Sounds like someone's coming."

"Maybe it's someone coming to rescue us."

"Maybe. Except the only people who know we're here are the

ones who put us here. More than likely, we're probably going to be interrogated."

The sound of the engine swelled until two Land Rovers appeared over the crest across from their dune prison. The tan SUVs rolled down the slope and came to a stop in the little valley between hills.

Four men with submachine guns hanging from their shoulders exited the SUV on the left. The other vehicle's doors remained closed for a moment as if the occupants were pausing while the other four made sure the area was secure. One of the men—a burly, bald man with a dark tan and even darker beard—looked over his shoulder at the other truck and gave a curt nod.

The doors flung open, and three more similarly dressed guards stepped out. The fourth man had to be the one in charge. He wore silver-rimmed aviator sunglasses and had a bandana over his mouth to keep the sand out. His tanned forehead ran up to a thicket of dark hair, streamed with gray. The guy was thin and walked with a wiry gait, like he had all the confidence in the world.

Sean realized who it was before the man said anything.

"I don't believe it," Sean said.

"Believe what? What's going on? Who is it?" Tommy rushed his words, eager to find any scrap of information.

"It's Dufort."

Chapter 2

THE EMPTY QUARTER

"Dufort?" Tommy asked as the man in question pointed to a few random places in the sand, issuing orders to his guards before making the ascent up to where his prisoners were tied down. "I thought he was dead."

"Nope. Should be. We aren't that lucky."

"So, he's the one behind this. Great."

Sean tilted his head forward as much as possible to get a good look at the man as he approached. "Ten bucks he says something clichéd like, 'So, Mr. Wyatt, we meet again."

"Book it," Tommy said. "Nobody says anything so clichéd in real life."

Dufort trudged the last twenty feet to his prisoners and stopped to the side, between both of them.

He pulled down the bandana and showed a crooked, toothy grin. "Well, well, well, Mr. Wyatt. We meet again."

Sean forced a dry laugh. "That counts!" he shouted back to Tommy.

Tommy chuckled. "You win. Definitely close enough to count."

Dufort eyed one man and then the other, clearly irritated at whatever joke they were sharing at his expense. He responded with a swift kick to Sean's side. The shiny black boot sent a surge of pain through Sean's body in an instant. All his muscles clenched at once, tightening the ropes for a second before relaxing again as his extremities collapsed to the sand.

"I'm well aware of your collective penchant for mischief and attempts at humor, so I'll be brief."

"Thank goodness for that," Tommy spat.

Dufort ignored him. "I trust it's hot enough for you out here."

Sean forced a couple of wheezing laughs. "Yeah, but it's a dry heat."

Dufort's eyes narrowed for a second, uncertain what the American meant. "You two have something I need," he said.

"A pair of—" Sean's grunted response to Dufort's comment was cut off by another kick to the ribs.

"You know what I'm talking about," the Frenchman sneered. "Where is the tablet?"

"Hold on," Tommy quipped. "Let me see if it's in one of my pockets. Nope, nothing here." Tommy jiggled his legs in a mocking manner.

Dufort took a few menacing steps up the hill toward Tommy. "I know you found the tablet. You didn't have it with you when you were in Dubai. So, you must have hidden it somewhere. Tell me where it is, and I'll cut you loose."

Sean snickered. "I'm sure you will. Just before you kill us."

Dufort glanced down at him and rolled his shoulders like he didn't have a care in the world. "It would be much more merciful than dying out here." He waved a hand around at the setting. "A death from exposure is slow, painful. You don't want to die that way."

"Slow and painful is having to sit here listening to you drone on," Tommy said.

Dufort took another step toward him and delivered a kick to his side.

Tommy grunted. His eyes squinted hard for a second before he started laughing. "Thank you. I think a bug had crawled in my shirt, and I couldn't reach it. Pretty sure you got it."

Dufort reached into his jacket and drew a pistol. He aimed it at the top of Sean's head. His finger tensed on the trigger. "The tablet! Where is it?"

"You kill us," Tommy said through clenched teeth, "and you'll never find it."

The Frenchman's right eye twitched. He knew Tommy was right, and there wasn't a single thing he could do about it.

"Well," Dufort said with a shrug, "that doesn't mean I can't torture the both of you for a while."

He moved his pistol an inch to the right, lining up his sights with Sean's right foot.

"Okay!" Tommy shouted. "Fine! I'll talk! I'll talk! Just don't shoot him."

Dufort looked across his shoulder at Tommy. The Frenchman kept the pistol pointed at Sean's foot.

"If you shoot him, I'll never hear the end of it," Tommy added with a thick layer of derision.

"What's that supposed to mean?" Sean asked, doing his best to sound offended.

"Shut up! Both of you!" Dufort boomed. He returned his attention to the matter at hand. "You were saying something about telling me the location of the tablet?"

Tommy nodded reluctantly. He licked his dry lips. "Yeah, but you have to let us go."

Dufort shook his head. "Not happening. Both of you are going to die here, in this place. How quickly that happens is the only leverage you have. You can die fast or slow. It's up to you." His finger tightened on the trigger.

"Don't tell this knucklehead a thing, Tommy. You hear me? Don't tell him anything."

Tommy swallowed. "I assume you already checked our hotel room."

Dufort gave a sideways nod to confirm.

"You didn't think we'd be dumb enough to leave it there, did you?"

Dufort's head bobbed back and forth from left to right. "Mmm, not really, but you never know, right? Might get lucky. You two were stupid enough to let me track you down. It was worth a chance to rummage through your things." His face twisted into a scowl. "Now stop stalling, and tell me where you hid the tablet. No one is coming to help you."

Tommy tried to swallow again, but his dry throat made it feel like he was swallowing a dagger.

"There's a locker," he gasped. "At Union Station in Dubai."

"What number?"

"Locker 247," Tommy said in a defeated tone. "You'll need the key." He hoped that fact would lend him and his friend a little more time to figure out a way to escape.

Dufort sighed, letting his chest drop in an overdramatic fashion. "Really? You mean this key?" He fished a set of keys out of his pocket and dangled the smallest one that was marked with the initials of the Dubai Metro Red Line. "We took your keys from you, remember? And now that we know where to look, there's no point in keeping the two of you around any longer."

The Frenchman turned his head back to his weapon's sights and made sure they were lined up with Sean's foot.

"Hey, Gerard, you're still aiming at my foot," Sean said. "You said you'd kill us quickly."

"I lied."

A gunshot rang out across the dunes.

It wasn't from Dufort's weapon, though. It came from a high-powered rifle.

The two Americans scanned the horizon for the shooter's location, but they saw no one. Down below, however, one of Dufort's men dropped to the ground, blood leaking out of the base of his neck.

The rest of the guards scattered, taking cover behind their vehicles as they searched the area with their eyes, desperate to find the shooter.

Another blast echoed through the sandy hills. The sand at Dufort's feet exploded just inches away. He nearly jumped out of his boots. His attention immediately shifted. The prisoners were no longer his primary concern.

Dufort ran down the hill, kicking sand up to his knees as his feet plunged into the dune slope with every step. Another shot thundered in the distance. Another of Dufort's men dropped to the ground by the SUV on the left.

"It's an ambush!" Dufort yelled. "Let's get out of here!"

He flung open one of the doors and dove into his SUV. His men clambered to get to the relative safety of the vehicles' interiors. Another man was too slow in getting out of the open as he grasped the door handle. He took a round to the side of the head, leaving little remaining of the other side of his skull. He was dead before his knees hit the ground. His torso wavered for a moment before toppling over into the sand.

Dufort's SUV tore away, all four wheels spitting sand out behind it as it surged forward through the valley of dunes and disappeared around the bend. The second SUV was right behind and hurried to catch up, vanishing behind the next dune a moment later.

The engines groaned as their drivers sped away. Within a minute, the sounds had subsided and the two friends were alone again in the vast desert wasteland.

"So...what do we do now?" Tommy asked.

"I'm guessing we wait until our savior shows their face."

"Yeah, except I'm getting the feeling that we were saved just so we could be thrown right into something worse."

Sean's eyes narrowed to nothing more than slits as he scanned the ridge of a dune about two hundred yards away. At first he thought his eyes were playing tricks on him. He focused with all his energy and saw it again. It definitely wasn't a mirage. There was a piece of beige cloth flapping in the wind just behind the dune's crest.

Then Sean saw the glint of sunlight off glass. The shooter was searching the area to make sure it was clear. Whoever the sniper was, they weren't being careless.

Dufort and his men were probably a mile away by now, and still the shooter hadn't shown himself.

Smart, Sean thought. If it was him, he'd give it another five minutes just to make sure the men in the SUVs weren't doubling back.

The sniper behind the dune only gave it two.

The figure rose behind the ridge, carrying a long rifle under his armpit. The weapon was wrapped with similar cloth to what the man wore—beige pants, jacket with cargo pockets, and a bandana wrapped around his face. His sunglasses were dark and didn't reflect the sunlight. He had a matching guerrilla hat on his head with a bill that kept additional light out of his eyes.

"Looks like our savior is coming out to meet us," Sean said.

Tommy looked out and saw the man approaching. He had an awkward gait, but that could have been attributed to the unsteady footing in the sand.

The sniper reached the bottom of the ravine and took another cautious look from right to left, making sure there was no one lingering to ambush him. He nudged the bodies of the dead men with his boot to make sure they weren't faking it—a little overkill for the guy missing a quarter of his head.

Satisfied the men wouldn't be causing any more problems, the sniper trudged up the hill toward the two Americans. He stopped close to Sean's feet and assessed the situation. After giving another wary look around, he reached to his belt and unbuckled a long hunting knife.

Sean watched him with curious unease. He didn't know if the guy was about to cut him free or just cut him.

"What do you want?" Tommy asked.

The man reached down and sawed through the rope tied to Sean's left ankle. He moved over to the other foot and freed it in seconds.

"Who are you?" Tommy persisted.

The man pulled his bandana down and removed his sunglasses. "Just a friend," the guy said.

A grin spread across Sean's face. "Hank!"

Hank's lips creased. "In the flesh."

"You're late."

Hank shrugged. "You know what they say about late versus never, right?"

"Do they say be early instead?"

A booming laugh escaped the man's mouth, and he quickly quieted himself as he set to work on cutting Sean's wrists loose.

"What happened to you last night?" Tommy asked. "You were supposed to be there."

"Yep," Hank said, sawing the knife edge through the rope attached to Sean's right wrist. "And if I'd been there on time, I might well be working on my tan with you two fellas right now."

"Fair point. That still doesn't explain where you were."

Hank freed Sean of his last bond and turned his attention to cutting Tommy loose.

Sean worked his fingers in and out to get the feeling back in his hands and forearms. The skin on his wrists was rubbed red from the bindings.

"I got held up. Some idiot tried to run his moped through a red light at a busy intersection and got hit. I was stuck in traffic with no way to get out. Had cars in front, back, and beside me. Must have taken them an hour to clear up the mess."

"You should have called," Tommy said.

"I didn't know how long it was going to take them. Anyway, I think the rider survived. And the good news is so did you guys. Win-win!"

He made quick work of the ropes and put the knife back in its sheath.

Tommy stood up, grateful to feel the circulation returning to his extremities. He rubbed his wrists for a moment, careful not to irritate the already raw skin.

"How in the world did you find us?"

"Luckily, the cops showed up and started redirecting traffic. By the time I got to our meeting spot, it was too late. Fortunately, I got there as those men were putting you two in the back of their trucks. I laid low and watched, thinking there was no way I could take them all out right then and there. I followed them for a ways outside the city, but I knew they'd see me if I stayed too close. Once they turned off the main highway, there was no way I could stay on their tail. Given the direction they were going, there weren't many places they'd venture other than into the dunes. So, I hired a friend to fly over earlier this morning. He spotted you two in less than an hour, gave me your coordinates, and the rest is...well, you know."

"You hired a pilot to find us?" Sean asked.

"Yeah, and he ain't cheap, either. I'd appreciate it if Tommy's agency would reimburse some of that funding."

Tommy sighed. "Happily."

Hank slid the sunglasses back onto his face. "We need to get back to town. Not safe out here. If I've got any sense about those guys who kidnapped you, my guess is they'll be back to finish you off."

Sean shook his head. "Maybe. My guess is they're heading to Union Station."

Hank's eyebrows pinched together behind his sunglasses. "Union? Why would they go there?"

"Because we told them to."

"Told them to? Why'd you do that? And why would they listen?"

"They're after the tablet," Tommy explained.

"The Zerzura Tablet?" Hank asked, his tone shifting to a more reverent sound.

"Unless there was another one we were here to ask you about."

Hank frowned. "But that tablet is incomplete. It's useless without the other half."

"We know that," Sean said.

"If they get your half, though, then you'll be up a creek."

"That's why we sent them to our decoy locker."

"Decoy locker?" Hank cocked his head to the side like a puzzled dog.

Sean flashed a toothy grin. "Yep. Decoy locker."

Chapter 3

DUBAI

"So, you sent them to Union Station and a locker there with nothing in it?" Hank asked, still trying to piece together the story.

"Yep," Tommy answered. "Sean figured where we were meeting you had the makings of an ambush or at least was the perfect place for one. So, we took precautions."

"Rented a locker at Union Station and another one at the last station on the other end of the line."

"Which is where we're going now, Jebel Ali station."

"Correct. So, while Dufort and his men are opening up an empty locker in the next half hour, we'll be on the other side of town."

"By the time they realize what happened," Tommy said, "we'll be on our way to the airport."

Hank shook his head. "Seems like you guys thought of everything. Guess it's not your first time doing this sort of thing."

"Helps to be prepared—especially when you're dealing with something like this."

"The Zerzura Tablet," Hank muttered. "Do you really think that's what it is?"

"If it isn't, it's caused a lot of trouble for it not to be."

"You're sure your connection has seen the other half of the tablet?" Sean asked.

Hank's eyes flashed up to the rearview mirror at Sean in the back. "That's what he said. When you guys sent me the picture and told me what it was, I had to use a bit of restraint. I mean, you're talking about a tablet that could help us locate the lost city of Zerzura." His voice drifted into a distant tone. "Rumor has it that city holds treasures from every ancient kingdom that ever existed."

"Yeah, yeah," Tommy said. "They've got gold discs from Atlantis and even items from the Library at Alexandria. I've heard the stories. Mostly as a child." He muttered the last few words in a disparaging tone.

"How did you come by the other half of the tablet, anyway?" Hank asked, casting Tommy a sidelong glance.

"On a dig," Sean answered for his friend. "Tommy was working the site of the old abandoned city near Dubai."

"Julfar?" Hank asked, surprised.

"Yep," Tommy said. "We thought most of that area had been searched. Then recently, I got a call. Another team was there and said a section of land collapsed near one of the ruins."

"Sounds dangerous."

"That's why they called us. Ordinary researchers aren't as inclined to go jumping into mysterious holes without things being checked out first. Since we keep a team of engineers pretty much on retainer, we had the area checked out pretty quick. When they gave us the all-clear, we went in and started looking around."

"What we found," Sean added, "was an underground labyrinth that predated the city of Julfar. From the looks of it, we think it goes back to around 3,000 BC. Most of the tunnels had been rigged to take out intruders."

"Booby traps?" Hank asked.

"Yep."

"Luckily," Tommy said, "those traps had either deteriorated or been so badly damaged in the collapse that they didn't function anymore."

"So, that's where you found the tablet?"

"Yeah, we found a burial chamber deep underground at the back of the tunnel system. The sarcophagus only identified the interred person as *Priest,* carved into one end of the long sandstone box."

"Priest?"

"From the looks of it and all the other inscriptions painted on the walls, we think he was a priest from a culture that was a precursor to Mesopotamia."

"Assyrian?"

"Earlier. Also, much farther south than the Assyrians."

"You don't think it's an Egyptian colony, do you?"

"No," Tommy said. "The site didn't have anything we could link back to the first Egyptian civilizations. The language and images used were far too different. Whoever these people were, they were ancestors of modern-day Arabia."

Hank's SUV rumbled down the road and merged into another lane that led toward the southwest side of the city.

The gigantic skyscrapers of downtown Dubai soared into the air. The largest building in the world, the Burj Khalifa, towered over the landscape. Construction on the massive hotel began in 2004 with an ambitious plan to make it taller than anything else on the planet. At just over twenty-seven hundred feet, the mission was an astounding success.

Sean stared at the building. A tremor of fear crept into his chest.

"You guys been up in the Khalifa?" Hank asked, pointing at the structure in the distance.

"I was just thinking about that," Sean said.

Tommy chuckled. "No way you'll get him up in that thing, Hank. Sean has a legendary fear of heights."

"It's not legendary."

"Fear of heights? But you're a secret agent. I thought you guys weren't afraid of anything."

"*Was* a secret agent," Sean corrected. "Even Superman has his weaknesses."

The other two erupted in laughter.

"Okay, Superman," Tommy joked.

"You know what I meant."

"Sounded like you were comparing yourself to a superhero," Hank ribbed.

Sean sighed and looked back out the window at the desert on the horizon. Such a stark contrast, he thought, between the innumerable wealth and opulent luxury of the city and the vast nothingness beyond its borders.

"Seriously, though," Hank said after he managed to quiet his laughter, "you're working for your friend here?"

"Yeah," Sean said. "I quit Axis a while back. Worked for Tommy for a few years, took a little time off from that. Now I'm back on board with IAA."

"That IAA is no small operation," Hank said to Tommy. "Impressive work you guys do. I checked out your website. You've got people all over the planet."

Tommy blushed. "Pretty much. Uncovering history is a nonstop gig."

"I can imagine. So, back to the tablet," Hank said. "Once we secure the piece you guys have, we'll meet up with my connection and see what he has for us. Speaking of, how in the world did you convince the Emirates government to let you take that piece you found in the tunnels?"

Tommy looked over his shoulder at Sean and then over to the driver.

"Oh no. You didn't steal it, did you?" Hank asked, suddenly horrified at the consequences. "Surely you guys know better than that."

"Relax," Tommy said. "We have clearance from the government. They're the ones who called us, remember? We're to secure the artifact, take it in for study and evaluation. Then we'll clean it up and bring it back here to Dubai so it can be put on display at one of their museums."

Hank let out a breath of relief. "You had me going there for a second. Last thing I'd like to do is have a run-in with the law."

"Shocker," Sean said.

"Hey, I've kept my nose clean since I got here. I've got a good thing going, a legitimate business. I sell antiques."

"And how did those antiques come to be in your possession?"

"Bought 'em," Hank said. "At auction."

Sean raised an eyebrow, pressing his friend for more information. He knew Hank wasn't giving the whole story. It was something Sean picked up about the guy within the first minute or two of meeting him in that Mexican cantina years before.

"Fine," Hank relented. "I get most of them at auction. The rest I get from this guy you'll meet tonight. Don't worry, you can trust him."

Tommy looked puzzled. "We can trust the underground artifact dealer?"

"I know. I know. It sounds shady."

"It *is* shady," Sean corrected.

"Okay, fine. It's shady, but I've been using this guy a long time. He's got a good eye for fakes, too. He knows when someone is trying to screw him."

"That must come in handy when he's doing business with you."

"Ha, ha. All I know is that when I showed him the tablet picture you sent me, he recognized it immediately. The only thing that concerns me is he said the symbols on the right side of your tablet are different than the ones on the left side of his."

"That would make sense," Tommy said. "There are seven symbols in all." He pulled out his phone and eyed the image of the tablet stored in his device's camera.

Seeing the images took him back to the first night he'd found them in his parents' study. It didn't matter how many times Tommy looked at it. The result was the same every single time.

He remembered seeing the stacks of paper, the books, the maps, and the symbols tacked onto the wall, attached by long colorful strings to one symbol in the center, the seventh symbol that represented immortality.

Tommy had been only nine years old at the time, but that moment made an impression on him. Long after his parents gave up their search for the secret behind the symbols, he kept it in the back of his mind, always watching—listening for a clue that would rise to the surface and shed new light on one of the biggest mysteries in Earth's history.

At least he considered it to be one of the biggest.

Most mainstream history books never mentioned Zerzura. From time to time he'd find a reference to Shangri-La or another famous lost paradise, but information on Zerzura was sparse—less than sparse. It was virtually nonexistent.

It took him years just to make the connection between the symbols on his parents' wall and what he believed was a map to the lost city.

Where his parents failed, Tommy would succeed.

Part of their problem was that they never narrowed down what all their information pointed to. Zerzura was one of the possibilities, but due to its mythical nature it was among the first hypotheses they eliminated.

So, when Tommy found the tablet inside the tomb of the priest at Julfar with an inscription mentioning the name Zerzura, he knew the path had just gotten a whole lot clearer.

He slid the phone back into his pocket and looked out the windshield again. "Once we know what is written on the other half of the tablet," Tommy said, "we'll be one huge step closer to finding the lost oasis city and whatever wonders it still may possess."

Hank's eyes grew wider at the possibility, but he said nothing. The other occupants in his SUV were more concerned with the historical value of ancient treasures than the monetary worth. Of course, if he tagged along it was entirely within reason for him to get some kind of reward.

"Except there's still one giant problem with all this," Sean said.

"And that is?" Hank asked.

"If there was a lost oasis city somewhere in the Sahara, it would have been found a long time ago. Heck, random nomads would have discovered it, not to mention satellites, aircraft, you name it."

"So, you don't believe it exists?" Hank did his best not to sound too crestfallen.

"If I didn't believe it was out there, I'd still be in the States right now. I believe Zerzura was a real place. Too many eyewitness accounts to dispute that. I just think we're going to have a difficult time locating it since it's probably buried under three thousand years' worth of sand."

"Have a little faith, buddy," Tommy said. "If we can find the location, we'll figure out how to dig it out later."

Sean didn't say anything else. He knew his friend's motivations. A big part of finding the lost city of Zerzura was to finish a journey his parents began long ago. Tommy wondered openly about the project on numerous occasions, even asking his parents about it from time to time.

"A quest like that," his father said, "is a young man's game. Not to mention I sank a lot of my life into the search for the lost desert city. The time I spent working on that was time I could have spent with you and your mother."

Tommy hadn't brought up the fact that his mom was heavily involved with the project, too. He didn't need to. He understood what his father was saying.

That didn't stop Tommy from trying to finish the job.

Hank turned off the highway and onto an access road leading toward a large train station to the east. The huge skyscrapers loomed in the distance behind them, giving way to the more modest accommodations on the outskirts of town. Rising just above the apartments, businesses, and houses in the industrial district was the Jebel Ali train station just to the north.

The station looked like some kind of giant space ship, birthing two railroad tracks out from either end. While it was the last stop on the line, expansion was always on the table with the Dubai city planners, though their focus was on creating three new railways before extending the current ones.

The golden glass dome stretched from the ground on one side all the way over to the other, overlaying on a pattern of regular glass windows arching directly over the tracks.

"I'll say this about Dubai," Hank said, "they don't do anything halfway. When they set out to build something, they really go after it."

"You can say that again," Tommy said as he admired the train station through his window.

Hank weaved his way through traffic, stopping several times for red lights. Finally, after navigating the stop-and-go mayhem, they reached the station. Hank pulled the car into an empty spot a hundred feet from the station entrance. There were dozens of empty parking spots to choose from since the last stop on the line was usually the least busy.

Sean stepped out of the vehicle and immediately began assessing their surroundings. The parking lot was flat and fairly open. Lots of places for a gunman to take a position behind one of the other cars. From his initial reconnaissance, he didn't see anything like that. Still, best to keep his eyes peeled.

He'd also kept a close watch on the road behind them as they left the desert and returned into the city. They hadn't been followed, of that Sean was certain. If they did have a tail, the pursuers were using something other than line of sight to keep up. Doubtful since that would mean they'd have anticipated everything that happened with Hank coming to the rescue.

No way Dufort was thinking that far ahead.

In Sean's limited encounters with the man, he'd learned that Dufort wasn't anything if he wasn't confident. The Frenchman had slipped through Sean's fingers in Morocco. Before that, he'd narrowly escaped by sheer luck from the basement of a castle in Denmark.

Now he was back and, apparently, trying to make a play for the Zerzura Tablet.

While Sean was certain Dufort and his men were safely on the other side of the city, no doubt inspecting the contents an empty locker, it was disconcerting that the man had resurfaced.

The sandbox in which Sean and Tommy played tended to be a small one, and bumping into familiar faces, even villains, was bound to happen from time to time. Dufort, however, was different.

If he'd been smart, he would have stayed hidden under whatever rock he'd crawled the last time he and Sean squared off. The fact that he was back out in the open merely reinforced the man's reckless overconfidence.

It wouldn't be a surprise if Dufort was simply out for revenge. Sean's actions resulted in the Frenchman losing millions from his human trafficking network in what was one of the largest busts of its kind. Dozens of girls were freed from his clutches, and piece by piece, Dufort's criminal network had come tumbling down.

Upon entering Hank's SUV, one of the first things Sean's friend had asked about was who the guy was that was about to kill them.

Sean spent about three minutes giving Hank the rundown, which was more than enough to cause the older man to drive a little faster out of the desert.

There were few places on Earth where Dufort could go without setting off a sequence of alerts that would result in his arrest. Dubai, it seemed, was one of those locations. That also meant he'd probably established a new network of some kind within the area.

Tommy led the way into the big train station as the sun in the west reflected off its shimmering glass panels. Once the men stepped through the doors, they were greeted by a blast of cool air that reminded them just how hot it was in the desert city.

The three men paused inside the station. Sean and Tommy took a quick inventory of their surroundings, making sure nothing or no one suspicious was lurking about. They must have looked a motley crew, with Sean and Tommy in their sweaty, dirty, and bloodstained clothes. Hank looked the most normal of the three.

The station's interior was as much a statement as the exterior. Bold, swooping lines of light panels, steel girders, rails, curving stairways—all amid an atmosphere that projected success—made a bold statement about Dubai and its intent to be a beacon of progress in the future.

"Where's this locker?" Hank asked, anxious to get in and get out before there was more trouble.

"Over here," Tommy said, pointing at a recessed area under an escalator.

They started walking, but Hank stopped them. "Wait. What about the key? Surely Frenchy didn't let you keep that one."

Sean's eyes narrowed with a mischievous smile. "No, he wouldn't have, which is why we didn't bring it with us."

Chapter 4

DUBAI

"Didn't bring it with you?" Hank blurted out. "How are we supposed to get in the thing if you didn't bring your key?"

"We didn't bring it with us to meet you," Sean clarified. "We left it here."

"Left it here?"

That explanation didn't seem to instill Hank with any more confidence than the previous one.

Sean's eyes twinkled. "Yeah," he said with an upward nod.

He strolled toward a giant fake palm tree that was placed at the bottom of the main stairway. The tree was situated in a huge pot. The pot was full of rubber mulch and fake moss.

Sean took a careful look around, backing up until he felt his fingers touch the lip of the planter. Then he reached back a few inches farther and shoved his hand into the narrow gap between the pot's inner wall and the foam keeping the tree upright. For a minute, Tommy and Hank watched from the other side of the walkway as Sean felt around in the planter.

He did his best to keep from looking awkward, but the way his body was bent to the side and the fact that he was clearly sticking his hand in the pot were hard to ignore. Luckily, the relatively few travelers who walked by didn't pay him much attention.

Finally, he felt his index finger touch something metal with a pointy edge. He stuck his hand in a little farther and wrapped his fingers around the key. Then he stood up straight, casually shoved the hand with the key into his pocket, and strolled back over to the other two.

"Smooth," Tommy said.

"I thought so," Sean said.

"Except not at all. Pretty sure everyone noticed the American standing awkwardly by the big flower pot while you sifted around for something."

Sean cocked his head to the side and pulled the key out of his pocket. "Well, I got it, so you're welcome. Come on."

He turned and stalked away toward the locker area.

Tommy and Hank exchanged a short laugh and a knowing glance before they moved ahead to catch up.

Sean turned into one of the rows of metal lockers. He counted down the numbers until he found the one he wanted and then bent down to open it. He slid the key in easily, swung the door out, and reached inside.

Hank stared with wide eyes and an equally gaping mouth at the bag Sean pulled out. It was just a normal daypack.

"You're keeping a priceless artifact in an ordinary backpack?" Hank asked. "I figured you guys would have some kind of airtight, metal, ultra-secure container for something like that."

Sean slung the bag over his shoulder and closed the locker. He stood up and put the other arm through the strap, securing the bag tight against his back.

"It's made out of stone, Hank."

"Yeah," Tommy said. "We don't have to worry about air damaging it or anything like that. I'd rather it not get wet, which is why we have it in a freezer bag inside the backpack."

"Huh." Hank sounded crestfallen. "Way lower tech than I anticipated, I suppose."

Sean shook his head. "Come on. We need to get out of here. Where are we going to meet your contact?"

"Working on that," Hank said as he pulled out his phone and checked his messages. "Hold on." A new message caused the device to vibrate in his hand. "He said to meet at the docks in an hour."

"The docks?" Tommy asked. "Won't there be workers there?"

Hank shook his head. "Not where he wants us to meet. This pier is all but abandoned. They haven't used it in three years, not enough boat traffic coming in to warrant it."

Tommy and Sean cast each other a wary glance.

"Okay, Hank," Sean said. "You're on point with this one. We're going to have to trust your lead."

"It'll be fine. No cops in that area, and if someone were to try to sneak up on us, we'd see them coming from a mile away. It's a good spot."

Tommy pressed his lips together and nodded. "Sounds like you've got a handle on it, Hank. Let's do it."

Back in the SUV, Sean tucked the bag down by his feet as Hank sped out of the parking lot and made his way back onto the road.

"You guys need to eat something," he said. "I know a good little place not far from here. You probably need to drink something, too."

Hank had provided each of them with a bottle of water, but that had been guzzled down within a minute of getting into the SUV. Sean hadn't thought about eating, but now that Hank mentioned it he realized how hungry he was.

Sensing their apprehension, Hank spoke up again. "We have plenty of time. I'm telling you, the docks where my guy wants to meet are minutes away from here. Let's get some food, and then we'll get there early, scope the place out, and make sure you're comfortable. Last thing I want is for you guys to end up tied to some stakes in the middle of the desert again."

"Avoiding that would be a good thing," Tommy said.

Hank steered his SUV through the quiet industrial streets until they reached an area where three- and four-story buildings lined the streets. Signs for restaurants, retail stores, and other businesses hung from the walls over the sidewalks.

"A few blocks up is the Dubai bazaar. That's not where we're going, but if you'd like to pick up some souvenirs for your visit that's the place."

Sean and Tommy chuckled at Hank's comment. The older man flashed a toothy grin in the rearview mirror.

Hank was probably in his mid-fifties, though Sean never brought up his age. That sort of thing didn't matter. What mattered was effectiveness. So far, Hank had more than proved himself as a useful ally.

He swung the SUV into an empty parking space next to the sidewalk and backed it into place.

"I'm impressed," Sean said. "Tommy usually takes three or four tries to parallel park."

"What?"

Before Tommy could protest, Sean climbed out of the vehicle and slung the bag with the tablet in it over his shoulder.

Tommy wasn't going to let the parking comment go. He hurriedly opened his door and hopped out with a scowl on his face.

"When have you ever seen me parallel parking, to say that?" Tommy asked.

Sean rolled his shoulders. "I don't know, every time I've ever ridden with you anywhere."

Tommy started to argue again, but Sean cut him off. "Hank, where's this place with the food you were talking about?"

"Omar's," Hank said, closing the door to his SUV. He hit the lock button on the fob, and all the doors clicked. "It's right down here." He pointed down the sidewalk at a blue-and-white sign hanging out over the concrete.

Hank led the way through the mobs of busy pedestrians. The people were dressed in all kinds of outfits. Some wore traditional clothing from the region, while others would have looked at home in a jeans commercial.

The three Americans turned into Omar's and found themselves

overwhelmed with the scents of onions, curry, beef, lamb, and garlic. There was a hint of smoky paprika in the air as well.

It was a simple enough restaurant. Tables with white tablecloths draped over them lined the walls on both sides, with two rows in the middle. Sean immediately counted nine customers—three in line ahead of them and six already eating.

Hank got behind the last customer and turned around to face his companions. "What do you guys like? Chicken? Beef? Lamb?"

"All of the above," Tommy said.

"What he said," Sean agreed. "Although that falafel looks pretty good."

"It's outstanding," Hank said. "I'll get a little bit of each. You guys go ahead and grab a seat."

The other two nodded and found a table in the back corner close to a hallway leading to the bathrooms.

Sean sat down with his back to the narrow corridor so he could face the window. It was an old habit but one he'd probably never change. Being able to see danger coming was the first step in surviving, especially in close quarters like this.

"Seriously," Tommy said as he leaned back in his seat, "when have you ever seen me parallel parking? And beyond that, when was I bad at it?"

Sean shook his head. "You're still on that? I'm already working on my next joke about you."

"Sometimes I don't know why I hang out with you."

That comment sent a thin smile across Sean's lips. "Because you love me. And because I saved your life."

"Last I checked, that debt was repaid."

"I'm not talking about the literal life-saving times. I'm talking about making you happy."

"Making me happy?" Tommy's voice rose to match his irritation. "How in the world do you figure you make me happy?"

Sean shrugged. "By coming back to work with you. Imagine if I hadn't. You'd still be out in the desert somewhere, staked to the ground instead of in this nice, air-conditioned building."

Tommy's head swiveled back and forth rapidly. "First of all, it's your fault...and Hank's," he hissed the other name so Hank wouldn't hear, "that we ended up out there. His little rendezvous nearly got us killed. Frankly, I can't believe I'm letting you two set up another one with this mysterious connection of his. For all we know, Hank's connection could be hooked up with Dufort."

The little bell over the door dinged as two men entered the restaurant. They were wearing sunglasses and apparently had no intention of taking them off despite being out of the blinding hot sun.

It only took one slip of body language to tell Sean why.

The second guy, probably in his early twenties, took a quick look back outside as if to make sure no one else was coming in. None of the other restaurant patrons noticed, or if they did they didn't let on. Hank was busy ordering food when the two men walked in and made their way toward the register.

Tommy was still mumbling about the gall Sean had to think he'd somehow made his friend happy.

"I mean, sure, I'm glad to have you along, and you're my best friend in the world. Just seems like a jerk thing to say," Tommy said, looking down at the table.

Sean barely heard his last comment. He was locked in on the two guys approaching the counter. He saw the weapons just inside their unzipped windbreakers as the air flapped the fabric up a few inches, just enough to reveal the black gunmetal.

Sean knew what was about to happen, but his weapons were back in the hotel. Come to think of it, Dufort and his men probably took them. He'd have to fix that as soon as possible. For now, he'd have to make do with whatever he could.

He took in the room in the blink of an eye: metal napkin holder next to his left elbow on the table, broom leaning up against the wall behind the register, gum ball machine five...maybe six feet away next to the corner of the counter, and then of course the tables and chairs. Not a lot to work with. Luckily, he already had a plan by the time the first man pulled out his gun and pointed it at the guy working the register.

"Hands up!" the first gunman yelled in plain English. "Everyone down on the ground!"

Hank was startled and nearly jumped out of his shoes at the sudden command. He instinctively spun around and came face to face with a gun. Hank's hands opened, and he raised them slowly, showing the gunmen he was trying to do as told.

The first guy grabbed Hank by the shoulder and shoved him to the ground. The second gunman drew his weapon a moment later and started waving it around the room.

It was a simple enough plan. One guy would handle the register and any workers behind the counter. The second would take care of crowd control. Sean watched the scene unfold. If it weren't so dangerous, he might have been amused. Instead, he was annoyed.

Tommy didn't budge, either. While the other patrons quickly dove to the floor, Tommy observed what was happening. He glanced at Sean, the question in his mind flowed from his eyes to his friend's. He didn't need to say anything.

"Second guy, napkin holder to the head," Sean whispered. "I'll take out number one."

Tommy gave a single nod.

"Hey!" the guy working crowd control shouted at the two men sitting at their table. "He said down on the floor!"

The gunman waved the weapon from Sean to Tommy and back again. As the weapon moved back toward Sean, Tommy snatched the napkin holder and in one fluid movement flung it.

There was no way the would-be robber could do anything to stop it. The metal object flew across the short span between the men and struck the guy in the forehead.

Stunned for a second, the second gunman instinctively reached up to grab the fresh wound and lowered his weapon.

Tommy exploded out of his seat and charged. He let out an angry yell and raised his arm parallel to the floor.

The first gunman saw the movement to his right and spun to address the situation. His reaction was too late.

Sean sprang from his chair, took one huge step over to the gum ball machine, and hefted it off the floor. Gunman number one was already aiming his gun at the charging Tommy when Sean swung the heavy machine and crushed the man's forearm with the base.

The first gunman shrieked as the bone in his arm cracked. His weapon dropped to the floor, and as he grasped at the broken appendage with the other hand Sean jumped into the air, planted one foot on the counter, pushed off to get even more elevation, and then swung his right shin around with an incredible amount of force.

His shin struck the man in the side of the head and sent him sprawling to the floor. Sean landed next to him and rolled the guy over onto his back.

Meanwhile, Tommy lined up his guy with the inside of his elbow and clotheslined him, driving the bone deep into the gunman's throat. The man flipped onto his back, his head smacking into the floor. His eyes instantly went hazy, desperately searching for something stable in what was now a spinning room.

"Call the cops," Sean said as he straddled gunman number one.

The manager shouted something to one of the employees, who hurriedly picked up the phone and started dialing.

The gunman under Sean tried to wiggle free, so Sean raised a fist and punched him across the jaw. The guy's body went limp, and Sean sighed through his nose.

He looked over at Hank, who was clambering to get up off the floor. "I guess we should probably get our order to go," Sean said.

Chapter 5

DUBAI

Dufort stood with his arms crossed as his men secured the perimeter around the locker area at Union Station. The building was full of people busily rushing about their afternoon to get to or from work. Some locals were rushing to meet up with friends, no doubt taking advantage of the public transit system. Travelers were easy to spot. They almost always carried too much luggage, or often had cameras dangling from their necks.

All the people were just a backdrop to Dufort. He saw the hustle and bustle going on but paid no attention to it. His ears drowned out the sounds of the busy station while his men made sure no one else could see what he was about to retrieve.

He stepped toward the locker and lowered his arms. The key he'd stolen from the Americans hung loosely in his fingers.

Dufort loomed over the locker for a moment. It was at knee level and didn't look like anything special, just like all the other lockers in the area. Inside this one, however, was something he'd been trying to find for a long time. Getting it would not only lead him to one of the most powerful treasures known to man, it would also be the final undoing of Sean Wyatt and his friend.

Wyatt had ruined everything for Dufort.

At one point, the Frenchman's wealth numbered in the hundreds of millions, nearly reaching the billion mark. With businesses in the sex slave trade and narcotics, he'd easily have reached that number in no time.

Sean Wyatt and his gang of miscreants changed all that. Dufort lost 90 percent of his wealth within just a few months. His associates, some with whom he'd done business for several years, disappeared. Dufort's criminal empire crumbled like wet cardboard. He couldn't even find a decent place to hide out during his exile from society.

Luckily, he still had more money than most ordinary people. While money wasn't as good as power, it still enabled him to buy his way into a few places where he could reinvent himself and come up with a plan to rebuild—and a plan for revenge.

His return to the top wouldn't be possible if he was just an ordinary man. Authorities in nearly every First World country had him on a watch list. He couldn't get on a commercial airplane without setting off a dozen red flags. With cameras everywhere in public places of travel, he'd be spotted and apprehended in no time.

If Gerard Dufort was going to make a return, he'd have to do it as someone else...and *something* else.

The first thing he focused his energy on was learning as much as possible about Sean Wyatt and his close friend, Tommy Schultz. Getting information about Wyatt was tricky, but money had a powerful sway on people who kept secrets. Schultz was easier and, as it turned out, held the key to Dufort's plan for revenge.

Perhaps it was providence or maybe just dumb luck, but Schultz had taken up pursuing something his parents worked on decades before. They'd been trying to find an ancient lost city called Zerzura that had disappeared thousands of years ago.

Dufort set about trying to learn as much as he could about this legendary city. Information was difficult to come by. Most of what he initially discovered was conjecture or hearsay. There were rumors about nomads who'd been lost in the desert and returned to civilization with stories of vast treasures within the ruins of the lost oasis. When they were pressed to give the location of the city, however, these men were unable to provide the exact spot on a map.

Treasure hunters from around the world spent fortunes on the search for Zerzura, every one ending up empty handed. Many of them went broke in their pursuit. The saga reminded Dufort of some of his own treasure hunts from the past.

One thing he'd learned along the way was how to leverage the hard work of others. Doing so allowed him to shortcut all the time and effort involved. Well, almost all of it.

The Schultz family, Dufort learned, had a significant weakness. They were sentimental. Tommy, in particular, was inclined to nostalgia. While on his self-imposed exile, Dufort hired a few mercenaries to keep an eye on Schultz, waiting for the right lead to come along that would give the Frenchman everything he wanted.

Nearly two years went by before Zerzura fell in his lap.

Tommy picked up something in the ancient town of Julfar, and the artifact led the younger Schultz to believe it was somehow connected to Zerzura.

While the lost oasis city was rumored to contain unimaginable wealth, it wasn't the financial gain that most attracted Dufort to the United Arab Emirates. Something else was rumored to be hidden in one of the temples at Zerzura, something that could grant mere mortals eternal life.

Dufort snapped back to the present. He'd planned and prepared for this moment where he would take the next step. Every move he'd made was precisely calculated. Everything was planned to perfection.

With this tablet, he would find the lost city of Zerzura, and from there he would become like a god.

Some people doubted the stories. He knew some of his own men didn't believe there was some magical artifact that could grant humans eternal life. But Dufort had seen too many unexplainable things to write it off. Besides, it didn't matter if his men believed or not. All they cared about was getting paid.

He shuffled one foot closer to the locker, keeping his gaze on the keyhole. His mind wandered back to a few hours before.

The incident in the desert had been a little too close, but after making their escape Dufort never turned back. Losing two of his men was disconcerting, but that was the price that had to be paid.

He leaned down and carefully slid the key into the keyhole. It clicked as each tooth rode over the mechanisms inside until the base hit the outer edge. Dufort held his breath for a second before he twisted it.

The key turned easily. Dufort half expected it not to work, a trick played on him by Wyatt and his friend.

He let out another long breath through his nostrils and pulled back on the locker door. His relief from the moment before quickly vanished as he stared into the little box.

It was empty.

Dufort sniffled and twitched his nose in irritation. He leaned down farther to see if perhaps the locker was deeper than he anticipated or if perhaps the tablet had been pushed to the back. Further inspection confirmed there was nothing to be found inside.

He swallowed hard and stood up straight. His spine stiffened, and he cracked his neck to the right and then left.

His right-hand man, a tall brute named Cody Dent, noticed his employer's reaction to opening the locker.

He stepped close and looked inside. His eyebrows lowered, confused at the empty box. "Where is it?" he asked.

"That is a good question, Cody. It would seem that we've been tricked."

"You don't think—"

"I would certainly hope not. Then again, anything is possible. I'll get to the bottom of this soon enough."

Dufort felt his phone buzz in his pocket. He fished it out and pressed the home button below the screen. With another tap, he opened the text messaging app and stared at the screen. His anger slowly dwindled like a wave dying to a ripple.

He took in a deep breath and stuffed the phone back in his pocket then turned to Cody. "Round up the men. We're going to the other side of town."

Cody's face scrunched in a frown, clearly not understanding why the sudden change of plans. "What's on the other side of town?"

"It would appear our friends Mr. Wyatt and Mr. Schultz tricked us. But we know where they are going. They only had one half of the tablet. The man they're meeting has the other half. While their trickery has caused us a slight delay, it's actually going to work out in our favor. We'll be able to—as you Americans say—kill two birds with one stone."

Chapter 6

DUBAI

Sean peered through his sunglasses from the shadows of an old warehouse. The sun was setting over the desert to the west. Soon, dusk would arrive and then darkness. He preferred not to conduct their meeting with Hank's connection in the dark. It opened up too many variables. Well-equipped assault teams would have night vision goggles and other tools that would tip the odds heavily in their favor. He could only assume Dufort's men would be outfitted for such an occasion.

It was a big leap to guess they'd show up. He hoped he was wrong. Most of the time when he found himself hoping for something like that, he was disappointed. Men like Dufort were like a pimple that kept popping up on the day of the homecoming dance. He'd been gone for a couple of years, but just when Sean thought he would no longer be an issue, boom! There he was again.

Their little ruse to send the Frenchman to the other side of the city certainly gave Sean and his friends a good head start, but that time was lost due to the delay in meeting Hank's connection. If Dufort was somehow able to pinpoint what happened and where Sean went, there'd be trouble.

Not only were he and his companions outgunned, they were severely outgunned considering they had *no* guns.

Well, that wasn't entirely true. Hank had a revolver. It was a .357 and could do serious damage up close, but it hardly leveled the playing field, and according to Hank he only had six additional rounds in his SUV.

Tommy stepped into view around the corner and walked up. His head was on a swivel, too, checking the grounds as he approached.

"It's all clear in the back. When is this guy getting here? I thought he was going to arrive ten minutes ago," Tommy said.

"I know," Sean said. "Tardiness is one of my biggest pet peeves."

"Mine, too. And it certainly doesn't make me want to trust this guy any more than I do."

"Yeah, I don't like it."

Sean leaned forward, placing his elbows on top of a big wooden crate. Hank appeared around the corner of another building fifty feet away and sauntered over, almost as if he didn't have a care in the world.

"See anything?" Tommy asked when Hank drew near.

"No, we're good. I walked the perimeter and didn't see a thing. If someone was going to ambush us, they'd be here. I told you, you were being paranoid," he said, directing his last comment at Sean.

"Paranoia has served me well."

"Yeah, yeah. Speaking of, good job in the restaurant earlier." Hank's eyebrows pinched together. "How in the world did you react so fast to those two would-be robbers?"

Sean shrugged. "Old habits, I guess."

"You seem to have a lot of those."

"When they walked in, they didn't take off their sunglasses," Sean explained. "Either they were trying to make some kind of fashion statement, or they didn't want people to see their faces."

Hank snickered. "We could see their faces, just not their eyes."

"I didn't say they were brilliant criminals, but you'd be surprised how much a single item like a pair of sunglasses could throw off eyewitnesses. You don't have to think too hard to recall a certain superhero whose only disguise was a pair of reading glasses."

"Fair enough. Still, not a very good disguise by those two, especially in the real world."

"Next, I saw the way they were walking. They looked antsy, like they were in a hurry. More than that, the second one had a nervous pace to his stride. I could tell they weren't there to eat. Then, of course, the breeze from the cool air inside the restaurant knocked back their jackets, and I saw the guns. Not to mention wearing a jacket in Dubai in the middle of the summer? Dead giveaway."

Hank turned to Tommy. "He always like this?"

"I don't know how to turn it off," Tommy said.

"Probably best you don't. Better stay alert. I trust my guy." He paused for a moment. "I mean...the number one rule in dealing with things like this is not to trust anyone. I know that much, but this guy is okay. I swear."

Sean and Tommy weren't so sure. They exchanged a dubious glance.

"Seriously, guys. It's fine. Me and Slater go way back."

Hank had given Sean and Tommy the rundown on how he knew Slater Ellis. Despite Hank suggesting they'd known each other for a prolonged period of time, the truth was he'd only known Slater for a few years. He'd bumped into him while trying to forge his new life in the Middle East. According to Hank, the two hit it off almost immediately. Slater had connections. Hank had drive. Together, they'd collected a tidy sum of money in a short amount of time from their underworld dealings.

Of course, Hank claimed that no one was ever hurt by what they did. They were high-end fencers, nothing more. Hank was fine with that. The way he saw it, he wasn't the one stealing things. As far as he knew, Slater wasn't either. Often, Slater would buy items of interest for a low price and then find the people he thought would pay a premium. It was easy for the two men to justify what they did without worrying over moral obligations.

Sean and Tommy weren't about to ask too many questions. If

Slater did have the other half of the Zerzura tablet, how he came about it didn't matter—even though they both wanted to know the answer.

"You do realize," Sean said, "that if he tries to screw us over, I'm going to kill him, right?"

Hank was taken back by the comment. At first he thought Sean was joking. The stern look in Sean's eyes told him otherwise.

Hank swallowed and nodded. "Yeah...well, you don't have to worry about that. Okay? You have my word. Slater is a good guy."

"A good guy who sells stolen artifacts?" Tommy asked.

"Hey, I don't judge you two over what you do on your own time. I know Sean is no saint. If you're running with him, it's a good bet you aren't either."

Sean smirked. "Okay, take it easy. I'm not going to kill Slater."

"Good." Hank gave a curt nod.

"Unless he screws us."

Tommy snorted a laugh.

Hank rolled his eyes. Before he could speak again, they heard a truck's engine groaning from the other end of the harbor. Yellowish lights flashed and bounced on the walls of the warehouses and outbuildings nearby.

The three men ducked behind the crates and waited until the cargo truck came into view around the building. It rumbled to a stop in the middle of the thoroughfare and sat for a moment. The engine churned and rattled, making the truck tremble like a teenage boy on his first date.

"Is that your guy?" Tommy asked without turning to look at Hank.

Hank continued staring out from his hiding spot in the shadows. His shoulders only offered the slightest shrug. "I have no idea. I can't see inside the cab."

"You don't know what your buddy is driving?"

"He didn't say. Okay?" Hank tried to keep his irritation to a minimum. "What does it matter what he's driving so long as he shows up?"

"It matters if that's *not* him," Tommy hissed.

"Settle down, you two," Sean said. "That's him."

The other two turned and faced Sean. "How do you know?" they asked simultaneously.

"Because if he was an enemy, he wouldn't show up so carelessly. He'd have stalked us like a hawk hunting a rabbit, watching us until the opportune moment to strike. He wouldn't drive up in the loudest cargo truck ever made and park it there in plain sight with the lights on." Sean turned his attention to Hank. "I guess he doesn't know we're trying to keep things subtle?"

Hank was embarrassed. "I probably should have warned him about what happened with that French guy."

Sean stepped out from the shadows and slowly raised his right hand, letting his palm face the truck. He noticed the silhouette inside suddenly twist his head. Then the truck's engine shut off, and the driver's door opened.

A guy with wavy brown hair and a red T-shirt hopped down to the ground. He took a casual look down both directions of the harbor, removed a black case from the cab.

"That's him," Hank said. "That's Slater."

"Let's just hope this friend of yours doesn't get us killed," Sean said.

Hank turned to Tommy. "Seriously, is he always like this?"

Tommy rose slowly from his position and tossed his head to both sides. "You have no idea."

Slater slowed to a stop and put his hands on his hips. He looked like he was in his early thirties. The crow's feet spreading out from the corners of his eyes were the only sign of aging. In broad daylight there may have been a loose strand of gray in his dark chocolate locks, but in the waning light of dusk none were noticeable.

"You're late," Hank said, stepping out to greet his associate. He put on his best disgruntled expression.

Slater sighed like they'd already been through it a hundred times. "I know," he said. "I'm sorry."

"No," Hank said, crossing his arms. "You're like twenty-four hours late. What happened to you last night?"

Sean and Tommy listened anxiously for the explanation.

"I ran into some trouble," Slater said in a matter-of-fact tone.

"*You* ran into trouble?" Hank thundered. "We were ambushed. I barely escaped. These two were taken out to the desert and staked to the ground, left for dead. And all you have to say is you ran into trouble."

"I can leave if you like," Slater said. His accent was definitely American, West Coast, probably Southern California.

Hank grunted.

"Look, I had the tablet stored in a safe place. When I got there, the building was closed. I didn't have a way to get in."

Tommy stepped forward. "You stored the tablet in a public place?"

Slater's head turned slightly, and his gaze fell on Tommy, sizing him up in seconds. "Yeah, sort of. I keep a lot of my inventory there."

"Where is this place, exactly?"

Slater let out an exasperated sigh. "It's a storage unit in the business district. I assure you, the place is extremely secure."

If Tommy were the fainting type, he would have toppled over right then and there. "You...you kept the tablet in a storage unit?" His voice started to rise as the anger swelled in his chest.

Sean put out his hand to calm his friend. "Hey, we kept our half in a locker at the train station. Not exactly Fort Knox, buddy."

Slater let out a short laugh.

"I thought you said these guys were pros," he said to Hank. "Train station locker? Those get broken into all the time."

"Look, we're all here," Sean said, "so let's just get on with it. I know you're not going to tell us where you got this, but do you have any idea where your half of the tablet came from originally?"

Slater considered the question and sighed. He looked in one direction and then the other before answering. "Okay, I've never told anyone this, but several years back, when they were excavating some of the ruins in the Valley of the Kings, they found my piece in one of the chambers. According to the rumors, it was discovered in one of the high priest's tombs near the pharaoh's. I don't know if that's true or not, but that's what I heard."

He set the briefcase down on the nearest crate, spun the combination numbers until they lined up the way he wanted, and then flipped open the case.

Inside, a stone tablet matching Tommy's half rested in black foam cushioning. It looked much like the one Tommy and Sean possessed, though the symbols on the corners were different.

Tommy recognized them immediately. They were the other set of symbols he'd seen on his parents' wall as a child.

He took out their half of the tablet and laid it down next to Slater's. The script engraved into the stone lined up perfectly.

Tommy's eyes widened as he read the ancient text, running his finger over the smooth stone.

"Where'd you guys find your half?" Slater asked Sean.

"Julfar."

"The ruins near Dubai?"

"Yep."

"What was that thing doing way down there? The lost oasis city was rumored to be in the Sahara somewhere. Not down here in the Middle East."

"We were wondering the same thing. I guess whoever created the tablet thought it best to keep the halves separated."

"Lot of good that did them."

"It served the purpose for several thousand years," Tommy said absently as he continued reading.

Sean noticed something move in the shadows over near the docks. He wasn't sure, but that didn't matter. He'd been on full alert since arriving at the harbor. He'd hoped they'd be the only ones there. Another shadow moved quickly into the darkness beside another building.

Another ambush.

"Read faster, Tommy," Sean said with a strong sense of urgency.

"Why?" he asked. Then he looked up and saw the look on his friend's face. "Aw, man. Not again."

"Yep. They found us. Not sure how, but Dufort's men found us."

"What?" Slater asked. "Who's Dufort?"

Hank pulled out his pistol and turned in the direction Sean was facing. "Where are they?"

"Two in the shadow of that building over there," Sean said. "Too far for pistols."

"Unless they have rifles," Slater said.

"Right. Speaking of, you wouldn't happen to have a few guns in the back of your SUV, would you?"

Slater's lips creased. "Yep. I've got a few in there. Or you could take this one." He reached into the other side of his jacket and pulled out an identical weapon to the one in his hand. He held it out for a moment toward Sean and then pulled it back. "You sure I can trust you?"

"I was wondering the same thing."

"Good," Slater smirked and handed the pistol to Sean.

Tommy looked up from the tablet. "Got it."

"Got it?" Sean asked. "Got what?"

"The translation." He looked expectantly at Slater. "Got one of those for me?"

Slater sighed and bent down to his ankles. He pulled up his pant leg and unfastened a small pistol from a holster wrapped around his shin. He spun the gun around and placed it in Tommy's palm.

Tommy frowned. "Seriously? This thing is a pea shooter."

"It's that or nothing," Slater said.

A gunshot popped from over behind another stack of crates fifty feet away. Sparks exploded off a metal light fixture and caused the thing to swing back and forth, creaking as it passed from left to right.

The four men dropped to the ground and scrambled to take cover behind the crates. Another shot rang out from the hill behind them. Sean turned and found the shooter's silhouette. He squeezed off a shot of his own, sending the man diving for safety near some thick bushes. The plants wouldn't stop bullets, but they'd make the guy harder to see.

"They've got us pinned down," Hank said. He poked his weapon around the corner of the nearest box and fired twice at the men across the thoroughfare. "What do you suggest we do?"

More shots came from two other angles directly across from their position. Now they were taking fire from four points.

"They're going to keep hitting us with suppressing fire and slowly close in, squeezing us until they can shoot us from point blank range," Sean said.

Tommy popped his head up and fired two shots at the men straight ahead. They dove behind a crane and a forklift but soon returned the volley with their own.

Rounds splintered the crates and sparked off the wall behind them. The air clouded quickly with acrid gun smoke.

"So, you're saying we're trapped," Tommy said.

"Yeah," Sean answered. "We're trapped."

Chapter 7

DUBAI

Sean spun around the crate and fired up the hill again at the man in the bushes. He squeezed the trigger three times before ducking back behind the big wooden boxes. The man on the hill yelled in pain. Sean must have hit him with one of his rounds, though he couldn't be sure which one did the damage, or where the man was hit.

More bullets poured in from every angle. They grew more frequent, the gun spray more hellish with every passing second.

"If you've got any ideas," Hank said, "now would be a good time."

Sean sat on the ground with his back against a crate. A blue metal door faced him with a rusty chain and a padlock keeping trespassers out. The door led into what he believed to be an old warehouse, not that that would do them any good. They'd be going from one kill box to another. It would only be good for buying them a little time, and that wasn't even a guarantee.

Slater popped up and squeezed off two more rounds at the men across the thoroughfare. They sprawled back behind the machines for safety.

"I have a guy with a boat waiting for us at the dock," Slater said abruptly. "If we can get to the water, we might be able to lose them in the gulf."

"You have a guy in a boat?" Tommy asked. He wasn't sure whether he should be in disbelief or be furious.

"Always have a backup plan," Slater said. "Although I didn't anticipate every path to the docks being cut off."

Sean drew in a deep breath. He stood up, slid over close to the door, and then fired a bullet through the rusty chain. The round ricocheted off the ground and into the ether as the chain fell limp on the door handle.

Wasting no time, Sean grabbed the handle and yanked the door open. "Hurry up, fellas. Gotta move."

Slater and Hank glanced at each other with suspicion, but another round of suppressing fire shook off any trepidation they may have had. The two men scrambled to their feet, keeping low as they hurried into the warehouse.

"Go, Tommy," Sean ordered.

"You go ahead. I'll cover you."

"Not happening."

"Fine," Tommy relented. "This hardly seems like the time to argue."

"Agreed."

Tommy sprang from his hiding place and rushed through the open door.

The bullets rained down on Sean's position. He ducked for cover and let the door close. It slammed shut with a loud bang.

Sean scurried back over to the crate. He popped up and fired a shot at the men across the way, hitting one in the shoulder and scaring the other back to safety. Then he spun and fired at the men in the other two positions near the crane and forklift. One more rapid turn, and he shot one of his few remaining rounds back at the attackers on the hill.

He'd only have a second before they resumed their assault. Sean reached up to the top of the crate and grabbed the black case with the tablets inside. He pulled it down as carefully as he could considering the pressure he was under. He closed the lid and locked it down and then rose once more, firing the last of his rounds at the men by the machines.

Then he slid back over to the door, yanked it open, and dove inside just as another flurry of bullets pinged into the thick metal.

Inside, the other three were waiting with wide eyes.

"You got the case," Tommy said, surprised. "You heard me say I got the translation, right?"

Sean gave a nod. "Yeah, but I didn't want those guys to get it."

"Good thinking," Hank said. "Now what?"

"Run," Slater said. "Go to the other end of the building. We can get clear of their line of sight through the other entrance. Once we're back in the shipping yard, we can lose them in the containers and machinery."

"You'll have to lead us to your guy," Sean said.

"That's the plan. Come on. Follow me."

Slater turned and took off at a furious pace. Sean and Tommy didn't have much trouble keeping up, but Hank lagged behind. He was a little older and not nearly in the shape his younger counterparts were. Even so, bringing up the rear he did his best not to slow down the others. He gasped for air and his legs ached, but he pushed on.

The others were already at the door. Tommy held it open while the other two ran through and back into the warm evening air.

"Come on, Hank. They'll be coming through any second."

"I'm...doing...the best I can," Hank said between breaths.

"I know."

The door at the other end burst open. Tommy raised his weapon and fired three shots as one of the gunmen appeared in the doorway. Sparks flew off the brick wall and concrete floor. He knew he wasn't going to hit the gunman from that distance, especially with the tiny gun Slater provided. It would have to be enough to scare the men for a moment to buy Tommy and his friends some extra seconds.

Hank lumbered through the door and out into the fresh air. Slater was already halfway across the thoroughfare when Hank made it out. Sean was in position at the corner of the building, watching the lane in case one of the gunman saw their play and came that way. He loaded a full magazine into his weapon, a second gift from Slater.

"Go, Hank," Sean said.

Hank swallowed and took off again, shuffling his feet at first before finally picking up his knees and trotting to a shipping container where Slater waited patiently.

"Give me the case," Tommy said to Sean. "I'll carry it. You cover me."

"I was just thinking the same thing." Sean set the case down and scooted it to his friend.

Tommy picked it up by the handle and then clutched it to his chest. "Ready," he said with a nod.

Sean acknowledged with a nod of his own. "Go."

Tommy darted out of from behind the building and sprinted to where Slater and Hank had been standing just a moment before. The other two were now weaving their way through stacks of crates and shipping containers like rats in a maze.

Tommy noticed a light flash for a half second out beyond the edge of the docks. That had to be Slater's boat. He stopped and turned around the steel container's corner and raised his weapon, pointing it down the thoroughfare where they'd been just a few minutes before.

He set the case down without looking and motioned for Sean to come across.

Sean did as instructed, gave one last look around the corner, and then darted from cover. His feet pounded the pavement and his arms swung hard back and forth to help with his balance and momentum.

Tommy saw his friend drawing near, and then his eyes locked on something else. A gunman came through the open warehouse door and raised his weapon to fire at Sean.

Tommy shifted his aim, swinging his puny weapon around toward the doorway. Sean charged toward his friend and then saw

Tommy pointing the gun in his direction. His eyes went wide. Sean knew Tommy could handle himself with firearms, but for a second it looked like Tommy was aiming the gun straight at him.

The muzzle erupted in a bright flash and a loud pop.

Sean dove to the ground as the bullet zipped through the air, whizzing by his head at a dangerously close proximity.

The round struck the gunman in the chest, and he fell back into the doorway.

Sean looked back at the downed attacker and then at Tommy. He scrambled to his feet and hurried to the other side of the shipping container where Tommy had retreated a second before.

"Are you crazy?" Sean asked. "You could have killed me."

Tommy rolled his shoulders. "But I didn't. I knew what I was doing."

"I'll say. You hit that guy from around forty feet away...with that tiny thing." Sean pointed at Tommy's pistol.

"That part was luck. Honestly, I was just trying to scare him."

Another gunshot exploded from the warehouse. Sean peeked around the corner and saw a second gunman standing in the doorway with his weapon extended.

"Get to the boat," Sean said.

He ducked back just as the shooter fired again. The bullet pinged off the steel container, narrowly missing the mark.

Two close calls in less than a minute, he thought. He spun back around and unleashed four retaliatory shots at the gunman, driving the guy back into the warehouse for cover.

Sean turned back toward the water. Tommy had already taken off and was running by the rows of containers. He made a sharp turn at the last row and disappeared from sight. Sean gave one more look back and then took off after his friend.

As he neared the water, he heard the gurgling sound of water churning accompanied by a boat motor idling its low, throaty tone.

Almost there.

Suddenly, another series of shots echoed through the corridors of containers. Sean stopped just before the last row and waited a second. He leaned around one corner and saw two gunmen rushing toward the boat.

Tommy and the others would be easy targets, although so would the onrushing gunmen.

Sean spun back around to the other corner of the steel box and fired down between the rows as one of the attackers passed by. The bullet struck the man in the leg and dropped him to the ground. The wounded guy managed to roll out of the way before Sean could hit him with another round.

The man's partner turned his head as he heard the shot ring out and ducked for cover behind the other end of the container. Sean knew he'd drawn attention. The second guy would no doubt be coming for him.

Sean took quick inventory of his surroundings. One row of containers was stacked two high. The row where the gunman disappeared only had one. Sean crept halfway down the row, and then stuffed his gun in his belt. Always one to take the high ground in a fight, he jumped up and grabbed on to the edge of the steel container. His shoulders, back, and biceps strained against gravity, and he hauled himself up over the lip to the top.

The gunman had the same idea, and both men rolled to a stop almost nose to nose on the ribbed surface.

Sean reacted first, reaching for his gun to get off the point-blank kill shot. The gunman was about to do the same but saw Sean's move so instead swung his leg around and kicked Sean's hand. The hard tip of the man's shoe struck the bridge of Sean's hand and sent a surge of dull pain through the bone and up his arm. He shrank back for a second and then saw the gunman reaching for his own weapon.

Sean sprang to a crouching stance and returned the favor with a swift kick of his own, striking the man's hand and then swinging his other leg at the guy's face. Sean's boot tip sank into the gunman's cheek and snapped his head sideways, but the guy wasn't done yet.

Dazed but not done, he rolled over onto his side and recovered quickly, pushed himself up, and shifted into a fighting stance.

Sean saw a thirty-foot cabin cruiser less than a hundred feet away. Tommy and the others were climbing on board.

With his friends safely on the boat, Sean refocused on the man inching his way toward him. Sean's opponent was clearly sizing him up, trying to figure the best line of attack.

Sean didn't give him the chance to strike first. He turned sideways and raised his hands. His feet shifted suddenly, and the gunman shuffled backward. Sean saw the slight retreat and used it to his advantage. His feet crossed one over the other, and then he swung his right foot around in a fake roundhouse kick.

The mercenary reacted predictably, twisting his body and swiping his left hand down to deflect Sean's foot.

Sean dropped his right leg, cutting the kick short and planting his foot on the ground. The move was too fast for the enemy to realize what happened. Sean kicked his left leg around, driving it into the man's abdomen. The guy doubled over as Sean spun toward him. He drove his fist into the henchman's jaw with a right, then a left, and another right.

The man stumbled backward, closer and closer to the container's edge. He felt his heels touching nothing but air and immediately shifted his weight forward to keep from tipping over.

Sean went for the finishing blow and swung his right arm around in a dramatic, wide arc. The gunman made a last-ditch effort and swung both arms around, partly to keep his balance and partly to fight off Sean's attack.

He blocked the right hook and then a jab before countering with a jab of his own, striking Sean in the lip. The blow knocked the American back a step. Unfortunately for the mercenary, it only made Sean's furious attack even more aggressive.

Sean pressed forward again. The man deflected a jab, but Sean used the block to grab the guy's forearm with his other hand and pull him into an elbow. The combined momentum of the man's forward movement with the sudden swing drove his nose squarely into bone.

The gunman staggered backward. The hazy world spun in his

eyes. His legs weakened, suddenly feeling heavy and unstable. He felt a warm breeze roll in from the gulf, washing over his back.

Sean took two fast steps forward and launched into the air. He extended his foot and struck the man in the chest. The blow from Sean's boot sent the man flying over the container's edge and toward the next metal box.

The back of the henchman's head struck the opposing edge with a sickening crack. The sudden impact flipped him forward to the pavement below where he landed on his face.

Sean wasted no time. He scurried to the other side of the container, grabbed his weapon, and jumped down to where the mercenary's lifeless body lay prostrate on the ground.

Sean nudged the guy's head with his boot, making sure he was either dead or unconscious. When the man didn't move, Sean darted over to the other end of the container, looked around the corner, and then sprinted to the boat.

The men were unhooking the moorings when they saw Sean come around the pier's gate and onto the dock.

Tommy waved his hand frantically in an effort to make his friend move faster.

"Hurry up!" Tommy yelled.

Gunfire erupted from behind Sean.

Tommy and Slater snapped their heads around and saw the men moving toward their position with guns blazing. Rounds plunked into the ship's bow and the cabin walls.

"We gotta go, Slater!" the captain said from inside the cabin.

"Ten seconds!" Slater yelled back over his shoulder.

He crouched down and made his way to the front of the boat to one of the storage boxes. A bullet tore through the fiberglass hull and sank into the cabin wall, missing his left arm by mere inches. He flipped open the box and pulled out a Colt AR-15 rifle.

Slater swung the barrel around and lined up one of the gunmen in his sights. He squeezed the trigger once, then again and again. The gunman dropped to the ground as one of the rounds found its way into his abdomen. Slater turned his attention to another attacker and fired again.

Hank and Tommy joined him at the front just behind the gunwale and opened fire with their smaller weapons. They didn't hit any targets and they both figured as much due to the limited range of their guns, but they could buy Sean some time.

Sean was close now. He heard bullets zipping by. The wooden light poles splintered as they caught some of the rounds. Others thumped into the wooden decking underfoot.

The boat was starting to drift into the water despite the captain doing his best to keep it close to the dock. Sean saw Slater and the others firing back at Dufort's men, doing their best to keep the attackers at bay.

"Come on!" Tommy shouted.

Sean's legs pumped harder the last few steps. His left foot stepped on the eye of the dock, and he jumped. His arms flailed in the air as he flew over the few feet of water and landed with a thud on the boat's deck.

As soon as the captain saw Sean safely on board, he shoved two levers forward and spun the wheel hard to the left.

The twin engines engaged with a throaty groan, and the black water instantly churned to white. The bow raised up as the captain steered the vessel around to the left and out to sea.

Tommy and the other two shooters fell back against the cabin from the sudden and unexpected acceleration.

Sean rolled back toward the rear of the boat and managed to plant his feet on the back gunwale to brace himself. The captain shifted the levers all the way forward and adjusted another to get the most plane out of the vessel as it picked up speed.

Back on land, the figures of the gunmen grew smaller and smaller. A few of them kept shooting until the boat vanished in the darkness of the Persian Gulf.

Sean gathered himself and climbed forward to the cockpit where the captain was staring out at the sea with analytic eyes.

"Thanks for bailing us out," Sean said.

The captain turned his head, and Sean saw his face for the first time. Even in the darkness the long scar that ran from the man's temple to his jaw could be seen.

"We were going to leave you in another thirty seconds," the man said. "Oh, and you're welcome."

Chapter 8

DUBAI

The boat dipped and rose through the sea's shallow swells. Sean and Tommy sat across from Hank inside the cabin close to the captain. Every one of them gazed back to the foaming water behind them and beyond, making sure they weren't being followed. Even after cruising at a decent speed for the last half hour, none of them were confident they'd completely lost Dufort and his men. Not yet, at least.

"How did they find us?" Sean asked suddenly, turning toward Hank on the other side of the boat. "They should have been on the other side of town."

Tommy echoed his friend's sentiment. "Yeah. Even if they found the empty locker at the other train station, how in the world would they have realized our exact location and when we would be there?" His eyes drifted to Slater.

"What are you getting at?" Slater asked with a sharp edge to his tone. "You saying I set that up, that I double-crossed you guys? I just saved your hides."

Hank put up his hands to calm everyone down. The boat's captain kept his eyes forward, although he tilted his head to the left a tad to listen in on the conversation.

"I'm sure there's an explanation for all this," Hank said. "So, let's just keep calm. Slater's right, Sean. He did just get us out of trouble. He and the guy behind the wheel here deserve our thanks."

"I already thanked him," Sean said. "That doesn't mean something strange isn't going on. First the ambush yesterday. Then this. How is it that Dufort keeps turning up at the right time and the right place?"

Hank leveled his gaze with Sean's. "I want to know the answer to that question, too, my friend. But I can tell you right now that no one on this boat is responsible for what happened yesterday or tonight."

"My name is Sid, by the way," the captain said over his shoulder, still keeping his eyes ahead. "In case you feel like throwing blame my way, might help to have a name to go with the accusation."

Sean smirked. He liked Sid's smug, unapologetic attitude. And he'd only heard the guy say a few words.

"Is it possible they planted something on us?" Tommy asked. "Maybe before they took us out to the desert?"

Sean took in a deep breath and sighed. "I suppose it's possible. Check your clothes, and see if there's anything attached. Or maybe there's something deep down in one of the pockets you didn't realize was there."

All the men stood up and ran through the process of checking every inch of fabric they were wearing. Then they sat back down and examined their shoes to make sure nothing was hidden in them, either.

No one found a thing.

"I didn't figure you had a bug on you, Slater," Sean said.

"Yeah, well, I didn't want you guys to think I was hiding something."

"So, what now?" Hank asked, throwing his hands up. "Proctology exam?"

Sean snorted and Tommy chuckled.

Hank's comment broke the tension and brought the men a much-needed break from the stress.

"Seriously, though," he went on, "they found us somehow. Maybe they followed us, you know...with a human being and not some tech gadget."

"It's possible," Sean confessed. "I'd have thought we'd have spotted someone tracking us."

"Would have been difficult for a tail to stay hidden from the desert all the way into the city," Tommy said. "And that theory has its own issues. How did they know you were going to come to our rescue?"

Hank shrugged. "Maybe this Dufort guy is a planner. Some people like to cover all their bases."

Slater shook his head. "Could be. But Sean's a pro. And it seems like Tommy here can handle himself, too. If they were followed, I'd think they would have seen someone."

"Then there's the little matter of the incident at the restaurant," Tommy said.

"Restaurant?"

"Yeah," Hank said. "These two thwarted a robbery at one of my favorite places to eat in the city. Stands to reason if someone was following us, we'd have seen that person in the melee."

Sean saw where his friend was going with the line of thought but didn't think it very valid. Somehow, Dufort anticipated their move to the docks. He knew when and where to strike. The pier was a big place, too. It would be easy to get lost in the maze of shipping containers, warehouses, and machinery. Yet Dufort went straight to them.

The only explanation is that they were followed. At least that's what Sean told himself. He knew that it was possible one of the other three men had betrayed him and Tommy, but as he looked into the eyes of Hank and Slater, he didn't see an ounce of dishonesty. The boat's captain was a bit harder to read. Sid was a salty fellow, and the scar on the side of his face belied a checkered past, probably filled with a criminal record. While Sean believed he could trust Hank and Slater, Sid was another matter—no matter how much Sean liked the guy's attitude.

He'd keep an eye on Sid just in case.

"How far until we get where we're going?" Tommy asked.

"Yeah. And where are we going?" Sean added.

"Down the coast," Sid answered without turning his head.

Sean looked out over the side of the boat and then back to the captain. "We're nowhere near the coast."

Sid cracked a frail smile. "Nothing gets past you, does it?"

"I've been known to miss a thing or two. Your accent...you sound like you're from northern England. Probably close to Liverpool if I don't miss my guess."

"Very good," he said. "Scouser for life."

Sean recognized the slang term. He knew a few guys who were big Liverpool Football Club fans. They called themselves Scousers. He'd also spent a little time there and quickly picked up on some of the differences with the accent and local culture.

"We're heading to Qatar," Sid said. "Quicker to stay farther out to sea like this. Plus, we're going to need to pick up some more fuel."

Sean and Tommy turned to look at the fuel canisters stored on the back of the boat, tied down with straps.

"You don't have enough on board?"

"Possibly," he said. "But it's a long ride to Qatar from here. Several hours. There's an island about seventy-five nautical miles away. We'll stop there to refuel before continuing on to the mainland."

Island? There weren't many islands out in the middle of the gulf. Sean knew that much. The only ones he was aware of were operated by...then the realization hit him.

"So, you're a smuggler?" he asked point blank.

Sid said nothing, but the smile on his face broadened.

"He prefers the term *entrepreneur*," Slater said.

"Of course he does," Tommy chirped. "I can only imagine what kinds of things you must smuggle in this part of the world. Weapons, I suppose?"

Sid shook his head. "No, nothing like that. Although I can see why you'd think that, what with so many terrorist camps in this region."

"Not to mention the weapons you have stored on board."

"Those are for defense. And it's a good thing I had them. Otherwise your friend here might still be on the docks with a few more holes in him."

"So, if you're not moving weapons, what are you smuggling?"

Sid turned his head for the first time in a while and stared at Tommy for a long moment. "What's the one thing that's difficult to get in this part of the world?"

Sean smirked. "Booze."

Sid raised a finger and pointed at him. "Bingo. Slater, show him what he's won!"

"So, you smuggle alcohol," Tommy said with a hint of derision in his voice.

"Hey, bootlegging is a profitable operation, especially in this part of the world. There are lots of people willing to pay a premium for good alcohol. I'm just filling a need. If you boys want a swig or two, I keep a bottle in the galley down below for personal consumption. Of course, I reserve the best for myself and my guests."

Tommy remembered how drunk he'd been in Australia during their adventure down under. The hangover had been brutal.

"Thanks, but I'll pass right now. Don't want to tempt fate with seasickness and all."

"Suit yourselves. We should be at the island in a little over an hour."

The conversation died off. The constant drone of the engines and the consistent slap of the waves hitting the hull were the only sounds the men heard for a while.

Sid occasionally checked the GPS screen on his dashboard to make sure they were going in the right direction. Sean got the impression their boat's captain didn't need the technological assistance. Experienced sailors knew their way around the seas and oceans like they knew their own bathtubs.

A little over an hour went by before Sid pulled back on the levers to slow the boat's speed. The other men on board stood up to look out through the windshield but saw nothing of interest in the black sea ahead.

The thickest blanket of stars Sean had ever seen stretched out overhead. The moon was nothing more than a sliver on the horizon to the east and did little to light up the waters of the Persian Gulf.

"Why are we slowing down?" Tommy asked.

"Because," Sid said with eyes locked on something in the distance, "we're here."

Tommy frowned and narrowed his eyes, trying to see what their driver was talking about.

Then he noticed it. There wasn't much, just a dark outline against the slightly less dark backdrop of the sky where it merged with the sea. It was there, though, a small land mass rising up out of the water.

As the boat drew closer, they could see the island was empty, vacant of any signs of life or civilization. It was small, probably less than two miles across, although it was difficult to see how long it was from their vantage point.

"This island has been used by smugglers for a long time," Sid explained before any of the men could ask. "There's an understanding between everyone who uses it. Don't mess with anyone, and no one will mess with you."

"So much for that old saying about no honor among thieves, eh?" Tommy chuffed.

"We're not thieves," Sid snapped. "Most of the smugglers in this region buy our goods and sell them for profit. It's an import/export business."

"He didn't mean anything by it," Sean said. "We get it. Booze is something that can be hard to come by in these parts. No judgment on our end."

The comment seemed to settle down the captain. "At any rate, we usually don't see other smugglers out here. It's pretty rare. My stash is straight ahead. I'll anchor the boat as close to shore as I can. You blokes wait here while I go get the petrol. Slater, you come with me to help haul the fuel cans."

Slater nodded and started rolling up his pants.

Sean frowned. He knew there were some other islands in this part of the gulf, not many, but a few. A couple of them were privately owned. One or two were part of the Emirates and were used as refinery installations.

This, apparently, was not one of those islands. It was rare to find any piece of land that wasn't owned by someone, especially of the island variety. That meant this particular plot must be especially worthless. Sean couldn't help but wonder why.

Sid shut off the engine as the boat drifted closer to the shore. There were only a few palm trees standing against the sparkling black backdrop. He could see the outlines of some buildings a few hundred feet away from the water's edge.

"What are those structures?" Sean asked as Sid dropped the anchor and started getting ready for his journey to the shore.

Sid looked up and followed Sean's gaze.

"They used to house people who worked at the refineries on the other islands," he said. "When production dropped and people started leaving, most of the homes were abandoned."

"Now it's a smuggler's paradise," Tommy said.

"I guess you could say that. Not a very hospitable place. Fresh water had to come from the ocean in big desalination machines. When everyone left, those machines were shut off. Now it's just a patch of desert floating in the sea."

He put one hand on the gunwale and swung both legs overboard, landing deftly in the water. Slater grabbed his AR and joined him. The two waded toward land through the knee-deep water, leaving the others in the boat.

When they were out of earshot, Tommy turned to Hank. "Listen, I know you and Slater are buddies, but how much do you really know about Sid?"

"Only what he just told you guys," Hank said. "I hadn't met him before today."

"And Slater?"

"Look, guys, I know what you're thinking, but you got it all wrong. Slater and me, we go way back. I trust him with my life. And like he said, he saved our necks back there. If he wanted the tablet for himself or to give it to Dufort, he woulda taken it and left us for dead or killed us himself. Same with Sid. He didn't have to take out that AR and start shooting at Dufort's guys, but he did. So, how about we give them the benefit of the doubt on this one? Okay?"

"Fair enough," Sean said. "He's got a point, Schultzie. They could have both killed us already if they wanted."

"Fine," Tommy relented. "I'm just trying to figure this out. Frankly, I'm a little concerned you two aren't."

"Oh, the gears are turning, my friend. They're always turning." He looked down at the case at Tommy's feet. "Speaking of, how about we take another look at that tablet."

"Sure." Tommy picked up the case and set it on his lap.

He flipped open the lid and stared at the ancient stones.

"Hank, let me borrow your phone. It's too dark to see out here, and I don't think we should turn on the boat lights."

"Why?" Hank asked as he fished his phone out of a pocket and passed it to Tommy.

"Call it a hunch."

"He's right," Sean said. "If there are other smugglers out here, or if, on the off chance, Dufort has a boat coming after us, it would make us an easy target. Let's go down below to look at this thing."

The others nodded and headed down the steps into the bowels of the vessel. Tommy laid out the case on the table, and the three men eased into the cushioned booth seats.

Tommy's finger ran along the lines of script once more, and this time he read the passages out loud.

"This part right here is key," he said. "At least I think it's the key to everything. It says that the four stones must be brought together where paths from the four corners meet. Only then will the oasis city reveal itself to the weary traveler."

"Four stones?" Hank asked. "What four stones?"

Tommy nodded. "I'm not entirely sure. The next part, however, gives us a clue as to where we should begin our search. It says the first will be found above the plains of the pharaohs, in the grandest of all their tributes to the stars, in the shadow of Anubis when the sun is setting to the west."

"Tributes to the stars?"

"The pyramids," Sean explained, "are thought to be laid out in a formation that matches the constellations."

"Exactly," Tommy said. "The three big pyramids near Giza are believed to be an earthly match for the three celestial bodies of Orion's belt."

"Really?" Hank said, sounding impressed. "That's pretty cool."

"Indeed. The pyramids are an incredible tribute to the engineering and technological capabilities of the ancient Egyptians. Scientists and archaeologists still aren't certain what other secrets those structures may hold."

"I thought they were just tombs for the pharaohs," Hank said.

"That's what many of the original theories suggested. Now, we're not so sure. It's clear there is a connection between the constellations and their designs. You can see it with their temples, cities, monuments, and other engineering works. Most of the great pharaohs were either buried in the Valley of the Kings or in their own tombs. That leaves the reason behind the pyramids to be a mystery."

"Fascinating stuff," Hank said. "I had no idea." He paused for a second and then looked back down at the tablet. "What about the other stones?" he asked. "Does it say where we can find them?"

Tommy shook his head. "It only gives vague information about them, referring to the other three corners of the land." He pointed to a specific collection of words and tapped on it with his finger. "This is what's really got me, though. There are some things missing from this part. See where the stone is blank?"

Sean and Hank nodded.

"I might be wrong, but it could be that when we find the first stone, we will also find what goes here."

"Why do you think that?" Sean asked.

"Because it says that the second stone can be found...and then there's nothing. It says that about the third and fourth stones as well."

"So, we have to find the first one to get to the second and so on," Hank whispered.

"Right. No shortcuts."

"Which means we could be in for a long haul," Sean said. "Would be nice to have some faster transportation. When we get to the mainland, I'll make a call."

He cut himself off abruptly. When he spoke again, his tone was hushed. "Do you hear that?"

The other two looked around and listened.

They nodded.

Another boat was approaching.

Chapter 9

THE PERSIAN GULF

Sean climbed back up to the deck and looked out across the gently rolling waters of the gulf.

At first he didn't see anything. As his eyes readjusted to the darkness, he made out the silhouette of a small boat off the starboard side. He could see red lights through the windshield, but it was difficult to make out any further details.

Sean ducked his head back down below. "We've got company."

Tommy's eyebrows furrowed. "Dufort?"

Sean shook his head once to the side. "I doubt it. Out in this huge body of water, we could be anywhere. If he's not tracking us, and I would hope he's not, I'd say it's more likely other smugglers."

"Sid said they don't usually cross paths out here," Hank hissed.

"Usually. That doesn't mean it never happens."

"What do we do?"

Sean thought for a moment before responding. "You two still have your guns, right?"

They nodded.

"Yeah," Tommy said, "but I've only got two or three rounds left."

"Same here," Hank said.

"Sid might have some ammo sitting around. Check the cupboards and the pantries down here. I'm going to check the compartment where that Colt was earlier. Maybe there's another one in there."

"Won't whoever is on the other boat see you?"

Sean cocked his head to the side and fired a derisive glare at Hank.

"Right," Hank said. "I forgot. You're awesome."

Sean didn't respond. Instead, he twisted around and got down on his belly. He crawled around to where he'd seen Slater get his weapon before. When he opened the hatch, he was disappointed at first. There wasn't another AR. There was, however, something else.

Shouting from the other boat drew Sean's attention away from the hatch's contents for a second. The masculine voices were speaking Arabic. A second later, a spotlight from the top of the boat switched on. It lit up Sid's vessel and would have temporarily blinded anyone on the deck if there'd been anyone there.

Sean stayed down, letting the light pass over him as the man controlling it passed it from one end of the boat to the other. They were looking for someone. Why, Sean didn't know. What he did know was that these guys weren't looking to be friends.

When the light passed back to the other end of the boat, Sean risked a peek over the edge of the gunwale. It was hard to tell how many were on board, but based on the silhouettes he counted, it looked like five.

Not the worst odds he'd faced, but certainly not in his favor.

The other boat drew closer, slowing its engines until they were almost idling straight at the starboard side of Sid's ship.

Sean slid back over to the open hatch and reached in. He pulled out the weapon hanging on a metal rack and checked to make sure it was loaded. Another peek over the edge told him the men on the other boat were armed with AK-47s. Pretty common, especially in this part of the world. For smugglers, they were well armed if all they were doing was selling goods to a needy consumer base.

He listened closely. One of the men was issuing orders to the others, saying something about searching the boat. He must have been the one in charge of their little operation. Then Sean heard the guy order his men to kill anyone on board.

That made Sean's next decision much easier.

He shouldered the weapon, rechecked to make sure it was properly loaded, and popped up from behind the gunwale. He lined up the sights with the cabin of the other boat and prepared to fire. Just as his finger tensed on the trigger, the spotlight swung around toward his position. He pulled the trigger.

For a split second he tensed, waiting for the weapon to fire, but nothing happened. "What the—?"

He ducked down just as the light reached where he was crouching. The spotlight kept moving until it reached the end of the vessel and then started back the other way again.

Sean looked at the weapon again and realized the safety was on. "Idiot," he muttered.

He cursed himself for the mistake and hoped the other boat was still far enough away. He raised his head just enough to look over the side of the vessel and saw the other smuggler's boat was still a good fifty feet away.

Sean readied the weapon again and prepared to fire, lining up the other boat in his sights. His finger tensed on the trigger again as the target vessel drifted a little, exposing the broad port side.

Before he could fire, a gunshot boomed from the direction of the island. The spotlight exploded in a flurry of sparks and shattered glass. For a second, it almost seemed brighter than before. Then just as quickly as it flashed, it went dark.

The men on board the other boat reacted instantly. Two of them rushed to the front of their vessel and started firing toward the shore. Sean risked another quick look overboard and couldn't see what or who they were firing at. He didn't need to see. He knew it was Slater who'd shot out the spotlight. Sean would recognize the sound of that Colt AR almost anywhere.

What he didn't expect was Hank and Tommy to rush up the steps to the deck and start firing their weapons at the other boat, which is exactly what happened.

The two must have found what they were looking for down below because they unloaded full magazines at the enemy ship, doing little more than alerting the other three men aboard to their presence.

It only took a few seconds for the enemy to react. While the two men at the front of the boat were focused on Slater—wherever he was—the other three turned their attention to Sid's boat.

Their Kalashnikovs blazed with thunderous booms like a midsummer gulf storm. Bullets pounded the hull of Sid's boat, ripping through wood and fiberglass like it was cardboard.

Tommy and Hank immediately saw they were outgunned and retreated, diving back into the wheelhouse and down below deck.

Sean knew he and his friends were in trouble. And he knew just how to get them out of it.

He waited for a few tenuous seconds while the enemy unloaded the rest of their magazines at Sid's boat. When he heard the bombardment slow, he knew at least one of the men was reloading— probably more than one. Even if they all weren't, their attention was on the other end of the boat, not where he was hiding.

Sean raised up and placed the other vessel dead in his sights. "Third time's the charm," he said to himself.

His finger squeezed the trigger.

A loud pop like a stack of two hundred phone books hitting a gym floor at once boomed across the water. The boat shuddered, and a surge of heat deflected off the inside of the portside gunwale and washed over Sean's back. The rocket propelled grenade whooshed out of the barrel in a fury of white fire and smoke. Sean didn't have to wait long to see what happened next. The other boat was so close, the munition reached it in a split second.

The ordnance detonated on impact. The three men on the port side were instantly consumed by the sudden explosion. The two on the bow were shredded by shrapnel just before the concussion blew them clear of the destruction. Their bodies splashed down in the water at least twenty feet from their burning vessel. A moment later, the boat's fuel erupted in an orange ball of fire.

Sean stood up, still holding the RPG launcher in his hands. The other smugglers' boat was close enough that he could feel the searing heat from the blazing wreckage. Thick, black soup roiled into the sky.

Standing on the front deck, Sean looked out toward the shore. He made out two figures wading through the water. They looked an odd sight—Sid carrying two canisters of fuel in the sea with Slater leading the way, holding his weapon to his chin.

"I see you found my RPG-7!" Sid shouted as he drew near the boat.

Sean exhaled and looked down at the weapon in his hands with a fond appreciation. "Yeah. Good thing you had this sitting around. We might have been in trouble."

Tommy and Hank appeared at the top of the steps on the deck and looked out over the fluttering waves.

Tommy saw the burning boat and immediately turned his head back to his friend. "You blew up the whole thing," he said, somewhat stunned.

"Oh, don't act so surprised. It's not the first time we've done something like that."

Tommy motioned to the RPG. "Where'd you get that?"

"Sid's weapons hatch." He twisted his head and looked down at Sid, who'd arrived on the starboard side of the boat. "I hope it's okay if I call it that, Sid. Unless you've got other places where you stashed weapons on this thing."

Sid ticked his head to the side. "You never know."

Tommy was incensed. "I thought you said smugglers didn't see each other out here. And you also said there weren't any hostilities between you, that you left each other alone." He threw up his hands in frustration.

Sid lifted a fuel tank, placing it on the back edge of the boat. "Hank, can you grab this?"

Hank shuffled over to the canister and hefted it out of the way, sliding it to the back corner where the others like it were housed.

"We don't usually see other smugglers out here," Sid explained. He lifted the second canister out of the water and placed it on the deck. He took a second to catch his breath after hauling the heavy fuel containers from the shore. "But it does happen." He wiped his face with his forearm and then climbed up the ladder.

"What was with the hostility?"

Sid shrugged. "Who knows?"

Slater climbed back on board and looked out over the sea. "Could be a vendetta. Or maybe they don't approve of your usual cargo," he said. "Some of these guys in this part of the world are on a religious witch hunt to rid the area of unholy things. According to some Islamic beliefs, alcohol might be considered one of those things."

"Or they're just terrorist pirates," Sean said, walking back to where the others were standing.

"Pirates?" Hank asked. "Shiver me timbers, arrr." He laughed at his own terrible joke until he saw no one else thought it was funny. Then he cleared his throat and straightened his neck.

"Right." Sean said. "You done?"

"Yeah. Sorry."

"Pirates in the Persian Gulf?" Tommy asked. "I knew there were some in the waters off the African coasts, Somalia and all that. I didn't know there were any out here."

Sean clenched his jaw, staring out at the flaming remains of the pirates' boat. "Yeah, there aren't many, but they like to travel in packs. We need to get out of here before anyone else comes by."

"That fire is sure to draw attention," Slater added. "And if it doesn't, the smoke will be seen for miles. Sooner or later, someone is going to show up."

"How are we on fuel right now?" Sean asked Sid.

Sid pouted his lips and nodded. "We're fine for now. I can top her off when we're in safer waters."

"Good. Let's get moving. Everyone look alive. If we encounter any more trouble, we need to be ready."

Chapter 10

DUBAI

"The bodies have been disposed of, sir," Cody said to Dufort. He waited with arms crossed, wondering what his employer would have him do next.

The other mercenaries had gotten rid of the bodies of their fallen comrades by taking them out in a dinghy, tying random pieces of heavy machinery from the docks to their ankles, and dropping the dead men in the gulf. The fish would take care of the rest, and no one would know what happened.

Dufort did little to hide his irritation. He was perplexed by the turn of events. First, he was taken on a wild goose chase to the wrong train station. Fine. That much he could deal with despite the fact that he ended up looking like an idiot to his men. Then he had Wyatt and company surrounded, yet somehow the Americans had managed to escape.

Where had the boat come from? Who was driving it? And how in the world did Wyatt and his associates slip through Dufort's men?

It was maddening. And for the time being, there was no telling where they'd gone. He shook his head, still staring out at the dark sea beyond the docks.

"We'll find them, sir. That cabin cruiser can't have a long range. They'll have to make berth somewhere."

"No," Dufort said after a long silence. "That ship can travel at least a hundred nautical miles before refueling, maybe more. They'll have prepared for that. I'd wager they have more fuel on board."

Cody gritted his teeth together, embarrassed. "Then what should we do next, sir?"

"We'll go after them shortly. You and your men get some rest. I'm tracking their movements. When they make a move, we'll know exactly where to pounce. Have the men sleep in shifts. We might have to leave at a moment's notice."

"Of course, sir. I'll tell the men."

"And get two more recruits," Dufort said. "We have to replace the ones we lost tonight."

"I'm on it."

The younger man spun around and trotted away. Dufort heard him issuing orders to the rest of the men, passing on their employer's message.

Dufort was annoyed. He didn't care about his hired guns on a personal level. They were nothing more than pawns to him. Those men were, however, expensive. And they weren't always easy to find. Many of them were ex-military from varying governments around the world. He'd found it interesting how men who may have once been enemies were so willing to unite under a common banner—money.

Cash changed allegiances, forged new friendships and allies. It was the great equalizer. It took men from often highly contrasted backgrounds and turned them into a sort of band of brothers.

Of course, that loyalty was easily broken. All it took was a higher sum of money, a better offer from somewhere else.

Dufort shook his head, snapping back to the current situation. Hopefully, Cody could find a few guys. He'd know the right places to look, and Dubai was ripe with former ex-special forces types. Many of them moved to the burgeoning city to start private security companies for the many billionaires and millionaires that populated the area. The men hated the work—babysitting wealthy brats or their parents. But the gigs paid well.

Dufort's edge was an offer to get back in the game, to do something somewhat dangerous again.

As much as so many former military guys were glad to get out of combat, life as a civilian was tougher for many. These unfortunate souls had a difficult time adjusting. In a strange way, being in a war brought a sense of normality to some.

Dufort couldn't relate. He'd never served in the military back in France, getting a medical exemption that relieved him of what he considered to be too dangerous and beneath him. As a child of privilege, making the exemption happen didn't take much, just rubbing the right people with the right amount of money.

He pulled the phone out of his pocket and checked it. The hour was getting late. He knew he wouldn't be able to sleep, but he had to try. Even with his resolute determination, Dufort was still human. He required the same necessities as any other person.

He turned and meandered back to his SUV and climbed in the back. The driver was already behind the wheel, waiting for instructions.

"Take me back to the hotel, Terrance," he said as he shut the door. His lips creased into a wicked grin.

Even with the loss of two of his men and the seemingly well-timed escape by Wyatt and his friends, everything was going according to plan.

Chapter 11

DOHA, QATAR

Slater had thought of everything. After landing in Doha, he and his new associates went straight to the airport where Sid had a small cargo plane ready.

The aircraft was older than Hank by at least a decade or more. Its silvery aluminum wrapper and twin prop engines were a reminder of flying days of yesteryear.

"You sure this thing is safe?" Hank asked as he climbed aboard.

"She'll get us where we need to go," Sid replied from the cockpit.

Sean and Tommy had been in sketchier airplanes, so they were comfortable with Sid's aircraft. Slater obviously was as well.

"No substitute for being prepared, eh?" Sean said to Slater.

"Absolutely," Slater said. "Sid runs a tight operation. Some people might say he's a micromanager, handling everything himself. In his line of work, though, it's probably safer that way."

Tommy was sitting in the seat closest to the cockpit. He leaned around and looked in at the array of controls. Sid was busily flipping switches, running through his preflight check.

"How long you been flying?" Tommy asked.

"Me? Oh, I've never actually flown a plane before. Just picked up this old jalopy last week on a whim. Thought it might be fun to try out flying."

Tommy's forehead crinkled, matching the concerned frown on his face. "Wait, what?"

Sid smirked. "I'm just messing with you, mate. Been flying over ten years now. Got a few thousand hours. You'll be safe with me."

Tommy offered a tenuous laugh and leaned back in his seat. Despite Sid's reassurance, now he wasn't as comfortable as he'd been before.

Once the plane was in the air and leveled out at cruising altitude, Sid spoke into the headsets. "Feel free to move about that cabin and all that. This flight will be a non, non-smoking flight. So, smoke 'em if you got 'em."

The men in the main part of the cabin looked at each other with quizzical expressions. Slater was in the copilot seat, and he turned around with a big grin on his face.

"You boys don't smoke, do you?"

The other three shook their heads.

"Then I suppose we'll wait until we land to light up."

"Thank you," Tommy said. "That's very considerate."

Slater snorted. "I wasn't being considerate. We just don't have any cigars on board."

"Cigars?"

"Yep. Never smoked cigarettes. But I do enjoy a good cigar."

He turned back around and stared out the side window at the vast wasteland below.

"It all looks the same, doesn't it?" Slater said.

The deserts almost seemed endless. Vast stretches of sand as far as the eye could see, only occasionally interrupted by a town or a small oasis with clumps of trees.

Hank stared out the window for a minute like all the others. His mind wandered back to the treasure they were trying to find, and he turned toward Tommy.

"You said that we're looking for the grandest pyramid, one that looks over all the others."

Tommy nodded. Sean listened through his headset but kept his eyes out the window.

"And you said something about Anubis. I think I've heard that name before," Hank said. His eyes were fixed on Tommy as he waited for an explanation.

"Yeah, so there are a couple of interesting things about this little riddle," Tommy said, tapping the case in his lap with an index finger. "Normally, when people think of the largest pyramid on the Giza strip, they think of the biggest of the main three that are grouped together."

"That's not correct?"

Tommy shook his head. "No. I mean…yes, it is correct in that the great pyramid of Giza is larger than the other three and is certainly the biggest of any of the mainstream pyramids."

"Mainstream?"

"Yes. You see, there is another pyramid that no one visits. It's actually not really a pyramid in the sense of how it's shaped. It's open, so the chambers, pathways, and corridors are all exposed."

Hank listened carefully. He'd never heard of such a pyramid, not that he was an expert on ancient Egypt. His knowledge on the subject was minimal at best.

"You're right, Tommy. I've never heard about a pyramid like that before."

"That's because the Egyptian government doesn't promote it. In fact, they almost go out of their way to make it seem like an unimportant part of history. There are no barricades to keep people out, no gates, no guided tours, nothing. It remains largely ignored by most visitors to the Nile River Valley."

Hank considered Tommy's explanation. "So, what makes you think that we're going to find one of these stones at this unusual pyramid?"

"It's bigger than the others, for starters. It's built into a mountain a few miles from the main three. The pyramid actually *is* the mountain in a way." He paused for a second and took a swig of water. "Whoever built it cut the passages and chambers straight out of the rock. The real key, however, is that it overlooks the other pyramids. If you stand on the top, you can see the big three off in the distance. It's higher than all the others."

"Which figures into that part of the riddle."

"Exactly."

Hank considered Tommy's answer for a moment before asking his next question. "What about Anubis?"

"One of the ancient gods of the First Dynasty," Sean answered. "For a time, he was considered to be the guardian of graves and ushered souls into the afterlife. By the time the Middle Kingdom began, he'd been replaced in that role by Osiris."

Hank turned around and looked at Sean, who was still staring out his window. Sean twisted his head slowly and gazed at Hank with an unnerving look in his eyes, like a wild animal about to devour his prey.

Hank whipped back around to face forward for a second and then turned to Tommy. "Is that true?"

"Yep," Tommy said. "He nailed it. Anubis is a strange figure in the grand scheme of Egyptian deities because he didn't have a well-defined role in many of their myths. It's thought that he was the guardian to the afterlife by some. Others consider him to be nothing more than a priest with an animal's head. One thing that remains consistent is that in many hieroglyphs, Anubis is present for the embalming process during mummification."

"Which is why he was considered to be the god of mummification by many," Sean added.

"Correct."

Hank was still confused. "Okay, so what's so important about Anubis in regards to the stones we're trying to find?"

Tommy shrugged. "I'm not sure yet. I do find it interesting that a deity that is considered somewhat unimportant in the history of Egypt is also mentioned in tandem with a pyramid that is as equally unimportant."

It was a lot for Hank to take in, and he still didn't reach any sort of clarity.

Tommy could see his associate wasn't connecting the dots. "Maybe it will help to think about all this in terms of what we're looking for from a zoomed out view. The lost city of Zerzura was said to be the final resting place for a relic that could give eternal life to humans."

"Okay."

"Since the dawn of time, people have been desperate to unlock the mysteries of the afterlife or to defeat death entirely and live forever. Zerzura was purportedly a place where the latter was made possible."

"Until it was swallowed by the desert thousands of years ago," Sean chimed in.

"Right," Tommy said with a quick look back at his friend. "The legend says that the king of Zerzura, a man named Hussa, offended the gods by boasting that he was one of them. He claimed to possess a relic that could keep him alive forever. According to the story, the gods sent an earthquake to destroy Hussa's temples, palaces, and the entire city. After that, the legend claims that the gods then sent a giant sandstorm to cover up any evidence that the place ever existed."

Hank frowned. "Sounds a little hokey to me."

"Indeed, but that's the story."

"And these stones," Hank said with a perplexed look on his face, "they're somehow supposed to magically make this city reappear?"

"That's what it sounds like."

Hank blew air through his lips, making them flap loosely for a few seconds. "Sounds like a wild goose chase to me."

"You would think that if you hadn't seen the things we've seen," Sean said. He was once again staring out the window at the desert below.

"Oh yeah? Like what?"

Slater was curious now and turned around in his cockpit seat to look back at Sean while he answered.

"We've seen all sorts of strange things in this line of work," Sean said. He twisted his head and leveled his gaze at Hank again. "We've seen a man eat a piece of glowing fruit that killed him. We've seen a terrorist speak to a plate, and the plate answered. It's easy to think of the supernatural as hokum or ridiculous until you see the unexplainable phenomena happen right in front of you. Then all your doubts just melt away."

Hank's eyes widened. "You've seen those things?"

"We've seen all sorts of weird stuff. Maybe someday we'll have answers to some of it. I have a feeling that we won't know it all until we meet the Almighty. But I know this: There are forces at work in this world that neither science nor religion can accurately explain. So, if I was you, I'd be prepared for darn near anything. Because if these tablets say that a desert city will rise from the sand, I'm inclined to think it's entirely possible."

Sean's words lingered in the cabin amid the drone of the plane's engines outside.

Hank hadn't expected an answer like the one Sean gave. It caught him off guard.

"Supernatural?" Hank said. "You guys have seen that kind of stuff?"

"Now and then," Tommy said.

"You say that like it's no big deal."

"I'm not a religious man, but I do consider myself to be a pretty spiritual guy. Sean does, too. We understand that there are forces at work in the universe beyond our feeble understanding. It's a bit strange when you see some of those things happening right in front of you, but believing it can happen takes a little of the edge off."

Hank shook his head. "I don't know about all that. Pretty sure I'd freak out if I saw some weird stuff like you're describing."

"The universe," Sean explained, "our reality, exists in a constant state of potentials. Only choices or observations change the reality. Our beliefs affect it. Many of the great spiritual teachers taught that. Even Jesus of Nazareth."

"Well, I don't know about all those miraculous things you guys are talking about, but if there's a treasure popping up out of the desert at this Zerzura place, you can bet your sweet caboose I'll be there to scoop up my share."

Sean smiled at his friend's materialistic sentiment. "If that's what you're looking for, maybe you'll find it."

"Anyway," Tommy interrupted again, "I didn't mean to make this a big spiritual discussion. Getting back to the pyramid in Egypt, I think we'll be searching for a statue or maybe a drawing of Anubis. This clue suggests we'll find the stone in the god's shadow."

"If it was in plain sight, someone probably would have already picked it up by now. Right?" Hank bounced his gaze from Tommy to Sean and back again.

"Probably. It's a good bet the thing is hidden underground. We won't know until we get there."

"One thing we do know," Sean interrupted, "is when we should look. Sunset."

"That doesn't give us a ton of room for error," Slater said.

"No, it doesn't. So, we should get to the site early and make sure we cover all the bases."

He didn't tell the others, but Sean had excused himself before they left the airport in Qatar and made a phone call. The way things had gone, it wouldn't hurt to have a little backup. And Sean knew just the person for the job.

Chapter 12

GIZA, EGYPT

"Like we never left, huh?" Tommy said as he and the others exited the beige SUV and stepped into the hot desert air.

The blazing sun beat down on them from the western sky, sucking the moisture from their skin and lips in a matter of seconds.

"Yeah," Sean said as he pushed his sunglasses closer to his eyes and took in their surroundings.

He'd been to Cairo more lately than he cared to remember. Each of the recent visits had resulted in some close calls. Based on the events of the last forty-eight hours, there was no reason to think this one would be any different.

Sean eyed the horizon but didn't see anything suspicious. "Let's move," he said. "The sun will be setting in a bit, and I'd like to know where we need to be when it happens."

"Good call," Tommy agreed.

Sid had remained at the airport to refuel the plane and keep things ready in case they had to make a quick exit again like they'd done in Dubai. That left the other four to handle things at the pyramid. Slater had brought up the idea of staying at the airport with Sid, but Sean insisted he come along for the ride in case things went sour. No such thing as too many guns on one's side in a fight.

The group took a short detour into the city to get new phones for Tommy and Sean since theirs had been confiscated by Dufort and his men. They also got cleaned up from their dirty, sweaty encounter in the Empty Quarter.

Sean looked up the remainder of the hill from where they'd parked. It was a few hundred feet to the top. They were already close to level with the top of the great pyramid off in the distance.

"It's just like you said, Schultzie. It's like they've completely ignored this place."

"I know. It's weird, isn't it?"

"Sure is," Hank chimed in. "No gates, no fences, nothing. Almost like the Egyptian government doesn't think it's important."

"And they reroute people to the other pyramids," Sean said. "Classic diversionary tactic. If no one thinks this place is significant, they won't come. The government promotes the other sites like crazy, and meanwhile this one sits idly by without much notice. It smacks of a cover-up to me, but I'm a bit cynical when it comes to things like that. So, I might be the wrong one to ask."

Tommy smirked and shook his head twice. "Come on, cynic, let's see if we can find a god with a dog head."

The four men trudged along the worn path up the slope. Sean brought up the rear. His head was on a swivel, eyes scanning everywhere an enemy could hide. Still, he saw nothing out of the ordinary. Deep down, he wished this one would be easy. One voice in his head kept saying that Dufort was gone, left behind in Dubai with no way to figure out where they'd gone. The other voice, however, was the one Sean usually heard more clearly. It was the voice that had saved his life on more than one occasion. That voice was telling him something wasn't right, that things were too quiet.

They reached the top of the hill and paused to catch their breath. Tommy was the first to turn around and look out at the scene below. The city was off to the left with the main three pyramids of Giza standing tall on the plateau across the Nile.

From their vantage point, the four men could clearly see that the mountain pyramid was easily higher than any of the others.

"Definitely the tallest," Slater said with his hands on his hips. "I hope your translation of those tablets was right. Otherwise we've just wasted a heck of a lot of time coming up here."

"It was correct," Tommy said. "I've looked over it several times. This has to be the place."

He led the way down into a passage lined on both sides by smooth cut stone. The rock was so precisely cut that it appeared to have been done by machines.

Hank noticed the craftsmanship and ran his fingers along the stone. "How in the world did they do this so perfectly thousands of years ago? It's like it was done with lasers."

"There are some historians and archaeologists who believe it *was* done by machines or some form of ancient technology we no longer know about."

They crossed a threshold into a more open area that would have been a chamber if there was a roof. Instead, it appeared more like a big open-air room. There were huge stones lying on their sides, strewn about in several places. They might have been pillars long ago but now appeared more like benches. Smaller rocks, possibly a fireplace, surrounded a pit carved into the floor.

Tommy noticed something over to the right and motioned for the others to follow. He stopped at a wall carved from the rock and pointed to some holes cut through it. He peered through the openings and saw there was a room on the other side.

"Look at these holes," he said.

Sean stepped close to one of them and ran his finger along the inner edge. "It's perfectly smooth."

"And even, too," Tommy added. "This couldn't have been done with hand tools, not for this depth of cutting."

Hank and Slater each raised an eyebrow and glanced at each other with a dubious expression.

"Over here," Tommy said, motioning to a recessed section in the chamber's floor. It had been cut into a perfect rectangle. "Here's another one. This entire chunk was cut right out of the rock."

"Like it was all done in one piece," Sean said, mesmerized.

"You two sound like a couple of those alien conspiracy theory guys," Slater said with a chuckle.

"I'm not suggesting it was aliens who did all this," Tommy defended. "What I *am* saying is that the people who were here long ago must have had access to technology we never believed possible. It's the only explanation."

"That or they just had some really skilled craftsmen."

Tommy shook his head and pointed at a nearby wall. "Look over here," he said, taking a few steps to the wall. "See this, where it looks a little blackened?"

The others nodded. "Those are scorch marks."

Slater shrugged. "Maybe they had a fire."

"Or maybe they had some kind of machinery we never learned about in school, something that made building the pyramids—their entire empire—much easier than we ever believed possible."

Slater sighed. "Okay. That's all well and good, but are we here to discuss ancient technology, or are we going to try to find that missing stone?"

Tommy raised a finger. "Good point."

He looked around, spinning in circles as he tried to get his bearings.

"Sun is setting over there," Sean said, pointing at the bright yellow ball in the sky. It was getting late in the afternoon. Darkness was creeping into the east. They wouldn't have much time.

"Yes, yes. I know. I'm looking for a keyhole."

"A keyhole?" Hank asked.

Tommy gave a curt nod. "Yes. The first clue says that the sun will point to the spot in the shadow of Anubis."

"So, we need to find Anubis and a keyhole?"

"There," Sean said, cutting off Hank's question. He pointed at a rock wall to the west where a tiny hole—about the size of a silver dollar

—had been cut into the stone. He shuffled his feet to get closer. Sure enough, he could see daylight on the other side. The sun was getting near the apex of the wall. Soon, it would be directly behind the hole.

"Good," Tommy said. "Now we need to find Anubis. Where could he be hiding?"

He looked all around the huge area but didn't see anything even remotely close to the deity or his likeness.

"Quick, fan out," Tommy ordered. "Search the entire area. Look for a painting, carving, statue, anything that has a dog head and a human body."

The others did as told and spread out, each taking a different section of the four walls surrounding the pyramid's interior.

Sean walked over to the end where the keyhole was located and started scanning the walls for a clue as to where Anubis might be found.

Hank moved slowly, worried he could possibly miss something and ruin the venture for everyone.

Slater was a little more relaxed with his effort, but he did the best he could and walked casually down the north wall, eyes panning the stone as he went.

Tommy took the farthest wall to the east. He spent nearly five minutes searching for a scrap of evidence as to Anubis's location. After he'd scoured the entire wall and the floor around it, he still had nothing.

Frustrated, he spun around and looked at the others. They'd finished their search and joined Tommy where he was standing.

"You guys find anything?" he asked.

They shook their heads.

"No. Not a thing," Sean said.

Tommy put his hands on his hips. "It has to be here. The clue wouldn't lead us here if there wasn't something to find."

"Maybe someone already got here before us and took it," Hank said.

"He could be right," Slater agreed. "Haven't grave robbers been coming to places like this for a long time, stealing valuable items and such?"

"Yes," Tommy said. "But this is something they would have missed. It wouldn't have been left around in a burial chamber or out in the open for someone to see. It was hidden with great care."

"How do you know that?"

Tommy sighed and rolled his shoulders. "I don't know. Call it a hunch."

"What if we're not at the right pyramid?" Hank asked. "It could be one of the others, and we're standing around here with our hands in our pockets while the stone is hiding somewhere else."

"I thought about that," Sean said. "Tommy's right. This is the correct place. We're just missing something."

Then Sean noticed something out of the corner of his eye. A little yellowish-white dot was inching its way down a column on the eastern wall—the wall Tommy had just been examining.

"What is that?" Sean asked, pointing at the dot.

The other three turned around and saw the anomaly.

Tommy's eyes went wide. He drifted back over to the wall and stood in front of the pillar. He looked over his shoulder at the western wall where the keyhole was located. He swallowed hard and then stared up at the column again. There was an ankh carved into it about eight feet up.

"That's it," Tommy said with an air of reverence in his voice.

"What's it?" Hank asked.

"The ankh. It's one of the most important symbols from ancient Egyptian religions and mythology. There's one on the tablet."

"And," Sean added, "we've seen a good number of pictures featuring Anubis holding an ankh."

"Right," Tommy said. "We were looking for Anubis when we should have been looking for the symbol he carried."

"Plus, Anubis was a god of the underworld. It would make sense he wouldn't be out here in the open if someone was trying to hide a valuable relic."

"Good point."

The men watched eagerly as the tiny dot made its way down the side of the column. The journey took several minutes, and more than once Sean turned his head to check the entrance, making sure no one was coming down the passage. The last thing they needed was some random tourists to show up on a whim while he and his companions were unearthing a lost treasure.

At the base of the pillar, the little dot came to a stop for a moment, right on the seam between the huge plinth and the floor. Then, just as suddenly as it had appeared, the dot vanished.

The four men gazed at the bottom of the pillar for a long moment before anyone said anything.

"So...what do we do now?" Slater asked in a hushed tone.

Sean drew closer to the column. He figured it was about ten feet tall, right around the same height as a basketball rim. The corner wall next to it was only three feet away, as best as he could tell. That gave him an idea.

He handed Tommy his gear bag they'd picked up in Cairo before coming to the site and then stood between the column and the wall.

"What are you doing?" Tommy asked.

Sean gazed up at the top of the pillar, making sure his assessment was correct. "I'm gonna push the column over. You three should probably step back."

"Push it over?" Hank chuffed. "That thing weighs several tons. We'd need a crane to get that thing out of the way."

"A crane or leverage."

Sean pressed his shoulders into the corner and then planted his feet on the side of the pillar. He shuffled one foot up and then the other, then shimmied his shoulders upward. When he repeated the process, the others realized what he had in mind.

"You'll have to get near the top to get enough leverage," Tommy said. "You sure you're okay with that?"

"Why wouldn't he be okay with it?" Slater asked as he and the other two took a step back.

"Sean's afraid of heights," Tommy answered, staring up at his friend as he continued his slow ascent.

"Afraid of heights? I thought he was some kind of super spy."

"Even superheroes have their kryptonite," Sean grunted. "And I'll be fine, Schultzie. This isn't too bad."

"Just checking," Tommy said. He turned to the other two. "Anything over 25 feet or so, and he gets a little sketchy."

"I can hear you," Sean huffed.

Sweat rolled down the side of his face. Other beads of moisture trickled into his eyes, causing them to sting and blur. He kept working his way upward, though, fighting the aching from his back and shoulders digging into the wall and the burning in his legs.

He locked his focus on the pillar in front of him to ward off the urge to quit and let himself drop to the ground. He was more than halfway up when he started to feel the pillar shift a little. It didn't give much, for which he was thankful. At this height, he wouldn't be able to get enough leverage to topple the heavy stone. He'd need to be at the very top.

The other three watched in mesmerized awe as Sean continued climbing. He was nearly to the top when one of his feet slipped. He started to fall. Tommy jumped forward first, ready to attempt a catch if his friend dropped. Luckily, he didn't have to. Sean pushed his neck and shoulders back even harder and steadied himself with his right foot to keep from falling. He let out a weary gasp and then kept working toward the top.

After what seemed like twenty minutes, Sean felt the top edge of the pillar with one of his boots. He swallowed hard. The perspiration was pouring off his head and face now. Fortunately, the warm, dry air evaporated it relatively fast. He bent his body forward as much as he could without losing pressure on both points of contact and then flexed his quads. He pushed with as much power as he could muster.

The column trembled for a second and then broke loose from the ground where it had been planted for thousands of years. The three men on the ground watched as the giant stone wobbled to the left and then tipped back to the right, bending Sean nearly in half.

One last push would do it. At least that's what Sean hoped.

He grunted and shoved the pillar again, this time a little harder.

The heavy stone swung back the other direction like a huge, upside-down pendulum. This time, it went far enough that Sean's feet came free. He fell as the pillar toppled beyond its tipping point.

The drop to the ground was considerable. Sean flailed his arms to keep his balance as he fell. When he hit the ground, he landed on the balls of his feet, bent his knees instantly, and rolled along the stone to absorb the impact. He tumbled clear of the destruction as the pillar crashed to the ground in a thunderous boom. Dust and debris erupted from the ground and clouded the entire chamber.

Sean and the others pulled their shirts over their faces to keep from breathing the dirty air. They watched and waited patiently as the dust settled. It took a few minutes before they were able to see everything clearly again.

The four men stepped forward once the air had cleared and stared down at the destruction. The big pillar was on its side and had split in two when it hit the ground. At its base, a hole slightly smaller than the diameter of the column was cut into the stone floor.

"Well, I'll be," Hank said.

Tommy moved ahead of the others and stopped short of the cavity. He gazed into it with wide eyes.

Shadows enveloped the chamber, and the sky above was turning darker by the second. Even so, there was enough light for the four men to see what was inside the hole.

A small stone box with the image of Anubis carved into the top.

Sean blinked rapidly, still trying to get some of the debris and sweat out of his eyes. "Looks like the right spot," he said, wiping his forehead with the bottom of his shirt.

Tommy nodded. "Yep. Time to see what's inside."

Chapter 13

GIZA

Tommy reached into the hole and clasped the ends of the box as tightly as he could. He lifted but was surprised at how heavy the object was, almost as if it were attached to the ground. He let go of it and tilted his head to the right.

"There are little handles cut into the lid," Sean pointed out. "Maybe just take it off."

Tommy snickered at his friend's helpful yet sarcastic comment. He worked his fingers under the edges of the lid and pried it off the main part of the container. It was much easier to pick up, and he set the top off to the side of the hole.

The four men held their collective breath, staring into the box.

"What is that?" Slater asked in a whisper.

Tommy almost didn't believe what he was seeing. Within the ancient container was an amulet of pure gold. It was shaped like an ankh but with one major addition. Just below the hoop at the top, a gem was embedded into the precious metal.

"Is that a ruby?" Hank asked, nearly licking his lips at the possibility.

"Might be," Tommy said. "Sure looks like it."

Tommy picked up the amulet, cradling it in both hands as if it were a newborn baby. The others circled around him as he held it in the middle for all to see. He waited a moment before flipping it over and examining the entire piece. On the back was an inscription.

"What is that?" Hank asked.

"Coptic," Tommy said. "And it's a slightly more modern version of it than what they might have used in the earlier kingdoms of Ancient Egypt."

Slater scratched his head. "Um...can you read it?"

Tommy looked up with his best *how dare you ask me that* face. "Yeah, I can read it."

He ran his finger along the yellow metal, taking a moment to process the information. He shook his head and ran his finger along the inscription again, this time with a scowl on his face.

"Something wrong?" Sean asked.

"Maybe."

"Maybe?" Hank asked. "What do you mean, maybe? Can you read it or not?"

"I definitely can," Tommy said with a slight hint of defensiveness to his voice. "That isn't the problem."

"Then what is?"

"The problem is where it's telling us to go next." He looked to Sean. "Hand me the tablets. I want to make sure this is right."

Sean jogged over to the middle of the chamber where they'd set down the case and retrieved it. He placed it on the ground next to Tommy and unlatched the clasps. Tommy took it from there. He set the medallion on his lap and carefully opened the case.

"Could one of you shine a light on this?" he asked.

Slater whipped out his phone and switched on the light, shining down onto the ancient script carved into the tablets.

"Right here," Tommy said, pointing at a blank space in the script. "It says the second stone can be found here."

"The line is blank," Sean said.

"Apparently," Tommy said, raising the talisman, "we use this to fill in the gap." He laid the relic down onto the tablet and then read it out loud. "The second stone of power can be found in the arch where Dorieus failed, a tribute of three."

Hank and Slater frowned. "What in the world does that mean?" Hank asked.

Tommy shook his head. "I'm not entirely sure."

"You're not sure? I thought you were some kind of expert in this sort of thing."

Tommy snorted. "I like to think I am, but world history is a broad and deep subject. I can't remember everything I studied. There's only so much space in this noggin." He tapped his head.

"So, what do we do?" Slater asked.

Sean and Tommy cast each other a knowing glance and nodded.

"The kids," they said at the same time.

"The kids?"

Tommy reached into his pocket and pulled out the temporary phone he'd picked up in Cairo. He tapped on the app to make the numbers appear on the screen and then started pecking away.

He paused after entering the area code and looked up, clearly trying to remember what the rest of the numbers were.

"Can't remember it, can you?" Sean asked with a hint of mischief in his eyes.

"Shut up," Tommy said.

"Seriously? It's your building, man."

"Do *you* remember it?"

"No, but I rarely need to call. And besides, it's not *my* building."

"What number? What are you two talking about? And who are the kids?" Hank was clearly getting frustrated by the lack of answers coming his way.

Sean sighed. "Tommy has a crack team of researchers working for him back at the IAA headquarters. Personally, I think there's something romantic going on between the two of them, but who knows."

"Sean," Tommy said.

"Sorry, tangent. Anyway, they're good at getting us fast answers when we need them."

"And since I have a cell signal here—barely—I can call them

much faster than I can probably get the internet to work on this thing." He paused again, and then his face brightened. "Oh, got it."

He typed in the rest of the numbers and hit the green call button.

The phone rang three times before a young woman answered.

"Hello, IAA labs, Tara speaking."

"Tara, it's Tommy."

"Oh, hey, Tommy. You sound a little crackly."

"I'm out in the middle of nowhere."

"Is this a Cairo area code?"

"Yeah, long story. Had to get a temporary phone. Listen, I need your help."

"That's why we're here."

Tara and her partner, Alex, had been working for Tommy for several years now. They were more than a decade younger than Tommy and Sean, which was how they received the nickname "the kids." Most of the time, they worked on analyzing new artifacts that were brought into the lab, but now and then they performed a different kind of task, the kind that required the use of the internet and a few other tricks they had up their sleeves. Aside from being experts in the field of archaeological research, Tara and Alex were brilliant with computers and other technology.

"I need you to find out what you can about a person named Dorieus. It sounds familiar, but I can't recall exactly who it is or what he did."

"And you're somewhere you can't look that up on your phone."

"Correct."

"Okay, give me a few minutes, and I'll call you back."

"Thanks, Tara. I appreciate it."

"Not a problem."

He could hear her say, "Hey, Alex," as he ended the call.

"She's going to call me back," Tommy said to the others who were hovering over him with expectant stares on their faces.

He opened the camera app and took a few pictures of the talisman and the tablet before closing the case.

"That name," Tommy said in an absent tone. "It sounds so familiar. I'm mad at myself that I can't remember it."

"Like you said," Slater chimed in, "world history is a big subject. You can't expect to remember every detail from every kingdom and culture that ever existed. And if you could, you should be on Jeopardy. You'd go undefeated."

Tommy chuckled. "Yeah, I know. Still, Dorieus sounds like a name I've come across before."

"Is it one of the caesars?" Sean asked. "I don't recall him being one of them, but I don't have that list of rulers memorized, either."

Tommy shook his head. "I don't think so. I mean, yeah, it sounds like a caesar, but that isn't it. He's from somewhere else."

"Persian? Greek, maybe?"

"Possibly Greek. It's driving me crazy."

While Tommy pined over the dilemma of recalling just who Dorieus was in the annals of history, Sean turned his head around, peering out at the upper reaches of the pyramid through slits in his eyelids. Something wasn't right. An old feeling he only got when trouble was coming started creeping up inside him.

"We need to go," he said abruptly.

Hank jerked his head back and scowled. "Why? What's the matter?"

"I don't like this place. It's a kill box. We need to get out of here."

"What's the worry? We're all alone here. And if someone were coming, we'd see them at the top of the passage."

Hank pointed up the slope through corridor leading to the upper end.

"He's right," Slater said. "We should move." He suddenly had a concerned look on his face as he scanned the pyramid's horizon.

"What's with you two?" Hank asked. "I'm telling you, no one is here. And who would be following us? We left that French guy way back in Dubai. No way he could track us here."

"It might not be him we have to worry about," Sean said.

"If not him, then who?"

Tommy knew his friend well enough to know when something

wasn't right. If Sean's danger-radar was going off, nine times out of ten that meant there was trouble on the way. He picked up the case and stuffed the medallion into a back pocket.

He led the other three back toward the passage and then stopped in mid-stride at the base of the slope. He stared up at a silhouette against the backdrop of the darkening evening sky.

The figure was dressed in black, loose fitting clothes. It appeared he had something wrapped around his face with one piece of fabric dangling to the right, flapping in the wind. It was impossible to see the man's face, but the weapons were easy to spot. A sword dangled from the figure's waist, and a Kalashnikov hung in his hands.

The four Americans looked around the chamber for another way out. That's when they saw the others begin appearing around the upper edges of the pyramid. Each one looked identical to the figure at the top of the passage, and they were all similarly armed.

They pointed their guns down into the pyramid at the Americans as if waiting for the four men to make a move.

"Them," Sean answered Hank's question from before. "That's who."

Chapter 14

GIZA

The man at the top of the passage remained there for what seemed like an eternity, staring down at the four trapped Americans.

Sean noticed Slater easing his hand back toward where he kept his pistol. "Don't provoke them," Sean said. "Besides. We're severely outgunned here. They'd cut us down in seconds."

"You don't want to take a few of them with us?"

Sean took a long, slow breath and assessed the situation for the third time in half a minute. "No. If they wanted to, they could have killed us already."

Slater gave a single nod, acknowledging Sean was correct. "What, then?"

"I think we're about to find out," Tommy said.

The man at the top started lumbering down the path toward them. His weapon swung from side to side, and the sword on his hip dangled back and forth with each step. When he reached the bottom, he stopped fifteen feet short of the Americans and looked into each man's eyes.

The guy had a black piece of fabric over his face. Combined with the head wrap, the only things that were visible were the top of his nose and his eyes.

"Why have you come here?" the man asked in a gruff, heavy accent.

Sean placed it from somewhere in the Middle East, but which country was hard to say based on one sentence.

"We're taking in the sights," Tommy offered.

The man shook his head. "You're not tourists. Tourists do not come to this place. They don't teach people about this place in history books. And no travel guide tells anyone to come here."

"You speak good English," Sean said. "Where did you learn that?"

The gunman raised his weapon and pointed it at Sean's face. Sean didn't flinch.

"Answer my question," the man said.

"You think that's the first time I've had a gun like that aimed at my head? You're not even in the top fifty."

He shouted something in Arabic, and the men around the top of the pyramid tightened their grip on their weapons.

"What did he just say?" Hank asked, suddenly panicked.

"He told them to ready their weapons," Sean said. "But they're not going to kill us. Are you, friend?"

The gunman cocked his head to the side. The four Americans could see a quizzical look in his eyes, as if he was unsure how to take Sean's assessment.

"That's right," Sean said. "Because if you were going to, you would have done it before. That tells me you're not interested in killing us." He paused for a second, sensing the case at Tommy's side. "That means you want what we have."

"You have trespassed on sacred ground," the gunman said. "Long have we watched this place to keep the secret safe from thieves like you. Now you have desecrated it and stolen something that doesn't belong to you, a relic more powerful than you could ever conceive."

"Oh, you mean the medallion?" Tommy said.

Hank looked like his head was about to explode. "Don't...why would you tell...don't let on...." He couldn't form a full sentence.

"We already know about the medallion," the gunman said. "What do you think we've been protecting for the last few thousand years?"

Sean raised an eyebrow. "Guardians, eh? We've encountered some of those in the past. Remember those guys, Schultzie?"

"Oh sure. Good fellows. Took a little getting to know them, but once we did they were real stand-up guys." Tommy's tone was as casual as he could make it for having a few dozen automatic weapons pointed at him.

"Give me the medallion," the gunman said, sticking his hand out with palm up. "And never return here again."

"No," Sean said. "Don't give it to him, Tommy."

"Oh, I won't," Tommy chirped. "He'll have to pry it from my cold, dead hand."

The gunman shook his head slowly back and forth. "Very well, Americans. Have it your way."

The guy started to step back and raise his weapon to waist high. Tommy suddenly whipped the case up. The hard edge struck the man's weapon, and he drove the gun up into the air, knocking it from his hands.

Sean stepped forward and in the same movement drew the pistol from his belt. He wrapped his arm around the gunman's neck and pressed the muzzle to the guy's temple hard enough to indent the skin.

"Now," Sean said as his companions gathered close around the hostage, "here's what's going to happen. Tell your men to drop their guns, and I'll let you go. Deal?"

"No. I am willing to die to protect that holy relic your friend has in his pocket. As are all my men."

Tommy wondered how the guy knew it was in his pocket. He figured the gunman and his followers were watching when he retrieved it.

"Tommy," Slater said, pointing at Tommy's leg, "look at your pocket."

A strange red glow was coming from Tommy's pants. It was in the shape of the gem embedded in the ankh.

"What in the world?"

"You see, foolish ones? The medallion contains a stone of power. You have no idea what you're meddling with. One order from my lips, and my men will cut us all down to keep it safe."

"We're not thieves," Sean said. "You called us thieves. We're not. We're archaeologists."

"Well, I am," Tommy argued. "You're more like the head of security."

"Anyway," Sean said, ignoring his friend. "We aren't looking for trouble. But if we don't secure this medallion, there's a very bad man out there looking for it, too. If he finds it, that will mean trouble for everyone. I'm talking on a global scale here."

The gunman's eyes narrowed as he assessed Sean's explanation. "You lie."

"No," Sean said. "I'm telling the truth. His name is Gerard Dufort, and he's the worst kind of human being. He sells children for money and who knows what else. He's looking for the lost city of Zerzura. And if he finds it...well, it's gonna be no bueno."

"That's Spanish for not good," Tommy clarified.

Sean loosened his grip on the gunman and let him go. Then he lowered his weapon to his side before stuffing it back in his belt. He raised his hands in surrender.

"What are you doing?" Slater asked. "He was our only bargaining chip."

"No," Sean shook his head. "We're on the same team as this guy. They're on a mission to protect a powerful item from the wrong hands. So are we."

He peered through the gunman's eyes and into his soul. In doing so, Sean let the man see the honesty in his own eyes.

The gunman raised a hand to the sky and held it there for a second. Then he called out a command in Arabic. The men around the lip of the pyramid lowered their weapons and relaxed.

"This man you speak of, Dufort. Why does he want to find Zerzura?"

"Same reason anyone else does," Sean said. "He wants to live forever."

The gunman nodded. "For centuries we have worked to keep the legend of Zerzura a secret. Men and women have come to this place investigating the works of the ancient ones. Television crews have even visited here, but no one has ever looked for the medallion or disturbed a single stone. Until you four showed up. Now, I fear, the secret will be undone."

"No," Tommy said. "We'll keep it safe."

"Why do you seek the lost city?" the gunman asked. "Do you also seek to attain eternal life?"

"No. I don't. I look to uncover history that has been lost to the world. I seek answers. And more importantly, I'm on a quest to fulfill a dream my parents had before they disappeared."

The man raised his head, assessing Tommy and his story. "Your parents disappeared?"

"Yeah, well, for like twenty years. They're back now, but that's beside the point. Before they vanished, they were working on something big. It took up most of their time." There was a hint of sadness in his voice. Maybe he'd lost time with his parents as a result of their relentless efforts. "Anyway, I'm trying to finish what they started. I need to find Zerzura. If I don't, someone else will."

"Not if you give me the medallion," the gunman said. "I will take it and throw it into the sea. Then no one will find it for all of eternity."

"That," a new voice interjected, "my good man, will not be happening."

The five men spun around and looked up the passage to where the nasally voice originated.

Sean and Tommy's hearts sank into the pit of their stomachs. They instantly recognized who spoke.

At the top of the path, the outline of a skinny, middle-aged man stood between the stone walls.

"Dufort," Sean muttered.

"How does he keep doing that?" Tommy wondered out loud.

"I don't know."

The gunman shouted an order to his men. They raised their weapons, ready to fire. Suddenly, a gunshot rang out from somewhere in the distance. Down in the chamber it sounded like nothing more than a balloon popping. One of the men around the top edge shuddered for a moment and then fell over into the pyramid. He landed on his face with a thud and never moved again.

The other men on the upper perimeter immediately spun around and searched for the shooter. Many opened fire on the unseen sniper, but they had no idea where he was or what they were shooting at.

Another man caught a round in the chest on the opposite side of the pyramid and fell backward into the chamber. Then another was shot in the gut, a fourth in the neck, a fifth in the chest, a sixth in the head. One by one, the men dropped from their perches, most dying before they hit the stone floor below, some on impact.

"Stop!" the leader shouted at his men. "Cease fire!" he yelled in Arabic.

The men stopped shooting their weapons and raised them up over their heads.

The cacophony of noise ceased, leaving nothing but an eerie silence and a cloud of gun smoke lingering in the air. The acrid fog drifted down into the chamber and then floated away, dissipating into the dry night air.

Dufort waited for a moment before he sauntered down the long path. He reached the bottom and stopped, looking with disdain at the five men before him.

He shook his head and wagged a finger, clicking his tongue as he did so. "You just never seem to learn, do you, Sean? No matter where you go, I will always find you. There is nothing you can do to stop that."

"You killed my men," the gunman said. "You will pay for this with your life."

Dufort looked surprised. Both eyebrows raised, and he almost chuckled but held it back. "I doubt that, whoever you are. Your men are lucky I didn't have them all executed. Tell them to lay down their weapons before any more of them die."

The gunman hesitated.

"You don't seem to understand, so I'll say it again. Tell your men to put their weapons down, or they will all die here tonight. One word to my snipers, and they'll cut down all of your rabble like weeds in a field."

The man in black blinked rapidly. The other four knew Dufort wasn't messing around. He'd have no problem ordering the deaths of all the remaining men on top of the pyramid.

"You should do as he says," Sean chimed in. "He's not a man to be taken lightly."

"Ah, very good, Sean. I'm glad to see you're finally coming around."

"And I'm glad to see you're finally calling me by my first name instead of the usual Mr. Wyatt crap."

"Well, you can't blame one for trying to be formal. Now, I believe we were about to have your men drop their weapons, hmm?" He tilted his head forward and stared at the gunman from under his eyelids.

The masked man shouted out an order, and his men immediately set their weapons down and put their hands in the air.

"Much better. Thank you for your cooperation. Cody, kill them all."

The masked man's eyes went wide with a mix of fear and rage. He surged forward, but Dufort whipped out a pistol from inside his jacket and pointed it at the man's face.

"Ah, ah, ah. I wouldn't do that. Did you really think I was just going to let your little horde go free?"

A gunshot fired from off in the distance. This time, however, none of the men around the upper perimeter fell. Dufort waited for a second and then frowned. There should have been more shots fired, more men dying. Something was wrong, and Dufort didn't do a good job of hiding his sudden concern.

"That didn't sound like the same weapon from before, did it?"

Sean asked. "If I had to guess, I'd say that was a 9-millimeter. Not sure about the make, but it certainly wasn't the big .50 caliber you had going off before."

Dufort took a wary step back. "Cody, come in. Do you copy?"

"Sounds like someone took out your boy."

"Shut up."

Another shot popped from the darkness, then another.

"Cody? What's going on out there?"

One of the men up top saw what was transpiring below and risked picking up his weapon. He took aim at the retreating Frenchman and fired. The round blew off a huge chunk of stone at the corner of the passage, narrowly missing the villain by a few inches.

The abrupt boom from the AK-47 caused Dufort to stumble backward and up the corridor, accidentally finding his way to safety behind the stone walls. He kept backing up, faster and faster, while waving the pistol at the five men still standing below.

The guy in the mask shuffled a foot toward his weapon on the ground, but Dufort fired his pistol. The round sailed over the group and harmlessly into the wall behind them, but the shot did what it needed to do—bought Dufort time to get away.

Near the top, he turned and sprinted into the darkness, disappearing from view the second he went behind the wall.

Sean and the others took off after him, running at full stretch up the slope until they reached the crest. At the top, Sean halted the others and peeked around the corner. An SUV was spinning out in the dust and whipped around in a fury of dust and taillights before speeding away down the hill.

Sean fired two shots, hoping he might get lucky and take out a tire, but at that distance that hope was fleeting at best.

The men caught their breath from the hard sprint up the hill and then looked around at the rest of the masked guys standing over the pyramid.

"We were lucky," Slater said. "I guess someone was watching over us."

"It wasn't luck," Sean said. "Before we left Qatar, I called in a favor. I had a feeling Dufort was going to show his ugly mug again. I figured having a little backup might be a good idea."

"Backup?" Tommy asked. Even he was confused about Sean's mysterious helper.

Sean flashed a stupid, toothy smile.

Tommy's eyebrows lowered for a second until the answer hit him. "Oh. Wait, no. Seriously? Where was she when you called her?"

"I didn't ask. I assume she was somewhere in Europe."

"You didn't ask?"

"I'm sorry, guys," Slater interrupted. "Who are we talking about here? Sean, you called someone in to help?"

"It's his girlfriend," Tommy explained. "I can't believe you called her."

"Um, first of all, you're welcome. Secondly, why not?"

"Well, one, because I would think keeping your girlfriend out of harm's way would be your first thought, and two, I was hoping this could be like the old days, just you and me working our way through a series of puzzles and clues."

"You know what you sound like right now?" Hank asked.

"Don't start with me, Hank."

Sean chuckled, and then he remembered the masked man was still standing there with them.

"Oh, sorry. You're probably completely lost right about now. My name is Sean, by the way. This is Tommy, Hank, and Slater. My girl-friend, Adriana, is out there in the dark somewhere."

"I am Alu Arshad, leader of this group." He looked out toward the vast stretch of blackness before the lights of the city took over. "Shouldn't you go help her, your girlfriend?"

"If I had to bet money, I'd say she isn't the one who needs help."

Then he saw two headlights switch on halfway down the hill and off to the side of the road. The second vehicle spun out and fishtailed onto the dusty trail, following the other.

Sean's face drew long. "Then again," he said. "Slater, keys." Sean held out his hand.

"Oh no. If you're going after them, so am I."

"Alu," Tommy said, "care to chase this guy down?"

"He will pay for killing my men." The determined look in Alu's eyes was almost scary. He pulled out a key fob from the folds of his clothes and pressed a button. A black Range Rover's lights flashed in the darkest corner of the parking area. "I brought my own ride," he said.

Chapter 15

GIZA

Sean and Slater rumbled down the bumpy road with Alu, Hank, and Tommy in the SUV just behind them. Dufort's vehicle was nearly a half mile ahead at the start with what Sean presumed to be Adriana right on his tail.

Slater's foot kept the gas pedal to the floor, flying over humps and potholes at breakneck speed. Sean gripped the handle with white knuckles. There was a sort of troubling grin on Slater's face as he stared straight ahead with both hands on the wheel.

"Uh, Slater? Why do I get the impression you're enjoying this just a little too much?"

Slater never looked over at Sean, fearful that any distraction could cause him to lose control. "Been a while since I had any action like this in my life. Most of the time we're just babysitting."

"Miss the thrill of the chase, huh?"

Slater's head twisted to the side like he was stretching his neck. "You know what it's like, right?" He jerked the wheel to the left. The SUV's back wheels slid around the turn, but Slater kept it straight.

"Not really," Sean said. "This sort of thing seems to happen more often than you might think."

"Really? Working for your buddy's archaeological group?"

"The world's full of greedy, terrible people. Sometimes they want treasure. Other times...they want something else."

"Power."

"Yep," Sean said with a nod. "And power can come in many different forms."

They were closing in on Adriana's vehicle along with Dufort's. Sean cast a quick glance into the side mirror and saw that Alu was having no trouble keeping up.

If Slater could have pressed the gas pedal any farther into the floor, he would have. The engine screamed as they barreled down the road in pursuit. Slater pulled the SUV alongside Adriana. Sean looked through the window and saw her, but she was preoccupied. Slater moved past her, taking the lead in the chase.

Dufort's SUV wasn't far ahead now, only a few hundred feet.

A bright flash came from the passenger side of Dufort's ride. Then it popped again and again rapidly. One bullet ripped through the windshield and out the back window. Most of them missed wildly. He knew accuracy in a moving vehicle was tough, but Sean also knew Dufort and his men were desperate. They were running out of options, and with Sean and the others now closing in, things had to look bleak.

The high-speed caravan reached the edge of the city, and the packed dirt road changed into asphalt. The driver of Dufort's vehicle jerked the SUV side to side, struggling to keep the thing on the road when the tires gained a sudden grip on the pavement.

Seconds later, Slater and the others hit the road as well and gunned their engines to catch up to the Frenchman.

The lead SUV reached an intersection where the road split in three directions. One way went into the city, which would result in a massive slowdown for Dufort and his men. Another road branched off to the right, heading due west and into the desert. The third road continued south, running parallel to the Nile just to the east.

Sean watched intently, wondering what the Frenchman would do. He'd already ruled out the city route. Too much traffic, too many people, and once he came to a stop, Sean would pounce. He knew

Dufort had already thought of all those things. That left two realistic options. It would be tough to lose the pursuers in the desert. Things were too open with not enough places to hide. The road was also fairly straight. With a full tank of gas, it would be a race to see who ran out of fuel first. If Dufort hadn't taken the opportunity to fill his vehicle, he'd be in trouble. The chase could take as long as needed until the Frenchman's SUV petered out.

That left the road south, heading along the riverbank. Sean knew little about the road. What he did know was that there were several places along the way where Dufort could pull off and try to hide. There were ruins, pyramids, temples, and many other locations that —during the day—were occupied by tourists and research teams. In the evening, however, things were much quieter and the spots essentially vacant.

Slater must have read Sean's mind. "He'll take the south road."

"I was thinking the same thing."

"Great minds."

"I don't know about great, but for a couple of guys who used to do this sort of thing for a living...yeah, we're on the same wavelength."

They hit the intersection, and Dufort's driver did the exact opposite of what the two Americans expected. The lead SUV veered left on the road heading back into the city.

Sean frowned and stole a glance at Slater, who had the same bewildered expression on his face.

"So much for experience," Slater said. He spun the wheel to the left and tucked in behind Dufort's vehicle on the bridge crossing the river.

The gunman in Dufort's vehicle popped out again and squeezed off another sequence of shots. Slater yanked the steering wheel to the left, then right, attempting to zigzag clear of the bullets.

"Anytime you want to shoot back is fine with me."

Sean was a step ahead, rolling down his window and bracing himself to lean out the window. "No sudden movements," Sean said, "or I'll be nothing but hamburger meat on the pavement."

"Roger that."

He stuck his head out the window and wedged one foot on the seat and the other on the floor to keep his balance. He pointed the weapon at Dufort's vehicle, lined up the back window, and fired. The first shot sailed wide. He squeezed the trigger again. This time, the round punctured the back window, splintering it into a hundred cracks. A second later, Dufort's driver jerked the vehicle to the left—a reaction to the bullet hitting the glass. The SUV hit a pothole, and the window shattered, scattering shards of broken glass all over the pavement.

Slater's tires crunched the pieces on the road and kept going. Dufort's shooter moved back into the interior of the SUV. Sean could see the man climb into the far rear seat, which was a much better place to shoot from than hanging out a window.

Sean fired again, but Dufort's driver was keen to his attack now. He kept the vehicle weaving back and forth as Sean continued to empty his magazine at the Frenchman's ride.

The gunman in the back opened fire again. Slater had to hit the brakes to keep out of range and whipped the wheel to the right, nearly losing control as the rear end fishtailed from side to side.

Behind them, Tommy and the others watched from a safe distance in their SUVs, staying close enough to follow but far enough away to not interfere.

Another bullet found its way through the windshield of Slater's vehicle and plunked into the leather in the backseat.

"That was too close," Slater said. "These guys are really starting to piss me off."

Sean knew he only had a few rounds left, plus one more magazine. The chase was closing in on the city up ahead. Once they were there, things would slow down. There were traffic lights and pedestrians, not to mention a bunch of cars still on the road. No chance Dufort was going to lose them there.

"Pull back a bit," Sean said. "Let them think we're trying to stop them, but don't give them an easy shot."

"Once we're in the city they won't be able to lose us," Slater said, finishing Sean's thought.

"Exactly."

Slater gently applied the brakes and weaved the vehicle to the right lane and back to the left, keeping up the appearance of evasive maneuvers. Sean leaned out the window again and fired another shot to keep Dufort's gunman honest.

Then Slater saw something strange in the left lane.

"Sean? Did you notice there's no more traffic coming from the city?"

"What?" Sean shouted back over the wind noise.

"The other road coming out of town. There were cars coming, but now there aren't."

"I wonder...." Sean stopped short in mid-sentence. He looked through the cracked windshield at the road on the left. "What in the world?"

He realized what was happening before it was too late. Two SUVs, much like Dufort's, were blocking both lanes, parked sideways on the asphalt. Three men were waiting with automatic weapons pressed into their shoulders and barrels leveled.

"Oh no," Sean said.

The men opened fire as he ducked for cover. Slater slammed on the brakes and yanked the steering wheel to the right. Bullets tore through glass and metal. Some struck the grill and plunked into the engine block. The SUV skidded sideways for a second before the whole world turned upside down.

The tires on the left side caught hard, and momentum did the rest, flipping the SUV up over its side, onto its top, and again two more times before it came to a stop on its wheels. The body rocked back and forth for a moment before coming to rest.

Tommy watched in horror. Adriana saw the whole thing behind the wheel of her SUV. Fear filled her mind, and her heart dropped into her gut. A second later, rage—irrational and righteous—coursed through her. She veered the vehicle into the other two lanes as the gunmen reloaded their weapons. They saw the oncoming vehicle speeding their way. Panic filled their eyes, and they hurried to get the new magazines into the guns.

One man finished before the others and raised his weapon to fire, but it was too late. Adriana plowed into him as the muzzle erupted in several rapid flashes. His head snapped back and then forward, striking the hood of the car before she smashed into one of their SUVs.

The other shooters dove clear of the deadly battering ram, rolling out of the way in the nick of time.

Adriana's airbag deployed on impact. Her face smacked into it, and for a second everything around her went black. Her ears rang, and after a moment of dazed confusion her vision began to clear. She looked around and heard men shouting. The shooters. Things suddenly came back to her. There had been three men.

She looked out the cracked windshield at the dead man crushed between her grill and the side of the other SUV. Where were the other two?

Gunfire blasted from somewhere nearby. She looked out the window to her left and saw one of the men approaching her with a gun raised. He spun to his right in the direction of the shots, but his reaction was too slow. Bullets pounded him in the chest. One found his neck and punched out the other side in a pink mist. He fell to his knees, desperately clutching his throat at the mortal wound.

The last gunman opened fire on the other shooter. Adriana couldn't see who it was, but she knew they'd be scrambling for cover. She unbuckled her seatbelt, silently opened her door, and climbed out. Things were still a bit woozy, but her equilibrium balanced quickly.

She moved stealthily across the pavement on the balls of her feet. The gunman's full attention was on an SUV parked sixty feet away. He was peppering it with rounds from his weapon and stalking toward the friendly shooter's position. Now Adriana was slightly behind the enemy. By taking the offensive, he'd opened himself up to an attack from behind.

Adriana ran, still staying on her toes to minimize noise. She closed the gap between herself and the gunman within seconds.

When she was within range, she leaped into the air, leading with her knee.

The guy never saw it coming. The next thing he felt was Adriana's hard knee bone crunching into the middle of his spine. He let out an involuntary grunt as the nerves in his body screamed out in pain.

Her weight combined with momentum drove him to the ground, where his face smacked the pavement. Most people would have been debilitated by the attack, but he was clearly a pro. The gunman felt Adriana straddle his back and swung the butt of his weapon around behind him, striking her on the right cheek.

The blow knocked her off balance and for a moment brought back the dizziness.

She rolled to her feet and lunged forward just as the gunman stood and raised his weapon to end the fight with one pull of the trigger. He was fast. Adriana was faster. She jumped, whipped her leg around, and drove the tip of her boot into the side of the man's weapon. The jolt knocked the barrel away as he pulled the trigger and fired a round harmlessly into the air. He tried to bring it back around to his target, but she was already on to her next attack. She spun around, leading with her left leg, and drove the heel of her boot into the side of the man's head.

The high roundhouse kick hit the enemy in precisely the right spot—or wrong spot for the villain. He collapsed to the ground and twitched for a few seconds before his body went limp. His eyes locked on the far wall across the other lanes on the bridge.

Adriana stood over him for a second, thinking the guy might be faking. She nudged his arm with the tip of her boot, but he didn't move. Tommy arrived first. He skidded to a stop near the dead man and stared down at him with his weapon pointed at the guy's head.

"He gone?" Tommy asked.

Adriana wiped her lips with her forearm. There was a thin line of blood oozing from her lip. She hadn't realized she was bleeding until the fight was over.

"Yeah," she said with a nod. "I must have hit him in the right place."

Then she turned her attention to the totaled SUV behind her. She ran over to the passenger's side and started to open the door when she heard the mechanism click inside. The door clicked before she could pull the handle. It cracked open for a second, and then Sean pushed it out the rest of the way. The hinges creaked, bending a piece of metal that had warped off of the door and into the sill.

He had a cut on his head and a burn mark on his face from the air bag. Sean set one foot onto the pavement and started to climb out. His eyes were open, blinking rapidly, but it was clear to Adriana that he was a little out of it.

Tommy arrived on the scene a moment later and put his hand out to brace his friend. He did so just in time. As Sean's other foot hit the road, he started to fall forward. Tommy and Adriana held him up for a second and then let him down slowly.

"Call an ambulance," Tommy said.

Sean was woozy, but he managed to move his head back and forth as he stared at the pavement just beyond his feet. "No. Don't call them."

"Sean, you're hurt. You need medical attention," Tommy insisted.

"I'm fine. Just get me out of here."

"Who's the driver?" Adriana asked Tommy.

"A guy named Slater."

"See if he's okay. I've got Sean."

Tommy gave a nod and rushed around to the other side of the vehicle. It took more than a few tries to pry open the door. The crash had severely dented the roof along the seam where the door met the frame. By planting his feet on the back door and putting all his weight into it, Tommy yanked the door open wide enough to get inside.

"Slater, you okay?"

Slater's head was tilted to the side at an awkward angle. He didn't respond.

"Slater? Hey, man. You all right?" Tommy leaned to the left to get a better look at the guy.

His chest wasn't rising, and his eyes were closed.

"Slater?" Tommy nudged the driver's shoulder with his finger. Then he pressed two fingers to Slater's neck and waited a moment.

Nothing.

Slater was dead.

"He's gone," Tommy announced.

Alu and Hank trotted up to the scene of the crash and took in everything that was happening within a few seconds.

"What?" Hank asked. "Did you say he's gone?"

Tommy pulled back his hand and looked over his shoulder at Hank. "Yeah. He's dead. Sean's alive, but he's pretty banged up. We need to get out of here. And Sean might need a doctor. He says no."

"He's right to," Alu said. "The police will be here any minute. Lots of witnesses. We need to get out of here. If your friend is hurt, I know someone who can help him."

Tommy was dubious, and he didn't try to hide that in the expression he let Alu see. Tommy also realized he didn't have many options. Sean didn't want to go to the hospital, either out of pride or fear he and the others would be caught by the cops or someone worse. Dufort had the ability to sneak people into secure places. It wouldn't take much for an assassin to get into a hospital. Alu's offer was their best chance.

"Okay," Tommy said. "Take us to your friend."

Chapter 16

CAIRO, EGYPT

Cody stumbled through the hotel room door with a grimace on his face. The bruise stung like a needle piercing his skin, while at the same time producing a throbbing pain in his chest.

He was lucky he'd been wearing a Kevlar vest when the woman attacked him and planted a round in the center of his torso. The blistering desert heat had caused him to consider not putting the protective equipment on, but he'd opted for safety over comfort. It turned out it was the right decision and one that saved his life.

He dropped the vest onto the floor and stumbled over to the bed, where he collapsed onto his face.

"Where have you been?" a familiar, edgy voice asked.

Cody blinked a slow, heavy blink. He rolled over and sat up on the edge of the bed. "She...she came out of nowhere," he said, fighting to find the words. His throat was parched. It felt like someone had shoved sandpaper into the back of his mouth. "Watkins is dead."

"She killed him?" Dufort asked from a club chair in the corner of the room.

Cody nodded reluctantly. "Yeah," he said in a defeated tone.

"She didn't kill you."

"She snapped his neck. I was lucky. She kicked a rock or something in the dark. I heard the noise and turned just in time." He talked about the scenario like he was reliving a bad dream. "She must have known the sound tipped me off. She pulled out her gun just as I turned to fire and planted one in my chest. Good thing I was wearing my vest, I suppose."

"Indeed," Dufort said. He leaned forward, planting his elbows on his knees. He brought his hands together and interlocked the fingers in a slow, deliberate kind of way. A pensive scowl crossed his face.

"What about the others?" Cody asked. "What about my brother?"

Dufort continued to stare at the carpet. His mind wandered for a moment, following the brown crisscrossing patterns in the fabric. "They're all dead," the Frenchman said after a long pause. "Wyatt and his friends...they killed them all."

Cody swallowed back a hunk of pain. It fell all the way from his throat to his stomach. A sickening pang fluttered in his chest.

"Are you sure Tim didn't make it? You probably thought I was dead, too."

"I'm sure," Dufort said. "Zoli and I barely made it out ourselves. He's in his room getting some rest. I waited up here in hopes that you'd somehow make it back."

Cody barely heard anything his boss said. His thoughts lingered on his younger brother, Tim. He'd brought Tim along with the promise of being set for life once the job was done.

Dufort had been convincing. He'd shown the recruits what he'd been working on and more importantly, what Wyatt and Schultz had already found. The two IAA men brought a huge amount of credibility to Dufort's story about Zerzura and made getting men to sign on for the job much easier.

Now Cody wasn't so sure. He'd led his brother to his death. Memories of their childhood flashed through Cody's mind. They'd grown up in a tough home. Their father was a former military man and raised his boys with a heavy dose of tough love. It was far more tough than love, that was for sure. Cody remembered the beatings, the whippings with a belt, and the unorthodox ways their father would keep his boys in line.

Their mother could do little to stop it. Because she felt so useless, she'd turned to drinking too much on a daily basis. She tried to tell the boys their father was a good man, that he didn't know any better or that he was raising them the only way he knew how.

Cody knew better. He knew his father was a horrible person. He hit their mother from time to time when she stepped out of line or at least when their father perceived she'd done so. When Cody got to high school, he started growing. Soon, he was bigger than his father.

One night—when the old man was in a drunken rage—Cody finally fought back. He'd had enough. Their father was in the midst of whipping Tim with his belt because the younger brother had brought him the wrong kind of beer out of the fridge. Tim was still too young to defend himself, but Cody wasn't.

He'd charged his father from behind and tackled him, driving the man forward with more force than he'd thought possible. Cody's dad was already leaning over. The momentum combined with his position put him squarely in line with the wall just beyond the sofa where Tim was squirming—tears running down his face.

The two guys tumbled toward the wall, and Cody heard a sickening thud as his father's head struck it hard. The next sound was like a low snap. Cody had his arms wrapped around his father's strong chest, and he felt the man suddenly get very heavy.

Cody fought to keep him up, but his father dropped to the floor like a sack of rocks. Something was wrong. His dad wasn't moving. Cody shoved the older man a few times, but he still didn't budge. Then Cody tilted his head around and looked into his father's face. The eyes were open, but they didn't move, didn't blink. They just stared at nothing.

Cody put the back of his hand in front of his father's nostrils. Nothing. No sign of life.

"Dad?" Tim said amid a series of sniffles.

Cody swallowed hard. His eyes flashed around the room and

blinked rapidly. Panic started to set in with the realization that he'd just killed his own father.

"Dad?" Tim asked again. "Is he okay?"

All Cody could do was shake his head side to side.

Their mother poked her head out of the next room and saw what had happened. She had a cheap martini glass in her hand, filled halfway with a pink alcohol concoction.

"Carl?" she said. "What's going on?"

"He's dead," Cody said. The matter-of-fact way he said it surprised even him. He didn't feel the slightest tick of remorse. The only emotion he felt was a twinge of fear that he'd be charged with murder. Visions of prison and a life without freedom rushed into his mind.

"Carl?" His mom yelled this time. "Carl?"

The drink in her hand slipped free and crashed to the floor in a million pieces of discounted glassware.

She crossed the floor to her dead husband in less than two seconds. Cody had never seen her move so fast or look so emotional about anything. The lack of emotions he'd felt upon killing his father was replaced by a sense of confusion.

Tim joined her on the floor, shaking the dead man's body in a desperate, futile attempt to revive him.

Cody didn't understand. The way he saw it, he'd just done them all a huge favor. No more beatings or drunken rage to deal with. His father didn't love them. He loathed them, all of them. Yet here his little brother and mother were, doing their best to keep this monster around.

A few years later, Tim had thanked Cody for what he did.

Cody was never charged in his father's murder. When his mother finally settled down, Cody told her that he was whipping Tim, lost his balance, and fell over.

The coroner's report revealed no sign of foul play and that the man had broken his neck as a result of the tumble into the wall. The exact words he'd used were "one of those freak accidents you read about now and then."

Cody felt no guilt over the incident.

Rather than following in his father's footsteps and enlisting in the military for a sense of purpose or duty, Cody enlisted because he realized he had a gift. He was endowed with the ability to take another human's life without the slightest sense of remorse. He figured it was a natural fit.

A few years later, Tim joined the army. By the time they'd done their tours in the Middle East, the young men were recruited by a private security firm based out of Virginia.

It was there Dufort had found them.

The Frenchman had spoken to Cody first. It was an easy sell. Two young guys with nothing to lose and the promise of fame and fortune were the perfect combination.

Now that bright future was nothing more than another pile of ashes in the smoldering fire pit of dreams.

All he'd wanted for himself and his brother was a better life. They'd found a beach house in western Senegal where they could retire and live off the grid, unbothered by anyone. They'd laughed about the bar they would open there and how much fun it would be to drink on the beach every day with their customers.

Those dreams were erased, wiped away by Wyatt and his crew. A new fire sparked in Cody's belly. A flicker flashed in his eye. The flames were fueled by one thought: revenge.

"Where is Wyatt now?" Cody asked.

"Right now?" Dufort shook his head. "I have no idea. But we'll know soon enough."

"Good. Because the next time I see Sean Wyatt and his friend, they're dead men."

Chapter 17

CAIRO

The first thing Sean saw when his heavy eyes opened was a disturbing visual. Tommy's figure was looming over him like the worst child's mobile of all time. Sean shuddered and shook his head for a second to clear the image.

"He looks okay," Tommy said to someone else in the room.

The room. Where am I? What happened?

Sean's mind was still a little foggy.

"Tommy? Where are we?"

"If I told you, I doubt you'd know."

Sean pushed himself up a little in the bed and grimaced. "My head hurts."

"That's because you had a pretty bad concussion," a new voice said. The man's accent was sharp with a heavy Arab accent.

The stranger appeared from the shadows on the right side of the room. The only light came from a single bulb fixed flush against the ceiling. The cracked beige paint on the walls along with the rudimentary lighting told Sean he wasn't in a hospital, not in a modern country, anyway. At least the bed linens were clean from what he could tell. The bed itself was a creaky old contraption, probably a relic from the 1960s.

"Take these," the stranger said as he stopped next to the bed and held out two white pills.

Sean frowned, uncertain as to whether or not he should trust the guy. "What are they?"

The man grinned, revealing a mouth full of crooked teeth. "Ibuprofen."

Sean hesitated another second and then scooped the pills out of the guy's hand. He popped them in his mouth and swallowed before the stranger could offer him a cup of water.

"You should probably take it easy for a while," he said. "You need to rest."

"Where am I?" Sean asked.

He pulled back the sheets and found he was in a hospital gown. Then he swung his legs over the edge of the bed and let them dangle for a moment, using his hands to keep his balance.

"My brother-in-law's place," Alu said as he stepped deeper into the room so Sean could see him better. "His name is Eslam. He practiced medicine for twelve years before he was banned from the profession."

"Banned?" Sean asked.

"Yes, but it was a big misunderstanding. He was charged with trying to drug a patient. In the end, all the charges were dropped, but his reputation was ruined."

"It turns out," Eslam said, "working in the medical underground pays just as well, if not better sometimes. Plus, no pesky taxes to deal with. All my clients pay cash to keep their identities and conditions kept out of the public eye. Not to mention some are afraid of being caught by the authorities."

"You mean like us," Hank said from a seat against the left wall.

"Yes, except I am doing this as a favor. No payment required." Eslam smiled happily.

"I...I don't understand. Why would you help us?" Sean asked.

"Because you saved my life," Alu said, stepping forward. "You will always be taken care of in Cairo should you ever need anything."

"I appreciate that," Sean said and let his feet drop to the floor. "Now where are my clothes? We need to get going."

"Hold on, Mr. Wyatt," Eslam said, holding out a hand. "You've had a very bad concussion. We had to keep you awake several hours for observation. You need rest."

Sean shook his head. "No, what I need are my clothes. There's a madman out there looking for the lost city, and we can't let him find it. If he gets there first...."

"He won't," Tommy said. "I still have the case, along with the first medallion. Dufort isn't going anywhere, not fast at least. And so far he hasn't traced us to this location, which means it's possible he lost our trail."

Sean clenched his jaw. Maybe that's what it meant. Or more likely, the Frenchman was waiting for them to make their next move. Dufort was deadly—a venomous snake lurking in the shadows, hidden until the opportune moment to strike.

"He'll be back, Schultzie. You know it as well as I do. We have to get the rest of the stones before he can." Sean noticed a stack of folded clothes on a rickety chest of drawers on the right. It was what he was wearing the day before. When he stood up, he wobbled and nearly tipped over. The world spun at a dizzying rate. Nausea hit him like a tidal wave. He fought off the gag reflex and stood still for a moment, focusing on the wall in front of him to keep his balance.

Tommy reached out and put his hand on Sean's shoulder to brace him. "Take it easy, buddy. You heard the doc. You need rest."

Sean shook it off. "I'm fine. Let's get moving. Would you all mind giving me some privacy so I can change? And where's Adriana?"

"She ran out to get us something to eat. She should be back any minute," Hank explained. "Nice girl, by the way."

Sean snorted. "Don't let the pretty package fool you."

"I kinda got that impression."

"What about Slater? Where's he?"

The other men glanced at each other, wondering who should be the bearer of bad news. Tommy volunteered by speaking first.

"Slater's dead, Sean. He died in the crash. There was nothing we could do. I'm sorry."

The news was heavy, but for some reason Sean wasn't troubled by it. He'd lost friends in the line of duty before. He'd seen more than his fair share of death, especially for a man his age. While he wasn't completely numb to it, there was a part of him that knew it was the way Slater would have wanted to go—in the thick of the hunt, chasing down bad guys. During what turned out to be their last conversation, Sean had picked up on that vibe. Slater was the kind of guy who would rather die with his boots on than in a hospital gown somewhere. That last thought brought Sean back to the present.

"Guys," he said, seeing the others were concerned about leaving him in the room alone, "I'm okay. Could you give me a second to get changed?"

Reluctantly, the others nodded and slowly made their way out. Tommy closed the door behind him, but before shutting it all the way he reminded Sean he'd be just outside if he needed anything.

Sean thanked him and then pushed the door the rest of the way. He ran his fingers through his hair and let out a long exhale. A million thoughts ran through his head. Dufort got away again. Slater was dead. Adriana was getting food. He wondered why Hank hadn't gone out for food. He probably knew the city better than Adriana. Then again, she'd been pretty much everywhere in the world and could find a side street faster than GPS.

He wandered over to his clothes and slipped out of the gown. Someone had washed his stuff. He could tell from the clean scent of detergent. When he was done getting dressed, he sat down on the edge of the bed and rested for moment. The simple act had taken a good deal of energy out of him. He wondered how long the effects of the concussion would last.

It wasn't the first time Sean experienced such a head injury. He'd had a few concussions in his previous career working for Axis. Then there were one or two from sports in high school and college. Most of them were pretty minor, unnoticeable even. One had been fairly serious and sidelined him from playing soccer for nearly four weeks before he was cleared to come back. By then his season was pretty much over, a fact that had irritated him at the time.

Now Sean thought about how frivolous all that had been. The stakes were much higher than a regional or conference title. This was no game. Dufort was still out there, which meant no one was safe.

A knock came at the door, and he picked his head up too quickly. The room spun again for a second but not as bad as the first time. Progress, he supposed.

"Come on in."

The door cracked open, and Adriana peeked inside. "You okay? Tommy told me you were awake."

"Yeah," he said with a meek grin. "I'm fine."

She stepped inside and closed the door quietly. "They said you were having some problems with your balance."

"Just got up too fast. Nothing to worry about." He noticed the brown paper bag in her hand. "What's in there?"

She offered a sheepish grin. "Grilled cheese and salt 'n vinegar chips."

"How'd you get that here in Cairo?"

"You'd be surprised what some of the sandwich shops in this town can do. It's made with goat cheese. I hope that's okay."

"Mmm. That actually sounds amazing. Or maybe I'm just starving. Either way, thank you."

Adriana padded across the room and set the bag down on an end table. She sat next to him on the bed and wrapped her arm around his shoulders. He leaned sideways, put his head on her shoulder, and took a deep breath.

"I'm glad you're here," he said.

"Well, you pulled me off a pretty pressing job."

"Really? Looking for more art?"

"I'm always doing that," she said with a chuckle. "But no, not this time. You actually caught me during some downtime."

"Seriously?" he asked, pulling his head away from her and giving her his best surprised face. "The great Adriana Villa was taking it easy for a change?"

She smiled from ear to ear and leaned in to kiss him but halted a few inches from his lips. "I doubt anyone calls me great."

"I think you're pretty great."

"Pretty great?"

"Okay," he relented. "You're really great."

"That's better."

She leaned in the last few inches, and their lips locked. After a few seconds, he pulled back and looked into her eyes. "Thanks for coming, especially on such short notice. There are few people in this world I trust as much as you. Even fewer with your...expertise."

"You mean my ability to take down bad guys with my bare hands?"

"That...and your skills with weapons, you're kind of the whole package."

"You need to bump your head more often," she said, tousling his hair with two fingers. "This is the most I've been complimented in a long time."

His lips parted in a weak smile. "You saved lives back there, mine included. I owe you."

"You'll never owe me, Sean. I hope you know that."

"And you'll never owe me."

His eyes diverted away from her and over to the bag on the little table. "I'm really sorry, but would you mind if I go ahead and eat that sandwich you brought? I'm pretty hungry."

She snorted. "Of course. Eat up, cowboy."

Sean devoured the sandwich and gulped down the drink she'd brought him. When he was finished eating, another knock came from the door.

"Are you two decent in there? Or do we need to give you a few more minutes?" Tommy asked.

Adriana and Sean laughed and shook their heads.

"You're an idiot," Sean joked. "Just finished eating, Schultzie. And no, I didn't save you any."

The door flung open, and Tommy stepped through. "She brought me my own." He held up his empty bag with a proud grin on his face.

"So, you feeling better?"

Sean nodded. "Yeah, much better. I just needed something in my belly."

"I see you took off the gown," Hank said as he returned to his previously occupied seat. "You look like you're ready to get back after it."

"He doesn't need to get after anything," Eslam said as he came back in the room along with Alu. He saw the insistent look on Sean's face and shook his head disparagingly. "But I can see you're not going to listen to me, anyway."

He produced a small translucent orange bottle with half a dozen pills inside. "Take one of these every twelve hours as needed. Try not to do more than that. They'll help with the pain."

Sean took the bottle from him and stared into it. "What are they? Painkillers?"

"No," Eslam said. "I already gave you those. I don't hand out pain pills. Too many people get hooked on that stuff. These are for nausea."

"Oh."

"I really think you need to take it easy for a few days," Adriana said with a look of deep concern on her face. She put her hand on the back of his neck, wrapping her fingers around the side.

Her skin was cold at first and sent a shiver down his spine.

"I'm telling you guys, I appreciate the concern, but I'm fine. We have to get moving." He turned his attention to Tommy. "Any word back from the kids about that thing we asked?"

"Spoke to them earlier this morning."

Sean waited for his friend to continue, but he didn't say anything. "And?" Sean said with eyebrows raised as if begging for Tommy to tell him what he wanted to know.

"We figured out where we need to go next."

"Which is?"

"There's a place due west that used to be an ancient Roman city. Originally, it was a Punic settlement, but a man named Septimius Severus turned it into a thriving metropolis for a while. Eventually, the citizens couldn't defend it from invaders, and so it fell into ruin."

"So...what makes you think that's where we need to go?"

"Remember our friend Dorieus?"

"Yeah...."

"He was a Greek prince, Spartan to be precise. You've probably heard of his younger brother, Leonidas."

Sean's eyebrows shot up at the name. Of course he recognized it. Leonidas was one of the most famous commanders in all of history. His ability to stave off more than ten thousand Persians at the Battle of Thermopylae was legendary. Books and movies had been made about the tale. People all over the world knew the story.

"Leonidas...as in the commander of the three hundred?"

"The very same," Tommy said. "His father had three boys. Cleomenes was the oldest brother, eventually became the king of Sparta. Dorieus had a bit of ambition to him. He wanted the crown, but since it went to his brother, instead of trying to kill off his own sibling, he requested he be allowed to take part of the army west and try to establish a Greek colony at Leptis Magna."

Sean gave a nod. "Makes sense. If you can't be king of your kingdom, go set up a kingdom where you can be king."

"Yeah, I guess that was the logic."

"Talk about an ego," Hank said.

"Right. Anyway, when Dorieus and his men arrived at the city, they fought hard but couldn't defeat the local defenders. The Punic army turned them back."

Sean processed the information. He turned his gaze down to the floor. "So, that's where Dorieus failed."

"Exactly."

"Okay, so we go to this Leptis...whatever you said, place."

"Magna."

"Right. Leptis Magna, find some arch, get the medallion, and go to the next spot. Sounds easy enough. Strange, I have a feeling it won't be."

Tommy cocked his head to the side. "What would be the fun in that? And you're right. There's a problem with where we need to go."

Sean raised his head and waited for the punch line.

Tommy sighed. "It's in Libya."

Sean's face reflected the sinking feeling in his chest. The relations between the United States and Libya had deteriorated in recent years, in no small part due to the fact that Libya was harboring known terrorists. Some political pundits speculated that the Libyans were even sponsoring some of the things those extremists were doing.

The relationship between the United States and Libya had been a tenuous one at best for nearly thirty years. Now it seemed the two countries were further apart than ever before.

That meant going into Libya would be dangerous for American citizens. Sean had been in tough places like that before. While he didn't embrace the thought, he knew they had to do it.

"So, what's the plan?" he asked. "I assume we're not going to fly into Tripoli on a commercial airline."

"Nope," Tommy said. "And we're not going to take my private jet there, either."

"Sid's going to take us in his plane," Hank explained. "He'll fly us over the desert to the most remote section of the Libyan border. The plan is to fly low to avoid radar detection."

"Which should work," Sean said, "since they're still fifteen years behind on their tech."

"Right. And we'll go in at night to avoid being seen."

"Okay," Sean said. "What about weapons?"

"You'll be fully equipped," Alu interjected. "We'll make sure you have everything you need: guns, ammunition, explosives, you name it."

Sean glanced at his friend with a surprised look on his face. Then he turned his gaze back to Alu. "Thanks for the help. And thank you to your brother-in-law as well. I appreciate you taking care of me."

Alu dismissed the gratitude. "You saved my life. I am happy to return the favor. And it is of the greatest importance that you stop this madman from finding the lost city."

Sean couldn't help but notice the guy said *you*. "You're not coming with us?" he asked. "I thought you'd probably come along, you know, to help protect the lost city."

Alu sighed. When he spoke, it was with a grave expression—his face drawn with anxiety and sadness. "I have many men to bury," he said. "They were my brothers. We served our cause many years together. While my duty is to stop this evil man, I also have a duty to honor those who have fallen. You, Sean Wyatt, are more than capable of taking care of Dufort."

Sean understood. He gave a nod and clapped his hand on Alu's shoulder. "We'll meet up again."

"That, I'm afraid, is probably a good bet."

Chapter 18

LIBYAN COAST

One of the most important skills to have in the field is the ability to adapt. The plan was to fly through the desert and into Libya, turn north, and then find a safe place to land without being noticed.

On the surface, it sounded like a simple enough plan. Okay, Sean didn't think it was a simple plan. He knew better.

In theory, flying low enough to avoid radar was a good idea. The problem was it would put the aircraft in plain view of any Libyan military below. Sure, they could find a flight path that would—most likely—be safe, but there was a civil war raging on the ground and that meant guerrilla fighters could be hiding anywhere, unbeknownst to some of the best satellite cameras in space.

So, Sean called an audible. He suggested they fly to the nearest port in Tunisia, rent a boat, and sail into Libya.

It was the more expensive of the two plans and not nearly as efficient on time. What his idea did, however, was keep them out of view from both the rebels and the loyalists in the civil war. With things as unstable as they were, the Libyan coast guard was almost nonexistent since most of the nation's military firepower was focused on the interior.

The only water transportation they could find for hire was an old fishing vessel. The boat was forty feet long with faded and flaking paint on the side. On first sight, Hank had been dubious about taking the vessel out onto the open sea. The motor looked like a relic from the 1960s. Little splotches of oil decorated its casing, and when the owner started it, huge puffs of white smoke tumbled out of the exhaust.

"Couldn't we find something...more reliable than this? And also faster?" Hank had asked.

Sean went on to explain that the antique fishing boat would be better than taking something newer. An old vessel wouldn't stand out. At first glance they would look like nothing more than local fishermen coming in from the morning's catch.

"If we make it to Libya," Hank responded in a grumpy tone.

Waves lapped against the boat's hull as Sid guided it through the shallow swells a mile off the Libyan coast. Sid had been saddened to hear about the passing of his associate, Slater. As a guy whose living was made from illegal activities, it was a bit surprising for the others to see him so emotionally affected by Slater's death. The friendship between the two men was, apparently, much stronger than Sean or anyone else figured.

When Sean and Tommy relayed their plan, Sid was an easy sell. It probably helped that there was a potential fortune waiting at the end of the trail, but Sean got the impression that money wasn't Sid's primary motivator for joining the voyage. Revenge, it seemed, was at the front of Sid's mind.

Off in the distance, the makeshift crew could see little lights shining from a small town.

"What's that?" Adriana asked, pointing to the coastal city.

"According to the map," Tommy said, "that village is just a few miles from Leptis Magna. We should be able to get there just before dawn." He pointed out the windshield of the wheelhouse.

Sean's eyes narrowed. The sky was already making its transition from night to morning. Stars that had burned brightly in the dark blanket above were now fading, giving way to the early light of the sun. Sean took a deep breath of the salty air. His senses were on high alert. He knew what was at stake. If the Libyans caught them, things could get bad in a hurry.

Sid spun the wheel a couple of inches to the right, steering the boat through another series of gentle swells. The engine—for all its visual shortcomings—had worked well so far. It puttered in the back, churning the water steadily, pushing the vessel ahead.

It didn't take long for the boat to pass the town on the starboard side. Everyone on board kept their eyes on the coast, waiting breathlessly for any sign of trouble. They'd already cleared their biggest hurdle, passing the Libyan capital of Tripoli under the cover of darkness. Getting by there had been nerve-racking. At one point the group thought they saw boat lights coming their way, but it turned out to be nothing more than a buoy tossing in the water a half mile off shore. Their heartbeats raced every time they glimpsed an airplane. The aircraft never came close to their boat. They'd made sure to keep all the lights off along with any devices that might give away their position.

Sean spied a piece of coastline with no lights and no signs of life. Based on their evaluation of the map, they had to be close to Leptis Magna.

"Take her in right over there," Sean said to Sid.

"Aye, Captain," Sid remarked in a horrible pirate voice.

He turned the wheel a few notches to starboard, guiding the vessel through the increasingly high swells as they drew nearer to shore. The sounds of waves crashing soon found the crew's ears. It was different than the noise from a typical beach. Sean recognized it immediately.

"Be careful through here, Sid," he warned. "That coastline is rocky, which means there could be more rocks out here in the water. Don't want to get stuck."

"That makes two of us," Sid said. "I'll drop anchor as close as I can, but you're going to have to take that lifeboat the rest of the way."

He jerked his thumb to the back where a rickety-looking dinghy was bouncing around in the wake behind the fishing boat. The smaller vessel was just big enough for Sean and his three companions, though he wondered how the thing had made it this far.

"Take the wheel for a second?" Sid asked Sean.

"Sure," Sean said. He stepped to the wheel and wrapped his fingers around it.

Sid shuffled around some boxes of tools and fishing gear, making his way out the back door of the cabin. He was only gone thirty seconds before he reappeared and resumed control of the boat.

"Okay, looks like the lifeboat is still good," he said. "I was worried about that rope keeping it behind us. Been keeping an eye on it through the night. It was frayed in several places. I'd say it doesn't have too many voyages left."

Sean thought it strange that Sid was checking the rope at this point. A moment before he'd poked his thumb in the direction of the lifeboat, assuming it was still there. Maybe that's all it was, just Sid making an assumption.

"Didn't look like the dinghy was taking on water," Sid continued. "I was concerned about that, too."

"That makes two of us," Tommy said. "That thing looks as old as...well, old."

Sean snorted a laugh. "Too early to think of anything clever?"

"Yeah," Tommy said. "Plus, I haven't had any coffee. You don't suppose they have a coffee shop nearby, maybe something with a drive-through?"

Adriana shook her head in derision. She knew Tommy was joking. She also knew him well enough to know he was also half-serious.

"There are lots of shops in Tripoli," she said with arms crossed. "If you'd like to go back there."

He chuckled. "Yeah, I think I'll pass."

"Okay." Sid interrupted the facetious conversation. "We're gonna stop here. You guys will have to paddle the rest of the way in."

The boat continued drifting toward the shore as Sid flipped a switch and then pressed a button just below it. The sound of chains clunking through a metal hole echoed into the boat's cabin. Sid grimaced as he kept his finger mashed against the button as the anchor dropped to the sea bottom. When the noise ceased, he tapped on another button to bring the chain up until it was taut.

"Anchor's down," he said.

He stepped back out through the rear door and leaned over to grab the frayed rope. Sean stuck his head out the doorway to check on their pilot to make sure he didn't need any help—and to see if he was up to anything else.

Sid was heaving the lifeboat toward the fishing vessel. He tugged on the rope, putting one hand over the other as he drew the little dinghy closer and closer.

Sean went to Sid's aid and helped pull the lifeboat the rest of the way until it butted up against the main vessel.

"Thanks," Sid said with a nod.

"No problem." Sean dusted his hands together and then turned to the others who were already joining them on deck. "You guys ready to do a little rowing?"

Sean and Tommy handled the oars with relative ease. They'd both done their fair share of flat-water kayaking, not to mention the time Sean had spent several years before running a kayak and surf shop on the Florida panhandle.

"Let's try to land over there," Adriana said to the two friends as they rowed. She pointed to a spot on the beach where the rocks gave way to a patch of dark brown sand.

They worked hard against the currents pulling the tiny vessel one direction and then the other. It was hard to keep the boat on target with the shore, but they fought their way through it and—after a twenty-minute ordeal—finally felt the underside of the craft scratching the ocean floor. It sounded like rocky sand. Better than just rocks. Hitting something like that would have easily punched a hole in the lifeboat's hull.

The sun was starting to peek over the horizon to the east, its rippling yellow-orange globe signaling the start of a new day, a day Sean and the others hoped would be filled with discovery. The fact was, however, they'd just entered the country illegally. If they were caught, getting out would be problematic to say the least.

Sean hopped out first, landing his boots in the shallows of the beach. Tommy joined him as Adriana and Hank moved forward. Sean and Tommy held the rope until the other two had jumped out of the boat. Then all four took a grip and pulled the vessel onto the sand until three quarters of it was out of the water.

According to Sid, they'd already passed high tide. The sea would be retreating through most of the day, although it would also fluctuate. Sean knew that if they pulled the boat too far out of the water, getting it back would prove far more difficult if they made it back when the tide was at its lowest. It could be the difference of twenty feet or more. That didn't sound like a lot, but he knew better. Dragging a boat over sand— even one as small as their lifeboat—would be nearly impossible.

The four trespassers trudged out of the water, splashing saltwater around recklessly as they made their way onto dry land.

"Now what?" Hank asked. "How are we going to get to this place? Doesn't look like there's a car rental nearby."

Tommy shook his head and smirked with a mischievous gleam in his eyes. "Dude, we're already there." He pointed over a rocky rise to their left.

The other three looked to where he was pointing and saw the tops of some ancient structures. There were pillars with huge beams of cut stone lying across them.

"Is...is that it?" Hank stammered.

"Part of it," Tommy said.

"Better to land close to the site than try to go into town, steal or rent a ride, and then come here. We want as few people to see us as possible."

"Makes sense."

Adriana marched ahead, climbing the hill easily. She stopped at the top and looked back out over the Mediterranean. It was a gorgeous sight: pale blue water giving way to a deeper shade near where Sid and the fishing vessel bobbed gently in the waves.

The others joined her on the crest. Less than a quarter of a mile away, the ruins of Leptis Magna stretched out before them. It was like looking back in time. Ancient roads spread through the city like a spiderweb made from bright gray stone. The most prominent structure of the ruins was the incredible amphitheater. It was less than half a mile to the seaside cliffs and presented visitors with a spectacular view.

"Whoever built that place sure knew how to pick their spots," Tommy said. "What an absolutely beautiful location."

"No kidding," Sean said.

"Imagine sitting there in the audience a few thousand years ago," Adriana chimed in. "Listening to someone sing, a speaker give a speech, or watching a play while the ocean waves crash into the cliffs."

The visitors let their minds wander for a short moment before Sean spoke up again.

"What is it we're looking for, Schultzie? Something about an arch?"

Tommy nodded. "It was an arch built by Septimius Severus. And if I had to guess"—he paused for a few seconds, narrowing his eyes against the brightening sun—"I'd say that's it over there."

He pointed at a structure confidently. It didn't take long for his proud grin to turn into a frown. "Or maybe it's that one over there."

As he looked out over the ruins, he noticed arches in several locations.

"Wait," Hank said. "You don't know which arch is the one with the stone?"

Tommy rolled his shoulders, suddenly sheepish. "Tara said we couldn't miss it. She acted like it was the only one."

"And you didn't think to maybe look it up on your phone, you know, so that we weren't guessing when we arrived illegally in another country that doesn't exactly have Americans on the top of their friends list?"

"Hey, take it easy. This is a burner phone. Not to mention I don't know how reliable the lines are out here. Getting online would take forever."

"And wandering around a bunch of ancient Roman—"

"And Greek," Sean interjected.

"Whatever, ancient ruins," Hank continued, "won't take forever?"

Adriana had subconsciously already started moving away from the three men. She shuffled along the sandy slope, making her way toward the ruins.

"If you boys are done arguing," she said, "maybe you would like to get out of this plain line of sight. We stick out standing up here."

The other three looked at each other, slightly embarrassed.

"She's right," Sean said, and he hurried after her.

Tommy and Hank passed each other one more irritated glare and then followed behind the others.

At the bottom of the hill, they made their way through a grove of small trees until the first remnants of the city appeared. Chunks of white-gray stone littered the ground, the last pieces of the outskirts road left thousands of years before.

Sean imagined the plan was to continue city expansion as the population grew, but those plans were cut short by war and constant invasion.

The group walked cautiously through an arch where the main road into the heart of the ruins began.

"You don't think this is the arch, do you?" Hank asked. There was still a hint of resentment in his tone.

"No," Tommy said. "I don't think it's an ordinary structure. From the sounds of it, I suspect the arch we're looking for is more ceremonial than designed for function."

"So, more like the Arc de Triomphe?" Adriana asked.

"Yes. That's exactly what I was thinking."

Hank shook his head. Now that they were down on the ancient city's ground level, it seemed to spread out as far as the eye could see. If it looked big from their view atop the hill; now it was even larger.

"We need to fan out," Sean said. "We can cover more ground that way." He pulled out his phone and glanced at the screen. "I've got a few bars. You guys have a signal?"

The others took quick looks at their devices and then nodded.

"Good. Then we can stay in contact. I suspect tourists will be showing up pretty soon. Mornings are popular in these hotter regions of the world."

"You think tourists will be here with a civil war going on?" Hank asked. He eyed Sean with a dubious stare.

"If life has taught me one thing, Hank, it's that people are crazy. They'll do whatever it takes, risk everything, just to do something that's on their bucket list or that they planned for a long time. I doubt many Americans will be here, but there could be other foreigners."

"Or locals," Tommy added. "So, do your best to look casual. And for the love of all that's good, don't speak English to anyone." He paused. "You know what, just don't speak."

"Don't speak?"

"At all."

Hank sighed. "Fine. Let's just hope we don't see anyone."

"I'll head down toward the coast," Sean said. "The rest of you spread out." He pointed at the path ahead that branched into several directions. "Take a road, and if you find the arch, call us and let us know or send a text."

The other three nodded and split up, each choosing a different stretch of road to follow.

Sean looked over his shoulder at Adriana and offered her a smile as they parted ways.

"You okay?" she mouthed with a look of concern written on her face.

"Yeah," he said back.

He took in how beautiful she looked. Even after being on a boat since the early morning hours, barely getting any sleep, and without the usual conveniences of home, she was still breathtaking. Her dark brown hair bobbed slightly in its ponytail as she padded down the road and disappeared from sight.

"She can handle herself," Sean said as he reached up and

grabbed the back of his head. His skull hadn't felt the same since he woke up in Eslam's makeshift hospital. He found if he looked up too fast, things would spin out of control. He'd never had vertigo before, but if this was what it was like, his condition couldn't go away fast enough. He'd not told the others that his head was still bothering him. He felt it was better if they just didn't know.

Sean took in a deep breath and pushed forward. No time to feel sorry for himself. They needed to find the next medallion before someone else did.

Chapter 19

LEPTIS MAGNA

Tommy knew he'd found what he was looking for before he arrived at the magnificent structure.

He and the others had been roaming the grounds of Leptis Magna for nearly forty-five minutes—not a long period of time, but considering the nature of their visit the search seemed to take forever.

His pace quickened, and he trotted down the path toward the arch. The narrow road was lined by a short wall on both sides. Beyond the diminutive barricade, huge shrubs and thick trees filled the landscape. The arch was not relatively close to the city center. In fact, it was pretty much on the outskirts on the opposite side from where he and his companions arrived.

Tommy slowed his jog to a walk as he reached the entryway to the old building. He could see through one side and out the other. It was built out of pale stone that wore an orange tint on the surface. The structure had four sides with an arched entrance built into each one.

He looked up at the intricate relief just over the opening. As with most Roman monuments, this one featured a story laid out with the images of different people, animals, objects, and events. It was hard to tell what story the designers of this monument were trying to convey, but that wasn't why Tommy was there.

He passed through the opening and into the cool shade the roof provided. More reliefs were carved into the stone, wrapping around the entire interior wall. His eyes passed over the imagery, momentarily letting his mind try to process what it all meant. His initial assessment was that the story was about the trials of the city, how the Romans came to gain control over it, and then eventually how it was settled and brought into the empire.

Tommy's eyes widened at the spectacular display of craftsmanship. He wondered how many times the structure had needed to be renovated through the years. Something as old as this surely would have gone through more deterioration than he was seeing.

Then he noticed something peculiar. On one section of the wall was a sequence of writing the likes of which he'd not seen in a long time. His heart rate quickened. He pulled out his phone and sent a group text to the others with directions on how to find the arch.

After the message went through, he took a step back and stared at the odd writing. Tommy knew what it was. As luck would have it, he understood what it meant as well.

It wasn't a language. It was a form of numbers used in the ancient world for counting purposes. What was on the wall in front of Tommy was a kind of numeric chart used for counting different items and adding up totals. The chart was simplistic in design, mostly just a sequence of boxes with different numbers of lines. In some boxes, the lines were horizontal. In others, they were vertical.

Tommy heard footsteps drawing near and let his fingers fall to the weapon hidden by his shirt hanging over the belt in the back. He drew the gun and waited in a corner, hoping it wasn't an enemy. He'd only sent the text message a minute or so ago. How could any of his friends have made it so fast? They were spread out all over the site.

Boots skidded to a stop on the dusty road just outside the entryway to Tommy's right. He focused on his breathing to keep calm, but that didn't change something he always felt in these kinds of situations. The possibility of being in a shootout or a fight always made him uncomfortable. More than that, it made him extremely anxious. His fingers twitched on the weapon, and he had to work extra hard to make sure he kept his composure.

Done this before a million times, he told himself. *You've got the element of surprise.* Then he had another thought. What if it was just a tourist? An ordinary person walking into the monument only to find an American with a gun in his hands could lead to big trouble.

Tommy made a quick decision and hid the weapon behind his back but kept his finger on the trigger, ready to fire.

The shadow drew closer, the footsteps louder. A bead of sweat rolled down Tommy's forehead and dripped into his eye. He winked hard to get rid of the stinging.

Then he saw one boot and then the other. They were attached to legs he recognized—tanned, slender, and strong. Adriana stepped into the monument with a leery look on her face. She held her weapon to the side.

"Oh, thank goodness it's you," Tommy said.

His sudden comment startled her, and Adriana spun to the right, whipping her weapon up to chest level. She held it there for a second, aiming the gun at Tommy until she realized it was him.

"Sorry," she said. "You startled me."

Tommy's eyes were wide with surprise and fear. "Yeah, well, you scared me, too. Mind putting the gun down?"

"Oh, sure. My fault."

She lowered the weapon and then started looking around. "This is incredible. So, you think this is the place?"

"Sure looks like it," he said. "The clue we found in Giza mentioned this place along with something about the number three."

"So, all we need to do is look for a Roman numeral three, right? Severus was a Roman emperor, so he would have used those."

Tommy clenched his jaw. "Not so fast. Under ordinary circumstances, I'd say you were exactly right. Except I found this." He pointed to the chart on the wall.

"What is it?" she asked while crossing her arms and stepping closer.

"It's essentially a counting chart they used a long time ago. This appears to have been something they put up to guide people who ran businesses."

Adriana cocked her head to the side while she gazed at the strange engraving. "You know how to read this? It's just a bunch of random lines. At least that's the way it looks."

"At first glance, yes. But it's more than that. What I think we need to do is find a place in this monument that either has the number three"—he tapped on one of the squares—"or we have to find a place that has two squares that add up to three. Make sense?"

She shrugged. "Seems simple enough."

Tommy looked out the nearest entryway. There was no sign of Sean or Hank. "I guess the other two must be farther away than you were when I sent the text."

"Yeah. I wasn't far. Just over the ridge back there." She motioned to the narrow road leading back up the slope.

"Well, no sense in waiting for them. We might as well have a look around and see what we can find. If you see anything that looks like these markings here"—he pointed at the chart again—"let me know."

"Got it."

The two split up and went to opposite sides of the monument. They scanned the walls and floor for anything that appeared remotely close to what Tommy discussed.

"Here's something," Adriana said as she neared the first corner.

"What does it look like?" Tommy asked.

"Four vertical lines."

"Nothing else?"

She shook her head.

"Then it's not what we want," he said. "Keep looking. It has to be here."

Tommy continued searching the engravings on the wall until he came to a place where two boxes contained the symbols for the numbers one and two. He froze for a second, making sure he wasn't interpreting things incorrectly.

He leaned down and stared at the symbols. They were etched into the wall on a piece of block near the floor. He set his gear bag down and ran a finger across the stone, then one of the blocks near it. The one with the numeric figures had a different feel. It was slightly coarser than the other. He checked another block and came to the same conclusion.

Adriana looked over her shoulder and noticed Tommy squatting near the corner—his focus locked in on something.

"What is it?"

Her sudden question snapped him back to reality. Tommy looked over his shoulder. "I'm not sure, but these two symbols add up to the number three."

She hurried over to where he was and hovered over him. It didn't take more than a second for her to notice what caught his attention.

"So, what do we do next?" she asked.

"This block is made from a different kind of stone," Tommy explained. "The rest of this feels like marble, but this one is sandstone."

"And that means...we have to remove it?"

"I think it might," he said with a nod.

They heard footsteps coming from outside. Instinctively, both reached for their weapons and took up positions opposite each other to cover every point of entry. Tommy was facing the direction where the sounds came from and saw the approaching person first.

"It's okay," he said. "It's only Hank."

Adriana lowered her weapon and stuffed it back in her belt.

Hank gasped for air as he trudged into the monument. "Jeez," he blurted out. "That was quite a run from the other side of town."

"You ran from the other side of the city?" Tommy asked, dubious.

"Well...maybe not all the way on the other side. But for me, any amount of running is a lot." He swallowed and wiped the sweat from his brow. "Find anything?"

"Sure did," Tommy said. "Take a look at this."

He walked back over to the corner where he found the numeric symbols and pointed to the block. "These add up to the number three. This"—he waved his hand around at the monument—"was built by Septimius Severus. It's gotta be the spot."

Tommy thought for a second. "Did you see Sean while you were out there?"

Hank shook his head. "No, we went in different directions. Cell coverage is spotty out here. Maybe he didn't get your message yet."

"Could be," Tommy said with a hint of concern. "We might as well get to work while we wait."

"Get to work?" Hank asked.

"Yeah." Tommy knelt down next to his gear bag and pulled out a mallet, chisel, and a few other tools. "These aren't the usual kinds of things I'm accustomed to using, but they'll do the job."

"What are you going to do?"

Tommy shifted his feet, twisted his torso, and faced the block. He placed the chisel along the narrow seam between the other blocks and whacked it with the mallet. Chunks of mortar flew out to the left, just as Tommy intended. The last thing he needed was to carelessly knock a bunch of debris into his eyes.

He fixed the chisel blade into place and swung again, careful to keep the edge angled safely away.

Over and over again, Tommy pounded the seam between the blocks until he'd removed most of the ancient adhesive. Hank and Adriana made themselves useful by keeping watch at opposite doorways, making sure no one heard Tommy's loud renovation project.

When all the mortar was gone, Tommy reached into his gear bag and pulled out a small crowbar. He worked the sharp edge into one of the seams and gave it a tug. The brick didn't move. He tried it again but still nothing.

"Something wrong?" Hank asked.

"It's stuck."

"Need me to help?"

"Maybe," Tommy said as he pulled harder on the crowbar.

Hank made his way back over to the corner. Tommy's face was as red as a lobster, and the veins in his forearms popped up on his skin.

"Let me give it a try," Hank said.

Tommy exhaled, stood up, and stepped away from the crowbar. "Knock yourself out," he said. "I can't get that thing to budge."

Hank rubbed his hands together and then yanked on the tool. He had the same luck as Tommy. He wiggled the crowbar a little to see if that would loosen the block and then tried again. Still nothing.

Adriana was watching their progress—or lack thereof—from the doorway while trying to keep an eye on the roads coming into the monument. The paths were still empty.

"No luck, boys?" she asked. Her Spanish accent sounded particularly thick on this occasion.

Hank had just recovered from his run to the monument and now was breathing heavily again. He shook his head. "No. That thing is well and truly stuck."

Adriana raised an eyebrow. "Mind if I give it a try?"

The two men shot each other a skeptical glance and then stepped aside as she approached.

"Sure, go ahead." Hank held back a snicker that tried to sneak up out of his mouth.

He didn't think there was any way Adriana could move the block if he and Tommy weren't able. They were both stronger than her.

She knelt down and looked at the block. Then she tilted her head and analyzed the seams, going as far as to put the tip of her index finger into one part.

"Mallet," she said like a surgeon. She stuck her hand out to the side, palm up, and waited for Tommy to put the requested tool in her hand.

Tommy's forehead crinkled. He bent down, picked up the mallet, and passed it to her. He stepped back to watch, still thinking she wouldn't be able to get the thing to move.

Adriana carefully wedged the crowbar blade into the seam, wiggling it a few times to get it as deep as possible. Then she took the mallet and gently struck the bar's handle a few times. The brick didn't move, and the two men passed each other a knowing glance.

Adriana raised the mallet a little higher and whacked the bar. This time, the block moved half an inch, and its corner jutted out away from the wall. She hit the bar again, and once more the brick shifted. Tommy and Hank watched with humility as Adriana continued striking the crowbar until the block was hanging on by a few inches of stone. She dropped the crowbar to the floor and swung the mallet one last time. The face smacked into the side of the block and knocked it free from its housing. It fell to the hard stone below with a loud clatter, chipping off one of the corners in the process.

The two men took a step forward to look into the gaping hole. Adriana craned her neck and gazed into the cavity. Just beyond the opening, the block below the one she'd removed had a rectangular hole cut into it. Something inside gleamed in the light coming in through the open doorways.

Adriana reached in carefully. She didn't want to scratch the object. When her fingers touched the medallion, it felt cold. She thought it odd that anything could be cold in such a hot place, but being buried in the stone for so long must have kept it cool.

She pulled it out and held it in her palm for the other two to see.

This medallion was different than the first. Its golden chain was attached to a six-pointed star, a symbol that was prominently displayed on the Israeli flag. Fixed into the center was another precious stone. It was blue, like sapphire, but had a deeper hue to it than any such stone they'd ever seen.

Adriana turned over the medallion and found more script just like with the first.

"Hold on a second," Tommy said. He reached into his gear bag and pulled out the tablets. He'd made the decision to carry the stones in his bag as opposed to the case on this occasion because of mobility.

He set the stones on the floor and took the amulet from Adriana. Cradling it in his hands, he cautiously set the symbol over the tablet with the next blank space in the text.

"The third is guarded forever by the great beast of the south; the tail on his face protects the power."

Tommy pulled his head back after reading the passage. "What?"

"The tail on his face?" Hank asked.

"An elephant," Adriana said. "It's the only animal with something that looks like a tail on his face."

"Could be an aardvark or an anteater," Tommy offered.

"Fair enough," she said. "Either way, that doesn't help us know where it is, other than it mentions the thing is to the south."

Tommy stared down at the objects. It was a puzzling riddle to say the least. If they were looking for some kind of elephant, it would likely be some kind of statue. That was the only way a beast could guard something forever.

He pulled out his phone and tapped the screen a couple of times. "Where in the world is Sean, by the way? It's taking him forever to get here."

"Maybe he still hasn't gotten the message," Hank said.

Tommy shrugged. "Well, he needs to get over here. The longer we stay here, the greater our risk of getting caught." He started to tap the green button to call Tara and Alex back at the lab when he glimpsed a shadow by the door.

"Sean? What took you so long?" Tommy asked in a loud voice. "We found something."

The person who came through the door wasn't Sean. It was a dark-skinned man with black hair and a matching mustache. He was in a Libyan military uniform and held a pistol in his right hand. As soon as the man saw the three people in the corner, he swung the gun around and aimed it in their general direction.

Then he barked out something in Arabic. Two seconds later, five more men rushed into the room. They wore black scarves over their faces and donned similar uniforms to the commander. They were armed with automatic rifles and immediately pointed them at the intruders.

The leader was shouting something at the three who slowly put their hands in the air.

"What's he saying?" Adriana asked.

"Sounds like we're under arrest," Tommy said.

Chapter 20

LEPTIS MAGNA

Sean was strolling along a path that ran parallel to the coast when he got Tommy's text. So far, Sean hadn't seen anything he thought would be the arch except for arches built into some of the other structures. Tommy said the arch would be a lone structure, so Sean ruled those out immediately.

He glanced down at his phone and read the text.

"Great," he muttered to himself. "I was starting to think none of us were going to find that thing."

He raised his head and looked out over the city. From his view, it was hard to tell where Tommy could be. There was a hill just beyond the amphitheater, but it was on the other side of town. It would take several minutes for Sean to get there—even if he ran.

That was the direction Tommy went when they split up so, it would make sense that was where he found the arch. Sean sighed and reached into his gear bag for a bottle of water. He took a few chugs and then put the nearly empty bottle back. He disliked being out in the desert. His lips cracked, and his skin felt like a reptile's. Working in the desert heat was one of the downsides of helping Tommy at his agency.

Sean licked his lips and marched ahead. He meandered through the old streets, walking by the amphitheater, old palace walls, columns, and what had probably been a temple a few thousand years ago.

The path gradually rose up the slope of the hill until it reached the top next to a thicket of trees and shrubs just behind the walls on both sides. Sean squinted against the bright sunlight. He put the bridge of his hand against his forehead to get a little shade and looked down the hill.

"There it is," he said.

A few hundred feet below was the arched monument of Septimius Severus. Sean noted the intricate entryways featuring two inward-facing triangular stones set atop columns on each side of the arches. It was difficult to tell from far away, but it looked like there were reliefs carved into the monument above the archways.

Then a frown shot across Sean's face. Without a second thought, he dove over the wall to his right and ducked behind the overgrown bushes.

He raised up just enough to be able to see over the wall and took another look. He sighed. "Oh man. Libyans."

Sean watched as five armed men marched Adriana and the other two out of the building at gunpoint. Four men were stationed outside the monument. Then another man appeared. This one didn't have on a mask like the others. Sean knew instantly that the guy must be the one in charge, probably a mid-ranking officer. Sean hated those types. In his experience, they were always the ones doing the dirty work and typically had enough ambition to want to do their jobs a little too well.

The leader was shouting something at Sean's friends. From his position, it was impossible to tell what the guy was saying. A troubling thought occurred to Sean. How had those men known where Tommy would be?

Sean pulled the phone out of his pocket and checked the time Tommy had sent the message. It said the message was sent about fifteen minutes before Sean received it. The point still remained that the Libyan soldiers holding his friends prisoner pinpointed their location and ambushed them with incredible speed.

Had someone seen the group when they landed on the beach? Perhaps a spotter noticed the fishing boat off the coast and alerted the authorities when the lifeboat made its way to shore.

There was no way to know the correct answer. What Sean did know was that his friends were in trouble.

He knew how many rounds were in his current magazine. A quick shuffle through the gear bag told him he had two more with a full complement of ammo—more than enough to take out the Libyans. The problem was distance. Sean was too far away for his pistol to do anything more than piss off the soldiers. Sure, he might get lucky and hit one, but it was just as likely Sean would hit one of his friends, too.

An attack from his position was out of the question without a long-range weapon. Even then, he'd probably only get off two shots before the soldiers either started shooting at him—or executed his friends.

Sean had faced long odds before, but these were nearly insurmountable.

For better or worse, Sean didn't get the chance to go on the attack. The armed men turned their prisoners and forced them to start marching down the path in the other direction. Sean risked sticking his head out farther and scanned the area. A quarter mile from the monument, three military trucks were parked by an outcropping of trees and a four-foot-high stone wall.

Okay, those belong to the soldiers.

That was an easy conclusion. If he was going to save his friends from the doom of a Libyan jail, he'd need a ride of his own.

Ideas poured into his brain like water from a fire hydrant.

He noted the supply racks on top of the military vehicles. One of them held a large cargo box. He could probably fit inside it if the thing was empty. The problem would be getting to it. He'd need a distraction.

Perhaps if he fired one of his weapons to get the soldiers' attention and then made a run for it through the bushes and trees, they'd come to the spot from where the shot came, and he could loop around behind the men.

No way that would work. Sean knew it. The base theory behind the idea was fine. The issue was that not all the soldiers would charge his position. The commander would only send a few men toward the threat, leaving the rest to usher Sean's friends to the trucks.

Sean considered throwing something like a small rock to one side of the men, but they were much too far away for him to reach with his ragged arm. He doubted he could even throw it halfway.

The caravan with its prisoners was nearly halfway to the parked trucks. Sean was running out of time and out of ideas.

He saw something coming down the road toward the parking area. It was another truck. Dust kicked up and rolled into the air behind it as it rumbled down the gravel road. Sean noticed an official seal on the side. It was the equivalent of a park ranger. Maybe the ranger was the one who alerted the soldiers to the presence of Sean and his friends—though he doubted it.

Why would he single them out over any other tourists?

Sean watched as the ranger drove his truck all the way to the lot, stopped his car, and got out.

From his vantage point, it appeared that the ranger tried to stop and talk to the soldier in command, but the officer blew him off and continued marching his captives toward their rides.

The ranger kept moving and walked over to a sign that was hanging nearby. The placard had lost a bolt and was dangling from a single point. After raising the sign and seeing what kind of tool he'd need for the job, the ranger returned to his pickup and ducked inside.

By now the prisoners were being loaded into the back of the trucks. Tommy, Hank, and Adriana were put in separate cargo areas and joined by guards to make sure they didn't try to escape out the back. Sean returned his gaze to the ranger. The guy was busily working on the sign, testing out various bolts and screwdrivers to see which combination would fit the best.

That was Sean's chance. If he could get to the ranger's truck, he might have a chance to follow the soldiers.

He didn't have a second to lose.

He climbed back over the wall and out into the open for a moment before crouching down just behind the opposite barrier. He wasn't completely hidden from view, but staying low made him far less visible.

Sean shuffled his feet as fast as he could, keeping his knees bent while he hurried down the path. When he reached the monument, he veered off the path and hopped the wall, making sure the soldiers and the ranger weren't looking his way. Nobody had seen him. The ranger was busy bolting down the broken sign, and the soldiers were almost done loading the trucks.

Sean knew he had to move faster.

The first military truck roared to life, then the others. One started backing up.

Sean threw caution to the wind. He took off at almost a sprint, still trying to stay as low as possible without being in plain sight. The first truck turned around and then inched forward at a snail's pace. A moment later, a second truck copied the movement of the first.

Sean was almost near the end of the wall where it wrapped around the parking area. He slid to a stop and peeked over the edge as the third truck started moving. Sean glanced over his shoulder at the ranger who was still fixing the sign.

Sean swallowed hard, planted his left hand on the top of the wall, and vaulted over it. The first two trucks had stopped just down the road to wait on the third. Now that it was on the way, the other two started creeping forward again.

In the open, Sean felt severely exposed, but he couldn't stop. His friends needed rescuing, and if he didn't get to them, no one would.

As Sean neared the ranger's truck, he realized the guy had left the engine running. Sean thought he was going to have to hotwire the thing. With the keys in the ignition, that wouldn't be an issue.

He opened the door as stealthily as possible and slid inside, plopping his gear bag in the passenger seat. He eased the door shut and shifted the vehicle into reverse, then started backing up.

The gravel crunched under the tires as the truck rolled backward.

Sean wasn't sure if it was the noise or the movement that the ranger noticed first. Either way, the man turned his head toward his runaway truck. He almost did a double take, half not believing that the vehicle was moving.

Then he saw Sean behind the wheel and reached for his pistol. The guy shouted something in Arabic as Sean shifted into drive and stomped on the gas pedal. Gravel shot out from behind the rear tires, and a cloud of dust exploded into the air. The ranger fired his weapon several times, but his truck was already too far away to even come close. The man trotted to a stop and pulled the radio from his belt to call for help.

Sean's attention was on the convoy of trucks down the road. They were already turning onto a stretch of pavement. As best as he could figure, they were heading in the direction of Tripoli. Not exactly the ideal place for three Americans and Adriana.

He sped down the gravel road and whipped the wheel around, skidding the truck out onto the highway. The military trucks were still at least a half mile ahead and rolling fast.

Sean's mind raced almost as fast as the pickup he was driving. Now that he was behind the convoy, he wasn't sure what to do next. He knew all the tactics, how to take down other vehicles in a high-speed chase, but none of that stuff was of any use with his friends in the other trucks.

He let his foot ease up on the gas pedal. The pickup slowed to a steady speed, just fast enough to keep the convoy in his sights but not so fast that he'd catch up right away.

For now, the only thing Sean could do was follow.

His knuckles whitened as his fingers squeezed the wheel. He felt helpless. As a man of action, he was accustomed to finding direct ways to fix a bad situation. In this instance, patience was the best course of action, and patience wasn't exactly winning the battle in his mind.

The woman he loved and his best friend were on their way to a Libyan jail. There was no telling what would happen once they were behind those walls.

Memories of the stories that surfaced in 1996 crept into Sean's mind. He tried to push them away, but couldn't.

That was the year that over twelve hundred prisoners were systematically killed inside the Abu Salim prison in Tripoli. It wasn't the first time something like that happened within the walls of a Libyan prison. The nation's leader at the time had a penchant for torturing those he deemed a threat or a problem to national security. More like a threat to his own job security.

It was an incident that drew the attention of people around the world. Human rights activists had a field day with it. In the end, not much could be done. It took more than a decade before the United States intervened and took down the dictator. Even then, the country was already embroiled in a vicious civil war in which no one knew who they could trust.

Sean lost sight of the convoy as they disappeared over a ridge. He sped up momentarily until he reached the top of the hill and the other trucks came back into view.

Off to the left, he could see where they were headed. His heart sank.

The Dar Falim prison was part of a military base just east of Tripoli. Off in the distance, Sean could see the sprawl of the Libyan capital stretching out into the desert. The good news was that Dar Falim wasn't in the city, which could make for an easier escape. The bad news was it would be heavily guarded and surrounded by Libyan military.

While Dar Falim wasn't a maximum-security prison like Abu Salim, it was still going to be like breaking into Fort Knox.

Sean saw one army helicopter sitting on a landing pad off to the side, just beyond the ten-foot fence that wrapped around the entire compound. A plan started to formulate in his brain. It would be risky, but there was no choice. All the risk in the world wouldn't keep him from going after the people he cared about.

Break into a prison/military base and get everyone out alive?

Sean had faced challenges before and overcome them.

He could do this. But it was just going to require a little help.

Chapter 21

DAR FALIM PRISON, LIBYA

Tommy sat with his hands bound behind an aluminum chair. His wrists were cuffed to one of the supports. To his left was Hank; to his right Adriana. Both were similarly attached to their seats.

Two soldiers with automatic weapons stood in opposite corners, staring at the three prisoners with cold, vapid eyes. Tommy knew the soldiers would have no problem cutting them down with a shower of bullets were they so provoked.

Being shot to death sounded merciful compared to some of the things he'd heard about Libyan prisons.

"What do you want with us?" Tommy asked for the third time. He used his best Arabic.

The men didn't answer.

"You know they're not going to talk to us, right?" Hank spat. "These morons just do what they're told." He directed the last barb at the two guards. "They're robots, dirty, smelly, non-thinking robots."

He shook his chair violently in a vain attempt to free his hands.

The guards didn't move. They just stood there like statues, staring at the prisoners.

Adriana maintained more composure than both men. It was a

difficult thing to do considering what could happen to women in a place like that. The men in that part of the world were sexually starved. The men in the military were even more so.

That made for a nightmarish combination for a pretty woman such as herself. Still, she remained stoic in the face of potential atrocities.

On the way into the compound, some of the soldiers had called out to her, saying despicable things in Arabic. She didn't let on that she understood their words. Her Arabic wasn't perfect, but she knew enough to comprehend their intentions.

Then there were the prisoners, men who'd been cooped up for so long they'd almost forgotten what a woman looked like. Seeing her was like finding an oasis in the desert.

The metal door in the center of the wall opened, and the man in charge of the arrest stepped into the room. He still donned his sunglasses despite being indoors. Tommy figured it was an image thing. The guy was probably trying to look as intimidating as possible.

"Your men here," Tommy said, "won't tell us what is going on. What do you want with us? We've done nothing wrong."

The officer reached up and slowly removed his sunglasses. His mustache twitched as he pulled the shades off and folded them in his hand. He raised his head and stared deep into Tommy's eyes.

"Nothing wrong?" the man said in English. "Is that what you call trespassing, entering the country illegally, and stealing?"

"Okay, first of all, we are just visiting your beautiful land. We wanted to check out some of the historical sites. Do a little research. You'll find that I'm—"

"I know who you are, Thomas Schultz. I know who all of you are." The man's voice thundered in the tiny room. "You think you can come into our country, destroy public property on a protected historical site, and then walk out of here without paying for it?"

"Oh, so I just need to pay for it? How much money we talking here? Few hundred bucks?"

"Silence!"

"Few thousand?"

The officer took a giant step forward and smacked Tommy across the cheek with the back of his hand.

"You think this is funny? We will see how funny you think it is when you and your friends are in the bowels of our prison for the rest of your miserable lives."

Tommy grimaced from the stinging sensation coursing through his face. That didn't keep him from sneering at the man.

"You're making a big mistake," Tommy said through clenched teeth.

"Huge," Hank added, albeit with less confidence.

"There's a madman out there who is looking for something at Leptis Magna. If he finds it, it could mean trouble for the entire world. Not just Libya. Not just America. Everyone."

He didn't have any proof behind the statement. For all he knew, Dufort had no idea where Tommy and his companions had gone after they left Egypt. It didn't matter if the story was credible or not. The threat was the point, not the truth behind it.

"This madman," a familiar voice resonated from the hallway, "does he have a name?"

Tommy's eyes widened as Dufort stepped through the doorway. He had a smug look on his face Tommy wished he could knock off with a right hook. Tommy felt his wrists tense against the metal cuffs, but there was no getting free from his bonds.

"Dufort," he said with disdain. "You just keep turning up, don't you?"

The Frenchman was holding a small metal case in one hand and the medallion in the other.

"Some people consider persistence to be a good quality," Dufort said. "I take it you don't agree."

Tommy turned his attention to the officer in charge. "So, that's it? You sold out to this guy? How much did he pay you? Huh? I guess everyone has their price."

"Mr. Dufort was kind enough to let us know there were criminals desecrating a historic site. In return for his assistance, we are allowing him to borrow the artifacts you tried to steal so he can research their origins and return them to the Libyan government."

"And you believe that?" Tommy's voice escalated.

"I can assure you that I have nothing but the best intentions for these items," Dufort said. He turned and faced the officer. "These tablets were stolen from another country by these three and their friend. I've been tasked with returning them as well."

"He's a liar," Hank said. "You can't trust anything that comes out of his mouth."

Dufort ignored him. "Speaking of their friend...where's Sean?" he asked.

"I have no idea," Tommy said. "But when he finds you—"

"Yes, I'm sure he'll do horrible things to me in the name of justice and revenge and all that. Except I'll be gone, and you three will be here."

The officer moved closer to Adriana. He'd been staring at her for the last few minutes with eyes full of lust. An old scar stretched from the corner of his right eye almost all the way down to his jaw.

He reached out and ran the back of his hand along her cheek. "What do you want me to do with these three?" he asked.

"Anything you like," Dufort answered. "We've been on their trail for a long time. I can't begin to tell you how many people they've killed. They are dangerous. Use the utmost precaution when dealing with them. That being said, feel free to be as creative as you like when it comes to how you treat them here."

Dufort turned and stepped toward the door.

"Sean's still out there," Tommy said, his tone full of warning. "No matter what they do to us in here, nothing will stop him from coming for you."

Dufort paused at the door's threshold and waited for a moment. He didn't turn around. "I hope he does."

The Frenchman stepped out into the hall and disappeared, leaving the three prisoners alone with the officer and his two guards.

"Don't worry," the commander said. "I'm going to hurt all of you in ways you never imagined."

"That sounds like the exact sort of thing we *should* be worried about," Hank said.

"You're right. It is."

He started unbuttoning his shirt while he continued to stare at Adriana.

"Um...what are you doing?" Tommy asked as he shifted uneasily in his chair.

"What do you think?" He turned to his guards and said something to them in Arabic.

The one on the right closed the door and resumed his position.

With all the buttons unfastened, the officer removed his shirt and tossed it at Tommy. It hit him in the shoulder and dropped to the floor. The guy leaned close to Adriana and ran his hand through her hair. She didn't flinch, didn't strain, just stared him in the eyes with unwavering intensity.

Near the base of her ponytail, his fingers wrapped around her hair and squeezed, yanked it back, and exposed her neck. Her nostrils filled with the stench of his breath and the obvious odor that came from days without a proper shower.

"You have courage," he said. "I admire that in a woman."

He ran the index finger of his left hand down the side of her neck, around to the front, and then to the collar of her tank top just above her breasts. He pulled back the fabric and looked down, getting a full view.

He looked over his shoulder at the guards. "I think she likes it."

"You leave her alone!" Tommy roared. "Don't you touch her, you sick freak!"

A knock came from the door.

The commander's face instantly turned to a scowl, furious that someone would interrupt his fun.

"What do you want?"

No answer came.

The officer turned his attention back to Adriana. He leaned in closer, sticking his tongue out to lick her face.

Just before he could, more rapping came from the door.

"What is it?" the commander shouted.

He turned around and motioned to one of his men to open it. "See what they want. Maybe our French friend forgot something."

The guy on the right stepped over and turned the doorknob.

The second he did, the door flew back and struck him in the face. He staggered back against the wall, momentarily stunned.

A man in a matching uniform with a scarf over his face charged in. He raised a pistol at the surprised guard on the left and fired a round into the man's head. Then he turned to the other guard and shot him twice, once in the chest and once in the forehead. Then the masked gunman stepped toward the officer with a pistol in each hand. He pointed the guns at the commander, who immediately put his hands in the air.

"Keys," the gunman said in Arabic.

The man's eyes widened with fear. His hands shook. He raised one index finger and pointed to the dead guard on the right.

The shooter sidestepped over to the body in the corner and eased the door shut. He kept one gun on the commander in case the guy tried to do anything stupid. When the intruder found the keys, he ripped them off the guard's belt and stepped back over to the leader.

"Uncuff them," he ordered.

The officer swallowed hard and turned his head from one side to the other. The gunman responded by lowering one of his pistols. He aimed it at the man's bulging crotch and tensed his finger on the trigger.

"Why is your shirt off? Is that...what is wrong with you?" the gunman asked in English.

The fear on the officer's face changed momentarily to curiosity.

Sean pulled the mask down and grinned. "Seriously, I would really appreciate it if you'd unlock those cuffs so my friends can go free. Otherwise, I'll have to shoot you first and then do it myself. If that's the way you want to do it, fine, but I'm going to start with... whatever it is you've got going on down there." Sean turned to Tommy. "I think he's aroused. Was he about to fool around with my girlfriend?"

Tommy and Hank were just as shocked as the officer to see Sean, but Tommy managed to get ahold of himself. "Yeah, you know, I think he was."

"Really? That's why you have your shirt off? I thought maybe it was just hot in here." Sean turned and looked at the dead guards for a second. "You were going to do that in front of all these other guys? What's wrong with you?"

The officer's tone grew brazen, his face replaced fear with resolve. "I don't know who you think you are, but you are a dead man. There are more than two hundred armed soldiers stationed here. You cannot escape. You will all die here. I swear it."

"You know, I think I asked you to uncuff my friends, but you're just not doing it fast enough."

Sean lowered the weapon and fired. The commander doubled over instantly, grabbing his groin with both hands. In less than three seconds, it was a bloody, mangled mess.

He screamed in agony as he dropped to his knees and rolled over onto his side, swearing in Arabic.

Sean went to work on the cuffs, unlocking Adriana's first then Tommy's and finally Hank's.

"Get those guns," Sean said, pointing at the guards. He handed one of his pistols to Adriana while Tommy and Hank scrambled to take the automatic rifles from the dead men.

Sean stood up straight and loomed over the writhing officer. "Oh, and when you said there were two hundred men, I think you may have overestimated. It was more like fifty...and they're all dead."

"You're the devil," the officer spat in Arabic.

Sean shook his head. "Me? No. I always heard the devil wears a dress."

He moved over to the door and waited.

Adriana hovered over the officer for a moment and then pointed her gun at his head. Her finger tensed on the trigger while the other three waited and watched.

"I don't think you deserve such an easy death," she said. Then she stepped to the door, leaving the man to squirm on the floor in his own blood.

Sean flung the door open and stepped outside. He checked to the right while Tommy cleared the left hallway.

"Clear," Tommy said.

"Clear this way," Sean said.

"How do we get out of this place?" Hank asked. "You heard him; there are probably guards everywhere."

"There were," Sean said. "Not anymore, although I may have missed one or two."

"Wait. You really did kill fifty guys?"

Sean sighed. "I wasn't keeping count, Hank. That sort of thing will keep you up at night. Best to just think of it like a ballpark estimate."

Sean started down the hall and made a left at the next turn. The others followed quickly behind with Tommy covering the rear. The next hall was shorter and split off in two directions. Sean took the right corridor and pressed ahead. They passed two dead guards lying facedown on the floor.

"You do that?" Hank asked.

"Do you really have to ask, Hank?" Sean responded.

Lights flickered overhead, and suddenly an alarm started blaring. Red swirling lights started spinning above the door at the end of the hall.

"That for us?" Tommy asked.

"No," Sean said. He kicked open the door and kept going.

"No? How is it not for us?"

"First of all, that officer is in no condition to raise the alarm. Second, the only way I could think of to get us out of here in one piece was to cause a riot."

"A riot?"

"Yeah."

The conversation died for a moment until they reached a set of windows along another corridor where they could see down into the cafeteria. The huge room was flooding with angry inmates who immediately took out the few guards occupying the area. The guards only managed to get off a few shots before they disappeared beneath the swarm.

"You let out all those inmates?"

Sean didn't answer immediately. When they reached the next door, he stopped, looked through the window, and then yanked it open.

"Well, most of them. We figured a diversion would be good. Not to mention they'll take out the rest of the guards."

Tommy looked horrified. "Yeah, and what happens when they decide to take us out?"

"Hopefully, we'll be long gone by then."

Sean rushed down the next hall toward the exit. He passed another passage on the left that was sealed off by a metal door. The door had a wire-reinforced window. That reinforcing was being put to the test by an inmate with a chair.

The man was banging the chair's legs against the glass in an attempt to break through. The window was severely cracked but still holding for the moment.

Sean kicked open the last door and motioned the others through. "Hank, take point. Get them to the helicopter."

"Helicopter?" Then Hank saw the chopper sitting in the middle of the courtyard. "Where in the world did you—"

"Just go, Hank. I'll be right behind you."

Hank nodded and took off, lumbering across the courtyard toward the helicopter.

Adriana went next, checking both sides of the facility as she ran. The second Tommy sprinted through the door, Sean gave one last look down the hall and then ran after him.

Inside the chopper, Sid increased the RPMs and readied the aircraft for takeoff. He saw Hank and the others running toward him and gave one last instrument check to make sure everything was good to go.

Sean was the last to climb aboard. He looked around the perimeter again, sweeping his weapon around to provide cover just in case.

He'd done a thorough job of clearing out anyone who could take down the helicopter during their escape.

Sid pulled the stick back a hair, and the chopper started to rise. At the door, Sean could see some of the prisoners spilling out into the courtyard. The reinforced door must have finally given way.

They rushed forward, hoping to catch a ride on the helicopter, but the skids were already twenty feet off the ground by the time the first inmate arrived.

Sid guided the aircraft over the walls and back out into the desert. Once they were clear of the base and prison, Sean eased into one of the seats and slid the door shut.

The other three stared at him in disbelief.

"How in the world did you pull that off?" Hank asked. "I mean, the guards must have been tough enough. But how did you find us in that place?"

Sean's lips creased slightly. "People will tell you anything you want to know when you apply the right amount of pain."

Tommy looked crestfallen. "I...I lost the medallion and the tablets, Sean. Without them...we have no idea where to go next. Dufort took them."

Sean sighed, frustrated.

"Luckily, I know we need to head south," Tommy added.

"South?" Sean asked.

"Yep."

Chapter 22

SAHARA DESERT, LIBYA

"**W**here did you get a helicopter?" Tommy asked into the headset. He leaned back against the headrest and stared at his friend.

"At the military base."

"So, what, you and Sid just snuck onto a high-security military installation and stole a chopper?"

"Wasn't as easy as it sounds," Sid chimed in.

Sean chuckled. "It's true."

"Come on," Hank said. "How in the world did you do that?"

"Do what?"

"All of it."

"I mean...do you want the whole story or just the abbreviated version?"

The others said nothing and continued to stare at him.

"Okay, fine. I was out by the water when I got Tommy's text. Apparently, I lost the signal while searching for the monument. By the time I found you guys, it was too late. Those soldiers had arrested you and were taking you to their trucks. I stole a ranger's truck, followed you to the prison, and then came up with a plan to bust you out."

He took a deep breath before continuing. "When I saw the helicopter, I knew that would be our best mode of escape, but I'd need Sid to help."

"I still can't believe you came all the way back out to the fishing boat," Sid said. "You could have just called."

"I didn't have your number. Besides, you needed the lifeboat to get to shore."

"Good point."

"Anyway," Sean went on, "I brought Sid back and told him my plan."

"Which was what?" Tommy asked. "Break in, take out all the guards, force one of them to tell you where we were being interrogated, and then come get us out?"

"Pretty much. I mean, there was a little more to it than that, but hey, it worked out."

The cabin fell silent as everyone processed Sean's tale. The only noise was the constant humming in their headsets.

"We were in there for nearly six hours," Adriana said. "That's a long time, but all things considered, I'd say you worked pretty fast."

Sean put his arm around her and pulled her close. "They didn't hurt you guys, did they?"

Tommy shrugged. "Slapped us around a bit, trying to get information. Nothing we haven't seen before."

"They didn't hurt her," Hank said, "if that's what you were wondering."

Sean was relieved to hear that. He didn't know what he'd do if something happened to Adriana. When he was fighting through the guards and soldiers at the prison, the thought of someone hurting her had fueled his rage, filling his veins with enough adrenaline to kill a mule.

The fighting had been a blur to him. He barely remembered much of it. Tommy called it a high-security installation. It was hardly Area 51. Difficult? Certainly. But Sean had faced difficult before.

While the men guarding the base and prison were well armed and probably well trained, they weren't exactly special ops. Once he was inside the walls, systematically taking out the threat one man at a time wasn't too much for him. He took out the first guy with his bare hands, sneaking up on him from behind and snapping his neck. The spine had snapped easily since the guy had no idea what was happening until it was too late. By the time he felt Sean's hands around his head, there was no time to tense his muscles or defend himself.

Sean had taken the guy's knife and proceeded to use it to silently take out most of the guards, eventually making his way to where the Libyans were interrogating his companions.

His muscles ached, finally catching up to the strain he'd put them through during the escape. Sean found as he got older that his body took a little longer to recover. It wasn't like when he first joined Axis. He could fall out of a second-story window and go run a marathon the next day. Now if he fell out of bed he'd be feeling it for almost a week.

"Where are we going?" Sid asked, cutting into the relative silence. "You said to go south. "We're getting close to the border with Chad."

"The Republic of Chad?" Hank asked.

"That's the one. I can turn west if you'd like, head toward Niger."

Sean knew there'd been some civil unrest in Niger recently. A warlord was wreaking havoc on small villages and towns. It was the last thing they needed to encounter.

"Stick with Chad," Sean said. "We can land there and rest for the night. You have enough fuel to get us there?"

"We should," Sid answered. "Won't be more than a few hours."

Sean didn't like the lack of absolute certainty from his pilot, but he didn't have a choice. They were flying over the Sahara Desert. It wasn't like there were a bunch of gas stations with aircraft fuel along the way. He also knew there was no point in worrying about it. They'd get as far as they could before having to set down. Preferably, that would be out of Libya.

He looked out the window, though there wasn't much to see. The vast desert stretched out all the way to the dark horizon where the rolling sand dunes became starry night sky.

"Why are we going south?" Sean asked as he continued to gaze out the window.

"Before those men took us," Tommy said, "I got a good look at the medallion and tablets."

Sean twisted his head around and faced his friend with a pleasantly surprised look on his face. "Really? What did it say?"

"It said the third stone is guarded forever by a great beast with a tail on its face."

"A tail on its face?"

Tommy gave a nod. "Yeah, we figure it's an elephant."

"Oh right. That would make sense."

"Only problem is we don't know where to find the elephant or even where to start looking. Best thing we could come up with is that the beast the riddle mentions must be made out of stone or something."

"Like a sculpture?"

"Yes. Nothing else would be permanent."

Sean thought for a moment. He didn't recall anything remotely close to that from his travels except for a fairly recent visit to Italy.

"It's not that elephant sculpture in Rome, is it? You know, the one at the base of that obelisk?"

Tommy laughed with a snort through his nose. "No, I don't think so. The clue said south."

"Right. My mistake. So, we're looking for a giant statue of an elephant somewhere in Africa. How far south?"

Tommy looked at Hank and then back at Sean. "No idea."

"So, this thing could be anywhere on this gigantic continent."

"Could be."

"Well, that sucks. Any ideas?"

"I have one," Adriana said. Up until then, she'd stayed relatively quiet. She stood up, grabbed a bar running along the center of the roof, and made her way to the cockpit. "There a map up here?" she asked.

Sid looked around for a second and then pointed to a folded map sitting in a side panel. "There," he said. "That should be one."

Adriana reached down and grabbed the map. She unfolded it to make sure it was what they needed before returning to the main cabin.

"You're welcome," Sid said in a sarcastic tone.

She ignored him and spread out the map on the floor, taking a seat next to it.

"If we're heading toward the border between Libya and Chad," she said, "and the clue told us to go south, what if the thing we're looking for is the same distance between Leptis Magna and Giza?"

The three men in the back leaned forward and peered at the map as they listened to her theory.

"What do you mean?" Hank said. "Same distance?"

Adriana nodded. She traced a line with her finger from the west bank of the Nile all the way to the region where they'd visited the ancient Roman ruins. "See that line?"

The others acknowledged with a nod.

"It could be that we have to find this elephant the same distance from Leptis Magna, or at least a similar distance."

"Why would that be?" Sean asked.

"I'm not sure," Adriana confessed. "Just a hunch."

"Okay," Tommy jumped in, "but even if the distance is correct, we still don't know which direction to go other than south."

"See if you can get in touch with the kids. If we can get them some general coordinates, narrow things down to a specific region, they might be able to find what we're looking for and cut our search time significantly."

The men glanced at each other and then turned their attention back to Adriana.

"That's a good idea," Sean said.

"Beats anything I came up with," Tommy added. "As soon as we land, I'll see if I can get a signal and call Atlanta."

The conversation died, and the cabin returned to silence. During the rest of the flight, no one said much of anything. A couple of times Sean noticed the others dozing off in short bursts. Adriana's head fell onto his shoulder more than once as she fell asleep for a few minutes and then woke suddenly, only to start the process all over again.

Sean couldn't sleep. He was exhausted, but his mind was racing. The others hadn't said anything about it since they got in the chopper, but Sean couldn't get it out of his head.

How was Dufort able to track them?

Sean eyed Hank from across the cabin. The former CIA man was leaning his head against the corner with his eyes closed. His lips flapped every few seconds, signaling he was fast asleep.

Could Hank be the one telling Dufort where they were going? Sean shrugged off the idea. Hank had been left for dead when Dufort made his getaway from the prison. If he was working for Dufort, the Frenchman would have helped his assistant escape—unless there was no more use for him. Again, that didn't add up in Sean's mind. Hank would have come clean or at least been irate at Dufort for leaving him.

No way Hank was the one.

That left Sid.

Sid was a wild card, an unknown. He'd been of great help so far, but that didn't mean the guy wasn't up to no good. Of course, if Sid had been working with Dufort, he would have left the second Sean and his friends got off the fishing boat. He may have even ditched the group sooner, all the way back in Cairo.

He hadn't, though, which caused Sean to think maybe Sid was okay. Heck, he was flying them to freedom. He didn't have to do that.

Sean knew that a smuggler like Sid had some kind of motive for helping out. It couldn't have been from the goodness of his heart. If there was treasure to be found in the desert, Sid wanted to get his share. Sid had hitched his wagon to Sean and the others, but that didn't mean he wasn't hedging his bets. Maybe he was helping Dufort *and* the Americans to ensure he'd come out on top.

Whatever the reason, Sean reaffirmed that he'd keep a watchful eye on their pilot, just in case.

A flash of light off in the distance to the west caught his attention. A moment later, a faint pop reached his ears. The sound didn't rouse his friends. Sean knew what it was. A tank had fired on something. Thankfully, the machine wasn't firing at the helicopter, at least that's what Sean believed. From the direction of the flash, it appeared the tank was aiming to the north. There was no way of knowing if it was a rebel tank or one belonging to the loyalists.

Not that it mattered. Both groups would be enemies to a random chopper flying through the area.

Sid must have seen the shot because he tilted the aircraft a little to the left to make sure they steered clear of the danger.

Sean closed his eyes, and he let his mind drift. The constant throbbing in the headset was like a hypnotic metronome, persistently begging him to dreamland.

He fought the urge to sleep and shook his head, but before long Sean had passed out like the rest while his subconscious took him to a lost oasis city somewhere in the middle of the Sahara.

Chapter 23

BARDAÏ, CHAD

Everyone in the helicopter's main cabin woke with a start.

"Setting her down," Sid said into the headsets.

Sean found Adriana asleep on his shoulder. His neck was stiff from leaning against the corner. He checked his phone for the time. He'd been asleep over an hour, closer to two.

The darkness outside was brightened by the light from a crescent moon high in the sky to the east.

"Where are we?" Tommy asked, rubbing his eyes.

"Far as I can tell," Sid answered, "we're just outside the town of Bardaï."

"Bardaï?" Hank asked as he stretched his arms and yawned.

"It's in Chad. Small oasis town, but it's the closest thing to civilization you'll find around here."

Sean and the others checked their phones, but they still had no signal.

"I got nothing on my phone," Tommy said, disappointed.

"Me either," Sean said. "This could be a problem."

"Sorry I couldn't get us farther," Sid's voice came through the headsets again. "Out of fuel. We should be far enough out of town that no one will bother us. We can get some rest here, and then I'll head into the village in the morning to see if I can find us some fuel."

The rotors above began to slowly wind down as Sid flipped a number of switches and began shutting off the controls.

"Sounds good," Sean said. He turned to the others. "Feel free to get some rest, guys. I'll keep watch for the next few hours."

"I'll take second shift," Adriana said with a yawn.

Sean slid the door open, hung his headset on a hook, and climbed out. The desert air was cooler than expected and sent a chill across his skin. He'd always known that nights in the desert brought about an extreme swing in temperature. It happened when he was in Vegas, though not as much as he'd expected.

Here—on the edge of the Sahara—it was much more extreme.

Sean wandered away from the chopper and looked out over the land. Sid had parked the helicopter on a plateau that overlooked a valley. They were only a few hundred feet above the town of Bardaï, but the view was still impressive. He tilted his head back and gazed up at the stars. The moment was short lived, however, as Sean's equilibrium revolted and sent the sky spinning in his field of vision. He lowered his head and squeezed his eyes shut for a second, trying to fight off the nausea that came with the sudden dizziness.

He took a deep breath and exhaled slowly before opening his eyes again. Off to his left was a cluster of boulders jutting up out of the ground. He wandered over to it and found a rock with a flat top where he could sit down and let his body adjust.

"How long is this going to last?" he asked himself as he eased down onto the hard surface.

He'd heard people talk about their experience with vertigo, but Sean never expected to go through it. He wondered how so many people could live with a permanent version of the condition.

He rubbed the back of his neck with his thumb and forefinger, hoping that would take away some of the dizziness. Then he looked out over the scene again. He'd visited places where there were more stars than a person could count in a lifetime. This spot would be added to that short list.

The Milky Way stretched across the sky overhead, running by the waxing moon from horizon to horizon. Down in the valley, a sparse smattering of lights flickered in humble houses or along the dirt streets. Sean was surprised anyone was still awake this late.

He rested his elbows on his knees. His vision stopped spinning almost as suddenly as it began, bringing him much-needed relief.

As he gazed out at the serene view, he thought he heard something jingle. Sean shook his head like he would if he'd been swimming and gotten water in his ear.

I must be hearing things.

No sooner had the thought popped into his head than he heard the noise again, this time more clearly than the first.

"What is that?" he muttered to himself.

Sean stood up and tiptoed over to the edge of the plateau where the slope rolled gently down to the plains below. Halfway down the mountain, he saw something moving amid an outcropping of boulders.

His eyes narrowed as he tried to focus on what had made the noise. His heart rate quickened. He stepped over the edge and crept downhill, keeping his pistol waist high in case whatever was down there was a threat.

Something moved again. It was white but still too difficult to discern. The metal clanking sound was more pronounced than before. If whoever was hiding in the boulders was an enemy, they were a pretty loud one.

Sean bent his knees and crouched behind the first big rock he came to on his descent. He peeked around the end, keeping his weapon extended and ready to fire. Some rocks shifted on the dirt on the other side of the boulder, and he pulled back his gun lest the enemy see him.

He pressed his shoulder blades against the smooth stone and waited for a second. He listened closely but didn't hear the movement again. Sean slowed his breathing, calmed his heartbeat, and tensed his finger on the trigger.

Slowing down the world around him was something he'd learned to do a long time ago. It was especially useful when shooting long-range weapons, but the technique also helped in close-quarters combat—hand-to-hand or otherwise.

The enemy was being incredibly silent all of a sudden. For someone who'd been carelessly lumbering about on the hillside, now it seemed they were intent on keeping quiet.

Had they seen Sean approaching? Did they notice him when he peeked around the rock?

Whatever the case, Sean had no intention of letting them make the first move. He spun around and flashed his weapon in front of his body, ready to squeeze the trigger at first sight of the target.

Every muscle in his body tensed for a brief moment. A second later, all those fibers relaxed. Standing in front of him in the center of the rock formation was a white-and-brown goat.

The surprised animal looked up at him and then made a bah sound before shoving its nose back to the ground to root around for more foliage.

Sean exhaled and lowered his weapon. He shook his head as he watched the goat rummaging in the rocks.

"A goat," he said. He was almost disappointed. He'd prepared for a gunfight. Instead, he found someone's pet.

Sean took a knee and made a clicking sound with his tongue. The animal looked up and trotted the short distance over to him. Sean ran his hand along the goat's head, rubbing his fur.

"What are you doing way out here?" he asked. Then he noticed the thing that had made the initial noise. A tiny silver bell dangled from a piece of twine on the goat's neck.

Sean shook his head, irritated at himself for getting so worked up over a farm animal. He let his fingers run down the back of the goat's neck and then dropped his hand to his side.

He stood up and started to turn away when he sensed something behind him. Sean spun around, expecting to see one of his friends. Instead, he found a boy in a white linen tunic and matching hat. The young man was holding a shepherd's rod in one hand, extended menacingly toward Sean.

"What are you doing out here?" Sean asked the boy, albeit with more suspicion than he'd used with the goat.

"What are you doing with my goat?" the boy asked in English.

Sean didn't even realize he'd spoken English to the boy. He was surprised the kid responded in kind, and sounded pretty fluent. The kid couldn't have been more than fourteen years old. It didn't take long for Sean to put two and two together. The boy was a shepherd, and Sean had stumbled upon his goat.

"I found your goat here in the rocks," Sean said as he stuffed his weapon in his belt. "I thought it might be lost."

The boy kept the staff extended, unsure if he should believe the American or not.

"Look, kid, I wasn't going to hurt your goat. Honest. My friends and I are just passing through."

"I heard your machine," the boy said. "It scared most of my animals back down into the valley. All except this one."

"Helicopters are pretty loud."

"Yes. What are you doing here?"

Sean decided to play things as casual as possible in hopes of getting the kid to relax. "My name is Sean. I work for an archaeological agency based in the United States."

"Archae...ological agen...cy?" The boy struggled to say the words.

"Yeah. See, we travel all over the world searching for relics, lost pieces of history, sometimes even treasure." Sean hoped the last part would spark the boy's interest. "What's your name?"

The kid gradually lowered the staff until the end rested on the ground. He stood his ground, keeping his feet planted.

"My name is Abdullah."

Sean could see the boy was still unsure of whether or not he should trust the American.

"It's okay," Sean said. "I'm not going to hurt you. Care to sit down?"

The boy didn't budge.

Sean decided to take a different tack. He looked out over the plains. In the distance, a huge rock formation rose up from the land and darkened the horizon.

"We're here to find something," he said after a moment of thought. "Do you know this area pretty well?"

Abdullah nodded. "I've lived here my whole life."

"You speak good English," Sean said. "How'd you learn?"

"An American missionary came to our town many years ago," he said. "He built a school and taught us how to read and write."

That was surprising. Then again, Sean knew that American missionaries did their best to cover the globe with their gospel message.

"Did this missionary convert many people?"

Abdullah's head went slowly left to right. "No, but we let him teach us anyway."

"I see."

Sean folded his hands and rested his forearms on his knees.

The boy took a cautious step forward. "What are you looking for?" he asked.

Sean raised his eyebrows and turned to face the young man. "I'm sorry, what?" He'd heard Abdullah's question. He just wanted to keep the kid talking.

"You said you were looking for something. What could you be looking for out here? There's nothing but desert and wasteland."

"Well, I'm not sure if what we're trying to find is close to here," Sean confessed. "But we are out of fuel and need to find more to continue our journey." He thought for a second. "There wouldn't happen to be an airport or something close by where airplanes land, would there?"

Abdullah nodded. "Yes. There is an airstrip in the village. They may have fuel for your machine there."

That was good news. Sean had figured they were a long way from any place that would have the right kind of gas for a helicopter. Based on what the boy said, they might not be as far away as he believed.

"What are you looking for?" Abdullah pressed his original question. "The treasure you seek, what is it?"

"Oh right. Well, we don't really know if there's a treasure or not, but the thing we're trying to find right now will hopefully lead us to the answer."

"Answer?"

"Yes. See, we found a clue that we believe will lead us to the treasure...or whatever it is that's out there. But first we have to figure out the next clue."

Abdullah was clearly lost. Maybe there was something wrong with the translation. Sean didn't know. So he kept going.

"We found a riddle that said we have to find a place where a great beast stands forever over the next clue."

"A great beast?" the boy looked puzzled.

Sean smiled as Abdullah drew near and propped his staff up against the rock. Then the young man planted his hands on the boulder and hoisted himself up. He looked expectantly at Sean as though the American was telling a bedtime story.

"Yeah, we're not entirely sure what that part means, either. We think it's talking about an elephant because the riddle mentions a tail on the beast's face."

"That's not a tail. It's the elephant's nose."

Sean chuckled. "Right. We know that. We just figured...you know, in the context of the riddle."

"Context?"

"Never mind. Not important. Anyway, that's what we're trying to find. We believe that there might be a large sculpture of an elephant somewhere in this region. Where it might be, we have no idea."

"Oh."

A gentle breeze rolled up the slope and washed over the two as they sat quietly for a moment, absorbed in their thoughts.

"I don't suppose your village has high-speed internet," Sean said. He didn't think the answer would be yes, but it was worth a try. Stranger things had happened.

"No," Abdullah shook his head. "The only thing we have is a radio, and it usually doesn't work because we have to create electricity with wind or by hand."

Sean figured that would be the kid's answer, although he wondered how they created electricity by hand. Must have been some kind of hand crank or something. It didn't matter. He and his friends were up a creek, with no sign of a paddle anywhere.

"There is a place not far from here," Abdullah said.

"Oh yeah? They have internet there?"

Abdullah shook his head. Sean's hope that had, for a second, sprung in his chest, sank back down again.

"No. It's a place in those hills over there." The boy pointed at the dark silhouette in the distance. "It is a sacred place. No one goes there except the old man who lives in the desert. They say he's a kind of priest from a religion no one believes in anymore."

"Why does he go there?" Sean asked.

"They say that the spirits of the people who lived here long ago walk among the columns."

"Columns?"

Abdullah nodded. "Yes."

"What columns?"

"They are giant stone formations, hundreds of feet high. I went there once when I was young but got scared and haven't been back since."

Sean almost laughed at the kid's comment about being young but kept the laughter to himself. "What's so special about that place?"

"You said you and your friends are looking for an elephant sculpture."

"Yeah...."

"Well, there's a big rock formation that looks like an elephant in those mountains."

Sean's heartbeat picked up the pace again. "Really?"

"Yes. No one goes there much."

"This elephant, is it hard to find?"

Abdullah shook his head emphatically. "No. You hike straight in and follow the path through the columns until you find it. The trail goes right to it."

Sean stood up and grinned at the young man. "Thank you for your help, Abdullah. I really appreciate it."

"You're welcome. Thank you for finding my goat. Father would be angry if I lost him."

"Glad I could help."

The boy stood up and trudged over to where the animal was munching on some dried weeds.

"It isn't often we get foreigners to this area," Abdullah said. "Now I've seen two in one day."

Sean had just turned to hike back up the hill when the boy's words froze him in his tracks.

"What did you just say?"

Abdullah looked a little surprised. "It's odd that we've had two visitors to the village in one day."

"Two? Who else was here?"

"It was a group of men. They arrived in two airplanes. One of them had gray hair, but his face didn't look old."

"These men," Sean said, "they were looking for the elephant rock, too?"

"I don't know, but they went to the mountains. I heard them tell my grandfather they planned on visiting the area to study it. They had a lot of equipment with them. Some of the men carried guns."

Sean already knew who the men were from the description of their leader. It matched Dufort perfectly.

"You said they had equipment. What kind of equipment?"

"It looked like tents and things for staying out in the wilderness. I think you call it camping in America."

"That we do, Abdullah." Sean stepped close to the point and put his hand on the kid's shoulder. He shook the hat loose atop the boy's hair and grinned. "Thank you for your help. I appreciate it."

"You're welcome, Mr. Sean."

Abdullah turned and led his goat back down the rocky slope toward the village. Sean watched for a second until the boy was nearly at the bottom before he turned his gaze back to the bulging silhouette in the distance. Somewhere in those hills, Dufort was sleeping snug in his tent. A plan started forming in Sean's mind. First, there were ideas of going over there in the dead of night, killing all his men, and smothering him with his own pillow.

Dufort wasn't stupid. He'd be expecting that if he even for a fraction of a second considered that Sean and company were still alive. The Frenchman would have taken precautions to protect his camp.

Sean dismissed the ambush idea and settled on another plan. It was one he believed Dufort wouldn't be expecting.

Chapter 24

BARDAÏ

Dufort stood with his hands on his hips, staring at the huge rock formation.

"Well, I'd say this is the right place," Cody said, standing just a few feet away from his employer. "It looks like a huge elephant." He looked over his shoulder at Dufort. "That's assuming that the riddle was talking about a huge elephant."

"Yes. What else could it be? Here we are, due south of the ruins at Leptis Magna, and we find a great beast standing here, permanently frozen in time. I'd say it's a good bet, wouldn't you?"

"Yes, sir." Cody felt stupid for suggesting otherwise. "Hard to believe that thing is a natural formation."

"How do we know it is?" Dufort asked with a sly look over his shoulder. "It's highly possible that the ancients had some kind of technology we don't yet know about. They could have crafted this thing in any shape they wanted."

"Why an elephant?"

Dufort rolled his shoulders. "That, I don't know. Perhaps it was the largest land animal they could find and wanted to project dominance to anyone coming to the area."

"To what end?"

"To protect the secret. Say someone was looking for the medallion and came to this place a few hundred years ago. Seeing that great beast might have been frightening. The only problem now is where to look." Dufort watched as his team scoured the area. They'd been up since dawn searching for the hidden relic, but in two hours hadn't found a thing.

"Did you manage to obtain the package?" Dufort asked, staring straight ahead at one of his men as the guy overturned a rock.

"Yes, sir. It's on the way to Cairo. It will wait there until we need it."

"Good," Dufort said in an affirming tone. "Never hurts to have a little insurance."

"I don't understand, sir. You seem concerned. And why the need for insurance?"

"Sean Wyatt," Dufort said. He folded his hands behind his back and stood up on his tiptoes then let himself sink slowly back to the soles of his feet. "Sean Wyatt is why."

Cody shook his head and stared forward at the other men as they worked. "His friends are dead. If they aren't, they will be soon. And I'm willing to bet they're in a terrible amount of pain right now."

"Wyatt wasn't there. That's troubling."

Dufort's second in command didn't share his employer's concern. "Wyatt is out of the picture, sir. I don't know why he wasn't with the others, but if he was with them and got separated, good news—he's still in Libya without a clue as to where we went. And besides, me and my men can handle one guy. Sean Wyatt is the least of your worries."

"Is that what you think?"

"He's just a man, sir."

"He is *not* just a man!" Dufort boomed. "Sean Wyatt is a ghost. He moves in and out of the shadows, striking when you least suspect it. You clearly underestimate him."

Cody didn't flinch. "Maybe you overestimate him. If the Libyans haven't picked him up yet, they will eventually. And even if they don't, like I said, he's not going to find us here. How could he? You have the tablets and the second stone. There is no way for him to find us."

"You know what your problem is, Cody?" The other man said nothing, instead staring ahead as he waited for Dufort to give him the answer. "You don't believe. And that unbelief will be your undoing if you don't change."

"Sorry if I don't believe in ghosts, sir. But don't worry. My men and I will make sure Wyatt doesn't interfere with your plans. If he's stupid enough to show up, we'll take care of him."

Dufort was fed up with Cody's lack of respect for the enemy. The Frenchman had learned the hard way not to underestimate Wyatt. He wouldn't let that happen again.

One of the men by the rock formation stopped at a wide crack near the bottom of the elephant's trunk. The guy leaned down and looked inside. Then he reached to his belt and unclipped a small flashlight. He shined the light into the dark recess and moved closer.

"Sir?" the man shouted, still staring into the hole. "I think I've got something! You might want to come take a look!"

Dufort drew in a long breath through his nostrils and then exhaled. "See?" he said. "The tablets don't lie." He glanced down at the case Cody held in his right hand. "Bring those up with me."

The two made their way through the loose rocks and occasional sagebrush until they reached the base of the massive elephant sculpture. The thing looked big from fifty feet away, but standing next to it gave a true sense of how gigantic it was.

The top of the head was easily eighty feet high. Whoever built it —if it wasn't an act of nature—must have possessed some high-level engineering skills, along with massive creativity.

Dufort stopped a yard away from where his man was still shining the light into the hole. "What is it?" he asked.

"Not sure," the guy said. "Looks like some kind of a box. I think it's stone."

"Can you pull it out?"

"I'll try. I just wanted to make sure you were okay with it."

Dufort gave a curt nod, and the man reached his hand inside the rock sliver. He had to twist his body sideways to reach the box. That meant he had to put the light behind his waist and was searching entirely by feel. His fingers ran along something smooth. Then he felt the edge of the box.

"I've got it," he said in a triumphant tone. Then the proud expression on his face abruptly changed.

He screamed, suddenly in an excruciating amount of pain. He jerked his hand back out of the hole and held it in the air. Dufort and Cody stepped back as the man waved his hand around. Attached to it was a huge sand spider, latched on by its fangs.

The screaming man managed to shake the arachnid free, sending the insect to the ground. It started to crawl away, but Cody stepped forward and crushed it with the heel of his boot.

The other men ran over to see what was going on and saw their comrade clutching his reddened hand with the other. The guy doubled over, squeezing his wrist as hard as he could to keep the venom from coursing into his veins.

"Gary," Dufort said, "it's going to be okay. I just need you to stop being so loud. Calm down. It's just a spider."

Cody knew different. "That's a sand spider, sir," he whispered into Dufort's ear. "It's the most venomous arachnid on the continent."

"Is there an anti-venom?" Dufort asked in a hushed tone.

Cody merely shook his head slowly from side to side.

"I see," Dufort said.

The Frenchman pulled out a huge pistol from a holster and pointed it at Gary's head. The bitten man's face was flushed red, and it looked like his eyeballs would burst from their sockets.

"I do apologize, Gary. But it's this or die an excruciating death."

"No. Wait," Gary begged.

The muzzle fired. The round drilled a hole through Gary's head and into the sand behind him. The man shook for a few second. Then his eyes fixed forward, and he fell facedown into the rocky sand.

"Johnson," Dufort said, motioning with his pistol toward the crack.

Another man stepped up. Johnson was a younger guy—mid-twenties—but his reddish beard made him look ten years older.

"Retrieve my box for me," Dufort ordered.

Johnson swallowed hard. He stared down at the dead man at Dufort's feet and then at the squashed spider. His hesitation was noted by the Frenchman.

"Those spiders don't come in groups, Johnson. It's unlikely there's another one inside. You'll be fine."

Johnson frowned and moved uneasily toward the crevice. He stopped near the rock and paused. Then he looked inside, inspecting the hole to make sure there weren't any other surprises.

Dufort and the rest of the men waited and watched as Johnson unclipped his flashlight and pointed it into the hole. He checked and rechecked before twisting his body sideways and sticking his hand into the cavity.

His fingers slid across the edge of the box, and he snatched it quickly. He yanked the object as hard and fast as he could, terrified there might be another spider inside the hole.

The narrow box came loose and slid out of the recess. The surface scraped the sides of the crack, but Johnson didn't care. He set the stone container down on the ground and took a step back.

Dufort grabbed the case from Cody's hand and laid it down next to the stone box. He took a knee and ran his finger along the symbol carved into the top. It was a circle with a four-point cross in the center.

He stared at the lid for nearly a minute, forgetting about the men standing around him and the dead guy a few feet away. He even let himself lose track of his concern over Sean Wyatt. He had the third stone. Now, nothing would stand in his way.

He lifted the lid and stared down into the container. Within it lay a medallion made from white gold. A green gem that looked much like an emerald was embedded in the center.

Dufort left the amulet where it was for a moment and turned to his left. He unlatched the case and opened it, exposing the other two medallions and the tablets.

Suddenly, the two medallions in the case began vibrating. A high-pitched sound rang in the men's ears, and they dropped their weapons to cover their heads.

"What is that?" Cody winced as he spoke. He stared down at the amulet in the stone box. It shook as if the ground beneath it trembled.

Dufort leaned closer, unafraid of the bizarre occurrence. He picked up the third medallion and held it high. The sun sparkled off the precious metal. A green hue appeared on the ground beyond the box as the light passed through the emerald.

The rest of the men stepped back, confused and terrified.

"Sir, maybe you should put that back."

"Don't you see, Cody? The stones are meant to be together. There is a power at play here that no science book can explain."

"Yeah, and I'm not so sure that power is a good thing."

"Nonsense," Dufort said. "These are a divine gift to humanity, lost for centuries—millennia, even. There is nothing to fear."

Cody wasn't convinced. He took another cautious step back along with all the other men.

Dufort picked up the other medallions and set them in the stone box. Then he placed the third one on the tablets in the place where the third blank appeared in the text. Reverently, he turned the jewel over onto its face to reveal the next clue. He traced the ancient script with his finger as he read the entire passage.

"What...what does it say?" Cody asked, still standing several yards back.

"To the east where kings meet gods in the shadow of the pharaoh, a fallen prince sits on his empty throne."

Cody's eyebrows stitched together. A perplexed scowl crossed his face. "What's that supposed to mean?"

Dufort drew in a deep breath through his nose and then exhaled as he turned his head side to side. He let a grin crease his lips despite his frustration. "I have no idea."

He closed the stone box and handed it over to one of the men standing next to Cody. Then he placed the first two stones inside the case, closed it, and passed it to Cody, who took it reluctantly.

"Relax, Cody. These relics won't harm you. Quite the opposite, in fact. They were designed to lead us to a place where immortality is attainable. Soon, we will be invincible and have more resources than we ever imagined."

The crazy talk about eternal life was a hard sell to the younger man. He didn't buy into the mystical mumbo jumbo—although he had to admit that what just happened with the stones was pretty incredible and terrifying all at once.

The resources part, however, was what Cody wanted. Dufort had promised him and his men a vast treasure with a value in the billions. He and the others would never have to work again. No more babysitting rich kids or running security for wealthy businessmen looking to exploit danger-ridden countries. With his portion of the treasure, Cody would disappear—probably to a remote tropical beach in the South Pacific or maybe Senegal. Not many tourists knew about the west coast of Africa, although he wasn't picky. Pretty much any beach would work so long as the drinks flowed and they were brought by someone young and beautiful.

"We'll need to do a bit more research," Dufort said. "Unfortunately, a good internet connection isn't available in this part of the world. We'll need to go somewhere that will have at least a Second World connection."

Cody was puzzled. They had more than enough equipment back at the camp. "I don't understand. Why don't we just use the satellite links? We can get online from here. The generators have plenty of fuel. What's the problem?"

Dufort stuffed the emerald-encrusted medallion into a pocket and forced a patient grin onto his face. "The problem, my dear Cody, is that satellite links are a fairly unique signature. Only a small percentage of people in the entire world have access to that sort of thing. Usually, they're in the military. We, however, are a private enterprise, which means if we get online with one of those things, someone is going to notice."

Dufort didn't have to say who. Cody and his men already knew. Some of them had worked for the various intelligence agencies around the world. One guy in particular had been given a job at the NSA before he decided to quit and make more money as a mercenary.

There was, however, a problem with Dufort's paranoid theory.

"For someone to track us, they'd have to have been alerted. I doubt anyone is watching this area for a SAT link to get thrown up. Who would have told them?"

Dufort shook his head. For all his skills as a killer and an enforcer, Cody wasn't the smartest person. He was brilliant when it came to tactics, strategy, in-the-field sort of stuff, but he lacked a good deal of common sense.

"Remember what I said earlier, Cody?"

"Which part?"

"Sean Wyatt," Dufort said. "He's still out there, remember? And he's the type to cover all the bases. So, do us all a favor, and stay off the internet until we can get to a place where there are lots of people. Okay?"

Cody's face flushed red. "Very well, sir." He turned to the rest of the men, still blushing from the embarrassment. "Let's roll out. Pack up everything."

The men trotted away, heading back to the camp they'd set up the night before among the giant stone columns.

"I'm going to go help the men, sir," Cody said and started to turn away.

"Good. And keep an eye out. I get the sense we're being watched."

"Watched?" Cody started to ask who would be watching, but he didn't have to. He knew who his boss was talking about and decided to skip the crazy.

"I'll put an extra man on guard," Cody said and jogged away.

Dufort watched him until he'd run around an opening in the rocks and disappeared. Then he reached into his pocket and pulled out the medallion. He held it high in the air, letting the sunlight catch the gem in the middle and once more splash a greenish hue across the rocks and sand.

He sighed with satisfaction. Soon, he would have control of everything.

Chapter 25

BARDAÏ

Sean crouched as low as he could, staying behind the truck until the guard turned and started pacing back the other way.

He looked over his shoulder. Tommy, Adriana, and Hank were all perched at the top of a huge rock jutting out of the ground. They watched as Sean darted between bushes, thin trees, and outcroppings of boulders as he approached Dufort's camp.

He knew Dufort would have guards stationed. Sean also knew that Dufort wasn't foolish enough to believe he was out of the picture yet. They'd done this little dance before, which was why Sean decided to change the tune.

Dufort would be expecting some kind of a brute-force attack, or at the very least an ambush. That expectation was why the Frenchman had placed men at the entrance into the sacred ground where the columns stood like tall stone guardians.

Lucky for Sean, he found another way in—several ways, actually. He knew Dufort would use as many men as he could to hurry the process of finding the third medallion. That meant he couldn't cover every entry point.

So Sean used an oldie but goodie tactic and flanked Dufort's camp and came in from the east. He encountered two guards using a standard patrol movement. It was easy enough to time when the men would be looking the other way and when they'd be coming back around. Once Sean figured that part out, getting into the main section of the camp was a piece of cake.

As soon as the shepherd boy gave him Dufort's description the night before, Sean came up with a plan. Figuring the Frenchman would anticipate some kind of ambush, Sean and Sid ripped out the transponder from the helicopter and broke it down into the smallest possible form they could without sacrificing signal and power. The latter was the least of their problems. Sean could jack the makeshift homing beacon into one of Dufort's trucks and hook it right into a power supply.

Tracking it, however, would be another issue. He didn't have anything on hand that could be made into a sort of monitor, which meant he was going to have to outsource that task to someone else.

The plan was to put the transponder on a truck and then follow from a safe distance until they reached a place with a cell signal. From there, Sean would call Emily and see if she could get a read on where Dufort was headed.

It wasn't an easy plan, but it was the best he could do with limited resources and time.

He unconsciously reached up with one hand and felt the device strapped to his chest inside his shirt to make sure it was still attached and in one piece, as if he couldn't feel the heavy hunk of metal and wires hanging from his skin.

The guard turned to the left and disappeared behind a tent.

Now was his chance.

Sean stood up and risked a quick peek over the truck's hood. No sign of the guard or any of the other men in Dufort's regiment. He reached for the door handle and pulled. Sean knew better than to expect the door to open right away, but he couldn't help himself. After all, why in the world would the mercenaries lock their doors? They were out in the middle of nowhere.

Unless they were afraid of the locals coming around and stealing some of their gear. Or maybe it wasn't the locals Dufort was worried about.

Sean sighed and ducked back down just as the guard reappeared around the other end of the tent. The guy had been looking the other way but could have just as easily turned his head and spotted Sean.

There was no backup plan. While his friends acted as spotters high on the cliffs a few hundred yards away, they were well out of range with their weapons. The only thing they could offer in the way of assistance would be as a diversionary attack. They could fire their weapons to draw the guards' attention, but it was unlikely Tommy and the others would be able to take anyone down. It would be a challenge for an expert sniper equipped with a .50-caliber rifle at that range, much less the smaller weapons Sean's friends carried.

The roving guard disappeared again, this time behind a huge boulder in the middle of the camp. Sean seized the opportunity and dashed over to one of the other trucks parked a few feet away. He slid to a stop in a patch of gravel and pressed his back against the tailgate. He panted for air and then glanced around the back of the vehicle. The two guards were at the intersecting point of their routes and passed each other. The first guard proceeded down his path, getting farther away with every step. Now the second guard was coming Sean's way, which meant Sean would have to work fast.

He slipped around to the driver's side of the truck and pulled the handle. *Dang it,* he thought. It was locked, too.

Only one left.

He stole another look around the front end of the truck. The second patrol was behind one of the tents. Sean took off and ran the ten steps to the last vehicle. He tucked in behind it just as the guard reappeared and started curving his pattern back around toward the entrance to the campsite.

Sean sidestepped around the back-left quarter panel and eased his way over to the driver side door. He watched the path he knew the guard would take as his fingers felt their way up to the door handle. He pulled the latch, but once again nothing happened.

Why on earth would these guys lock all the doors?

It was a pointless question and one to which there was no answer. Wondering why didn't help the current situation. Sean was going to have to go with Plan B.

The guard turned to his right and started marching toward the trucks. Within seconds, Sean would be in plain sight if the guy diverted his gaze.

Sean didn't wait for that to happen. He dropped to the ground behind the tire and waited. His fingers gripped his pistol tightly as he waited with his back against the wheel. If he engaged the enemy, the entire plan would be shot. Dufort would be alerted to his presence, reinforcements would flood the camp, and Sean would be up against odds even he couldn't overcome.

His muscles tensed, and he leaned over onto his forearm. The rocky soil dug into his skin, but he ignored the pain, keeping most of his body off the ground so he could crane his neck and see the oncoming guard. The man's torso and face were blocked by the truck's undercarriage. He was visible from the waist down, though, and Sean watched patiently as the guy meandered in his direction. When the guard vanished behind the front right wheel, Sean carefully swung one leg around and then the other, careful not to kick any rocks or make a sound. Even the slightest noise would cause the patrol to raise an alarm.

Sean lowered himself to the ground and rolled just as the guard's boots appeared on the other side of the truck, mere feet away from where Sean had been crouching just a moment before.

Sean watched as the guard took ten more steps, spun around, and paused. He'd seen him and the other guy do the exact same thing several times while trying to figure out their patrol's timing. The guard was too close to see Sean underneath the truck, but if he moved out of his usual path—even just a couple of feet—the jig would be up and Sean would be exposed at point blank range.

He looked up and realized that under the chassis there were several places he could use as handholds. He deftly rolled onto his back, stuffed his pistol into his belt, and grabbed the metal bars next to the drive shaft. Then he raised one foot, planted it on a bar going across the center of the truck's underbelly, and pulled himself up.

His muscles strained to hold him in place, but Sean didn't give in. He squeezed as hard as he could while keeping his head bent back in order to see the guard's boots.

The man started to walk back down his path when something caused him to stop and reroute.

Sweat rolled down Sean's head, and his forearms bulged. His muscles screamed for relief, but he gave none. The guard walked around to the passenger side of the truck and stopped again. Sean watched as the man bent down and picked up a cigarette butt from the rocks. If the guy even twitched to the right, he'd see the former government agent hanging under the truck and shoot him on sight.

Fortunately, the guard straightened up and started back down his path. Sean slowly lowered his body back to the ground. As soon as his tailbone hit dirt, he let go of the chassis and let his head fall. He clenched his fingers over and over again to get the blood flowing normally through his arms.

That was too close, he thought.

He looked back up at the underside of the truck's motor and found what he wanted. These particular military vehicles featured an enormous amount of space between the frame, body walls, and engine. They were designed that way to allow for easy maintenance or repair work.

In his early years, Sean had spent enough time working on Japanese cars to appreciate an open design when he saw one. He'd owned a beat-up Japanese hatchback in high school and soon learned that the cars made over there were designed to last a long time, not be tinkered with by an amateur.

The oil filter was almost impossible to reach without being double jointed, and switching out spark plugs was equally as challenging.

This truck, however, had tons of space to work. The only problem was Sean didn't have a lot of time.

He reached into his pocket and pulled out the wire cutters he'd taken from the helicopter tool kit. Finding the battery from the underside of the truck was difficult, but thanks to the open motor setup, Sean managed to locate it quickly above his head and to the right.

Next, he traced the wires running to the distributor, spark plugs, and other areas of the motor until he found the ones he needed. The transponder only needed a little juice, which meant the lines running to the truck's headlights would be perfect. The only problem with that was that the lights would have to be turned on for it to work. That meant tracking the vehicle at night was the only option since older trucks didn't have automatic daytime running lights. Of course, some people turned their lights on in the day as a safety precaution, so it was possible he could get lucky. Sean knew the device wouldn't provide any resistance to the current so there would be no dimming effect to the beams that might draw suspicion.

He took a quick look out from under the passenger side to make sure the other guard hadn't returned yet and then shoved the wire cutters up into the array of lines and hoses. Carefully, he pinched his chosen wire with the two blades and then pulled it toward the truck's rear. Squeeze the cutters too hard, and the wire would be severed. If that happened, the truck's headlight would go out, and then there could be trouble. A driver would notice that, and if he didn't one of the other men in Dufort's little army certainly would.

Sean pulled the wire coating back an inch or two and then opened the cutters once more. He set them on the ground next to his waist and set to work on the next part of his plan. He tugged his shirt up with both hands, exposing the makeshift device, and then pulled on the tape keeping it to his skin.

He grimaced as the adhesive tugged on his chest hairs. He had to bite his lip to keep from making a noise. The process seemed to take forever, probably because of the agonizing pain each tug put into his skin. Finally, he held the transponder up to a crossbeam on the chassis and wrapped the excess tape around the metal several times until it was used up.

Then he took another glance out to his left and noted the first guard would be coming back around again soon. Sean knew he was running out of time. Not only that, but the longer he stuck around, the greater his chances were of being caught.

Sean grabbed the wire he'd prepped on the transponder the night before and wrapped the bare copper around the newly exposed section running to the headlights. Then he used his fingers to pull the insulation back as close as possible to where he'd cut it.

Next, he tore a piece of tape off the device and used it to wrap where he'd attached the two wires. He reached up and grabbed the homing beacon and gave it as hard a shake as he could without making the entire truck gyrate.

Satisfied the device was as secure as he could make it, Sean rolled out from under the truck and made his way to the rear. He stopped, looked around the back, and then sidestepped to the back-right taillight.

He removed the weapon from his belt and held it down at his side, just in case. He leaned around the back corner of the truck and saw the first guard step behind the tent. Now was his chance.

Sean took off at a dead sprint toward the rock formation about twenty-five yards away. It would be close, and acceleration had never been Sean's strong point. He reached the edge of the rock wall just as the guard stepped out from the other side of the tent. Sean skidded around the corner and disappeared from sight before the guy could turn and see him.

Sean's chest rose and fell rapidly as he gasped for breath. He wiped his forearm across his head and took a second to let his breathing calm down. Then he had a terrible epiphany. He checked one pocket and then the other. It wasn't there.

He twisted his body enough to be able to see back to the truck he'd been under and caught a glimpse of what he was missing.

The wire cutters were lying on the ground underneath the chassis.

Idiot, he thought. *How could you be so careless?*

Sean ducked back behind the rock to avoid being spotted. If he left the tool there under the truck, one of Dufort's men could find it. If he ran back to retrieve the thing, he could be spotted, and he'd already pushed the envelope with that.

He snorted angrily and peeked around the rock once more. The guard strolled aimlessly along his path like he'd done at least a dozen times already. Then, inexplicably, he stopped right in front of the truck with the transponder. For a second Sean wondered if the guy had seen the tool. If so, Sean would have no choice. He'd have to rush the guard and take him out. Doing so would mean Dufort would notice one of his men missing or dead.

A plan formed in Sean's mind. He'd make it look like an accident. His eyes flashed around, desperate for a device that would make the plan work.

Then he saw the guard reach into a shirt pocket and pull out a pack of cigarettes. Sean sighed. The guy was just stopping for a smoke.

The guard put the cigarette to his lips and reached into his pocket, fishing out a lighter. He cupped his hands and started to light it when the cigarette suddenly slipped out of his hands and fell to the ground.

Irritated, the guard bent down and grabbed the cigarette. Sean's heart stopped. The guy was almost at eye level with the tool. All he had to do was turn his head to the side and he'd see it. Then things would hit the fan.

Sean gripped his gun and readied himself to charge. He started regretting the complicated plan of tracking Dufort's movement. Maybe they should have just rushed in with guns blazing. Perhaps a night mission several hours before would have been a better option.

Just as he pushed aside his regrets and second guessing, he heard some shouting from beyond the other side of the camp. A moment later several men ran into the area, waving their hands around in a circle. Sean ducked back behind the rock and listened closely.

The shouting voices were saying something about packing up and leaving. Sean risked one last look around the big rock and saw the guard he'd been watching trotting away from the truck.

He hadn't seen Sean's handiwork.

Sean let out a relieved sigh and let the back of his head rest against the stone for a second. Then he perked up and sprinted toward the plateau where the helicopter waited.

The game was on.

Chapter 26

ASWAN, EGYPT

Dufort took a long sip of water. The cool liquid washed over his tongue and soothed his parched throat.

He hated the desert. He came from a region in France that was much cooler, much greener, and much more humid than the hot, sandy climate the Sahara offered. Fortunately, Aswan was an oasis town, a place where wasteland was temporarily interrupted by a thin patch of trees, grass, and life. And it all came from the Nile River —the lifeblood of a nation for thousands of years.

He set the clean glass down and stared at his computer screen.

Dufort and his men had driven all afternoon and into the night to reach Aswan. As soon as the caravan arrived, he'd dismissed his men to their own rooms in a resort he doubted many of them could afford with their usual salaries.

While he was the only one with a room to himself, he made sure the men were comfortable. After all, they were going to be in for a long day tomorrow.

He knew one of the men would be outside his door all night. They'd go in rotations of two hours each to stand guard, and so his mind was at ease.

He was even more relaxed because there'd been no sign of Sean

Wyatt since leaving Libya. Dare he hope the American had met his demise at the hands of Libyan nationalists or perhaps a group of zealous rebels?

It was certainly possible.

Wherever Wyatt might be, it was becoming increasingly apparent that the troublemaker wouldn't be bothering Dufort any longer. Worst-case scenario: Wyatt's friends were dead in the prison outside of Tripoli, which tilted the odds more in Dufort's favor.

That caused another fanciful thought to pop into Dufort's mind. Maybe Wyatt risked a daring prison break to save his friends and was killed in the process. Would he be so bold, so foolhardy? It was certainly in the American's MO.

Dufort's lips parted slightly at the thought. He imagined Wyatt rushing into the prison with guns blazing, being cut down by dozens of bullets before he even reached the front steps.

Maybe he didn't need the insurance policy in the other room after all. If Wyatt and his friends were dead, it would make sense to cut the dead weight.

Finding the woman was easy enough. Dufort's team in the United States knew exactly where to look. Getting her, on the other hand, was considerably more difficult. It was nothing his men couldn't handle. After all, they were some of the best in the world. The woman, though, was also well trained.

His team leader had received a broken nose as a result of underestimating the target. Once that happened, the rest of his team took her down in a less-than-gentle manner. At least that's what Dufort was told. The girl had a few nicks and bruises to corroborate the story.

He snapped his head around to rid his mind of the wandering thoughts. He needed to focus.

He stared down at the tablets laid out on the desk to his left. He'd separated the medallions from the sacred stones, keeping them in different rooms to eliminate the odd vibrations and noises the things were emanating.

Dufort had to admit he'd never seen anything quite like it in his life. And he'd seen some strange stuff.

The way the amulets interacted, however, was like looking into the face of the supernatural, a higher level of science that only the divine could understand. He snorted a short laugh.

Science, he thought. *Humanity knows nothing about the real power of the universe.*

His eyes scanned the page on the screen, but he didn't find what he was looking for, not even a scrap of useful information.

He clicked the back button and then clicked on another link in the search query he'd performed almost forty-five minutes ago. He read through paragraphs, zoomed in on images, and made a few mental notes. Still, nothing that related to his search.

Dufort leaned back in his chair and ran his fingers through his hair, pulling on it at the end to force his weary eyes to remain open. He glanced over at the clock and noted the time. It was almost 1:30 in the morning. He'd have to sleep soon, although he knew that if he didn't solve the riddle of the tablets, they'd be stuck in Aswan for another day—or longer, depending on how much time it took him to figure it out.

He shook his head and clicked the back button again. This time, he did it twice, returning to the search engine.

"What is the secret?" he asked himself. "What am I missing?"

He glanced down at his notepad. Few people could read his scribbling, but he knew exactly what it said. It was the riddle from the third amulet.

"To the east where kings meet gods," he muttered. "Fine, we're east."

That much was true. Aswan was far to the east of Bardaï, Chad. The problem was that the riddle didn't tell him how far east he was to go in order to find the next part of the clue.

"In the shadow of the pharaoh, the fallen prince sits on his empty throne."

Dufort frowned. His eyebrows knitted together and wrinkled his forehead as he rested his temple in his right palm. "What does it all mean?"

He reached over and took another drink of water. Then he put his fingers back on the keyboard and started typing again.

Fallen prince of Egypt.

He hit the return key and waited for the search results to populate on the screen. Aswan didn't exactly have the fastest internet in the world, but at least they had it. He half expected to hear the nerve-crushing sounds of a dial-up modem echoing through the room.

Ten seconds after entering his search, he had a new page full of links. He scrolled through them and shook his head. All the results were focused on movies, books, and other forms of entertainment. None were what he was looking for.

He sighed and hit the back button again, nearly ready to give up. He'd been at it for hours now and with no success.

His thoughts wandered back to Wyatt and his friends. "How do those two idiots manage to figure this stuff out so easily?" The thought only furthered his anger.

"To the east where kings meet gods in the shadow of the pharaoh, the fallen prince sits on his empty throne."

He said the riddle out loud again to see if it would spark something in his mind—a connection he'd not yet made that would reveal the secret.

"Empty throne?" he whispered. Then he shook his head. He'd already searched for that. It brought up several results in Germany from the fabled Neuschwanstein Schloss, the castle that had inspired fairy tales, movies, and cartoons. He'd been there once in the mountains of Bavaria. Pretty place, epic location, and some of the most inspiring vistas he'd ever seen.

None of that helped him with his current dilemma.

"Shadow of the pharaoh," Dufort said.

When he first read the passage, his immediate thought was that he and his men needed to return to Egypt. That seemed to make the most sense. After all, Egypt was home to the pharaohs.

Another thought occurred to Dufort, and he raised his head from his hand. What if the riddle wasn't referring to Egypt? What if the shadow of the pharaoh had a different meaning altogether?

To get a clearer answer, he had to erase any preconceived ideas about his original idea. He stood up and paced around the room with his hands on his hips. It still wasn't coming. Then he walked over to the balcony door and swung it open. The warm night air washed over him, and he took a deep breath. He looked out over the town.

There were a few streetlights lining the sidewalks, a night-light on in an occasional apartment or house. A dog barked in the distance, probably at a cat or another small animal. To the southwest, the desert sprang up from the river and rolled to the horizon where the stars met sand dunes.

Dufort sighed, and he rested his hands on the guardrail. Out beyond the limits of his vision was the nation of Sudan. It was a wretched place, full of crime, disease, murder, and filth. As much as Dufort craved power, he couldn't understand the mindset of the warlords who decimated that poor nation. What were they trying to prove? He assumed it was about proving something since Sudan didn't possess a litany of resources. The land was mostly useless wilderness.

Sudan had been in the news more and more over the years as Hollywood actors and celebrities from the music business did their best to bring awareness to the refugee crisis centering around the African nation.

No government would intervene. Why would they? There was no profit in it for them.

Dufort had seen nations like the United States rally its allies to go in and rescue people of countries with vast oil reserves. Sure, they'd assist other countries if they didn't have oil, but it was always for some other reason—something under the table that none of the mainstream media knew about.

Then it hit him like a brick to the face.

"Sudan," Dufort said with renewed energy. He could feel his pulse quicken as he was hit with a sudden rush of excitement.

He turned around and hurried back to his laptop. His fingers flew across the keyboard until he'd entered the search query. Once more, he waited a long ten seconds until the internet connected him to a page of results. This time, he found several new things he'd not seen before. All of them contained information he thought might be useful.

Dufort ran his finger down the screen, keeping it a centimeter away so he didn't smudge the surface. On the fourth result, he noted something of interest and clicked the link.

Another lengthy ten seconds later, a new page displayed on the monitor. He read through the first few paragraphs and then hit the back button. Then he clicked the images tab and waited until the screen brought up dozens and dozens of pictures. Most of them were of ancient ruins. There were sharply angled pyramids like he'd never seen before. The odd-looking structures were narrow and featured steep sides. They were also much smaller than the pyramids in Giza. These pyramids almost appeared to be scale models of their larger cousins in north Egypt.

Dufort clicked one of the images to enlarge it. "Fascinating," he said.

He returned to the previous page and read further.

Sudan was home to ancient ruins that Dufort had never heard of before. The Kingdom of Kush had apparently been a thriving nation right about the same time as Egypt was also growing.

According to historians, the ancient Sudanese people emulated the Egyptians in many ways, including with their construction of pyramids similar to the ones found in Giza. While the structures in the nation to the south were much smaller, they did possess some unique qualities aside from the steeper design. The Kushites created elaborate entryways into their pyramids—perhaps as an artistic differentiator or possibly because of religious reasons.

He shook his head to refocus.

The area that kept popping up in the images and text was an ancient city called Meroë . According to the website, Meroë was the capital of ancient Kush. Their proximity to the Nile made irrigation possible as well as trade and travel with the larger kingdom to the north.

Dufort's eyes widened as he continued reading. He clicked on another image and zoomed in on it—a picture of what was believed to be the ruins of a palace dating back to the time of the first Egyptian kingdom.

"Fascinating," he said again.

He continued scrolling through the images, occasionally stopping on one that looked interesting before moving on to the next. He had no idea the Kushites built so many pyramids, temples, and other advanced structures. Outside of ancient Egypt, Babylon, Greece, Persia, and Rome, he wasn't aware of older civilizations in that period of time that constructed such things.

Some of the Kushite buildings were better preserved than the ones in Egypt.

Dufort moved his fingers along the mouse pad until he saw an image unlike the others on the page. He leaned in closer to the computer monitor to get a better look. The picture was of a giant statue sitting on a throne. The figure was dressed much like a pharaoh, with a few minor differences. Clearly, the smaller culture mirrored the larger in many ways. There was a second sculpture on the right, but it was different than the one on the left.

It featured a massive stone seat with a crumbled statue sitting in it.

"Who are you?" Dufort asked as he clicked on the image.

The link took him to another website that featured information on the ancient Sudanese civilizations close to the border of Egypt.

The picture was displayed prominently at the top of the page, which allowed Dufort to get a better view of all the details. After reading the caption, Dufort's eyes widened.

He read the paragraph just below the image. His heart raced.

The two giant stone figures were Kushite royalty—brothers whose rivalry resulted in the shame of one and the elevation of the other.

Dufort read more. He learned that the man on the left was the older of the two. By birthright, the throne was to be his and he would be made the king of the empire. The one on the right—what was left of him—was the younger brother who had ambitions to be king.

According to the historian's comments on the blog, the younger brother tried to take the crown forcibly from his brother—an action that turned out badly for the young sibling.

Knowing he couldn't trust his younger brother, the king had him banished from the empire and sent him into exile where he died some years later. Because of his disloyalty, the king tried to erase all memory of his brother from Kushite history.

The king had his brother's face removed from engravings, temples, and chronicles. The sculpture was essentially destroyed, leaving nothing but a pair of legs and part of a torso for visitors to see.

It was a huge statement by the king. Anyone who tried to undermine his rule would not only be punished, they would be wiped from the face of the earth.

Dufort didn't care about the brotherly squabble or the king's desire to intimidate anyone who got in his way. What he cared about was the context of the story in relation to his own quandary.

The Kushite prince had been removed from his throne but was still sitting atop it. It lined up perfectly with the riddle.

"Shadow of the pharaoh. East where kings meet gods," he said. That last part was still a bit strange. Then he remembered what he'd learned about pyramids. Many archaeologists and Egyptologists believed that the pyramids weren't tombs but gateways to the afterlife. If that was the case, pyramids were a place where kings met the gods. Dufort recalled something he'd learned long ago from Egyptian lore, about how when a king died they had to be judged before they were allowed into the afterlife.

"Who better to judge a king than a god," Dufort muttered. "This has to be the place."

He closed his laptop and stretched his arms. Another look at the clock told him he needed to get some rest.

Rest? How could he rest? He was energized with adrenaline. He'd figured out the riddle! He needed to get his men ready.

Dufort fought to calm himself down. He needed to sleep. His men needed sleep, too. What was the hurry? He'd waited this long for eternal life. He could wait a little more.

First thing in the morning he would call Cody and tell him about their next destination.

That thought brought up a new issue. Getting into Sudan might not be an issue, but getting out certainly could be. He'd have to make sure they were prepared for any contingency before making the journey south to Meroë .

Chapter 27

ASWAN

"What are they doing?" Hank asked.

Sean and Tommy watched from their perch on a balcony of a cheap hotel a few blocks away. They had the perfect view of Dufort's trucks in a parking lot down below the hotel where the Frenchman stayed the night before.

The Americans had tracked Dufort all the way across the Egyptian border thanks to the help of Emily Starks back in Atlanta.

Luckily for Sean and company, the closest big city to where they'd been in Chad happened to be Aswan. There were a few in the other directions, to the west in Niger and Nigeria, and back to the north in Libya.

The latter wasn't an option, and Sean didn't care to return to Libya any time in the near future.

As to the other options, he and his companions watched as Dufort's convoy headed east after leaving Bardaï. So, going the same direction was an easy decision. That meant Aswan was where Sean would call Emily. It hadn't taken her long to track the signal and pinpoint the Frenchman's location.

Dufort's men scurried around on the sidewalk like ants in a rainstorm. They loaded gear, supplies, munitions, everything they thought they would need for the journey.

The question was, where were they going? And why would they need so much stuff?

Unfortunately, there was no way for Sean to know. They were going to have to follow their target to the next site. The good news was that based on the furious nature of the load up, Dufort and his men had to know where they were going. That meant the Frenchman figured out the third piece to the puzzle, which was what Sean hoped would happen.

After no contact with Sean and the others for a few days, Dufort probably assumed them all to be dead or at the very least, stuck in a Libyan prison. That's what Sean hoped, but he wasn't going to make any assumptions. That's how things went awry.

"Hello?" Hank said, interrupting Sean's thoughts.

Sean lowered his binoculars and handed them to Hank. "See for yourself."

Hank frowned as he peered through the lenses. "Yeah, I can see they're in a big hurry to get somewhere. That still doesn't answer my question."

"Doesn't it?" Tommy answered for his friend. "You asked what they were doing. Looks like they're packing up and getting ready to go somewhere."

Hank let out an exasperated sigh. "Yeah, okay. Fine, wise guy. I can see what they're doing. *Where* are they going?"

"I guess we'll have to follow them to find out."

Hank lowered the binoculars and looked at the two friends. Adriana was sitting on a deck chair behind them, snickering to herself.

"Obviously," Hank said. "I just don't understand why we don't go over there and take the medallion from them. Or why we didn't do it in the middle of the night."

Sean pulled the magazine out of his weapon and rechecked it to make sure everything was in order. He slid it back into place and then pulled the slide back to chamber a round.

"For one," Sean said, "Dufort has a few more men than he did two days ago. He's brought in reinforcements. That will make things tougher on us if it comes down to a gunfight."

"Okay, yeah. We're outnumbered. So? I thought you were some sort of super spy."

Sean laughed off the notion. "Super? No. Spy? Not anymore. And technically, I was never really a spy."

"You know what I mean."

"If we go down there," Adriana interrupted, "Dufort's men will mow us down in seconds. He would have posted guards last night as well."

"Fine. But wasn't the point of all this to lull him into some kind of false sense of security about you all? I mean, if he thinks all of you are dead, shouldn't that lower the guy's defenses?"

"You'd think," Sean said. "But I'd like to play things safe."

"Besides," Tommy said, "we're always the ones doing all the work. Let him figure out an ancient mystery or two."

"Have you two been drinking? You love this sort of stuff, the ancient riddles and clues and all that."

"True," Sean said. "It's part of why we do what we do."

"Yet you're just going to let that guy head on down the road and find the next relic, risking everything you've worked for?"

Tommy and Sean glanced at each other and then looked at Hank. "Yeah," they said together.

Hank shook his head and rolled his eyes. He handed the binoculars back to Sean. "Okay, fine. What *is* the plan?"

Sid opened the balcony door and stepped out into the fresh warm air.

"Got the vehicles you guys wanted. They're not much to look at, but they'll run. I did a quick check on the motors. Everything seems to be in order."

"Perfect timing, Sid," Adriana said.

"Don't be too excited. The guy who sold 'em to me charged way too much. He wouldn't bend much on price."

"Not a problem," Sean said. "Right, Schultzie?"

"Meh," Tommy muttered.

Despite his wealth, Tommy was frugal about certain things, which was an ironic characteristic in someone with a private jet.

"Let's load up and hit the road," Sean said.

Tommy and Sean stood up and walked back inside the building, leaving Hank alone on the balcony wondering what was going on.

After standing on the ledge for another minute, he realized he wasn't going to get the answers he wanted, so he rushed inside and started collecting his things.

Sean pulled Sid out into the hall and closed the door behind them while the others finished getting ready.

"Did you get the device I asked for?" Sean asked.

"Yeah," Sid said. "But why all the secrecy?"

He reached into a vest pocket and pulled out a metal box about the size of a large cell phone. There was a screen on it with a map and a blinking red dot. He put it in Sean's palm and looked up and down the hall.

"Let's just say I'd prefer to keep this between the two of us. Okay?"

"Sure thing. I found the signal from your transponder and programmed it in, so now anywhere they go, we'll be able to track 'em."

"Perfect."

"That thing was actually easier to get than the trucks." Sid pointed at the device. "You wouldn't believe the military-grade stuff you can get around here."

"Oh yeah?"

"Loads of Cold War-era stuff. It's not as good as the current technology, but it gets the job done for what we're doing."

"This Russian made?"

"Saudi," Sid said. "Little better quality. I know a guy here in town who owed me a favor. He made a few calls." Sid waited for a moment as Sean inspected the device. He leaned in a little closer. "You're welcome."

Sean nodded and then tucked the device into his back pocket. "Thanks, Sid. Big time."

The door opened and the others came out into the hall.

"You two done with your little moment?" Tommy asked.

"Yep. Just wanted to give him a little kiss goodbye."

Hank frowned, standing in the doorway. "Sid's not coming with us?"

"No can do, amigo," Sid answered. "I've got some stuff coming into port near Dubai. Can't miss that one. Too much money involved."

"I'll compensate you for the trucks," Tommy said.

"I know you will." Sid grinned. "And if not, I know where to find you." He winked and then turned to walk away.

"Thanks for all your help, Sid," Sean said.

The smuggler waved without turning back around and disappeared at the next corner.

"Just like that, he's leaving?" Hank asked.

"The man's got a business to run, Hank," Sean said. "Come on. We gotta catch our rides."

Bewildered, Hank followed the rest of the group down the hall toward the stairs. He was going to ask why they weren't taking the elevator but decided to leave it alone.

The stairwell of the old hotel put the four out on the ground floor in the back of the building. Tommy pushed through a creaky door and stepped out into the bright sunlight. He slid on some sunglasses and held the door for the others as they exited.

The door slammed shut behind him, and everyone stared at the two SUVs parked by the door.

The vehicles were Toyotas from the 1970s. There were a few rust spots on the doors and hoods of the beige paint, but the tires looked like they were in good condition.

"Awesome," Sean said. "I always wanted to buy one of these and restore it." He ran his hand along the hood until his fingers reached the grill. Then he slapped the metal.

Tommy opened the driver's door to the nearest SUV and tossed his bag in. "Dibs on this one," he said. "Hank, why don't you ride with me?"

Hank was still standing by the door, staring in disbelief at the two beat-up vehicles. "Are we really riding in these?"

"Come on, Hank," Sean said as he stepped to the other SUV and tossed his gear into the back. "Where's your sense of adventure?"

"Being stuck out in the middle of the desert with no form of communication to civilization doesn't sound like adventure to me. It sounds like insanity."

"Funny how often those two get confused."

"Suit yourself," Tommy said. "Sure would hate to see you miss out on the treasure of Zerzura, though."

Hank cocked his head to the side. He knew what Tommy was doing. Even so, the tactic worked. Nothing could change a person's mind like greed.

"Just hold on a second," Hank said as he flung open the passenger side door. "I'm coming. I'm coming. Doesn't mean I have to like it."

He climbed up into the truck and slammed the door shut. The hinges creaked as it closed, and for half a second he thought the thing might fall off onto the pavement. The door stayed put, though, and Tommy turned the ignition.

The engine protested for a moment as it turned over several times. Finally, it coughed and sputtered to life until it was groaning consistently.

Hank shook his head. "We're going to get stuck out in the middle of the desert. I just know it."

"We'll be fine, Hank," Tommy said. He patted the dashboard. "These machines were made to run forever. That's half the reason so many people buy 'em and rebuild 'em. They can take a beating and keep on running."

In the other truck, Sean revved the motor to life and buckled his seatbelt. When Adriana was in, he passed the device Sid had given him earlier over to her.

"Is this what I think it is?" she asked.

"Yep."

"Sid get this for you?"

Sean nodded. "Yeah."

"I thought you didn't trust him."

Sean shrugged and shifted the SUV into reverse. "He's not so bad. Besides, the device works. Have a look."

She glanced down at the tracker and saw the dot moving along the map. "We'll be able to follow them at a safe distance with this."

"Yep."

"How in the world did he find this thing?"

"I don't like to ask too many questions, hon," Sean said with a wink. "Besides, the thing works, okay?"

She rolled her shoulders and ticked her head to the side. "I'm good with it if you are."

Sean backed the SUV out of the parking space and turned out onto the road with Tommy right behind them.

Ten minutes later, the two-truck caravan was out of the city and heading south into the desert.

Adriana glanced down at the homing beacon every few minutes to make sure they were on track, although there weren't many other side roads or paths for a vehicle to take.

After a half hour, Sean's face scrunched into a scowl. Adriana happened to look over at him and noticed.

"What's wrong?"

Sean clutched the wheel. His fingers squeezed it tight.

He sighed before he spoke. The realization had only hit him a few minutes before.

"Do you know where this road leads?" he asked.

She shook her head. "No. Should I? I mean, we're going south...." Then she had the same epiphany that had caused him so much distress.

"Yeah," Sean said. "They're going into Sudan."

Chapter 28

BORDER OF SUDAN AND EGYPT

"Are you out of your minds?" Hank asked. He nearly yelled the question at Tommy. "Sudan? Do you want to get us all killed?"

"Ideally? No," Tommy quipped.

Hank shifted in his seat, unable to get comfortable. "Great. We're dead. Every one of us is dead."

"We've been in worse places, Hank. Relax."

"Worse places? I doubt it. Don't you watch the news? Do you have any idea what's been going on in Sudan for the last twenty years?"

"One, no, I don't watch the news. Not often, anyway. Two, yes, I have a vague knowledge of the political and social stuff going on there."

"Then you know this is a horrible idea. We can't go in there. We'll stick out like four sore thumbs."

"Dufort doesn't seem worried."

Hank let out a short, frustrated sigh. "Yeah, well, he's crazy, too. Maybe crazier than you all."

Tommy turned his head to the side and looked at Hank with his best deadpan stare. "I can stop and let you out if you want to walk back to Aswan."

The idea was so ridiculous, Hank knew he was kidding. That fact did little to ease his fears.

"We have to be getting close to the border by now. They're not going to let us in the country. And if they do, they'll take our guns. Once that happens, we'll be screwed with a capital S."

Sean's voice came through the walkie talkie sitting between the seats. Sid had picked them up when he grabbed the makeshift tracking device for the transponder.

"Looks like Dufort and his men are taking a smuggler's road," Sean said. "Over."

Up ahead, Sean veered his SUV off the main road. Tommy slowed down and cut to the right to follow. The side road was nothing more than a couple of ruts worn into the dirt and sand. Rolling sand dunes rose on the horizon to the west, now in front of the two-truck caravan.

"Roger that, buddy," Tommy said. "You'd think he'd have done this crossing at night. Way less inconspicuous. Over."

"Yeah, I was thinking the same thing. Then again, you don't know what kind of people you'll meet on this road at night. It's obviously not a tourist thoroughfare. Over."

Tommy chuckled. "No kidding. I bet a lot of drug runners use this road. Over."

"Or human traffickers. Big part of the crisis in Sudan involves refugees being offered safe harbor, and then they're sold into slavery. Over."

"It's a sick world." Tommy decided to change the subject. "How far ahead is Dufort? Over."

"From the looks of it, I'd say just under two miles. Adriana is keeping an eye on him. He won't get too far away. I wonder how he knew about this little detour. Over."

"Who knows? Seems like that guy has connections all over the world. Maybe he has them here. Over."

"Could be. Over."

The conversation fell silent as Tommy followed Sean around a dusty field of dead brush, rocks, and sand that seemed to stretch out forever. The road curved to the south and continued toward the border between Egypt and Sudan.

"Don't you think the Sudanese border patrol will see all the dust we're kicking up? Over." Tommy was concerned about the issue. They weren't far from the border now, and watchful eyes could see the dust from their tires kicking into the air for a good distance.

"Yeah," Sean said. "I thought about that, but I can't see Dufort's dust, so maybe we're okay. Besides, from what I understand, it's going to be more of an issue when we try to get out as opposed to getting in. No one's trying to get in. Over."

Tommy shook his head. "Then why the detour? We could just drive right through. Over."

"Probably better safe than sorry," Sean said. "And besides, they'd take all our weapons. Plus, I don't like the idea of Adriana going through a security checkpoint. Over."

Tommy had thought of the weapons confiscation, but hadn't even considered anything happening to Adriana. He grinned as he thought about her turning to Sean in the SUV ahead and telling him she could handle herself.

"I'd feel bad for them if they tried anything with her. Over."

Sean laughed into the walkie talkie. "Me, too. Over."

Up ahead, a rock formation jutted out of the flatlands. It was one of the only things that looked like a mountain in the area.

"According to the map," Sean said into the radio, "we go around that big rock, and the border will be just beyond it. Over."

"Roger that. Lead the way, Bandit. Over."

Sean laughed again through the radio. "Nice. Does that make you Snowman? Over."

It was Tommy's turn to chuckle. He glanced at Hank to his right. "I'm not hauling a truck full of beer if that's what you're asking. Over."

Hank shook his head and wiped the side of his face with a napkin. "I'm glad you two think this is just fun and games. We could have been killed in that Libyan prison. Now we're going back into another lion's den, and you're cracking jokes about a B movie from the 1980s?"

"B?" Tommy sounded appalled. "B? Are you serious? That movie was a classic."

"Our definitions of classic are widely different," Hank said as he crossed his arms and kept looking nervously out the windshield.

"All I know is all of us growing up in the '80s wanted one of those Trans Ams. That car was awesome."

Hank sighed and shook his head while Tommy started humming the melody to Jerry Reed's "East Bound and Down."

The Americans' convoy rounded the big rock and slowed down once they reached the far side.

"I just don't understand how you two can be so relaxed about things," Hank said, breaking into Tommy's song.

"What do you mean?"

"You almost died! And odds are, you're going to almost die again. Or might actually die. Yet you and Sean don't seem to have a care in the world."

"You sound scared," Tommy said.

"Of course I'm scared!" Hank thundered. "I got out of the intelligence game because I didn't want to have a never-ending string of near-death experiences with bad guys trying to kill me."

"Oh. Well, if it helps you sleep better, I'm scared all the time."

Hank raised an eyebrow, expecting a punch line.

"Sean and I get into all sorts of trouble. Not often, but more often than I'd prefer."

"I doubt that. If you asked me, you two have a death wish. That's why you keep finding yourselves in these spots."

"Honestly," Tommy said, "I would love nothing more than to never have to use a gun again. I'd love to never be in another fight again. I got into this line of work to recover artifacts for people so they could learn more about the past. I didn't start the IAA to run around the globe playing cowboy."

"Yet here we are, chasing down bad guys."

"Sooner or later, Hank, you realize that what you want and what you're meant to do don't always coincide."

"Oh, so that's how you justify it? You tell yourself that no one else can do this sort of thing?"

Tommy shrugged. "I don't see anyone else chasing Dufort right now. Do you?"

"No."

"Here's the thing. We may never really know how many other people like him are out there and how many people like us there were that stopped those bad guys. I have to believe we're not alone. And I'm not talking about spies or people like Sean who worked for agencies. Their job is to put down bad guys like Dufort. Sometimes I wonder if there are others out there who aren't paid to do what we do but do it anyway."

Hank snorted derisively. "I can't imagine anyone out there being as crazy as you two."

"Maybe. I guess we might never know. For now, though, we'll do whatever we can to stop Dufort. If someone else like him comes along with some kind of sinister scheme, we'll deal with that person, too."

Hank grunted and looked out the window to his right. He stared into the flats that seemed to go on forever. Then something caught his eye in the mirror, and he turned around to look out the back.

"Um...Tommy?"

"Yeah?" Tommy looked into the rearview mirror to see what caught Hank's attention.

"Are you guys sure Dufort is in front of us?"

Tommy saw the three light tan pickups rolling down the hill behind them. Once they'd descended the rocky slope, the trucks dipped in and out of the rolling dust cloud behind Tommy's SUV. Even so, he could make out the figures of two men in the truck bed with rifles.

"That's not Dufort," Tommy said.

Hank peered through the back window and saw the pickups closing in. "How do you know?"

"Because Dufort's men had SUVs. Those are pickups. And if he was behind us, Sean would have said something."

Tommy picked up the radio from between his legs and pressed the button. "Sean? We've got trouble. Over."

"What kind of trouble? Over."

"Not sure. But they don't look like they're here to throw us a welcoming party. Over."

Tommy stepped on the gas, pressing his foot to the floor. In front of them, Sean also accelerated.

"You think we can lose them?" Sean asked. "Over."

With their increased speed, the SUVs kicked up more dust than before, and soon the pickups disappeared behind them.

Tommy peered into his mirror. All he could see was the rolling cloud. Suddenly, the first pickup appeared again. No sooner did he see it than the two men in the back started firing their weapons.

"Nope," Tommy said into the radio. "Pretty sure we're not going to outrun them. Over."

"All right," Sean said. "How many we dealing with? Over."

"Three trucks," Tommy said. "Shooters in the back. Looks like AKs."

"Probably bandits," Sean said. "Ironic."

Tommy looked back in the mirror again and saw the men aiming their rifles. The muzzles flashed repeatedly once more.

Instinctively, Tommy ducked down for cover as if his seat and headrest would keep him safe from the deadly barrage.

"Ironic?" Tommy asked. "And you didn't say over. Over."

"Ironic since you called me Bandit," Sean said.

Sean's SUV abruptly jerked to the left and off the road. It jumped a few feet into the air for a second before landing on the parched desert dirt and sand. The wheels turned sharp to the left and the tail end of the SUV swung around, kicking up a small wave of sand.

"What is he doing?" Hank asked.

"Bandit stuff," Tommy said.

Chapter 29

BORDER OF SUDAN AND EGYPT

Sean spun the wheel around to straighten out the SUV and pointed it straight at the three bandit pickups.

The lead truck stayed on Tommy's tail while the one in the middle turned off the road to pursue Sean.

"You want to do the honors?" Sean asked Adriana.

She smirked. "Well, I certainly don't want you trying to drive and shoot at the same time."

She leaned out the window and aimed her weapon at the oncoming truck. The two men standing in the back opened fire. Bullets sprayed wildly all over the place as the men were jostled and bumped around in the rough terrain.

Adriana's eyes were locked on the oncoming truck but also noted the path Sean took. Doing so enabled her to anticipate nearly every bump. She wedged her shoulder against the door frame to keep steady and let her arms act like springs with every dip and swell in the dirt.

Sean kept the hood aimed straight at the oncoming pickup, challenging the other driver to a life-or-death game of chicken.

Adriana squeezed the trigger as the front end dipped down and then up. The round sailed into the desert air, missing the target. She fired again, this time with a more stable base. Still, the round missed.

The two trucks were on a collision course and closing fast.

"Anytime, honey," Sean said. He gripped the wheel tight, ready to jerk it in one direction or the other.

"It's not as easy as it looks!" she shouted back. Her finger tensed again, and she squeezed.

The weapon popped three times in a short burst. Two rounds plunked into the grill of the oncoming pickup. The third went through the windshield. A billow of steam shot up out of the hood. Between the busted radiator and the round narrowly missing the driver, the other guy behind the wheel was spooked enough to give in first.

He yanked the wheel to the right before his gunners could get off another shot. Sean veered his SUV in the opposite direction just as the other truck flew by to his left.

The other driver had been too zealous with his evasive maneuver, and the pickup's tires sank into the ground. A second later, the truck was airborne—flipping side over side through the air.

One of the gunmen was thrown clear into the desert sand. The other wasn't so fortunate. The truck hit the ground on its top and crushed him instantly before rolling three more times until it came to a stop on its side.

Sean didn't turn around to look back. He saw the crash happen in his rearview mirror.

Adriana climbed back into her seat and looked ahead and to her left at the remaining two pickups chasing Tommy.

"Nice shooting," Sean said as he hit the gas pedal again.

The SUV lurched forward even faster.

"Thanks for giving me a hard time about it," she said with a devilish grin.

She pulled out the magazine and shoved five new rounds into it before pushing it back in the pistol grip.

Sean fishtailed the SUV around and stomped the gas pedal. The other two pickups had closed the gap between themselves and

Tommy. The lead truck's gunners were emptying their magazines at Tommy's SUV. It was only a matter of time until one of the wild bullets found its way to the target.

Sean guided his ride back onto the old road and into line with the chase. Now he and Adriana were tucked in behind the second pickup. Dust from the other three vehicles enveloped the last vehicle in line, making it almost impossible to see.

"I can't get a good line of sight like this," Adriana said.

"Yeah," Sean said. He spat out a mouthful of gritty dust. "I can barely see anything." He glanced out his window. The land next to the dirt road was mostly flat. While he couldn't determine how long that flat stretch lasted, it was worth chancing it.

"I'm gonna pull up next to them," he said. "That will give you a better angle and a clean line of sight. Take out the gunmen first."

"Check," she said.

Sean veered the SUV off the road. It bounced up over a ridge lining the old path, but once he was off on the side, it smoothed out and almost felt better than the road. The SUV accelerated, drawing ever closer to the second pickup.

"They'll have a clear line of sight, too, once we're next to them," Sean warned.

Adriana didn't need to be told. She knew to be careful, but he couldn't help it. He wasn't overprotective. He just didn't want anything to happen to her.

Then again, she kind of lived for this sort of thing.

Adriana leaned out her window, leading with the pistol as Sean pulled up next to the other truck. It only took a second for the men in the truck bed to realize what was happening.

Adriana fired, squeezing the trigger rapidly. The muzzle popped repeatedly as she peppered the enemy. The gunmen turned to fire, but their reactions were too late. At such a close range—even at high speed—Adriana wasn't going to miss. The deadly barrage ripped through legs, arms, and vital organs in seconds, dropping both gunmen immediately. The second guy's weapon fired wildly into the air as he dropped to his knees and then fell over. The closer shooter wavered for a moment and then toppled over the edge onto the road. His body tumbled in the dust for a second and then stopped.

The truck's driver saw what was going on—albeit too late for his comrades—and yanked his steering wheel to the left. His plan was to knock Sean off course or maybe spin him out, but the guy didn't consider the road's lip. Hitting it at that angle and at that speed turned physics against him. Before the enemy made his move, Sean saw the guy turn his head to the left. He saw the look in the other driver's eyes and knew what he was going to do.

Sean slammed on the brakes as the man veered left and hit the hump. Time slowed down. The pickup virtually floated for a what seemed like an eternity. Then it hit the ground at a bad angle. The other driver panicked and tried to over correct, but it was too late. The front wheels caught with most of the truck's weight already going down and forward. The vehicle flipped end over end, corner over corner, sending dirt and debris twenty feet into the air.

Sean stepped on the gas again and wove past the wreckage. He glanced back and glimpsed the pickup on its top, smoke roiling out of the hood.

Up ahead, the first truck was still pursuing Tommy and Hank. From the side of the road, Sean could see the gunman firing on his friends. He kept his foot to the floor. Now what had been a smooth patch of land turned rough, with big ruts cutting across the path before them.

The SUV jostled and bounced over the terrain but still closed the gap quickly between the vehicles.

Sean picked up the radio between his legs and hit the button. "Tommy?"

"Yeah. Kind of busy right now."

A bullet smashed through the back window of Tommy's SUV. A moment later, the glass shattered and littered the dirt road with thousands of broken shards.

"Let them get a little closer, and then slam on your brakes."

"What? We'll be sitting ducks."

"I know. We'll draw their fire. Just do it."

"Okay, Sean."

Sean set the radio back down into the seat and looked at Adriana. He pulled out his weapon and handed it to her. "Here," he said. "This one's full."

She took the gun and poked it out the window. The hot desert air blew through her hair, pulling strands out of her tight ponytail like an industrial-strength blow dryer.

Sean steered the SUV closer to the road until the other truck was only twenty-five feet away.

Adriana opened fire. The bumpy terrain caused her weapon to flail, sending bullets over and under the target, and everywhere in between. A few rounds pounded the side of the pickup. One hit the rear window and immediately drew the gunmen's attention.

They turned their weapons at the second SUV and readied to fire.

"Hitting the brakes," Sean said.

Adriana braced herself as he mashed the brake pedal down.

The gunmen did their best to keep their sights on Sean's vehicle, which took their attention fully from the road ahead.

Sean grabbed his radio and hit the button. "Now, Tommy!" he ordered in a loud voice.

They watched as Tommy hit the brakes. The pickup's driver reacted as fast as he could to the unexpected move and tried to slow down as well, but his reflexes were too slow. He slammed into the back of Tommy's SUV.

The momentum was too much. The shooters in the back were thrown over the top of the pickup's cab. One hit the top of the back door of Tommy's SUV and fell to the ground. The pickup bounced as it rolled over his body. The second gunman flew farther, soaring over the SUV with arms and legs flailing. As luck would have it, the guy hit the top of the SUV and rolled down to the hood. The bandit's rifle flew out of his hands and disappeared into the desert sands. Losing his weapon was momentarily fortuitous. He scrambled to clutch the top edge of the hood near the windshield wipers. His fingers wrapped around the thin metal, holding on as tight as he could.

Tommy frowned and jerked the steering wheel to the left and then back to the right.

The bandit's eyes were wide with fear, but he held on despite his legs whipping from one side to the other as Tommy tried to shake him loose.

Tommy tried again, this time veering right and then left. He hoped changing the pattern would throw his unwanted passenger off, but the man kept holding on.

He was about to turn the wheel again when the pickup behind them rammed into the SUV's rear bumper again.

Tommy and Hank's heads hit the headrests. Tommy instinctively hit the brakes for a second. Metal crunched in the rear, but the sudden slowdown broke the bandit's grip on the hood. The man screamed in terror as he slid forward down the hood.

Tommy stepped on the gas again to get away from the pickup behind him, which helped the bandit on the hood momentarily regain his grip with fingers pressed hard against the smooth metal. The guy's feet dangled over the SUV's grill. He flailed them around until he felt his toes touch the bumper and give him a foothold.

His right hand went back quickly to the folds of his nomadic clothing and pulled out a pistol. He started to aim it at Tommy when the SUV went over a big hole in the road. The bump knocked the bandit loose and sent him into the air for a second. The next moment, his torso struck the front edge of the hood in a jarring blow. He desperately snatched at the air to find something to keep him from going under, but it was too late. Gravity won the battle and pulled him under the SUV. The bandit's driver never saw him until it was too late. Even then it was just a mass of clothing rolling under the right tire, crushing the man instantly.

Sean's SUV bounced over the dead man and stayed close behind the pickup. He eased his vehicle up over the lip on the side of the road and accelerated. The SUV was tilted at an angle with the left tires on the desert plains and the right ones on the road. He pulled closer to the pickup, narrowing the distance between the two vehicles to less than twenty feet. Adriana stuck her weapon out the window and fired. Rounds thumped into the truck's tailgate. One found its way through the back window.

Spooked by the sudden gunfire, the driver whipped the wheel to the right. He almost went up over the lip like the other pickup, but he skillfully corrected and brought the truck under control back on the road.

"Do that one more time," Sean said. He guided the SUV to where his front right quarter panel was almost touching the pickup's back end.

Adriana fired again, but Sean hit a bump. She jostled in the seat as she fired. The bullet sailed harmlessly into the desert air.

The other driver repeated his same evasive maneuver as before. This time, however, Sean pulled the SUV back onto the road. When the other driver tried to merge back into the center, Sean was waiting. He flipped the wheel to the right just enough to strike the back end of the pickup. At that speed, it didn't take much. The other driver felt the truck bed turning out of control. He attempted to correct the motion, but there was nothing he could do. Once the pickup was sideways, it was all over.

The truck's tires dug into the dirt and flipped the vehicle in a violent crash. Dirt and sand flew into the air along with chunks of metal, plastic, and glass.

Sean slowed his ride down and eased it back onto the plateau by the road. A second later they zoomed by the wreckage as the truck came to a sudden stop. It landed on its tires, but there was no sign of the driver, who'd most likely been thrown clear of the crash. Even if he'd survived, the pickup was useless now.

Sean pulled his SUV in line with Tommy's, and they kept driving another five minutes.

"I think they're gone," Sean said into the radio. "I don't see anyone else coming. Over."

"Glad to see you're back to using proper radiospeak again," Tommy joked. "Over."

"Sorry," Sean said, realizing he'd been speaking so quickly before he didn't use proper etiquette. "Was just trying to save your neck. Next time I'll worry about formality. Over."

"Thanks for the assist, good buddy." Tommy used his best trucker impersonation. "Looks like they won't be bothering anyone again. Over."

"Roger that. Let's stop up here and make sure our rides are okay. Over."

"Ten-four."

Tommy slowed his SUV to a stop, and Sean eased up behind him. They left the engines running as they hopped out onto the dusty road.

Sean peered into the distance behind them. He could still see smoke billowing into the sky from the second pickup, although he could only find the top of the vehicle now that they'd put some distance between them and the bad guys' destroyed ride. He and Adriana walked around the SUV, checking it for any damage that might keep them from continuing.

Tommy and Hank did the same, and then the four met between the two vehicles.

"You guys are out of your minds," Hank said. "And you might be the two luckiest idiots I've ever met in my life."

"Better lucky than good," Sean said.

Hank shook his head. "Maybe. But eventually your luck is going to run out. I'd prefer not to be there when that happens."

"You're welcome," Sean quipped.

"Speaking of luck," Adriana said, pointing off to the left. "Looks like we just crossed the border."

A hundred feet away, a black-and-white-striped pole stuck out of the ground with a matching triangle sitting atop. The Arabic words for Egypt and Sudan were painted on it in black lettering and divided by a solid black line representing the border.

"Huh," Sean said. He looked at Hank and slapped him on the back. "Welcome to Sudan."

Chapter 30

MEROE, SUDAN

Dufort stood with his hands on his hips. He did his best to be patient while one of his men chatted with the translator. The Frenchman could read Arabic better than he could speak or write it, so it helped to have a man in his group that had spent a good amount of time as an interpreter for the military.

He turned his head and looked over the dirty, weary faces of the men on his team. They'd been well compensated for their work. Some had been lost along the journey—a fact that didn't sadden Dufort as much as it irritated him. He'd replaced the men who died, at least for the most part. Now he had a squad of eight working for him, not including the local expert who was speaking to his translator.

It hadn't been difficult to find the local historian. He was Egyptian but had been working on the site at Meroë for nearly two years and living in a temporary camp close by.

Dufort couldn't imagine living in a camp for more than a few days, much less years. There was no questioning the man's commitment—or his insanity. Dufort had once heard someone say how those two words were often confused with one another.

The man's name was Raj. He was older with a chubby, wrinkled face, gray hair, and dark brown eyes set in sockets that were deeper than most.

"He says the place you're looking for is just beyond those pyramids over there," Cody said after talking to the translator.

Raj smiled and nodded. He was being surprisingly friendly and unafraid for being surrounded by men carrying automatic weapons. Then again, it was Sudan. Being accustomed to that sort of thing was probably a necessity.

"Tell him to lead the way," Dufort shouted over to his interpreter.

The man immediately started talking to Raj again, relaying his employer's request.

"Be sure to tell him he will be well paid for his assistance," Dufort said.

The translator nodded and continued talking to the guy. When he finished, Raj gave another naive nod and motioned for the others to follow.

He led the way up a narrow path that wound its way between tall, skinny pyramids, columns with statues, and eventually, a building that looked like it had once been a place of worship for the ancient people who lived in the area.

Raj turned at the end of a row of pyramids and continued walking until they reached another structure.

It reminded Dufort of Greek and Roman buildings from antiquity. Its tall pillars propped up a giant stone slab that ran from one end to the other. Some of the walls were still intact, though, unlike many of the ruins from other ancient cultures. This building was constructed against a natural rock formation that rose up another thirty feet over where the roof would have been thousands of years before.

Raj motioned for them to go ahead through the entrance and spoke to the translator while the others crossed the threshold onto the smooth stone floors.

"He says this was the palace for the kings of Kush," the translator said to Dufort.

"Excellent."

"He also said that the throne room we're looking for is in the back. He claims the people who built this place used a lot of Egyptian influence for their designs and architecture."

Dufort didn't care about the last little fact his interpreter threw in. He wasn't there to study ancient Kushite architecture. He was there to get the final piece to unlocking the greatest treasure in the history of mankind.

He turned to one of his men and ordered him and another to stay behind at the entrance to make sure no one else followed them in. The henchman gave a curt nod and grabbed one of the other guys by the sleeve to keep him back. They stood guard, one on each side of the doorway, while the others proceeded deeper into the palace.

Raj stepped in front of the men and began giving a tour as he would to a group of random tourists visiting from a foreign land. He talked about the different hieroglyphs on the walls and what they meant, along with how they believed the stones for the building came from a faraway land.

Dufort did his best to be patient. He was tempted to put a gun to the man's head and tell him to take the group straight away to the throne room when Raj finally turned a corner through a high arched doorway and led them into a massive chamber.

He pointed at the two thrones with a huge smile as if proud of the stonework.

Dufort stepped forward, staring at the half-destroyed prince's sculpture. "Ask him what happened here," Dufort said to his translator.

The assistant asked Raj the question. After a long-winded answer, the interpreter turned to face Dufort.

"He says that this prince brought shame upon himself and the family. As a result, his face was removed from everywhere it could be seen and the conspirators also tried to take his name out of the kingdom's chronicles."

"Interesting."

Dufort didn't buy it. He understood that what Raj was saying was probably the truth. That wasn't the problem. The real issue was that their guide most likely didn't know the entire story. The Frenchman realized that with the fourth medallion here in this very room, it was highly probable that people had been searching for it. Maybe they weren't specifically looking for the lost amulet and its stone of power, but it could have been treasure hunters who'd heard rumors about the place.

Then again, he may have been reading too much into it. One thing Dufort had learned in life was that things were hardly ever what they seemed.

He gave a nod to Cody, who set his gear bag down on the floor. The other men carrying cases and duffel bags full of equipment did the same, placing their stuff on the ground. They began pulling out tripods, lights, shovels, picks, mattocks, and other tools.

Raj suddenly looked concerned. He asked the translator a question that was relayed to Dufort.

"He wants to know what we're doing. He said this site can only be disturbed with a permit."

"Permit?" Dufort asked. "Really? Is this country even capable of such organization?" He turned to Cody and gave a nod.

Then Dufort turned back to his interpreter. "Tell him I said thank you for his service. I truly appreciate it."

The interpreter gave the message to Raj, who forced a smile as he continued to watch Dufort's men set up their gear. The forced smile disappeared suddenly as Cody stepped up from behind the man, wrapped one forearm around his head and the other around his jaw. Raj didn't even have a chance to struggle. Cody snapped the man's head to the side. A sickening pop came from Raj's neck, and the man dropped to the floor.

"Drag him into the next room," Cody said to two other men who'd finished unloading their gear and were standing by their bags waiting for further instructions.

The men grabbed Raj by the ankles, dragged him carelessly out of the throne room, and disappeared in the next corridor.

"He wouldn't have approved of the next part," Dufort said to Cody.

"Which is?"

Dufort stepped closer to the giant figures and ran his fingers along one of the knees. He tilted his head to the side and examined the stonework. He shifted his feet and moved to the sculpture's back end, scanning the wall and the figure for any sign of a seam.

There wasn't anything unusual, so Dufort returned to the front of the thrones and went around to the other side, repeating the same check he'd done beside the first figure.

Still, he found nothing.

He put his hands on his hips and stared at the carved stone as if by simply looking at it long enough the answers would come.

"What can we do to help, sir?" Cody asked.

Dufort shook his head. "I'm not sure. But it has to be here. I know it." He looked up at the remains of the ceiling but still saw nothing that would help his cause.

"If I were hiding that medallion," he muttered, "where would I put it?"

His gaze drifted down to the floor and stopped on the stone beneath the royals' feet.

He got down on all fours and ran his fingers along the seam between the sculpture and the huge tile. He scooted to the right and lowered his face to the point that his nose almost touched the floor. He examined a thin line between two tiles and noted a few scuff marks on the edge. The blemishes were almost invisible, probably worn down over the ages. Dufort wouldn't have thought anything about the tiny notches except that as he looked at the other pieces of the floor he saw nothing similar. The other stone flooring was flawless.

Dufort returned to the tile in question and asked for a magnifying glass from one of his men. Dufort bent over the seam in the floor and peered through the glass. Sure enough, there were scratches along the edge, a dead giveaway that this tile had been moved after the rest were laid.

"Why would someone move it?" he asked himself, although he felt he already had the answer.

"What was that, sir?" Cody asked.

Dufort stood up and returned the magnifying glass to the man who'd given it to him. "Pull that tile up," he ordered.

Cody frowned but obeyed. He motioned for the other guys to grab their tools and set to work.

At first, they attempted to remove the giant slab with crowbars and wedges, but the seam was so narrow they couldn't get any leverage. Shovel heads fit into the tiny gap, but as soon as the men tried to use them as levers, the metal snapped free from the fiberglass shafts, rendering the tools useless.

Frustrated, Dufort crossed his arms and watched as one of the men tried to use a pick to get the tile to budge free, but the effort— like all the others—was in vain.

Finally, Cody spoke up. "Sir, that thing isn't going to move. We're gonna need to bust it up."

Dufort had been wanting to avoid that option. They'd brought hammers and other tools that could chip away at the stone, but taking such measures would put the medallion at risk. One wrong blow could smash the thing into pieces, potentially rendering it useless.

Still, it didn't seem like they could access whatever lay beneath the heavy tile without breaking it up into pieces.

Dufort gave the go-ahead with a nod, and his men set to work with their sledgehammers and picks.

The work was slow at first. Initially, they were only able to break off small chunks of stone at a time. Once some larger pieces were broken free, however, the work sped up. The men labored tirelessly, rotating in shifts every few minutes to give each other a rest and keep the job moving forward.

After a half hour of intense demolition, one of the men swung his sledgehammer into the tile, and the head sank through into the subfloor beneath. He froze for a second and waited, hoping he hadn't damaged whatever was hidden below.

Dufort took a step forward and stared into the small opening with wide eyes. The henchman pulled out his hammer and peered into the hole.

"It's okay," he said. "I didn't hit anything other than more rock underneath."

Dufort released a relieved sigh. "Carefully now," he said. "Keep chipping away until we find what's under there."

The men did as instructed, swinging their tools with increased caution. The progress sped up with every chunk of tile that was knocked free until they caught sight of something in the hole underneath the floor.

"Stop," Dufort said. "I see something."

He stepped between the men. They parted as he came through. Dufort took a knee next to the new cavity and got down on his elbows to look inside. The darkness of the recession made it hard to see, but there was still enough residual sunlight that he could make out what it was. He reached in and started to grab the box when Cody stopped him.

"Sir, remember what happened at the last place."

Dufort cocked his head to the side and gave his second in command an annoyed *no kidding* glare.

Then he shoved his hand back in and wrapped his fingers around the box. He had to wiggle it back and forth a few times before the object loosened. At last, the thing was freed, and he pulled it out of the hole.

Dufort set the stone box on the floor next to its hiding place and remained on his knees. He stared down at the box's top and the symbol carved into the surface. It looked like a sideways figure eight, but Dufort knew what it stood for. It was the universal symbol of infinity. Or as it applied to his current quest, the emblem represented life eternal.

He slid his fingernails into the seam between the lid and the main part of the container and pried it open. The top came free easier than he expected. He set the lid aside and stared into the open container. The rest of his men shuffled closer and leaned in to get a better view.

The golden medallion shimmered in the diffused sunlight. A purple stone was embedded into the center, just as precious gems had occupied space in the middle of the other pieces.

He reached into the box and retrieved the amulet. For a long moment, he held it in his arms as if the mere act of touching it would break the thing. Then he turned it over and stared at the engraving on the back.

"Cody," Dufort said without looking over his shoulder at his man.

"Yes, sir?"

"Bring me the tablets."

Cody spun around and rushed over to the case containing the two pieces of stone. He opened it and removed the tablets, then took them back to where his employer was still kneeling on the hard surface.

After carefully setting the tablets down next to Dufort, Cody stepped back and watched along with the others.

Dufort placed the amulet's long stem into the final blank space on the tablet they'd yet to decipher.

"Immortality awaits the one who brings the stones together." Dufort frowned. He stared at what was engraved into the golden stem but couldn't understand it. "This can't be right."

"What's the problem?" Cody asked.

Dufort shook his head. "It's just a series of random numbers."

Cody frowned. "What do you mean? It doesn't give a location?"

Dufort didn't answer immediately. "I don't understand. I did everything right. This medallion should give me the exact location of the lost city." His frustration was building in his voice. His breathing quickened, and his face flushed.

"Maybe there's something we're not considering, sir."

Dufort wasn't so convinced. "Everything we know about this riddle, the treasures, says that once we find the four stones the location of Zerzura will be revealed. This reveals nothing!"

"Is that a fact?" a new voice echoed through the chamber.

Dufort's six men spun around, raising their weapons in the process, but they froze before they could squeeze off a shot.

Standing in the doorway was Sean Wyatt and his three companions—all with guns pointed at Dufort and his men.

Chapter 31

MEROE

"I'd ask how you found this place, but I suppose it doesn't really matter. You're here. The how is moot." Dufort tipped his nose up into the air, reinforcing his belief that Sean and the others were beneath him.

"Oh?" Sean said. "Sounds like someone's being a poor sport, eh, Schultzie?"

"Definitely. Talk about a sore loser," Tommy said.

"Now, before we continue this little conversation, Gerard, I'd appreciate it if you'd have your men drop their weapons."

"I'm sure you would, Sean. But we have what you would call a classic stalemate, don't we?"

Sean tilted his head to the side and then stiffened his neck. "Actually, no. See, the second one of your guys makes a move, I'm going to drop him. When another one tries something, he goes next. We have four guns on you, and despite the fact that you have us outnumbered we could take all of you out before you even pulled a trigger."

Dufort inhaled deeply through his nose and then sighed.

"Oh, and your two guys at the door are dead or unconscious. I'll be honest, I didn't really stop to ask if they were still alive. Condolences on your loss."

Sean's words seemed to have little or no impact on Dufort other than to serve as an irritant. Sean could see the guy was trying to decide whether it was worth the gamble to have his men open fire and risk their lives along with his own, but he was giving off the distinct impression that he was going to surrender. It would be foolish to do otherwise.

"Lower your weapons, men," Dufort said.

"That's right," Tommy said, suddenly full of confidence. "Put them on the floor nice and slow."

The mercenaries reluctantly obeyed and put their guns on the stone at their feet.

"All of them," Sean said. "I know how you guys operate. Every single one of you has at least another gun or two on you, not to mention the knives. Why don't you just go ahead and put any and all weapons on the floor for me. Thanks." He said the last word with a heavy frosting of sarcasm.

The men did as instructed, each pulling weapons from different parts of their clothing until there was a fairly significant pile on the floor.

"That all of them?" Sean asked, motioning with his weapon.

"Yeah," Cody said. He was obviously frustrated at having to hand over his weapons.

"Gerard...come on," Sean urged. "I'm sure you've got some kind of weapon on you. What's behind your back?"

Dufort cocked his head to the side and offered a sardonic grin. He reached behind his back and pulled out his .50-caliber Desert Eagle. He held it for a second as if hesitating to cough it up, then set it down on the floor in front of his feet and kicked it forward into the mass of other weapons.

"Whoa," Adriana said. "That's a big pistol. Looks like someone's compensating for something, wouldn't you say, Sean?"

"Hardly a practical weapon, Gerard," Sean said. "Planning on hunting elephants later? I have to say, poaching might be the perfect hobby for someone as vile as yourself."

Dufort said nothing in response, instead simply offering the same crap-eating grin he'd been wearing for the last minute.

"So," Tommy cut in again, "before we interrupted you, it sounded like y'all were having some trouble deciphering the last medallion."

Dufort's eyes narrowed as he fired a glare at Tommy. "I had no problem deciphering the final piece."

"That's not what it sounded like from down the hall. In fact, I heard you. You didn't sound happy. Something about how it didn't make sense and it was just a bunch of numbers?"

"Precisely," Dufort said. "It's a nonsensical list of numbers, nothing more. If you ask me, I'd say this entire operation has been one huge wild goose chase."

"Good thing we didn't ask you," Tommy said. "Would you gents mind stepping aside and letting me take a look?"

Dufort and his men didn't move right away, which caused Tommy to wave his weapon around in a dramatic fashion as he tried to hurry them along.

"Men," Dufort said, "step aside and let our friend Mr. Schultz and his merry band have a closer look."

The men stepped out of the way as did Dufort, stepping to the right to give Tommy a clear path to the tablets on the floor. The medallion was still sitting on top of the tablets, right where Dufort left it just moments ago.

"Keep an eye on 'em, will ya?" Tommy said to Sean.

"Absolutely," Sean said. "And if any of you so much as blinks the wrong way, you're going to die. Understood?"

No one said anything. They didn't need to. Every man in Dufort's operation knew who Sean Wyatt was, along with his capabilities. There were no doubts that he would do what he said.

Tommy stepped forward, keeping a watchful eye on Dufort and his crew until he reached the tablets and nearly kicked them by mistake.

He crouched down and then took a knee to read the passage more closely. It didn't take him long to finish it, and when he did he stood up and turned around. His face looked weary, and there was something in his eyes that told the rest of the people in the room that he was perplexed.

"He's right," Tommy said. "It's just a number...a long, strange number."

Sean walked over to the tablets, keeping his gun trained on the bad guys. He leaned over the tablets and medallion and then looked at Tommy. "You sure it's not something else? Maybe it's a cipher."

Tommy shook his head. "If it was a cipher, there'd be a key, and we haven't found or even heard about anything like that."

"May I have a look?" Adriana asked.

The guys motioned her over, and she crossed the room with a graceful stride. Hank followed, not wanting to be the only one standing by the door.

He stood behind Sean as Adriana knelt over the tablets and translated the inscription.

"Ah," she said. "Very interesting."

"What?" Tommy asked. "What's interesting?"

"Do you remember how I found Coronado's cave outside of Las Vegas?"

"Yeah...."

"Well, the clue that led me to the cave was a sequence of numbers, much like this one. It's not a code. It's the numeric sequence for longitude and latitude. They must have understood it thousands of years ago, which is pretty remarkable."

"So, where is this place?"

Sean and Tommy kept staring down the enemy.

"Well, I don't know right off the top of my head, but if you give me a minute I can probably find it."

She pulled out her phone and tapped on the screen several times. After waiting for nearly a minute, she shook her head.

The entire room waited breathlessly to see what she'd discovered.

"I can't get a signal here," she said, finally. "But those are definitely coordinates. We'll need to get somewhere that has a cell signal or internet connection to pinpoint the exact location."

"How in the world were they able to understand that sort of thing thousands of years ago?" Hank asked from behind Sean and Tommy. "Are you sure that's what those numbers mean?"

Adriana looked up from her phone. "The ancients had greater knowledge about the earth and universe than we do. History teaches us that they were rolling things around on stone wheels and wooden carts. We're taught that all the incredible megalithic structures all over the globe were built by slaves pulling sleds across sand and round sticks. The truth is that they probably had vast technology that we're only now becoming aware of."

"Technology?"

"She's right," Dufort interrupted. "Long ago, the ancients had secrets that many believed came from God himself. Some say they even understood the power of a geometric grid that covers the earth and that's why sacred sites like the pyramids at Giza, the big stone lines at Carnac, Stonehenge, and many others were put where they are. The grid lays out places of great natural energy that we still don't fully understand. It makes perfect sense that these people under-stood how to use something as simple as longitude and latitude."

Tommy turned to Sean. "What should we do with these guys? Tie them up and call the authorities?"

"I wish it were that simple," Sean said with a shake of his head. "Unfortunately, I'm not sure there are any authorities we could trust around here."

"So, just tie them up and leave them? We're not going to kill them...are we?"

"I never kill an unarmed man."

"So, the tying thing?"

"That sounds like a good plan," Dufort interrupted. "Tie us up and leave us here to starve or die of thirst. I'm sure with our friend Raj gone that it would be some time before anyone came around, although you never know. However, I have a better plan."

"This ought to be good," Tommy said and looked across the room at Dufort.

Tommy's smirk disappeared as he felt something stick into his back.

"What the....?"

He started to turn his head around, but Hank stopped him.

"Uh, uh, uh, Tommy. Keep your head forward. "Sean, Adriana, that goes for you two as well."

Sean peeked out of the corner of his eyes. Adriana was already standing sideways in relation to the others and saw Hank holding the weapon against Tommy's lower back.

"Now, if you do anything stupid, I shoot your friend here. As best I can tell, his spinal cord is on the other side of this barrel. So, if I pull the trigger, it will either kill him or—best case scenario—he'll be paralyzed for life."

"I knew you and Sid were up to something," Tommy said through gritted teeth.

"Sid? That simpleton? He's got nothing to do with this."

"So, that's the game, huh, Hank? Working for Dufort? Branching out to a life of working for the bad guy?" Sean sneered.

"Don't be so high and mighty, Sean. For a guy who lost everything, he pays remarkably well. Better than you two. And please, spare me the diatribe about how you and I go way back and all that. I'm tired of playing the game, tired of being a low-level guy in everything I do. Do you have any idea what my government pension will buy? Not much. With what our French friend here has promised, I'll be able to retire and drop off the grid permanently."

"I hope he paid you up front," Sean said.

"Oh, he did, but that's only an appetizer. The treasure from the lost city is the main course."

"Sean," Tommy said. "Kill Dufort. Don't worry about me."

"You know, Tommy, we thought you might say something like that," Hank said. "That's why I suggested to our friend Mr. Dufort that we bring in a little extra insurance so you don't go trying to be a martyr."

He turned his head toward the entrance. "Hey, bring in the girl!" he shouted.

Sean and Tommy frowned. Adriana watched the entryway with

intense curiosity. They didn't have to wait more than a few seconds to see what Hank meant by "insurance policy."

A henchman appeared in the doorway holding a gun to a young woman's head. Her eyes were full of fear. Mascara was streaked down her cheeks from crying, and her normally silky blonde hair was frazzled and shooting off in every direction.

"Tommy," she said. "I'm so sorry." Tears started rolling down her face again.

"June," Tommy said. "Let her go, you animals." He started to take a step toward her, but Hank pressed the gun deeper into his back. "You already have us," Tommy protested. "Let her and Adriana go."

Dufort took a menacing step toward the Americans and shook his head. His arms folded across his chest as he stared into the barrel of Sean's gun. Slowly, he reached out and wrapped his fingers around the weapon.

Sean's finger tensed for a moment as if he might pull the trigger. He knew what that would mean. Tommy would die. And so would June.

"Fine," Sean relented. He let go of the weapon.

Dufort pulled it away from him and pointed the gun at Sean's chest. "You know...you've been a thorn in my side for a long time now, Sean. How many years has it been since you took my empire away from me?"

"Your operation was built on the backs of innocent people. There's no telling how many lives you ruined along the way. And for what? Money? Power?"

Dufort snickered. "Of course for money and power. What else is there?"

"Must be a lonely life."

"I guess you've never been rich. Those two things can buy whatever companionship a person could ever need."

"It can't buy loyalty, friendship, love."

"Pfft," Dufort scoffed. "Really, Sean? I expected more from you than some sentimental clichéd response like that. I disagree with the first, though. If you pay people enough, they'll be loyal."

"I guess."

Dufort motioned to Adriana. "Now, if you and Thomas don't mind, please put those guns on the floor."

They reluctantly obeyed, seeing there was no way out of it.

Hank looked at his watch. "We need to get moving, Gerard. He's stalling."

"Yes, I'm well aware of what Mr. Wyatt likes to do...biding his time until he can catch you in a moment of weakness. The problem here is that he's surrounded and we have three pressure points that he simply couldn't bear to have pushed."

Sean fought hard to keep his breathing as calm as possible. More than anything, he wanted to take a big step forward and punch Dufort in the jaw, drive him to the ground, and beat him until his arms couldn't swing anymore. That fantasy wasn't going to happen. His friends would die. While that was a distinct possibility anyway, it didn't have to happen yet.

"So, what now, Gerard?" Sean asked. "You going to take us out into the middle of the desert to find the lost city for you?"

"You're half-right," Dufort said. "I'm going to take them out to the desert with me. You, however, are staying here."

The muzzle fired. Sean flew back several feet, twisting as he fell onto his chest.

"No!" Tommy shouted and reached out his hand. Hank jammed the gun into his back, keeping Tommy from moving farther.

Adriana screamed. She started to make a move toward Dufort, but Cody stepped in and smashed his elbow into her jaw. Stunned, she fell backward onto the floor. Her eyes blinked rapidly as she tried to get her bearings. Two of Dufort's henchmen grabbed her under her armpits and dragged her out of the room.

"Leave the women alone," Tommy urged. "They have nothing to do with this."

"Ah, but they do, Thomas. They do. You see, if you don't do what I ask you to do, I'll torture them. Sure, eventually I'll give them the mercy of death, but not before I let my men have some fun with them. Feel free to use your imagination."

Tommy's breathing was coming faster than he could control. He glanced down at Sean's lifeless body on the floor. A pool of blood collected under his chest and oozed across the stone. Tommy couldn't cry. He couldn't do anything except feel rage. His arms and legs went numb as he stared at his dead friend.

"Please forgive me if I don't give you time to mourn his death," Dufort said. "But like Hank said, we should probably get going. Not to worry, though, Thomas. You'll be joining him soon enough."

Two more men rushed over to Tommy and bound his hands behind his back. After he and the women were dragged out of the room and his men collected the artifacts, Dufort lingered for another minute. He stared at Sean's body with amusement.

"I have to say, Sean, you really were so predictable. I expected a better effort from you." Dufort looked around the room one last time as if savoring the moment and then disappeared out the door.

Chapter 32

SAHARA DESERT, EGYPT

The chopper kicked up huge clouds of sand and dust on first landing, which forced the vehicle's occupants to wait until the wind died down. Cody shoved Tommy out of the helicopter as the rotors overhead came to a stop.

Tommy lost his balance and fell onto his face. His hands were still tied behind his back. He struggled to stand but a second later felt Cody's grip on his forearms along with one of Dufort's other men. In an instant, he was back on his feet, being held by the two mercenaries.

Dufort approached from a second helicopter on an opposite dune. The Frenchman waded down the slope, kicking up sand with every step until he reached a basin between the two mounds.

His men dragged the two women down the hill to join him and the rest of the group.

"Just one big happy family, eh, Thomas?" Dufort flashed a crooked grin. "The whole gang is here. Well, I suppose there is one notable absence."

Tommy surged forward, but he didn't make it more than a few inches before Dufort's men yanked him back.

"I'll kill you!" Tommy shouted. "You murdered my friend in cold blood. So, you better kill me, too. Because if you don't, I'm going to make you suffer."

Dufort's right eyebrow ticked up a notch. "Well, that's not much motivation for me to keep you alive, now is it?"

The Frenchman turned his attention to Cody. "So, this is the spot the coordinates from the medallion gave us?"

"Yes, sir." Cody kept his thoughts to himself. There was nothing out there, no treasure, no oasis, just an endless sea of sand and a few rock formations a hundred or so feet away.

"I wonder, Thomas," Dufort said, "if you'd be so kind as to help us understand what it is we're to do next."

Tommy sniffled, fighting back tears that begged to push through the dams behind his eyes. He wanted to tell Dufort where to go. More than that, he wanted to break loose the bonds keeping his wrists together and pounce on the Frenchman. Sadly, there was nothing Tommy could do. He resigned himself to the fact that he and the woman he loved were probably going to die out here, along with Adriana.

What would Sean do if he were in my shoes? The question resonated in his mind over and over again. The answer came to Tommy faster than he expected. It wasn't profound. *He'd wait for an opportunity. Just stay alive until one presents itself.*

The one thing he could do to stay alive was the one thing he didn't want to do. He had to help Dufort.

"The riddle on the tablets said that when we're here, we have to take the medallions to four specific points," Tommy said.

"Tommy," Adriana said in a chastising tone. "Don't lead them to the lost city."

"It's okay, Adriana. I have to do this. It's my family's legacy. It's my legacy. If I'm going to die, I want to die finding the thing my parents gave up on so many years ago."

"That's the spirit," Dufort said. "So, where are these four points?"

Tommy narrowed his eyes against the glare of the searing desert sun. He gave a nod. "I'd start with those rock formations over there," he said after careful consideration. "They're the only thing that stands out in this sand ocean."

"Good idea," Dufort said. "Glad to see you're willing to cooperate." He turned to his men and motioned for them to move.

The group trudged through the sand, making their way to the two overhangs. The ledges looked like twins, both sticking out of the sand and pointing at the other. Underneath were the only spots where shade could be found for hundreds of miles in any direction.

Once the group was underneath the ledge on the right, Dufort turned to Tommy again and put his hands out wide. "Okay," he said. "What next?"

"You think I just pull all the answers out of thin air?" Tommy asked. "This sort of thing takes a lot of time. We don't just roll up to a site and immediately figure everything out."

Dufort pulled a pistol out of his belt—the same one he'd used to kill Sean. He pointed it at Tommy's head. "Have you ever done this routine, Thomas? The one where someone tells you to do something and imagine you had to do it with a gun to your head? Good news: You don't have to pretend. What do we do with the medallions? The tablets say a gate will open when the medallions are brought together. Tell me where they go."

"You figured out as much as I did," Tommy said. "So, go ahead and kill me if you want to, because frankly, it's better than listening to you. Besides, if you do shoot me, you won't find anything. Or at least it will take you longer."

Dufort nodded. "Okay, okay. I understand." His French accent grew particularly nasally. "This is the part where I threaten you, you push back, and then I tell you that if you don't do what I say, I'll kill your girlfriend. Then I'll kill the late Sean Wyatt's girlfriend. Then you decide that you couldn't bear to see that happen and choose to help me. There, I just saved us at least three minutes. So, now that we have that settled," his finger tightened on the trigger, "find where we place the medallions."

"I need my hands," Tommy said.

"Fine," Dufort relented. "You have all these eyes and guns on you and your friends." He turned to Hank. "Cut him loose."

Hank sighed. "I don't think that's a good idea, boss."

Hank stepped behind Tommy and produced a knife from his pocket. He cut the rope in a few slices and backed away.

Tommy clenched his fingers, finally feeling the circulation flow through them. He shook his hands a few times to speed up the process.

"I don't pay you for your ideas, Hank," Dufort said. "Now, Thomas, please. The medallions. How do they open the gate?"

Tommy had no idea. He wasn't about to tell Dufort that again. Deep down, he knew that the Frenchman stood just as good a chance of finding the way to open the gate to Zerzura as he did. Maybe Dufort already knew that and his reason behind this whole charade was all part of his ego-driven power trip. It wouldn't be out of character for Dufort to make Tommy do his bidding just for the sake of it.

With a deep breath and a steely resolve, Tommy slowly made his way farther under the overhang, leaving the rest of the group behind. He looked up at the rocky ceiling and traced it to where it ended in a sharp point. Only ten feet across, the other pointy ledge began and recessed back to a nearly identical natural shelter.

Under the overhang was a stone wall, carved out in a sort of half circle. The walls were roughhewn, probably not created by human hands but by thousands of years of nature's work.

He scanned the jagged surfaces in hopes of finding some kind of clue, a drawing, painting, or carving that would tell him what to do next. There was, however, nothing out of the ordinary.

Tommy sighed. They were in the right place. Dufort and his men pinpointed the location the night before, using several different maps online and offline to double and triple check. Tommy had to hand it to Dufort. The guy wasn't going to take any chances. If they were going to commandeer two helicopters and fly out into the middle of the Sahara, they'd better be darn sure that was the place they needed to go.

Yet here he was, standing in the exact location referenced by the tablets and stones with nothing to show for it. Tommy looked back over his shoulder at June and Adriana.

Dufort stood near them and put out his hands wide. "Well?"

Tommy averted his eyes and looked down at the sand. Deliberately, he lowered himself to one knee and pressed his fingers into the gritty earth. He scooped up a handful of sand and let it fall through his fingers until his hand was empty again. He frowned and sighed. "This has to be the place," he muttered. "What am I missing?"

He ran through the script from the tablets once more in his mind. While he didn't have an eidetic memory, he could paraphrase things closely enough to be accurate. "The tablets said that the amulets were to be placed at the four points. Or was it corners?" Tommy whispered to himself to keep Dufort unaware of his uncertainty. Sometimes, he felt like he thought better when he spoke rather than just keeping things inside his head.

He turned and looked over at the edge of the overhang where the wall rose up to the ledge. If there was a point or corner in the area, maybe that was it. He stood up and walked over to the corner where the rock wall came to an end. He knelt down and ran his fingers over the stone. Leaning in closer, he noticed something unusual. It was so small he might have missed it had he not been so near. It was a curve cut into the rock. The indention was no more than an inch long, but it was definitely put there by human hands. It appeared to continue down below where the sand met stone.

Tommy's hopes rose, albeit cautiously, in his chest. He got down on all fours and started sweeping away the loose sand with his hands like a dog digging for a bone. He worked furiously, pulling away the gritty soil until he could make out a little more of the carving in the rock.

"What is it?" Dufort asked, taking a step closer. His mouth was agape as he stared at Tommy while he toiled.

"I don't know," Tommy said between hard breaths. "Something."

The group collectively moved a few feet closer, curious to see what Tommy found.

Tommy kept digging away the sand, realizing that millennia of sandstorms and shifts in the earth's crust must have buried any ancient evidence that would have pointed toward the lost city.

After several minutes, he found himself in a shallow hole staring at a carving in the rock. It was a symbol, much like one he'd seen so many times throughout his life and especially of late. An Egyptian ankh had been cut into the wall with incredible precision.

"Whoever put that there must have been quite the craftsman," Dufort said.

Tommy'd been working so hard he didn't notice the Frenchman walk up behind him to see what he was doing.

"Yes," Tommy said without even a glance over his shoulder. "It's flawless."

"What does it mean?"

"It's an ankh," Tommy answered. "It's an ancient Egyptian symbol for—"

"I know what it means," Dufort interrupted. "I'm not stupid."

Tommy wanted to debate his last point but kept quiet.

"I want to know why it's here and what we do next."

Tommy leaned over again and craned his neck. He stuck out his hand and pulled away a few more scoops of sand. Underneath the base of the ankh was a hole about the size of a nickel.

"Bring me one of the amulets," Tommy said.

Dufort's eyes turned to slits, full of suspicion.

Tommy sensed the man's doubt and turned to face him. "Look, Gerry, you can either trust that I know what I'm doing, which—by the way—you obviously do because you brought me here and set me loose to figure this thing out. Or you can shoot me and my friends and do everything on your own. Now bring me an amulet. The one that has the ankh carved into it."

Dufort sized up the American and then gave a nod. "Cody. Bring me one of the cases with the relic in it, the one with the ankh."

A minute later, Cody rushed to his employer's side and handed him a small metal case.

Dufort noticed Tommy eyeing the case with curiosity.

"It's lead lined," Dufort explained. "We experienced a strange phenomenon when we brought the stones together. To keep that from happening while traveling, we put them in these cases."

Tommy accepted the explanation with a slow nod.

"Set it on the ground," Dufort ordered Cody.

The younger man did so and stepped back away from the case.

"May I?" Tommy asked with heavy layer of sarcasm to his voice.

"Just be sure you don't do something stupid like break it."

Tommy sighed and knelt down by the case. "This was my family's life work, Gerard. Like I said before, if I'm going to die here, I at least want to see it through to the end."

He flipped up the two clasps and cautiously lifted the lid. Inside was the amulet with the symbol that matched the one cut into the wall. Tommy swallowed as he lifted the jewel out of its case and held it in his fingers as delicately as possible.

He pivoted around and faced the wall once more, gazing at the symbol on the rock and the hole just below it. Carefully, he slid back into the shallow hole and held the amulet a few inches away. The gem in the center of the jewelry began to radiate with a bizarre glow. For a second, Tommy was afraid he might be doing something wrong. He'd seen his fair share of strange things, but glowing gems were a rarity.

Tommy let out a long breath and aimed the bottom of the amulet's stem at the hole in the wall. He swallowed again, pushing the lump in his throat down into his chest as the metal tip slid into the stone. The gem glowed brighter until he'd shoved the amulet all the way to its hilt.

The earth trembled beneath their feet, and sand shook from the ledge overhead. Cody's eyes filled with fear, and he stepped farther away from the recess.

Dufort remained stoic. His eyes darted around to make sure he wasn't hit by a falling object, but he was oddly comfortable with the occurrence.

Tommy stood up and faced the Frenchman. "Tell your men to find symbols that match the ones on the amulets. They should be located in corners just like this one. If they don't see them on the walls, tell them to dig. We're dealing with thousands of years' worth of sand that has been blown all over this area. I'm actually a bit surprised I was able to find that one." He motioned with his thumb to the amulet sticking out of the wall. "The others might not be so easy, but they'll be there."

Dufort nodded. He had a triumphant, smug grin on his face.

"Men!" he shouted. "Get the shovels. We have work to do."

The men scattered, some returning to the helicopters, others setting gear bags down on the ground to retrieve their tools. Dufort kept his eyes on Tommy to make sure he didn't try anything.

"See?" Dufort said. "Helping me isn't so bad."

"Yes it is, Dufort. Yes it is."

"Don't worry. You won't have to much longer."

"Good, because if I did I think I'd probably vomit."

The Frenchman shook his head. "Always so dramatic."

"Listen, Gerry," Tommy made sure to say the name with as much disdain as possible. He could tell it got under Dufort's skin. "Just make sure your goons don't damage the artifacts, okay? When we get out of here, and we will get out of here, I want to make sure those things are taken to a lab where they can be studied."

Dufort snorted in derision at Tommy's remark. "Your confidence is admirable, Thomas. I'll give you that. But I assure you that you and your friends will never leave this place."

Chapter 33

SAHARA DESERT, EGYPT

Tommy nodded at Dufort, who in turn gave a nod to the rest of his men positioned at the corners of the rock formations.

Some of his henchmen had been digging for the better part of an hour in search of the symbols carved into the rocks. Tommy was glad he'd started with the easiest one. The mercenaries dug in shifts, stripping away large piles of sand until they located the ancient markers.

Now, three of Dufort's men were kneeling in front of the holes with amulets ready to be inserted. All they needed was his go-ahead. With the nod, the men simultaneously pushed the metal stems into the respective holes.

The earth trembled again, this time more violently than the first. Tommy kept his eyes on June and Adriana. They stood in the shade under the ledge, just ten feet away under the watchful eyes of Dufort's men.

Two of the mercenaries stood in the middle of the basin to keep an eye out—just in case someone happened to stumble upon their little project. It was a one in a million chance that would happen, but Dufort wasn't about to leave anything to chance.

"What's happening?" June asked. The fear in her voice had disappeared, and now all that was left was fierce determination.

Tommy knew Dufort's men were handling venomous snakes when it came to the two women. He'd seen June in action, and while she wasn't as skilled in hand-to-hand combat as Adriana, she could still hold her own. One misstep, and the mercenaries would end up dead.

"I don't know," Tommy said as he shuffled his feet back a few inches, deeper into the shade.

Dufort turned his head and looked out into the basin. "This is it," he said in a booming voice. "The gateway to Zerzura!"

The air suddenly filled with a high-pitched whine. Everyone immediately covered their ears to protect themselves from the painful sound.

The ground continued to shake under their feet. The two men in the middle of the basin looked around, confused as to what was happening. They kept their weapons at their hips, ready to fire if any danger appeared. There was no way they could have anticipated what happened next.

The earth opened up beneath them, and the men vanished in the blink of an eye. Their screams were drowned out by the whine. Dufort watched with wide-eyed wonder as the ground continued to open. A massive hole appeared and kept growing wider and wider until it nearly reached the shelter of the ledge.

Tommy looked up and noticed a strange glowing orb between the two rock points.

Then as suddenly as the bizarre event began, it came to an end. The ground shook no more, and the glowing orb disappeared. Some of the men had crouched low to the ground to gain stability. Others braced themselves against the rocks. Now everyone stood up straight and looked out into the opening in the earth. A warm gust of wind blew through the basin, carrying away the loose dust and debris that lingered after.

"What in the name of—" Cody said.

"The entrance to the lost city," Dufort cut him off.

The Frenchman moved instinctively toward the edge of the giant hole in the ground. He leaned over with only the slightest hint of caution and stared down into the abyss.

He laughed—quietly at first—and then louder.

Tommy risked taking a step forward. "What is it?" he asked.

Dufort turned around and grinned from ear to ear. "Zerzura."

He ordered his men to grab as much rope as they could and tie it to the overhangs above. The mercenaries on both sides of the opening did as instructed, and soon they'd fastened hundreds of feet of rope to the rocks above.

Tommy gazed down into the hole with the two women standing close by. Below, the light of the sun illuminated a narrow river running through a canyon. There were paths about sixty to eighty feet down inside the perimeter of the opening. Dufort's plan was to climb down to the paths and then find their way to the bottom.

Tommy tried to see the bodies of the men who'd fallen in, but there was no trace of them. Based on where they'd been standing, it was likely they fell into the river.

Then another sobering thought hit him. "No way Sean could stand here," he said to the women. "He'd have been terrified."

Neither Adriana nor June said anything.

"Cody," Dufort said from nearby, "have two of your men go down to that first path and make sure everything is safe."

"Yes, sir." Cody shouted orders at one of the men across the way and then relayed the same message to one of the mercenaries standing nearby.

These guys had been hardened soldiers, their steel nerves forged in the fire of intense training and combat. A drop of a few hundred feet to the bottom of a desert canyon wasn't enough to scare them. Most of them had faced more frightening scenarios.

The men worked their way around to the top of the overhangs and began their descent while everyone watched with bated breath. Hand over hand, the men lowered themselves into the giant cavity until they reached the ledges below. The one closest to Dufort landed first. He flipped on the flashlight attached to his weapon and swept the area. The second guy to touch down did the same. After a quick check, they waved up to the rest of the group that it was all clear.

"Tommy?" Dufort said with a glance over his shoulder. "You're next."

Tommy's forearms burned as he lowered his body down into the canyon. He didn't dare look down. Scared of heights or not, this sort of thing would terrify anyone. He knew there was no way he'd have been physically able to perform the task a few years before. He'd been in no condition for something so extreme.

He knew June and Adriana would be fine, barring some kind of freak accident. That possibility lingered in the back of his mind as he neared the path below.

His feet touched down, and he felt a surge of relief course through his body. He swung his arms around to get the tightness out of his tendons and muscles.

"Over here," one of the henchmen said.

Tommy stepped to the side and stole a quick look down to the canyon bottom. They were in a huge room that was probably the span of an American football stadium. He recalled football games he'd attended at the Georgia Dome in Atlanta and figured it was close to the same size.

The river flowing from one end of the cavern-like space to the other was clear as glass. It rippled gently, meandering through the canyon until it reached a dark opening in the shadows on the other side and disappeared through the rock.

"Truly an oasis city in the middle of the desert," Tommy said quietly to himself.

He heard a zipping noise from above and looked up. Adriana leaped out over the edge of the opening and dropped at a frightening pace. Tommy started to make a move to get under her, but one of the guards grabbed him by the shoulder and forced him to stay put.

Adriana fell until she was only ten feet from the landing when she squeezed her gloves and instantly slowed. The rope bobbed for a second under her weight as she gradually lowered herself the final few feet. Once her boots touched the ground, she unhooked a rappelling brake and whipped the rope around to signal she was off.

Tommy looked incredulous. "They gave you a rappelling brake but made me climb down like these guys?"

Adriana shrugged and joined him off to the side while the rest of the group came down the same way she had.

Tommy wanted to stand under June as she slid down the rope at a less aggressive pace than Adriana, but again Dufort's henchmen kept him away. Fortunately, she knew how to operate the mechanism, and after a thirty-second drop she found herself standing on the narrow stone path that spiraled down into the chasm.

What Tommy'd said was true. No way Sean would want to find himself in this situation. It was a small consolation, but Adriana and Tommy needed anything they could find at this point.

When everyone was on the path, Dufort turned to Tommy and waited for instructions.

"What?" Tommy asked, uncertain of what the Frenchman wanted.

"Where do we go next?" Dufort asked. "You're the expert."

Tommy's initial instinct was to slap him with some smart aleck remark or tell him to jump. He knew that wouldn't get him anywhere. The real issue was that Tommy was just as in the dark as everyone else. Getting to the gate was difficult enough. Once inside the opening, he had no idea what to do next.

The one thing he did know was that he couldn't share that information with Dufort. The second Tommy and the ladies outlived their usefulness would be the second Dufort cut the cord.

Tommy looked over his shoulder toward the wall where the path wound down to the bottom. "This way," he said with as confident a tone as he could muster.

"Good. Lead on."

His eyelids widened for a second as he passed the two women a look that told them he had no clue what he was doing.

He spun around and started marching down the path, keeping

one hand on the wall as he moved along to make sure he kept his balance.

The group had to walk in single file since the ledge was only wide enough for one person at a time. The trail bent back around in the previous direction with a sharp turn at each end. More than anything, Tommy wanted to twist around, grab the mercenary behind him, and shove the guy over the cliff, working his way back until he tossed Dufort to his death.

It was a fanciful daydream and one that had absolutely zero possibility of happening. But Tommy and his friends were still alive, which meant the window of opportunity could come at some point. He'd just have to stay alert.

After a long and sketchy hike down, the group stopped and stared straight ahead.

They'd seen it from above but couldn't tell what the structure was. Now it was clear.

A massive stone temple, carved straight from the canyon rock, towered over them against the wall. There were ruins of other buildings, mostly just blocks of stone toppled over from years gone by. The temple, however, remained intact.

Tommy stared up at the impressive structure and examined the figures standing guard over the staircase that ascended to an entryway. The statues—figures of lions—were made from granite, which was definitely not native to the area and stood out as a stark contrast to the sandstone that surrounded them. The gigantic cats were permanently frozen with their mouths open wide, brandishing menacing teeth to any trespassers who might dare to enter the temple.

"Assyrian?" Dufort asked as he stood next to Tommy, looking up at the stone sculptures. "Babylonian, perhaps?"

"The style is similar," Tommy said, "but no. Too far from where those empires were founded, and this stuff is much, much older. And then there's the question of the granite. Where did *that* come from?"

"So?"

Tommy shook his head. "I have no idea. Precursors to the Egyptians, I'd guess. Although the style is far more developed than any pre-Egyptian stuff I've seen."

"Can we hurry along with the art lesson?" Hank asked. "Maybe get to the good stuff?"

"You know, Hank," Dufort said, sounding annoyed, "I would have thought after that incredible display of supernatural power you witnessed above that you'd be a little more invested in what's really at play here."

Hank took a step forward with a cold, intense glare in his eyes. "I came here for one reason and one reason only, Gerard. Money. Now show me where this treasure is."

Dufort rolled his shoulders and faced Tommy. "You heard the man, Thomas. Lead the way." He motioned forward with his hand.

Tommy drew in a deep breath and started up the stairs.

When the group reached the top of the short flight, they were greeted by an open doorway. It was dark beyond the threshold, unlike the rest of the canyon that was well lit by the blazing desert sun above.

Strange hieroglyphs were etched into the stone frame over the open doorway. Dufort scanned them multiple times before turning to Tommy. "What does it say? It's not like anything I've seen before."

Tommy gazed at the images and symbols. "I have no idea," he said with an absent shake of the head. "It's new to me, too. Probably says something about where we are and what this place is."

"Well, obviously it's a temple of some kind."

"To which god, though?"

"Does it matter? Come on. Keep moving," Hank urged with another wave of his pistol.

"I'll need a flashlight," Tommy said. "It's dark in there. Don't know what kinds of things may be lurking in the shadows."

Dufort turned to one of his men and motioned for a light. The guy stepped up and placed it in Tommy's palm.

"Thanks."

The mercenary said nothing in response and simply returned to the middle of the pack.

Tommy turned on the light and moved cautiously over the threshold and into the first room.

He was immediately struck by the almost complete lack of imagery anywhere. There were no idols, no mosaics, no frescoes, no reliefs, nothing related to who the building was constructed for or why. The bare walls matched the cylindrical stone columns that rose high into the air and supported the ceiling. The only difference in the plain appearance of the place was the floor, which featured huge stone tiles. The rows of squares were colored differently with paint that had barely faded through the thousands of years since it must have been put down.

Tommy wandered over to a row of white tiles that wrapped around the outside of the room. Hank and Cody followed him, along with the two women and another henchman.

Dufort stood at the entrance to the room and looked around while two of his men walked up the middle, down a row of red tiles. They'd no sooner stepped on the first square when the floor gave way. The tile tilted down, and both men slid into the darkness below, screaming until the hinged flooring swung back up to flush with the rest of the surface.

Everyone in the room noted the sudden stop of the men's voices.

"Quick," Dufort said to Cody. "Come back over here. They might still be alive."

Tommy knew Dufort didn't care about the men or their lives. But with two men already dead from falling into the canyon, losing two more started to make things a little less comfortable for the Frenchman.

"Hank," Dufort said, "Watch them."

Hank nodded and wielded his weapon at the three captives.

Dufort knelt down on the neutral tile next to the rows of colored ones and waited until Cody and two of the other three mercenaries joined him.

"Press down on this corner," he ordered. "You, press on this one," he said to a younger guy with a ponytail.

The two men obeyed and pushed down on the heavy slab. Dufort turned on a flashlight and pointed it down into the opening. He immediately saw why the two men who fell stopped screaming. Their bodies were pierced in multiple places by tall stone spikes.

"Let it go," Dufort said. "They're dead."

"Dead?" Hank asked from across the room. "What happened?"

"See for yourself. This whole place could be a deathtrap, so you better be careful." Dufort gave his warning in a way that made it sound like he almost wished Hank would fall prey to a trap.

Tommy passed a knowing glance over his shoulder at Adriana and June. They didn't know what the look was for, and he couldn't tell them at the moment.

"Keep moving," Dufort said.

They pushed forward. This time, the entire group followed Tommy to the other end of the room until they reached the far wall. Two doors were cut into it, one on the right and one on the left.

Over the doorway was another symbol. It looked like the head of a bird looking down on them. The animal's features were made from sharp geometric lines.

Dufort pointed his flashlight into the dark corridor. Then he looked over at the other doorway. "Which one do we take? Or do they both go to the same place?"

"You know," Tommy said, "you keep asking me all these questions like I've been here a million times."

He shuffled his feet to the right, heading for the other door.

"Where do you think you're going?" Cody asked, stepping in his way.

"Um, the other door. Where do you think?"

Cody flashed a questioning eye at his boss. Dufort nodded, and the young man stepped aside.

Tommy stopped under the doorway and looked up at a different image carved into the rock.

"What is it?" Dufort asked.

"Looks like a cat...maybe," Tommy answered. "These drawings are pretty elementary."

"So, which door?"

Tommy thought hard. He didn't know the right answer. What he did know was that he was running out of time.

He remembered what he knew about Egyptian mythology regarding cats. They were the guardians of the underworld, which could mean that this cat was protecting something related to death. The bird, on the other hand, could have been an early reference to Horus, the falcon. In the ancient Egyptian religions, it was believed that the pharaoh was the human embodiment of Horus and when the king died he'd return to the sky god.

Both symbols looming over the doors represented the potential for death if Tommy's reasoning was correct. Of course, this temple could have nothing to do with ancient Egypt, which would change everything.

He walked slowly back over to Dufort and looked him in the eyes. "Both of those symbols could mean death," he said. "There's only one way to know."

Dufort leveled his weapon, pointing it at June's chest. "Which tunnel will you take?"

"It's a 50/50 chance either way, Gerard. You choose."

Chapter 34

SAHARA DESERT, EGYPT

"I'm tired of waiting on you two," Hank blurted. He turned to two of the other mercenaries. "You two, come with me. We'll take the tunnel over there. You all can take this one with the bird."

Dufort considered challenging Hank but decided splitting up might not be such a bad idea. He'd force Tommy and the two women to go ahead of him, and if there was something dangerous along the path they'd be the ones to die.

"Go ahead," Dufort said to two of his men. "Cody, Simpson, you're with me. Keep an eye on these three."

The other two mercenaries followed Hank across the room and cautiously stepped into the corridor.

"Now," Dufort said to Tommy, "shall we continue?"

Tommy gave the faintest of nods and started moving forward into the passageway.

The stone walls were clean, free of the cobwebs and dust that usually blanketed ruins such as this. Then again, Tommy couldn't imagine how spiders or anything else would get down there.

He scanned the walls and floor as he tiptoed forward, keeping June close behind. He reached back and grasped the tips of her fingers to give her a little comfort—and if he was honest, to give himself a bit of courage as well.

Dark lines were painted into the walls on both sides. The passage curved around toward the center of the temple. Tommy expected the floor to give way or the walls to collapse at any second—another trap triggered by their mere presence in the corridor.

Nothing happened, though, and soon the group of six found themselves standing in the middle of another large room. It was half the size of the first chamber. There were the same cylindrical pillars reaching up to the ceiling. While the first room was empty, however, this one wasn't.

The flashlight beams drifted across shiny objects lining the walls. Each person in the group stared with wide eyes at the incredible treasure before them. Gold bars, coins, crowns, jewels, encrusted swords and shields, armor, and every type of treasure imaginable wrapped around the room at least eight feet deep until the mass of unimaginable wealth stacked up against the walls.

Cody swallowed hard at the sight. He'd never seen anything like it. Dufort sighed in relief. He'd found it. He'd found Zerzura.

The treasure, though, was only a small part of what he sought.

A loud thud came from somewhere in the temple, and everyone jumped with a start. Their heads snapped around in all directions to see what happened, but after the loud noise and the momentary vibration through the temple there were no other anomalies.

"What was that?" June asked Tommy in a whisper.

Tommy didn't know, but he had an idea. If he had to guess, Hank and the other two men just set off a trap. They'd gone the wrong way.

"Watch them," Dufort said as he wandered deeper into the treasure room.

Cody and the other guard kept their weapons trained on their prisoners, watching their employer venture on.

Dufort stopped and cocked his head to the side. He turned back to the others. "Switch off your flashlights for a second."

"Sir?"

"No. You know what? Muffle the light with your shirt. I want to see something."

The two guards did as they were told and pressed their lights against their shirts to diffuse the beams. Tommy hoped that might be his chance to make a move, but the men could still see him and the two women.

With the lights turned down, the group realized there was something else illuminating the room.

A faint eerie glow emanated from the far wall, between the pillars. Tommy craned his neck to the right to see down the middle of the room.

Dufort padded reverently down the aisle toward the source of light. He stopped short of a five-foot-tall stone cube. In the center, a stone embedded in a medallion glowed, casting a pale corona on its immediate surroundings. The sound of water accompanied it.

"Bring them over here," Dufort ordered.

Cody shoved Tommy forward. Tommy's fingers slipped away from June as he was marched ahead. The second guard forced the women forward as well.

They halted a few strides short of where the Frenchman stood, staring at the bizarre relic on the altar.

"How?" Cody asked. "How is that possible? Where is the light coming from?"

Dufort took a step closer. He looked up at a stone pipe jutting out from the wall. A steady stream of clear water flowed from it, dropping three feet until it hit the amulet and dispersed through four troughs on the altar—each delivering the water to a respective drain in the floor.

"Sometimes, it's best not to wonder how," Dufort said. "Just accept that it is." He reached out his hands to touch the shiny yellow metal and the crystal-clear gem embedded in its center.

"Maybe you should leave that where you found it, Dufort," Tommy said. "I doubt the people who put it there wanted it moved."

Dufort didn't look back at his prisoner. His eyes were fixed on the prize. He was in a trance now, unable to avert his gaze.

"Immortality," he said to himself. "The Athanasia Symbol...it's mine. I will be like a god."

"Whoa!" a familiar voice shouted from the back corner near the doorway. "Look at all this loot!"

Tommy, the two women, and their guards twisted around to look at Hank. He stood in the doorway with a hand on his hip.

"What happened to the others?" Cody asked, unconsciously lowering his weapon a few inches.

"Oh, they're dead. Flat as pancakes," Hank said. "Which is fine. More booty for us, right?"

"Dead?"

"Yep. They set off one of those traps. Huge slab of rock fell on them from the ceiling. I was lucky it missed me." He stuffed his gun in his belt, hurried over to the nearest pile of gold, and started stuffing his pockets and a small shoulder bag he'd brought.

Dufort barely even heard the conversation. His fingers rubbed the precious gold, interrupting the flow of the water from above.

Cody started to turn around to see what his boss wanted him to do about Hank and the others, but he'd already made the mistake. And Tommy made him pay.

Tommy lunged forward and plowed his shoulder into Cody's chest, driving him backward into the nearest column. Cody grunted as his upper back struck the stone. His arms shuddered on impact, and the gun in his hand fell to the floor with a clack.

The other henchman saw what was happening and turned to fire a bullet into Tommy's back.

Adriana reacted faster. Her foot snapped into the air with a sharp kick and hit the base of the pistol. June joined in a second later and drove her fist into the mercenary's jaw.

The man's head whipped to the side at the same moment his weapon tumbled to the floor fifteen feet away. While his initial reaction was slow, his second wasn't. Adriana was swinging her knee forward to hit him in the groin when he pivoted on his right foot and twisted out of the way. Her attack missed, and he swung his hand around, smacking her in the back of the head and grabbing a fistful of hair. He tugged on the ponytail and then shoved her at June just as the blonde was about to throw another punch.

The two women crashed into each other and tumbled to the floor.

A few yards away, Tommy tried to keep Cody pinned against the column while delivering a blow to the midsection. The second he released Dufort's guy, though, Cody threw a hammer fist at Tommy's head. Tommy dipped his head to the side enough to dodge the intended blow, but still caught Cody's forearm just above the ear.

The strike did enough to weaken Tommy's grip. He staggered sideways momentarily while Cody doubled over and caught his breath.

Dufort was oblivious to the melee going on just behind him. He was standing with his torso pressing against the altar, both hands cradling the amulet as he stared into the light.

Cody saw his weapon lying on the floor near a pillar ten feet away and made a dash for it. Tommy realized what his opponent was doing and cut him off with a swing of the foot that caught Cody on the ankle and sent him tumbling through the air.

The victory was short lived.

Cody rolled to a crouching position and bounced up, ready to finish the fight. Knees bent, hands ready, body twisted to the side to minimize himself as a target, he stepped sideways, crossing one foot over the other, and he and Tommy circled in a stalemate dance, waiting for the other man to make a move.

Tommy's eyes narrowed. He faked a lunge forward and drew Cody out of his stance. The younger man went to make a counter move with his own step, but Tommy anticipated it. He spun, swept his leg around again, and caught Cody on the heel.

The move would have worked had the enemy been off balance. Cody, however, was ready for the counter. He jumped and did a back-flip. He landed on his feet, and as Tommy stood to recover, Cody whipped his leg around and planted the top of his foot across Tommy's face.

The temple blurred in Tommy's vision. He put his left hand out to brace his fall, but the ground didn't come. He stumbled to the side until he felt his shoulder hit a column. Letting all his weight push against the pillar, he tried to refocus his vision.

Cody came at him fast, fully intent on finishing his opponent. He jumped into the air to deliver a boot to the head that would drive Tommy's head into the stone behind him. Instead, Tommy reached deep within and found enough energy to drop to the floor and roll clear. A split second later, Cody's foot struck the column with a crack.

He howled in agony as he fell to the floor, immediately grasping his ankle with both hands. Tommy blinked slowly as his vision started to clear. He could see his opponent's leg bent at an awkward angle.

Across the room, the other henchman grabbed Adriana by the ponytail again and dragged her to her feet. He delivered an uppercut that sent her flailing back to the floor then kicked June in the face as she tried to get up.

The man wouldn't let June get a break. He bent over and grabbed her by the neck and lifted her up, pinning her against a nearby column. Her face flushed red, and she gasped for air. Veins and muscles bulged from his arms from the strain, but he had no intention of letting go.

Adriana staggered to her feet and shook her head to regain her bearings. She saw June being strangled and rushed to her aid. Adriana jumped and wrapped her arms and legs around the strong man's neck and torso, squeezing with every ounce of energy she could muster.

His thick neck made it hard to choke him, but she found the windpipe and focused the force of her arms straight back into it. Her feet dug into his midsection to enhance the pain, and a second later he let go of June.

She fell to the floor in a heap, reaching for her neck to make sure she could breathe again.

Now the mercenary spun around in circles, hoping to throw off Adriana from his shoulders. When that didn't work, he backed up quickly until her tailbone smashed into the wall. Her grip loosened. He took a step forward and another hard step back, once more driving her into the wall. This time, she gasped and let go, falling again to the floor on her hands and knees.

The mercenary bent down and grabbed her by the ponytail for a third time. He yanked it hard to force her head up and exposed her neck.

Adriana looked into his eyes without fear. A trickle of blood seeped out of her nose and from the corner of her mouth. Her chest heaved, taking in huge gulps of air.

The guard reached to his belt with his free hand to grab his knife. His fingers felt around the sheath, but it wasn't there.

Suddenly, his eyes shot wide, and his head trembled. The grip on Adriana's hair weakened, and his hand dropped to his side. June stood behind him with her hand planted at the base of his skull. She stepped back and let go of the knife handle with the blade shoved all the way into the hilt. The mercenary was dead before he hit the floor, dropping to his knees and then over onto his side with the knife handle still embedded in his head.

Tommy turned to Dufort. With his opponent immobilized, only the Frenchman remained. Hank was still in the corner getting as much loot as he could carry.

"Dufort!" Tommy yelled. "It's just you and me now!" Tommy's breath came in huge gasps. His eyes were full of vengeance and resolve.

Dufort didn't turn around. Instead, he lifted the medallion from its cradle and held it into the air with his arms extended.

Suddenly, the light from the gem faded, and the floor beneath them trembled. A deep rumble came from deep inside the earth. Dust shook from the ceiling. Dufort snapped out of his trance and looked around. He saw the dead man near the two women on one side of the room. Cody was dragging himself away. Hank crouched over a pile of gold and jewels, looking around, suddenly curious as to what was going on.

"Put the medallion down, Gerard," Tommy said. "It's over."

Dufort shook his head. "You're right. It is over. And I've won."

He raised his pistol and squeezed the trigger. The muzzle

erupted, and the loud pop caused everyone in the room to wince. Tommy instinctively put his hands over his ears. Then he realized something. He'd not been hit. He checked his chest, stomach, face, everywhere within a second.

Dufort frowned. He fired again. Once more, the bullet didn't hit his target. He fired a third and fourth time, spilling gun smoke into the room. But Tommy was unharmed.

"How is this possible?" Dufort thundered.

Tommy's lips creased with a sinister grin. "Looks like your luck has run out, Gerry."

Suddenly, a huge slab of stone dropped from the ceiling and crashed to the ground between the two men. Tommy fell backward in a cloud of dust and debris. The temple shook violently. He collected himself and stood up in time to see Dufort rushing toward the doorway. The Frenchman tossed aside his weapon and picked up the one that belonged to the dead man. A second later, he disappeared through the entrance.

Hank collected his things and hurried through the door, not willing to risk his life for a few more riches.

Tommy rushed over to the two women and helped them to their feet. "You two okay?"

They both nodded. "Yeah. Nothing a hot bath won't fix," Adriana said. "We need to get out of here. This place is going to collapse."

On cue, another piece of the ceiling fell to the floor with a boom.

"Come on," Tommy said. He started toward the door and then stopped in his tracks.

Cody was lying on his side between the three and their only way out. He couldn't stand, but he'd managed to drag himself over to his gun, which now pointed at Tommy, Adriana, and June.

"Like he said," Cody shouted over the rumbling, "it's over!"

His finger tensed on the trigger, and Tommy forced the women behind him, ready to use his body as their shield. One of the pillars broke free from the roof and toppled sideways.

Cody noticed the sudden movement but couldn't get out of the way fast enough. The massive stone cylinder crashed to the floor, crushing him under several tons of rock.

Tommy stared, almost not believing what just happened. He snapped out of it a second later and ushered the women forward toward the passageway. He leaped over the fallen column and on his way out the door snatched the weapon from near Cody's limp hand.

Chapter 35

SAHARA DESERT, EGYPT

Dufort pumped his legs as fast as he could, sprinting through the dark corridor and out into the next room. He hurried past the columns and through the falling debris, narrowly dodging a few large chunks of stone that fell from the ceiling.

Once Athanasia, he ran down the stairs, taking them two at a time until he was on the canyon floor again.

The gigantic room shook. Sand spilled in through the opening like a golden waterfall in the rays of the desert sun.

He looked up at the winding path leading back up to the ropes. Then he glanced around the cavern, and his eyes fixed on an opening far to his left. "Another way out," he said to himself.

Suddenly, a blow to his back knocked Dufort forward toward the river. He tumbled head over heels and dropped the medallion on the ground to brace himself. The weapon in his hand also fell free and slid across the stone, coming to a stop close to the water's edge.

He scrambled to pick up the weapon. His fingers wrapped around it, and he popped up, whipping the gun around as he did so.

Dufort's eyes widened with shock. "No," he said, shaking his head. "That's impossible."

Sean stood twenty feet away, a pistol in one hand and the Athanasia medallion in the other.

"I saw you die," Dufort stammered. "I shot you in the chest. I saw you bleed."

Sean's head turned side to side. "You really should check your magazine before you fire a weapon," he said. "Those were blanks in the weapon you fired. I replaced the live rounds before our little encounter in Sudan."

Dufort didn't believe it. His forehead wrinkled as he frowned in confusion. "No."

"Yes."

Dufort took a cautious step to the side. Sean mimicked it in the opposite direction.

"You must really think I'm predictable, Gerard," Sean taunted.

"You are," Dufort sneered. "That's how I've bested you."

"Yet here I am with the medallion you want."

The ground shook hard again, and the men bent their knees to keep their balance. The weapons in their hands remained aimed at the other.

"That belongs to me," Dufort said. "I will be a god among men."

Hank emerged from the temple and descended the steps. At the bottom, he saw the standoff and paused. The other two men were facing each other, circling in a duel to the death. Sean's back was now to the water. At first, he'd not seen Hank standing at the base of the stairs, which meant he could still get away. Sean surely saw him now, but his focus was on Dufort. Hank's eyes averted to the left, and he noticed the opening in the wall. Cautiously, Hank made his way along the temple wall as fast as he could until he reached the passageway. He took one last look back before disappearing into the darkness.

Tommy and the two women appeared at the top of the steps. They looked down and saw Sean and Dufort standing several paces away from each other. Tommy put his hands out to stop them in case they accidentally caught a stray bullet. All three turned a pale white as they stared at the apparition across from Dufort.

"Sean's alive?" Tommy whispered.

Adriana wanted to rush down the stairs and wrap her arms around him, but Tommy held her back.

"So, what now, Wyatt?" Dufort shouted above the rumble. "This place is going to collapse any minute. Is this where you want to die?"

"Seems like as good a place as any," Sean said. "Everyone's gotta go sometime. Might as well be today."

"You don't really believe that," Dufort said. "You have too much to live for. You're still young. And besides, you hold the key to eternal life in your hands. Everyone doesn't have to die. You could live forever."

"No man is meant to live forever, Dufort," Sean said. "We gave up that right a long time ago."

Dufort snorted. "Spare me the religious talk about the fall of mankind and how we've strayed from God's path. I will be god!" His voice echoed amid the constant noise resonating from the canyon.

Sean shook his head. "No, Dufort. You'll be dead."

"What are you going to do, Sean? Shoot me? You realize if you pull that trigger, I'll pull mine. We'll both be dead. What good will that do?"

Sean kept his weapon trained on the Frenchman's chest.

"It will rid the world of one more horrible person."

"Ah," Dufort said. "So, that's the plan, then? A Mexican standoff until one of us pulls the trigger? Then we both die? I have to say, Sean, that's pretty imaginative for you. The problem is if we stand here too long this whole cave will collapse in on us."

"Works for me," Sean sneered.

Dufort decided to try a different tack. "You know, if you hurry, you might still have time to save your friends. They're just inside the temple."

Sean didn't flinch, but inside he wondered. What if Dufort was telling the truth? What if Adriana and the others were still inside?

"Don't listen to him, Sean!" Tommy shouted from the top of the stairs.

Sean's eyes remained locked on the enemy. In his periphery, he saw Tommy, Adriana, and June standing at the entrance to the temple amid the chaos.

A gun fired. Something struck Sean hard in the chest with the force of a wrecking ball. He stumbled backward as the pain turned from dull to sharp and burning. He looked down at the hole in his chest. Crimson started spreading through his shirt. Then he looked up at Dufort standing there with his pistol. A thin trickle of blue-gray smoke wafted out of the barrel and disappeared into the air.

"Noooo!" Tommy yelled. He fired his weapon as he descended the stairs. The first round missed and ricocheted off the stone floor.

Dufort spun around to return fire, but Tommy's barrage was too much. The second round tore through Dufort's shoulder and spun him to the side. The third struck him in the ribs. A fourth ripped through his leg and dropped the Frenchman to one knee. He tried to raise his weapon again to ward off the attack, but Tommy kept shooting, pouring hot rounds at his target until one caught Dufort at the base of the neck.

The Frenchman dropped his weapon to the ground and grasped the mortal wound with both hands, desperately trying to plug the life from leaking out of him.

Behind him, Sean looked up at Adriana, who was rushing down the steps. He smiled at her as he fell backward into the rushing water.

"Sean!" she yelled, hysterical.

Tommy reached the bottom of the stairs and panted for air. Tears streamed down his face.

Dufort raised his head and looked into Tommy's eyes. "Do it," he mouthed.

"With pleasure, you piece of—"

The gun popped loudly. A pink spray shot out of the back of Dufort's skull. He wavered for a moment, the hole in his forehead still smoldering. Then he fell backward, his legs bending at an impossible angle.

Tommy swallowed and then looked over at Adriana, who skidded to a stop at the river's edge.

"Sean!" she yelled again. She was about to dive in after him, but June rushed to her side and wrapped her arms around her.

"No, Addy! You'll drown. The water...the current is too fast now. He's gone."

"Let me go!" Adriana shouted. She struggled, swinging her arms at June to break free.

Tommy rushed over to them and put his arms around Adriana. He held her still in his strong grip and forced her to look into his eyes. "We have to go," he said. "This place isn't going to hold up much longer."

June saw the passage over Tommy's shoulder. "Over there," she said. "It's a way out."

Tommy took a quick glance back and then looked in Adriana's eyes again. "He wouldn't want you to die here. We have to go."

She resisted for a second. Her eyes drifted back to the water. There was no sign of Sean's body. He was gone. She'd watched him die twice, and it was almost more than she could bear.

Tommy looped his arm under her armpits and started dragging her toward the exit with June helping from the other side. Huge rocks fell from the ceiling. A massive slab dropped down and crushed part of the temple roof as the three made their way into the dark corridor and out of the canyon.

Once they were in the passage, Tommy took one last look back. He was overcome by one resonating, heart-wrenching thought: Sean Wyatt was dead.

Chapter 36

CHATTANOOGA

The southeastern Tennessee sky was a gray soup overhead. Tommy stood with his hands folded in front of him as he stared down at the hole in the dirt at his feet. Tears streaked across his cheeks. He couldn't swallow, could barely breathe.

Next to him, Adriana sobbed uncontrollably.

June couldn't do anything to ease their pain. She stood quietly between the two, occasionally squeezing Tommy's hand or putting her other arm around Adriana.

The minister had left along with the sparse collection of friends and colleagues Sean had met through the years. His parents hung around a long time before heading back to their home, where everyone would be meeting for dinner. Joe and Helen McElroy lingered for a while, only choosing to leave because they thought it was best to give Tommy and Adriana a little time alone to say their final goodbyes.

"I can't believe he's gone," Tommy muttered after what seemed like a year-long silence. Thunder boomed in the distance, and a heavy drop of rain splattered on his shoulder.

"I know," June said.

"I like to think he did it to protect us," Adriana said between sobs.

"But that doesn't make me feel better. It actually makes me feel guilty, like I should have been the one to die."

Tommy shook his head. "No. He knew the score. He knew exactly what he was doing. Sean was going to take down Dufort no matter the cost. None of us would be safe if that guy was still out there, not to mention the countless others that guy would have harmed."

What Tommy didn't say was that he felt responsible. If he hadn't yelled at Sean from the top of the temple steps, his friend might not have been distracted. He may have shot first and taken Dufort out on his own. He'd seen his friend snake his way out of worse situations. Tommy's stomach turned at the thought and he had to fight hard to keep from throwing up.

It was something Tommy would never know.

He stared into the grave. The empty coffin sat at the bottom with a pile of roses on top of it.

"I don't know how I can ever go back to work again," he muttered to himself. "It will never be the same."

"I know," June said. "Give it time. There's no rush. Joe and Helen will run things for a while with the kids. When you're ready, you can come back. Just take your time."

"No," Tommy said in a distant tone as he shook his head slowly back and forth. "I don't think I can. Sean and I did everything together. How can I walk back into that building, board our plane? I don't think I can even find the will to do my job anymore."

"You love what you do, Tommy," she said, looking deep into his eyes. "Sooner or later, it will pull you back."

Six hours later, darkness had descended on the city. Tommy sat alone in Sean's south side condo, staring out the window as a heavy rain fell on the streets. Adriana and June were asleep in Sean's room after finally giving in to extreme fatigue.

Tommy glanced at the pictures hanging on the wall. Most of them were of him and his friend at various places around the world. There were a few from their childhood, too. One that struck Tommy in the chest was a picture of him and Sean in their little league baseball uniforms. They were only seven years old at the time, oblivious to the world around them.

He bit his lower lip and drew in a deep breath. A second later he exhaled and took a drink of water from a bottle dangling in his hand.

Tommy was exhausted. He'd not slept in days, other than for a few random moments where his body gave in and dozed off.

He turned away from the window as lightning flashed in the distance. He collapsed into the leather couch and stared at the black television screen. His fingers fumbled over the remote on the armrest, and he picked it up.

"Maybe a little television will help," he said to himself. "Staring at the wall doesn't seem to be doing any good."

The screen flickered to life, and he flipped through the channels until he arrived at the news.

"Haven't watched the news in a long time," he muttered. "Might as well see who else is miserable in the world."

A guy in a tight gray suit with perfectly cropped black hair was talking about flooding in Southeast Asia.

"Switching gears now, a former American agent was found dead this morning in his home in Grenada. Authorities released the name just minutes ago. We're learning that Hank Tillis was killed in the early morning hours yesterday. The CIA director has yet to comment on the tragedy, but is expected to release a statement soon."

Tommy's ears perked up. His right eyebrow lifted slightly, and he grunted. "Got what you had coming to you, eh Hank?"

"Tillis appears to have been the victim of an execution, though authorities say they have no leads in the mysterious murder. All evidence suggests that the killer broke into his home and shot him in the chest three times."

Tommy switched off the television and set the remote back down. The news of the traitor's murder gave him a sliver of satisfaction for a microsecond.

"In all fairness," a voice said from across the room, "his front door was open."

A chill shot through Tommy's spine and tingled every inch of skin on his body. *No,* he thought to himself. *I'm hearing things.*

Tommy shook his head, refusing to look up. The tears behind his eyes broke through and poured down his face. It sounded just like Sean.

Then he heard a footstep, deliberate and heavy from near the doorway.

"I'm sorry, Schultzie. I couldn't risk coming back until he was gone," Sean's voice echoed from the shadows. "I had to take him out."

Tommy's head kept turning as the tears streamed down, rolling off his chin into his lap. "Stop it!" he yelled, grabbing both sides of his head. "You're dead! I saw you die! What is this?" A billion emotions washed over Tommy like a tsunami.

"It's me, Schultzie. I know you must be...confused."

"No. We had a funeral for you," Tommy blurted. Globs of saliva spat out of his mouth. "Everyone was there."

"I know," Sean said. "If I'd been able to get back in time, I would have sent you flowers."

Tommy's chest surged with a short laugh. "You are such an—"

"We've made it this far without using profanity," Sean said as he stepped into the light. "No sense in starting now."

Tommy finally built up the courage to look over at his friend. "How?" he asked. "I saw you die, really die the second time. I don't understand."

Sean grinned and stopped by the island in his kitchen. He reached into a jacket pocket and pulled out the amulet he'd taken from Dufort. It radiated with a bizarre, yellowish glow.

"I know, Schultzie. Turns out...Dufort was right about this thing."

Tommy still didn't fully understand. "So, what? You're like a zombie or something? Are you immortal? I gotta be honest, man, this is too much for me." He choked again, unable to hold back the tidal wave.

Sean shook his head. "No, I don't think I'm immortal. But this thing does have some kind of healing properties. I don't remember much after the gun fired. All I know is I fell in the water with a hole in my chest. I saw the cavern ceiling, water flowed over my face and eyes. It was cold. I know that much. The pain in my chest...it was terrible. When I woke up I was on the shore of an oasis and the hole was gone. No bullet, nothing." He lifted his shirt and showed his chest. "It didn't even scar."

Tommy processed the story for a moment before speaking again. "I...I don't understand."

"I don't either. If you can ever find a way to forgive me for putting you through this, maybe we can figure out what this thing can do. This might be the cure to every disease on the planet."

Tommy's head still shook back and forth. His fingers trembled and his lips quivered. "I have so many questions."

"So do I. For now, though, would it be okay if I hugged my girlfriend?"

Tommy stood up and made his way across the room. He nodded. "Yeah, buddy. But I get one first."

Tommy had cried so much that his eyes were nearly dry, reddened and swollen from the torment.

He wrapped his arms around Sean and squeezed him tight. The second he felt the apparition, Tommy lost control again. He sobbed into Sean's shoulder, squeezing him tighter than he'd ever squeezed anything or anyone before.

"Adriana's probably going to kick your butt. You know that, right?"

Sean nodded as he let the tears flow down his cheeks. "Yeah, I know."

Tommy tensed his muscles again, unwilling to let his friend go. They'd known each other their whole lives, more like brothers than friends.

Sean returned the gesture and slapped his friend on the back. "Not so hard, Schultzie. You're a lot stronger than you used to be."

"Shut up, wuss."

The two laughed amid a river of tears as the rain spattered against the windows.

"Just shut up."

THANK YOU

Writing a book is a challenging thing.

It takes an incredible amount of time, research, energy, and mental focus. That last one is extremely difficult for me.

When I say thank you for reading my work, I truly mean it and I cannot express how much I appreciate you choosing to spend your time with my words.

Perhaps you're a loyal reader who has read every single book in the series. Maybe this is your first one. Either way, at some point you took a chance on purchasing a story from a guy you'd probably never heard of. I can't thank you enough for that.

I've always been a storyteller, no matter the career in which I worked. To be able to write books for a living is an honor and a privilege. I owe that to good people like you.

Again, thank you for trusting me with your time. It is the most valuable resource a person has. And you chose to spend some with me.

Sincerely,
Ernest

OTHER BOOKS BY ERNEST DEMPSEY

Sean Wyatt Adventures:

The Secret of the Stones

The Cleric's Vault

The Last Chamber

The Grecian Manifesto

The Norse Directive

Game of Shadows

The Jerusalem Creed

The Samurai Cipher

The Cairo Vendetta

The Uluru Code

The Excalibur Key

The Denali Deception

Adriana Villa Adventures:

War of Thieves Trilogy

AUTHOR'S NOTES

As a fan of great fiction that mixes history into the story, I love to read other writers' notes about what is true and what isn't in regard to their tales.

Over the years, many readers have told me the same thing about my books.

So, here are a few little tidbits from this story about what is real and what isn't.

Locations:

All the locations in this story are real places except for Zerzura. While the lost oasis city might be out there, hidden in the sands of the Sahara, it has never been found. The legends, however, have been passed down through the centuries. The ruins in Libya, Egypt, and Sudan are all accurately portrayed in the story, as well as the huge stone elephant in Chad.

The great mountain pyramid in Giza is a very real place. And as I described in the story, very few people visit it or even know it's there. I've heard many explanations as to why tourists don't frequent this unique and incredible structure, but none of them add up. I personally believe there is something at that site that the Egyptian govern-ment and even researchers want to be ignored. Maybe it's the evidence of ancient technology, as described in the story. I'm not sure, but it's definitely an item of curiosity.

Relics:

The amulets and the stones of power were a creation of my imagi-nation. While there are certainly fascinating pieces from history such as the Ankara stones, the crystal skulls, and many others, these particular items don't exist—to my knowledge.

Power and Supernatural Things:

The event that occurred at Zerzura when the sands opened up is not something that has been recorded, at least not that I know of. However, the glowing ball of light, the sounds the amulets made, and the idea of a global power grid are not new things. In World War II, pilots saw glowing orbs over Nazi Germany. They called them Foo Fighters, but no one knew what they were or why they were there.

In regard to the global grid, there are many historians, archaeolo-gists, and scientists who are trying to better understand exactly how this grid works. Perhaps the most fascinating thing about the grid is that almost every sacred site from antiquity ranging from the earliest Egyptians all the way down through the Incan empire was built along this grid. Coincidence? You may have to decide that for yourself.

As far as other supernatural occurrences in the story, I personally believe that things modern science can't explain doesn't make them any less real. A thousand years ago, Vikings believed that thunder and lightning were signs that Thor and his father, Odin, were waging war. Now we know what those things really are.

Someday, I hope that we are able to understand even more about the higher science that we now call miraculous or supernatural. After all, the design of the universe wasn't meant to be ignored. It was meant to be understood and appreciated.

The General Premise:

As with any fictional story involving locations and history, an author takes a fair amount of liberty in tweaking things to meet the needs of the tale.

Often, people will search the internet for more information about the plot devices I use or the locations involved in my books.

Allow me to save you some time.

It is uncertain whether Zerzura actually exists. There was an account from a man who said he got lost in the desert and woke up surrounded by pale-skinned men in a city of light.

Were these men angels? Were they immigrants from another land?

Based on the accounts I found, it isn't clear.

Part of my imagination wanted them to be Templars guarding an ancient secret in the vast Sahara. The Templar story, however, will have to wait for another time.

The account of this lost man was reported to occur around the year 1481. When he tried to lead people back to it, the city had vanished, possibly swallowed by the desert sands. Or perhaps he was merely a charlatan, leading people on a wild goose chase, pursuing a figment of his imagination.

Based on the few accounts available regarding the lost oasis city, I chose to blend the two possibilities. The romantic historian in me chooses to believe there really is a lost city in the desert and that when the man left, it was covered up—either on purpose, or by a sand storm. In the story, it is clearly both.

The Athanasia symbol or amulet was a creation of my mind, which I mentioned before. Unlike some relics in other stories, this one doesn't exist as far as I know. So, whereas the Ark of the Covenant, the Sword of Peter, or other artifacts could potentially be found someday, I doubt this amulet will be.

Anything, however, is possible. Which is why I love writing these kinds of stories.

For my sister, Ember. I love you more than words can say. And I write books so that's saying something.

ACKNOWLEDGMENTS

None of my stories would be possible without the great input I get from incredible readers all over the globe. My advance reader group is such an incredibly unselfish and supportive team. I couldn't do any of this without them.

My editors, Anne Storer and Jason Whited, must also be thanked for their amazing work and guidance in crafting these stories. They make everything so much better for the reader.

Last but not least, I need to give a big thank you to Elena at Lı Graphics for the incredible cover art she always delivers, along with beautiful social media artwork.

Made in the USA
San Bernardino, CA
14 March 2020